FROM DUTY TO DADDY

BY
SUE MacKAY

CHANGED BY HIS SON'S SMILE

BY
ROBIN GIANNA

With a background of working in medical laboratories and a love of the romance genre, it is no surprise that **Sue MacKay** writes Mills & Boon® Medical Romance™ stories. An avid reader all her life, she wrote her first story at age eight—about a prince, of course. She lives with her own hero in the beautiful Marlborough Sounds, at the top of New Zealand's South Island, where she indulges her passions for the outdoors, the sea and cycling.

After completing a degree in journalism, working in the advertising industry, then becoming a stay-at-home mum, **Robin Gianna** had what she calls her mid-life awakening. She decided she wanted to write the romance novels she'd loved since her teens, and embarked on that quest by joining RWA, studying the craft, and obsessively reading and writing.

Robin loves pushing her characters to grow until they're ready for their happily-ever-afters. When she's not writing, Robin's life is filled with a happily messy kitchen, a needy garden, a tolerant husband, three great kids, a drooling bulldog and one grouchy Siamese cat.

To learn more about her work, visit her website, www.RobinGianna.com.

FROM DUTY
TO DADDY

BY
SUE MacKAY

MILLS & BOON

Published in Great Britain 2014
by Mills & Boon, an imprint of Harlequin (UK) Limited,
Eton House, 18-24 Paradise Road, Richmond, Surrey, TW9 1SR

© Sue MacKay 2014

ISBN: 978 0 263 90740 7

Harlequin (UK) Limited's policy is to use papers that are natural,
renewable and recyclable products and made from wood grown in
sustainable forests. The logging and manufacturing processes conform
to the legal environmental regulations of the country of origin.

Printed and bound in Spain
by Blackprint CPI, Barcelona

Dear Reader

Taupo is one of those places from my childhood that I've never forgotten. We went there so my dad could go trout fishing. It was a much smaller town than nowadays; the houses were small, plain holiday homes, the footpaths unpaved, and no one was in a hurry. I have been back often for holidays, staying with my brother and his family, and seen Taupo grow into a busy, vibrant town. Despite the changes it is still the same wonderful place at the edge of a stunning lake and with a backdrop of mountains.

I chose Taupo for Charlie and Marshall's story as it seemed the perfect setting for a wounded hero trying to find his place in life. It's the antithesis to his constantly changing army life. It's where Charlie grew up, where she went to school, learned to sail on the lake, where her mother is buried, where her daughter was born.

Marshall has never lived in the same place for much longer than a year at a time. Charlie has never lived anywhere else than in the house that was her mother's family home. Does Charlie give this up to follow Marshall's erratic lifestyle? Or does Marshall take the plunge and learn to stay put in one place long enough to get to know it and the inhabitants well? Follow these two as they nudge their way towards the right solution for them both.

I'd love to hear from you at sue.mackay56@yahoo.com

Or visit my place at www.suemackay.co.nz

Cheers!

Sue

Dedication

Hannah, Phil and Austin—you rock. Love you heaps.

Also by Sue MacKay:

THE GIFT OF A CHILD
YOU, ME AND A FAMILY
CHRISTMAS WITH DR DELICIOUS
EVERY BOY'S DREAM DAD
THE DANGERS OF DATING YOUR BOSS
SURGEON IN A WEDDING DRESS
RETURN OF THE MAVERICK
PLAYBOY DOCTOR TO DOTING DAD
THEIR MARRIAGE MIRACLE

**These books are also available in eBook format
from www.millsandboon.co.uk**

CHAPTER ONE

CHARLIE LANG FOLDED her laptop shut and put it aside on the outdoor lounger she sat on, but continued to stare at the blasted thing as though it was to blame for all of her problems. Angst at her continued failure ate deep inside. 'I'm never going to find him, am I?'

Dad sat back on his haunches at the edge of the overgrown flowerbed he was weeding below where she sat. 'Aimee's father? Who knows, love? You've got so little to go on.'

Make that next to nothing. 'How many doctors are there in the US army called Marshall Hunter?' Her head spun with the frustration of it all, whizzing the ever-present fear into a maelstrom in the pit of her stomach. 'I must've sent hundreds of emails.'

'I take it the latest one bounced.'

'Yep.' Like every one before it. 'Why did he give me that address if he intended shutting it down?' Why had Marshall given her an address at all when he'd gone to great lengths to ensure she'd understood there couldn't be any contact between them after their fling finished?

On that last day, when he'd been heading back to war and she would shortly return to New Zealand, had he felt a sense of losing something special? She'd certainly been gripped by an awareness of impending loss. Had he suddenly found it impossible to walk away without some way of reaching her again? His note with the email address had been slipped into her shirt pocket while she'd been too busy kissing him goodbye and trying desperately not to cry. Trying to ignore the heat flaring through her body that one touch from Marshall had instantly triggered. Had always triggered—right from the get-go.

But he must've had another change of heart after he'd left Honolulu because not once had an email of hers got through to him. Fickle? Doubtful. Unsure of himself? Definitely not. Marshall had to be the most self-assured man she'd ever come across. Except when she'd asked about his family. Uncertainty had filtered into his steady green gaze then, only to be hurriedly blinked away and replaced with a cold, distant glare.

She'd understood instantly that to remain onside with him meant talk of his family was banned. Naturally, living with the outcome of that fling, she often wondered what he'd been hiding. Not that that was important right now. Only finding him was.

'Ever thought that the guy doesn't want to be found?' Dad never minced his words when he wanted to make a point.

'If I'm honest, it's blatantly obvious that's exactly what Marshall intended. In this day and age everyone puts their name, photo, even excruciatingly personal details out there in cyberspace so they can be found.' Everyone except Marshall Hunter. Which kind of told her what she'd been avoiding all along.

He really hadn't had any intention of ever having anything to do with her again—even in passing. That note had been an aberration she could put down to the emotional goodbye they'd been going through. Each kiss had been their last, only to be followed by another, and another, until Marshall's friend had hauled him away and into an army truck.

She'd stood, fingers pressing his kisses deep into her swollen lips, trying to keep Marshall's touch, his scent with her. Swallowing buckets of tears as the truck had disappeared round a corner, taking Marshall away forever.

Dad broke into her memories. 'Maybe you should drop your search.' He'd been sceptical right from the start about the man who'd got his daughter pregnant. Fair enough, she supposed. Fathers expected every man coming within reach of their girls to treat them carefully.

But what Dad wouldn't concede was that Marshall didn't have a clue she'd had his child, wouldn't believe that Marshall was a good man at heart. Of course, Dad hadn't met him.

She knew different. Or so she told herself regularly. 'No, I refuse to contemplate that.' Marshall had affected her deeply the very first time she'd laid eyes on him in the ED at the hospital in Honolulu where she had been doing post-grad work. His intense gaze had locked with hers and they'd both stepped closer as he'd teased her about her accent. When he'd smiled at her she'd felt as though she'd found something, someone she'd been unwittingly looking for all her life.

At the end of their shift he'd taken her hand and led her out of the department, out of the hospital and along the road to the beach. Walking barefoot in the warm sand, the waves crashing only metres away, her hand firmly held by Marshall's much larger and stronger one and her shoulder brushing his arm, she'd thought she'd died and gone to heaven.

And in the warm air, with laughter and chatter spilling out from the restaurants dotting the foreshore, he'd taken her in his arms and kissed her so thoroughly her body had melted. She'd held onto him like he was a lifeline. Her body had wanted his, craved the release she'd known he, and only he, could bring her. Every nerve ending had desired his touch. Every muscle had trembled with anticipation.

Then he'd swung her up into his arms and run up the sand, across the road and into the first hotel they'd come to. She had always wondered what might've happened if a room hadn't been available. There'd been no way they could've made it all the way to the tawdry apartment block where the hospital provided rooms for temporary doctors before they gave in to the pulsing heat gripping them.

Their affair had started that night in a burst of passion that had been insatiable. It ended as abruptly two weeks later when Marshall had been sent away to some unknown place with his army troop.

She'd missed him ever since, as though he'd taken a chunk from her heart with him. Damn it. That hadn't been part of the deal. Neither had coming home pregnant.

'I wouldn't be looking for him if not for Aimee.' Yeah, sure. Her pride would've prevented her chasing after him like some lovelorn teenager. Did she love him? She'd enjoyed him and the things they'd got up to in bed. But love him? Unfortunately she had a feeling she did. Otherwise why else did she still dream of him most nights? What other reason was there for daydreaming about him moving here and sharing her home? Maybe marrying her?

Reaching for the laptop, she opened it and waited for her program to reboot. Reality sucked. And hurt. Her love wouldn't ever be returned, and yet it was vitally important she track him down. For Aimee's sake, at least. 'I always knew there was no future for us.'

Dad gave her one of his 'This is your father talking' looks that she'd known all her life. It would lead into something she should probably take note of. Except she was an adult now, didn't need her father's wisdom. Much.

'Why don't you stop trying to find this guy for a while? Save your energy for getting completely well again and then maybe it won't be essential for Aimee to have her dad here.' He tried to hide the quiver of fear colouring his voice but she knew him too well.

Staring at her dad, holding onto the surge of her own fear, she ground out, 'I have to find him. Aimee deserves a father, even if only a remote one.' Would Marshall be thrilled or furious when he finally learned her news? There was only one way to find out and so far that hadn't gone too well.

'You've put too much time and effort into this for most of the past year. Let it go for a while. Put it out there and see what comes back.'

'Dad? Put it out there?' Despite everything, a giggle spilled across her lips. 'Where did you get that idea?'

Dad's cheeks coloured. 'From your pal, Gemma.'

'That's typical of Gemma, but I never thought I'd hear you say it.' Gemma and Dad? Had she missed something? Gemma often dropped by on the pretext of seeing her and Aimee but what if her older friend's real interest was Dad? How did that make her feel? No blinding pangs of anger or disappointment struck. Surely that had to tell her something?

'Charlie,' Dad called loudly to get her attention back. 'What I'm saying is there are other things you could be doing with your time rather than getting obsessed about something you've got no control over.'

She sat back in the lounger and stared at the laptop screen. Her finger hovered over the pad, ready to open the internet link. Could she stop searching? For a while at least? Take a break from the heart-wrenching negativity that failure to find Marshall regularly dumped on her when she already had enough to deal with?

It wouldn't be easy when finding Marshall had dominated her thoughts for what seemed like for ever. This campaign had driven her to get up in the mornings when her body ached so badly she wanted to swallow pills and dive back into sleep to avoid the real world.

Doing what Dad had suggested might free her. Enable her to see the situation for what it was. She was a solo mother whose first priority was her daughter. Aimee needed her healthy and focused, not slumbering in self-pity and trying to do the impossible.

She closed down the laptop. Then she looked at her father, really looked, and saw the extra lines on his face, there because of her. Her chest swelled with love. 'Okay, Dad, here's the deal. I'll…' she emphasised her words by flicking her forefingers in the air '…put finding Marshall out there if you start focusing on getting your old life back. I don't mean working longer hours at the medical centre. I'm talking fishing, hiking in the mountains, meeting your pals for a round of golf.'

Pausing, she watched the longing flick through his eyes so fast he probably thought he'd got away with it. She really had wrecked his life since coming home from Honolulu. Sticking her tongue in her cheek, she added, 'Did I mention dating? Definitely need to find time for that.' Should she bring Gemma's name into it? No, best leave that to Dad to sort out. For now anyway. She could give him a prod later if necessary.

'Dating?' he snorted. 'Me? At my age? You've been taking too many painkillers again.'

'Yeah, Dad, you. At your ripe old age of fifty-nine.' Thankfully right then a sound came from inside the house. Charlie usually heard her daughter crying almost before Aimee opened her mouth. Motherhood was so connected. As though a fine but strong strand of love ran between them so that deep inside she felt everything Aimee did.

'There goes my peace and quiet.' Charlie smiled, completely unfazed by the interruption.

Despite helping other women bring their babies into the world during her medical training, the overpowering strength of her love for one special little individual placed into her arms moments after the birth had been a revelation. And something Marshall had missed out on.

Her father chuckled as he returned to weeding the flowerbed beneath a pohutukawa tree. Obviously not too fazed by the dating suggestion, then. 'Go on with you. You've been waiting for Aimee to wake up for the last hour.'

'True.' Driven by a sense of panic, of time running away on her and not knowing how long she'd be around for Aimee, she desperately wanted to grab every minute she could with her little girl. That same panic caused her to pause now. Was she forcing too much on Aimee? Rushing her through life instead of letting her learn to wait? To take each day, each little step slowly?

'You should let her cry for a bit.' Dad unwittingly underlined her thoughts. Sitting back on his haunches, he winked to take the edge off his comment. 'Never hurt you to wait for your mother to come and get you at that age.'

Charlie laughed, and deliberately refrained from standing up, even though she itched to do so. 'Maybe that's why I used to hate lying around in bed once I woke up.'

'Nah, that was because you were too active for your own good.'

'I got that from you. Aimee's the same. Guess it's in the Lang genes.' A yawn rolled up her throat and over her lips. It had been a long time since she'd been anything like too active. So long she'd forgotten how it felt to have abundant energy, not to need to go to bed till well after midnight.

When she'd finally gone back to work at the Taupo Family Medical Centre after her illness she'd truly believed she was ready for anything and everything, but her days off couldn't come round soon enough so she could catch up on sleep. Not easy to do around a toddler with the energy of a trailer load of Energiser batteries.

'Want me to get Aimee?' Worry tainted Dad's voice, adding to her sense of inadequacy. Not to mention her guilt for letting him see that yawn.

She tried for a grin, didn't do too bad a job. 'I'm making her wait, like you said.'

Dad grinned right back. 'Look at you. Almost bouncing in the seat with wanting to go pick her up.'

He did way too much for her. It broke her heart, knowing that when he'd decided to take early retirement so he could start having some fun she'd messed up his plans. Not that she'd asked him to cancel the big trip to Europe he'd looked forward to for years. But being the awesome father he was there'd been no question of what he'd do when they'd learned her dreadful news. He had stepped up for her all her life. More especially after Mum had died. And now he did the same for Aimee.

Would she be half the parent he was? Some days that worried her sick. On the really bleak ones it frightened her to think she mightn't get the chance to find out.

Aimee had evoked something primal within her. Like flicking a switch, bang, the love had turned on. Never to be turned off. A deep, unconditional love that had fine-tuned Charlie's protective instincts, while also bringing so much joy to her life. She couldn't wait for the years ahead to unfold. Already she watched with avarice as Aimee learned to feed herself, to stagger up onto her own feet and totter around the house, to give sticky hugs with those little arms—it all gave her so much pleasure. There'd be plenty more great things to come. She just knew it.

Wearing her Pollyanna hat? Definitely, though *she wasn't so naive as to think her daughter was going to be perfect.* Actually, perfection was a fault in itself. Not so long ago she'd believed her life couldn't get any better and look how that had blown up in her face. She was still recovering, might never return to the peaceful state of mind she'd innocently thought was hers for ever.

She shivered, rubbed her arms. Forced a smile. Pollyanna had quickly disappeared. The black worry that lurked at the edge of her mind expelled her happy moments all too quickly. Would that change one day? One day soon?

'Charlie?' Concern laced her dad's voice. 'You okay?'

With a lightness she didn't feel she replied, 'Sure am.'

Another cry from down the hall. This time Charlie didn't hesitate. Jumping up, she headed for the door. 'Yippee. Get up time. I want that first sleep-scented snuggle from Aimee.'

'Okay.' Dad conceded quickly enough. 'Now that my grandgirl's awake, I'll get the hedge trimmer out and tidy up out the back.'

Charlie paused, turned back. 'Dad, why don't you go play a round of golf instead? The hedge can wait another few days. Take a break from the chores and enjoy yourself.' Those lines around his mouth hadn't been there a year ago. They were all due to her. Guilt spread through her like wildfire. 'I'm so sorry.'

His face softened as he crossed to stomp up the steps to the deck, where he hugged her. His tone was gruff. 'Cut that out, Charlotte Lang. There's no point beating yourself up for something you had no say over.'

Sniffing in the dad scent she'd known her whole life, she blinked back tears and dredged up a smile. 'Have I told you that you're the best father ever?' The familiar line fell easily between them.

'Never.' That too was the usual response. 'Tomorrow, if the weather stays fine, I'll take the boat out on the lake with Billy to do a spot of fishing. How's that?'

That was progress. 'Great. I'll order up a perfect January day just for you. And I'll get the barbecue ready.' Of course the trout weren't so easy to catch in midsummer but the men would have fun trying. At least trolling meant a bigger chance of success than river fishing. And she'd get in steak as a back-up.

Yeah, she had a plan. Plans were good, kept her on track through the rough patches. Then it dawned on her to look around, see the day for what it was. The sun shone bright and hot in the clear blue sky, making everything appear brand new and the flowers on the pohutukawa sharp red. And her tiredness wasn't dominating her quite so much. In fact, she felt the best she had in a long time.

She surprised herself with, 'I'm going to start getting fit. Take my bike out of the shed and pump up the tyres.' She grinned, feeling the most relaxed she had for a long time. 'That will probably take all my energy and I'll have to have a nap afterwards, but it's a start.'

Until the advent of Aimee she'd loved nothing better than to fall out of bed and hit the road on her cycle before going into work. And on her days off most of her spare time had been spent sailing her Paper Tiger across Lake Taupo, catching the erratic winds.

'Don't overdo it,' said the doctor in her dad as he stepped away, averting his face in a vain attempt to hide his worry.

'As if.' Nowadays she took naps and spent her free time playing with dolls and building things out of plastic blocks with Aimee.

How drastically her life had changed since she'd returned home pregnant. She rubbed her tummy. Felt the surgical scar on her lower abdomen. Tried to ignore the flare of anguish. At least she'd had a child before her hysterectomy. She'd loved being pregnant and watching all the changes that had happened to her body. The months had flown past and then Aimee had arrived and she was in love.

Unfortunately, someone else had missed out on all that. Aimee's father. Marshall Hunter, US Army medic.

If only he'd been able to share in the excitement, to be around to put his hand against her expanding belly and feel his daughter kick. Even if she found him tomorrow, he'd never get any of that back. Aimee was eighteen months old and nothing like the tiny scrap of arms and legs placed against her breast moments after the birth.

How stupid of she and Marshall to agree to going their separate ways at the end of their fling. Despite her heart breaking, she'd gone along with him. He'd assured her he was single, that they weren't hurting anyone else, but he didn't do long-term relationships. Rightly or wrongly, she'd believed him. He'd come across as genuine. But no one had told her she'd have a child from that liaison. There'd been no thunderclaps to warn her she'd need Marshall Hunter back in her life nine months later.

Had Marshall flown to the moon? Even if he had, he'd still be contactable. Wouldn't he?

Well, she could be stubborn if it was important. And finding her daughter's father ranked at the top of the scale. But as of today she wasn't going to let the continual failure to achieve her goal get her down. She'd done with all that. It was time to start living full on, not half pie.

A louder shriek from down the hall told her Aimee was fed up with waiting. She wanted out of her cot—now. Being a determined little lady—wonder where that had come from?—she would quite likely attempt climbing out of her cot soon. Charlie moved fast. A broken head would only add to the worries this little household already faced.

'Hey, beautiful, how's my girl? Have a good sleep?' Reaching for Aimee, Charlie's heart squeezed at the sight of the little creases made by the pillow on the side of her baby's face, and at the red cheeks and sleep-filled green eyes staring out at her over the edge of the cot. So like Aimee's father's eyes. Piercing green, reminding her of a polished emerald.

Aimee's father. MIA. She shuddered. Wrong term. She might be doing everything in her power to find him, but MIA? That was definitely tempting fate. Especially if he was back in another war zone with his unit. She touched the side of the cot with her fingers for luck, definitely needing to push away that cloud of dread.

'Mum-mum,' Aimee instantly gurgled, and raised her arms high. 'Mum-mum.'

Thoughts of Marshall kept trekking through Charlie's head as she lifted her daughter up. She couldn't really imagine anything happening to him. 'Your dad is so virile, so much larger than life, strong and full on. He looks the world in the eye, as though daring it to throw the worst at him.' He always acted as though nothing could touch him.

Stupid Charlie. Trying to get the man hurt now?

'Mum-mum.'

'Time you learnt a new word. How about Grandpa?' How about Daddy? If only there was a need for that.

Aimee wriggled and tightened her arms around Charlie's neck, almost choking her.

Carefully unravelling them, Charlie grinned. 'You've

got a very wet bottom, my girl.' She kissed Aimee's brow and headed for the bathroom.

Blowing kisses on Aimee's tummy took up a few minutes. Giggles rent the air and made Charlie grin more widely. 'You're worth it all, my girl. I'd go through everything again if I had to.'

Careful, you might have to yet. No guarantees out there.

The dark thought lifted goose-bumps on her skin. It was this fear that kept her acting on the side of caution, kept her refusing to relax and accept she was over the worst so that she could get on with life, and that drove her to keep trying to find Marshall despite the unlikelihood of ever succeeding in that quest.

'Mum, up.' Aimee's well-aimed foot banged against her jaw, making her jerk back, and refocused her on where her mind should be. On her daughter.

'Hey, mischief, watch who you're kicking.' Yep, definitely an active kid.

Her baby girl, whom she'd do absolutely anything for. Along with Marshall's green gaze Aimee had inherited a whole dose of stubbornness from him. Otherwise she was her mum with the dark blonde hair, button nose and freckles dotting her cheeks.

'One day, my girl, we're going to find your dad. Won't he be surprised?' Surprise might not cut it. There was a myriad of other emotions Marshall would no doubt feel when he learned he was father to this gorgeous bundle of joy. Hopefully love would eventually come out on top.

But first she'd get her strength back. She sighed. Nothing was easy these days. Hadn't been since the day the lab results had come back with all the medical jargon screaming out at her: cervical cancer.

Charlie's world had instantly imploded. The future, in particular Aimee's future, had become a priority in case the worst happened and Aimee lost her mum. Fear had driven Charlie throughout her surgery and treatment, had got her back on her feet. Losing her mother to cancer at seven had been dreadful, but she'd had her dad to love and cherish her. If Aimee lost her to this terrible disease then she'd need Marshall in her life.

He was out there. He'd held her in his arms, made love to her a lot, kissed her senseless. He hadn't been an apparition.

Oh, no. Not at all. Her fingertips traced her lips. Her insides melted as her skin remembered his large hands caressing, teasing, loving her body.

Aimee needed to know both her parents. And… Charlie's fingers brushed the bathroom cabinet…if the worst came to the worst, Marshall had to be there for Aimee if she couldn't be.

If only she could find him.

She had to. No argument.

CHAPTER TWO

CAPTAIN MARSHALL HUNTER turned onto Spa Road and slowed, checking which side of the road he was driving on. 'Goddamned Kiwis. Why can't they use the right-hand side like everyone else?'

Someone tooted at him and he pulled to the kerb. 'Yeah, yeah, give me a break. I'm a tourist.' A tired smile stretched across his mouth. The trouble with being overtired was that everything got that much more complicated. Twisting the cap off the bottle of soda he'd purchased at the petrol station a little way back, he poured half the contents down his parched throat. At least that tasted the same as back home. Jet lag, and lack of sleep for the past six months, played havoc with his body. And his mind.

The military plane out of Kansas that he'd hitched a ride on had touched down at Whenuapai Air Force Base at the ungodly hour of five that morning.

Which only went to show how crazy he'd been. Why had he hopped a plane going in the opposite direction from Florida, where he'd intended spending some of his leave checking up on his buddy's family? A sudden aberration of the brain? Had to be. No other explanation for finding himself in this place called Taupo. On the long-haul flight, squashed amongst gear and guys, he'd tried not to dwell on his uncharacteristically impulsive action. Like that had been possible.

What had happened to Mr Cool, the guy who planned every move of his life? He didn't do random. Random got you shot in a war zone. Got you in all sorts of trouble anywhere. Besides, he was an officer in the army where lateral thinking didn't go down too well with the top brass.

Marshall grimaced. All control gone in a haze of yearning for something intangible, for someone who regularly flitted through his mind. So close yet so far away. Charlie Lang. Woman wonderful.

She'd been responsible for the fog in his head and the gnawing sense of finally reaching a destination he'd been aiming for ever since he'd waved her goodbye back in Honolulu more than two years back.

Closing his eyes, he leaned back against the headrest. Charlie. 'Because of you I've come all this way with no idea if I'm even welcome.' Of course he'd be welcome. Charlie would be thrilled to see him. Why wouldn't she? They'd got on well.

'You spent all your time together in bed.'

So? That had worked out just fine. Could be that they might do some more bed gymnastics while he was here. Unless she'd got hitched to some dude in the intervening years. Air caught in his lungs. She wouldn't have. Would she? Why not? Charlie was one very sexy lady who any man would be happy to get up close and personal with.

Okay. Don't go there. Presume until told otherwise that Charlotte was still single and willing. They *had* been very compatible. He'd never known sex like it.

She'd pressed every button he had and some. One look
at her across the ED and he'd been a goner, falling into
those deep blue pools blinking out at him from under
a thick blonde fringe.

His belly rumbled with hunger. Snatching up the
BLT sandwich he'd picked up at the same time as the
soda, he bit into it. Chewing thoughtfully, he hoped it
was hunger and not nerves making his gut carry on
like a washing machine. Like he ever did nervous. Not
even on a recce when he knew armed insurgents were
waiting to take a crack at him.

The sandwich went down a treat, making him feel
almost human again. Ready to do battle. If it came to
that. As if it would. Charlie would be happy to see him.
But he'd been on edge for so long he couldn't quite get
a grip on things. He'd come off that flight feeling like
rubbish, knowing he should hop on the next plane out
of the country, no matter where it went. But he hadn't.
Instead, he'd gone looking for a way to get to Taupo.

A New Zealand officer at Whenuapai had organised
a room on the base so he could scrub up, shave two
days' growth off his face, change into civvies and have
a decent meal. Then that same guy had driven him to
the nearest car rental place.

Marshall knew he should've stopped overnight and
caught some proper shut-eye. Instead, he'd been driving
on foreign roads through a sprawling city, then through
amazing countryside to reach this small town nestled
on the edge of the country's largest lake. He might've
been more prepared to cope with what he'd travelled
so far for if he'd waited until tomorrow.

He snorted. 'For sure. If you're not ready to see Charlie by now, know what you want to say to her, you're

never going to be.' How else was he ever going to sleep properly again? 'But what am I going to say to her? Hey, buddy.' He looked up at the sky. 'Rod, you own this idea so help me out here.'

Sweat beaded on his forehead as his heart thudded against his ribs. Charlie was the woman he went to in his head at night after a hideous day on patrol. She was the woman who'd touched him like no other ever had. She'd gotten under his skin and wouldn't go away, no matter that he'd known he mustn't have her again. He had obligations that didn't include her. And yet here he was.

'It's not too late to turn around and head back up to Auckland.' But then he'd never have closure. Would always wonder what he might've gained by seeing Charlie one more time. This time he'd say goodbye properly so as his heart understood exactly where it stood. No notes slipped into her pocket.

Back in Honolulu he'd done the right thing by deliberately telling Charlie nothing about himself, not even which state he'd grown up in. He'd been strong, tough, thinking he was doing her a favour.

Their fling had been short, sweet, exciting and hot, not to mention mind-numbing. At the end of it he'd hopped a plane ride out of Honolulu bound for the base in Kansas to prepare for his next posting to Afghanistan. He'd been so damned confident he could walk away from Charlie Lang without a care in the world, never to think of her again. Right? Wrong.

Glug, glug. The remaining soda coursed down his throat. Coming here had to be right up there with being totally selfish. But he didn't know any other way to exorcise Charlie from his brain, where she seemed to have branded him—with images of her gut-twisting smile, her light laughter, her very sexy body. Hell, even thinking about that turned him on. The heat south of his belt had nothing to do with his head and all to do with being closer to Charlie than he'd been in a very long time.

So he'd come to get her out of his system? Not to get back in the sack with her?

'Yeah, well, I'm a little confused right now.'

Not once in those passion-filled weeks had he asked where Charlie was headed after she'd finished her time in Honolulu. So sure had he been that he'd never follow up on her. But she'd told him anyway, making it scarily easy to locate her when he'd given in to the deepening need clawing at him. The world could be a very small place at times.

Now here he was at the bottom of that world, around the corner from Charlie's house. Soon he'd see her for real and realise his dreams had lied, that those wonderful memories were vapour, not real. That she'd been a very ordinary woman out for a bit of fun. Then he could get on with life the way he needed to live it, following his army career as hard as possible, even if it wasn't so rewarding any more. Especially as Rod hadn't made it. Guilt was his constant companion. Duty to his men his creed.

Voices washed over him as kids on bikes wheeled past the open window of his rental. Free as the birds they were. Sometimes he missed being a kid and being able to ride horseback around the ranch with his grandfather.

'Aren't you forgetting something?'

Yup. The weeks when Dad had come home on leave from the army and forced his discipline on his son.

Harsh, unforgiving, relentless. That was the old man. He'd ruled by his fists. Hard to believe Granddad had spawned his father. Couldn't get two more dissimilar men.

Flick. His mind returned to the nagging questions that refused to die down. Would Charlie greet him with open arms?

Or would she give him a bollocking for breaking the pact they'd made in Hawaii?

Let's have fun and leave it at that. No contact afterwards, no regrets.

In the deep of the night when he couldn't sleep— most nights—he wondered if Charlie's willingness to go along with his ultimatum had meant there had been someone else in her life back here in New Zealand. Some guy she'd wanted to set up house and raise a family with. Had she been sowing some oats in Honolulu before coming back to marry? Whatever she'd been looking for at the time, he'd been a willing partner.

'Never going to know what she thinks while sitting here.'

Reaching for the ignition, he hesitated. Whatever it was deep inside his psyche that had brought him this far seemed to have suddenly deserted him.

Finally the engine turned over, purred loudly as though mocking this vacillation. He eased the vehicle back onto the road. His heart rate increased. Excited? Yeah, bring it on. He really wanted to see Charlie, no matter how she reacted. If she sent him packing he'd deal with it.

'At one hundred metres take the right-hand turn,' droned the GPS.

'Yes, sir.'

In Hill Road Marshall slowed, peered at letterboxes as he cruised along, finally finding Charlie's number. Lifting his foot from the accelerator, he glided the vehicle to the kerb and parked. Not stopping to overthink this any more than he already had, he pushed out of the clammy interior and leaned back against the hood, his arms crossed over his chest. He studied the house where Charlie supposedly lived. An old villa in good nick, surrounded by a recently cut lawn and weed-filled gardens, and with huge unusual trees equally spaced along the side fences.

Female laughter reached him, snuck under his skin, thawing the cold places deep inside. Charlie's laughter. He'd know it anywhere. It had warmed him, tickled and delighted him. Haunted him. Hungry for his first glimpse of the woman he'd flown halfway round the world to see, he scanned the veranda running across the front of the house. Movement from the side caught his eye.

A toddler, dressed all in pink, running and stumbling, shrieking with joy while waving a plastic bucket, heading straight for—for Charlie. Beautiful Charlie. There at last, right in his line of sight, was Charlie. In the flesh.

The air trickled from his lungs as he sank further down onto the front of the car without shifting his gaze. An exploding landmine couldn't have made him look away now. Memories of holding her close bombarded him, pummelling him with the sheer joy of her. Warmth crept into his body. Had he done the right thing coming here after all?

Charlie.

She seemed to still in her movements. Hell, had he

called her name out loud? Then she said something to the little girl and jerked backwards as she was rewarded with another ear-shattering shriek of delight.

Marshall began breathing again.

And continued watching Charlie, recalling how she'd race back to him after a long day in the ED and leap into his arms, kissing him senseless, before dragging him into bed. Not that he'd been reluctant, far from it. But he had enjoyed being seduced. It had been novel and exciting. She'd teased him blatantly with her body, but had always given what she'd promised. Then there had been the times she'd gone all coy on him and he'd had to woo her into bed.

He ran his hands down his face and re-crossed his arms. Was Charlie thinner now? Nah, probably not. His memory wouldn't be that accurate. But her hair was very different. What had she done to those stunning long, honey-coloured tresses that he'd spent hours running his fingers through? Gone, replaced with a shorter, curly cut that framed her beautiful face. Different and yet equally attractive.

His heart slowed as he watched the woman of his nights reach down and lift the hyperactive bundle into her arms. Even from here he could see the love for the child all over Charlie's features.

Her daughter?

Pain slashed at Marshall. He was too late. Too damned late. Charlie was a mother. Which meant there'd be a man somewhere in the picture. She was taken. She hadn't changed the rules. Instead, she'd got on with life, made a family. That hollowed him out. Made him realise how much he'd been hoping she was free and available. Great. Now he knew, what did he do?

'You could just say hi.'

Sure. Now that he had admitted he'd been fooling himself all along, it hurt big time. His heart rolled over, cranked up enough energy to pump some much-needed oxygen around his body. Disappointment flared, mixed with the pain and despair, underlining the whole stupidity of coming here on a whim.

Getting reacquainted with Charlie again was not an option.

The reality struck, blinding him. He'd wanted to get to know her properly this time, to learn what made her tick. The doctor side of her, the serious Charlie, the loving, caring woman who enjoyed having a good time. All the Charlies that made up the woman who'd caught his attention when he hadn't been looking.

Another movement snagged his attention. Someone was walking towards the back of the house from under a big, bushy tree. Tall, thin, and, even from the back view, definitely male. Marshall's stomach dived. His arms tightened in on each other, holding himself together.

Damn it. He'd thought about worst-case scenarios and taken a punt anyway. But Charlie was now a mother and there was a man in her life. Marshall could no longer deny the obvious.

'You, Marshall Hunter, have to walk away. Now. Before she sees you and the trouble starts.' It would be so unfair to knock on her door and say, 'Hi, remember me?'

No way did he want to hurt her. And he surely would if he stayed now. Truthfully, he'd hoped for another fling, something he could walk away from. So now he'd have to suck it up and walk away sooner than he'd expected. Get on with life and put Charlie out of his head permanently.

But his boots remained stuck to the tarmac, going nowhere. He'd come too far just to walk away without a word.

'Oh, buddy, did you really think Charlie was sitting around, waiting for the day you might step back into her life?'

An image of her standing outside the hospital, blinking back tears and saying the sun was in her eyes as she'd waved him goodbye, slapped across his brain.

A little bit, he had. Okay, make that a big bit.

He needed to get over it. He'd had an absolutely sensational fling with her. One that he'd willingly walked away from with few qualms. And then she'd emailed. A month after Rod had been killed. Two days after he'd visited Rod's wife and kids and seen the anguish caused by Rod's passing. He'd deleted Charlie's message without reading it, knowing he never wanted to be responsible for causing her the same pain Karen suffered.

As Marshall watched Charlie and the little girl chasing around the lawn he thought of the hurt she'd been saved from by finding another man to share her life with. No doubt that man wouldn't miss birthdays and Christmas, would be around to fix the car when it broke down or to dig the garden, take her out to dinner. Things no woman would ever get from him. The army regularly sent him off to some hellhole in a bleak part of the world where he had to be strong for his men, not worrying about how he might be letting down the woman in his life.

'Time to go, buddy. You made a mistake coming here.' He blinked. Took one last, long look at the woman

who'd unconsciously drawn him to Taupo, saw the
things his memories hadn't been particularly clear on.
The way she held her compact body as though ready
to leap into his arms at any moment, except now it was
her child she seemed ready to leap after. The gentle tilt
of her head to the right as she concentrated on whatever
the little girl was saying.

'Get the hell out of here,' he croaked around the
blockage in his throat. Dropping back inside the car,
he reached trembling fingers to the ignition. Blinked
rapidly as the heat inside the car steamed up his eyes.
Damn it to hell. He was too darned late.

CHAPTER THREE

CHARLIE HEARD A car moving slowly past the gate and glanced up. Not recognising the vehicle, she made to turn away but hesitated. Something about the driver's profile caught at a memory. What was it about that face that stirred her? Absolutely nothing. She bit down on the temptation to go out onto the street for a better look.

Losing her grip on reality now? Wishing Marshall Hunter back into her life wasn't actually going to bring him to her doorstep. No matter what Dad said.

Thump. Crack. The sound of metal crunching metal screeched through the air.

'What was that?' Charlie placed Aimee in the sand-pit and raced for the gate.

'Sounds like someone wasn't looking where he was going.' Her father spoke from right behind her.

The car Charlie had noticed moments earlier was now parked with its nose deep into the side of their neighbour's SUV, the bonnet folded back on itself. 'John's not going to be too pleased about that. At least it doesn't look like anyone's been hurt.'

'Unless the driver had a medical event,' Dad pointed out as he strode past her. 'I'll go and check.'

Charlie glanced back at Aimee but she'd become

engrossed in pushing a toy truck around the pit. Locking the gate latch, Charlie spun around to join her father. And froze.

The driver had climbed out of the car, cursing quietly as he surveyed the damage he'd caused. His American accent sliced into her.

'Marshall?' The name squeaked off her tongue as her heart slowed. 'Marshall?' Louder this time but just as scratchy.

He turned in her direction and took away any lingering doubt as his intense green gaze locked with hers. In that instant she saw the man she'd shared a bed with for so many wonderful hours. Her body remembered all the heat and passion, the sensual touches and her deep, bottomless hunger for him. Marshall Hunter. The man she'd spent untold hours trying to find for their daughter had turned up outside her gate. Just like that? No way.

Put it out there. Yeah, right, Dad.

The ability to stand upright deserted her. Her hand flailed through the summer air as she reached for the fence to hold onto, and her heart stopped. It must have because suddenly she couldn't breathe any more.

'Charlie.' Then he was there, directly in front of her, reaching for her, gripping her arms to hold her upright. 'How're you doing, babe?'

How am I doing? That's it? No *I came to see you.* No *Crikey what a long way from good old US of A to find you.* No *I'm just cruising through and thought I'd drop by.* Just how am I doing? Swallowing was impossible with the lump blocking off her airway. Her eyes widened as she stared at this smiling apparition with eyes that were deep green pools sucking her into an exciting world. An unrealistic world, she knew, but one she couldn't deny while so close to him. Her arms were heating where those strong hands gripped her. Her breasts seemed to be straining to be up close to that chest she'd once fallen asleep against in the wee hours of the morning.

'Charlie? I've surprised you.' Did he have to sound so pleased with himself?

'I'm fine,' she managed to croak out at last. Couldn't be better, in fact. Who did she think she was fooling? Not knowing whether to laugh or cry, she continued to stand there, stunned.

Then those wonderful arms she'd spent many hours longing for wrapped around her and tucked her against that expansive chest threatening to pop the seams of the black T-shirt he wore. That's when she knew this really was Marshall.

Something wet oozed down her cheek. Tears? She didn't do tears. Not once throughout her pregnancy when she wished Marshall by her side. Hardly ever during the harrowing days of waiting for the diagnosis of cancer. Hadn't cried while going through radiation and chemo. Must be the realisation that she didn't have to keep searching the phone records of every state in America to find numbers for every Hunter listed that was causing this leakage. 'You came,' she whispered.

'Were you expecting me?' As he leaned back at the waist to peer down at her, his mouth cracked a smile. A genuine, warm, toe-curling, Marshall smile.

And her heart went from slow to rapid in one beat. Heat rushed up her cheeks, dried her mouth so that when she spoke it sounded as though she'd sucked on helium. 'Don't be daft.'

'I'm daft now?' His smile widened, his eyes twinkled.

'I tried to find you. Except it seemed like you'd vanished into thin air. Even the army wouldn't help.' But what were the odds of Marshall turning up on her patch? Should she be buying a lottery ticket?

Marshall's arms fell away and he stepped back so fast she staggered. His tone was clipped. 'Of course not. They won't give out information on my whereabouts unless you're on my list of contacts.'

The temperature had suddenly dropped a few degrees. Of course she wouldn't be on that list. Hadn't expected to be, but Marshall voicing it reminded her how far apart they were, how little they'd had in common, or even knew about each other, except great sex.

And the sweetest little girl. Whoa. Red-flag warning. Her shoulders pulled back and her spine clicked straighter. She'd spent so much time trying to find Marshall that she'd never stopped to consider how she'd tell him about Aimee. Who knew what his reaction would be? What she wanted from him and what she might get could be poles apart.

Rubbing her arms, Charlie studied him. He looked exactly the same as the last time she'd seen him, the day she'd kissed him goodbye. Except then he'd worn army fatigues, not butt-hugging, thigh-accentuating jeans and a tee shirt that framed his size and muscles. His face was bronzed, his buzz-cut hair darker than midnight, that mouth that had done sensational things to her skin was still full and enticing. Marshall was still heart-stoppingly attractive.

Behind her someone cleared his throat. Dad. She'd forgotten all about him. Forgotten even where she was. And Aimee. Was she still in the sandpit? A quick look over the fence and Charlie relaxed a notch.

Aimee. Marshall's daughter. The tension rewound tighter than ever. And anger pounced. 'Why are you here? Turning up with no warning, as though you expected me to be happy to see you.' Her hands clenched and her breaths were short and sharp. After all this time of searching for him and here he was, looking wonderful, not to mention cocky. So darned sure of his welcome. 'Well, I don't want to see you.'

Her petulance rang in her ears. So much for being mature and sophisticated. Too bad. Right now Marshall bloody Hunter deserved worse.

Marshall was staring at her as though she'd grown horns. She probably had. 'Charlie, I'm sorry. I never thought to phone ahead.'

She gaped at him, her jaw dropping hard. A fish out of water probably looked more attractive. 'You have no idea what you've done.' She spun round on the balls of her feet and nearly slammed into her father, who looked puzzled as he glanced from her to the man and back.

'Charlie, didn't I tell you to let it go and see what happened?' That Dad grin he gave her calmed her temper the tiniest bit. 'Happened a lot quicker than we expected, didn't it?'

He was taking the credit for Marshall's sudden appearance? No, Dad was being Dad, gentling her when her temper ran away on her. Thank goodness for fathers. On an uneven breath she said, 'You're right. I don't know what came over me.' Now, there was a fib. Marshall was no longer MIA but standing a metre away, watching her from those intense eyes that missed nothing.

Both men seemed to be waiting for her next move. She didn't have one. Her heart was thumping so loudly in her chest she couldn't hear herself think. Her stomach was doing loop the loop while her hands shook so hard she had to clench them into tight fists again.

Finally Dad made the first move. He strode towards Marshall, holding his hand out in greeting. 'I'm Brendon Lang, Charlie's father.'

Marshall's eyes widened with something Charlie could've sworn was relief. Glad of the diversion? With startling alacrity he took Dad's hand and shook it. 'Marshall Hunter. Pleased to meet you, sir.'

Dad returned the handshake, said, 'Marshall, what happened? One moment you were parked on one side of the road, the next you've slammed into John's SUV on the opposite side.'

Embarrassment flushed through Marshall's eyes. 'I got distracted.' His gaze fell on Charlie. 'Forgot which side of the road to drive on. Do you know the owner of that vehicle? I'll need to sort out repairs with him.'

'John's our neighbour. I'm surprised he's not out here already.' Dad glanced up the drive.

'He went out on his motorbike hours ago.' She'd growled when John had roared down the road moments after Aimee had finally fallen asleep.

Dad crossed to the merged vehicles. 'Let's see what the damage is.'

Marshall looked embarrassed as he called after him, 'I'll shift the rental and then leave the guy my contact details. He's not going to be too pleased when he sees that dent.' He didn't move to join Dad, instead remaining beside her, playing havoc with her senses. He was an eyeful, for sure.

Tightening her stomach muscles in an attempt to gain some control over her wacky emotions, she looked up at him, and instantly wished she hadn't as her eyes clashed with his. A girl could get lost in those eyes. Heavens, she once had. And look where that had got her. Focus on the bent cars. Nothing else.

'I think you'll survive. It's John's work vehicle, supplied by his company. If you'd hit his Harley you'd be swinging from that tree in his front yard already.' The words spilled out in a rush.

Marshall grinned that mesmerising grin she'd never forgotten. 'Really? A Harley? Awesome.'

Great. Another motorbike freak. And something she hadn't known about him. Along with just about everything, she realised. A doctor in the US army didn't cover much about this man at all. Hang on, don't forget his energy, athleticism and how gorgeous he looked first thing in the morning with stubble darkening his strong jaw.

A shiver rocked through her. Stop it. None of that had anything to do with Marshall suddenly turning up unannounced. Why now? She shrugged. Plenty of time to find out. Or was there? He could be passing through. Of course, Waiouru. The military base was only a few hours down the road. This would be a fleeting visit. She'd have to make the most of it and grab the opportunity to tell him about Aimee. But why was he here? Then reality hit—hard. 'You were driving away. You weren't stopping by to see me at all.' What had he been planning on? A reunion? Changed his mind when he'd seen how suburban she actually was?

'Caught.' His smile faded as his lips pressed into a line. His gaze drifted to Dad, back to her. 'Sorry, Charlie. I decided I'd made a mistake.'

'Marshall.' She grabbed his forearm, shook him to get his undivided attention. When those eyes that reminded her of hazy summer days met hers this time she all but yelled at him, 'Don't think you're disappearing out of my life that quickly. Not when I've spent months trying to trace you.'

There was no way she'd let him walk away now. Her gut rolled, which had absolutely nothing to do with Aimee and everything to do with the wickedly hot memories of Honolulu that touching his arm brought to mind.

'You have?' Shock dropped his jaw. 'Why?'

Gulp. Not out here on the street. The man deserved some lead in before she dropped her bombshell. She shrugged, trying for nonchalance and failing miserably. 'If we sort out the vehicles first, will you promise to give me a few minutes of your time?' A few minutes? She'd better come up with a succinct explanation for why she'd been searching for him if that was all the time available.

'Yeah, sure.' Marshall's tone lightened as though he thought he'd been granted a reprieve.

As if. How could he know that? He was very astute, remember? Said it was part of his military training to always be looking for a hidden agenda. What he hadn't worked out yet was that it would be a very short reprieve. But first the cars. 'Think you'll be able to back your car away from the SUV without causing more damage?'

Then he leaned closer, traced a fingertip over her lips. 'How have you been, Charlie? Really?'

Her stomach thrummed. Her lips opened under his finger. Just like that, she was his. Or would be if she wasn't standing in the street with Dad watching warily. Jerking her head back, she glared up at him, saw the man who was used to getting what he wanted when he wanted it, and started to spew out two years' worth of desperation. 'I couldn't be better, what with—'

Aimee interrupted, 'Mum-mum. Up.'

Charlie spun around to find Aimee half-draped over the fence. 'You little monkey. That fence is supposed to keep you in.' Seemed she'd be arranging for the new, higher fence to be built sooner than she'd expected. Opening the gate, she bent to lift Aimee into her arms. 'Come here.'

Her heart was pounding as her blood sped around her veins. She'd nearly blown it then, had been about to spill it all thoughtlessly, without due consideration for Marshall and his reaction. That would definitely not earn her any points and make it harder for Aimee in the long run.

'Your daughter?' Marshall stood right behind her.

'Yes.' She saw disappointment cloud his eyes. So he didn't like the idea she had a child. Didn't that fit in with his plans? Whatever those were. Tough. She had more bad news for him yet. When he heard the whole story he wouldn't even be thinking about how he felt about *her*.

Charlie held Aimee tightly against her chest. A shield? Did she need protection from Marshall? Now the moment of truth had arrived she suddenly wondered how he might react to being told he was a father. He might go absolutely ballistic and deny flat out he could ever be a father. Or say there was no way in hell he wanted a part in Aimee's life. Or he might insist they move to the States to be near him. Not a hope in Hades, Marshall. Not a hope.

'Go sort out your car, Marshall.' Now she sounded bossy. But what was she supposed to do? Tell him everything here and now, standing on the footpath? Hand him Aimee and say, 'Meet your daughter'? 'Will you stay long enough for a coffee afterwards?'

Marshall's eyes widened. Struggling to keep up with her? 'Sure.' He turned towards the vehicles, turned back. 'It's great to see you, Charlie. Really great.'

Take my breath away, why don't you?

Her eyes feasted on his broad back and narrow hips as he walked away. A shiver of excitement rippled through her. But there was so much she didn't know about Marshall. Once she'd tipped his world upside down with the news he was a father, would she get the chance to find out anything? Or would he storm off, never to be seen again?

Her gaze drifted to the entangled vehicles. He wouldn't be storming anywhere in the next few minutes. Her spirits lifted. He had to hang around for a bit. At least until a new car had been arranged, surely?

Marshall headed for his rental, still trying to collect his scattered brain cells. This tall dude was Charlie's father. Hell, he'd nearly shouted with laughter when he'd heard that. All the disappointment gripping him since he'd spied the guy under the tree had dissipated in a flash.

You're not in the clear yet, buddy. That cute little girl has to have a father. Kids don't just arrive in the letterbox.

His smile slipped. True.

'Right, let's get this sorted,' Brendon muttered, just as a Harley shot around the corner.

'This your neighbour?' He tilted his head in the direction of the bike. What a way to introduce himself to Charlie's father. If the man had any sense he'd make sure he never went near his daughter again.

'Yes. Come and meet John.' Brendon seemed preoccupied. 'Are you staying in town, son?'

Straightening his shoulders, Marshall studied the man before him. There seemed to be a lot more to that question than was apparent. Until he got a grasp on the situation he'd give away little about his intentions. Intentions? Hell, they were as clear as a sandstorm. 'Yes, sir.'

'For long?'

So the guy did want him gone. Wasn't happy about his sudden appearance. Protecting his daughter? 'Two days. Maybe three, depends on my ride out of the country.'

'So you're flexible?' Was that hope lightening that steady gaze? Nothing made much sense here.

'Depends on the air force.' Not to mention Charlie and her situation. 'I'd like to spend some time catching up with your daughter, if that's at all possible.'

'You'd better stay the night with us, then.'

I don't think so. In the circumstances that's way too close and personal. 'Won't Charlie object?' What about the kid's dad?

Brendon gave him a knowing smile. 'Probably, but then she'll calm down and see the merit in my idea. You might have to weather her temper first, though.'

'Seems like I've already had a wee dose.' Marshall shook his head. He'd never once seen her get angry back in Honolulu. 'Let's talk to your neighbour about his wrecked SUV first.' And give me time to decide whether I go for broke or head for a hotel in town.

Stay in the same house as Charlie? And not be able to touch her, or to hold her, kiss her like he ached to do?

Because if he did he was sure he'd be history. It would go down a treat with her old man. The guy seemed decent enough but touch his daughter and there'd be hell to pay. Marshall just knew it.

Then he was being introduced to John and they got down to the nitty-gritty of sorting out his bad steering problem.

Charlie stood at the window, peering through the trees. Spying on the men. Pinching herself. That really was Marshall out there. With Dad. Talking as though they'd always known each other. There didn't seem to be any animosity from Dad, just his regular caution.

She grinned despite the tension gripping her. Dad must've just about wet himself when she'd spoken Marshall's name. For all his saying to leave it up to the universe to sort her problem, he would never actually have thought anything would come of it. She'd better remember to tell Gemma. She'd enjoy a good laugh.

But Gemma could wait. The man the universe had delivered to her doorstep was about to take all her attention. Strange that now he was here she felt reticent about telling him about Aimee.

Once Marshall knew he was a father Aimee was no longer hers alone. Someone else would have the right to make decisions about her life. Talk about selfish. She definitely wasn't being fair to Aimee or Marshall. There again, if Marshall wasn't interested in being a hands-on father, nothing would have changed. Except that if her health turned to custard, Aimee would still have a parent to go to. Marshall would have to take her then.

But it had been one thing wanting to find him with the intention of explaining the whole situation. It was a completely different issue to actually front up to him and turn his day upside down, if not his life.

More than two years ago he'd been adamant he didn't wanted commitments and she was about to ask him for the biggest one possible. Part of her felt sorry for the guy. If only she'd probed a little to learn what lay behind his statement. But every time she'd started to ask serious questions he'd leaned in and touched her, with the resulting heat turning her brain to molten desire. By the time they'd made love she'd forgotten everything else.

'Mummy.' Aimee tugged at the hem of Charlie's shorts. 'Want dink.'

'You want a drink,' Charlie enunciated clearly for her little miss. Hard to believe how quickly Aimee was learning to talk. Almost overnight she'd gone from saying nothing to these funny little sentences. Aimee was a gift. A joy. She had to get that message across to her daughter's father so he wouldn't miss out on anything else as Aimee grew up.

Male laughter filtered through the trees. Seemed everyone was getting on just fine. No surprise there, with John being so easygoing and Dad acting as middle man. Marshall could also charm anyone when he put his mind to it.

Including her. Not that he'd had to try very hard. She'd been his in a blink. Never before had she known such excitement with a man. Marshall had truly shown her past lovers to be beginners. He'd known all the buttons to push or caress or kiss, turning her into a sex addict overnight. A Marshall sex addict. There had not been even a hint of anything sexual since.

Trying to ignore the old but familiar sweet tension in her tummy, she turned away and headed for the kitchen and the juice, tidying away toys as she went. Aimee tended to spread everything far and wide when she was playing, making it a constant job to keep the floor clear enough to get from one room to another. Normally just thinking about it made Charlie feel tired but not today. Right now she felt more invigorated than she'd felt since she'd first become ill.

Must be something in the air, she hummed to herself. Or a certain American on her doorstep. Her lips twitched. Marshall Hunter was here. In Taupo. Outside her home. Unbelievable. And then the tears really started, pouring down her cheeks, dripping off her chin.

Brendon told Marshall to go on inside the house, and that he'd be along shortly. Marshall could feel his antennae twitching. It was as though Brendon was pushing him and Charlie together—for a catch-up chat? Or was there more to it? But no one had known he'd turn up this afternoon so that couldn't be right.

Did Charlie mind him being here? Or was she about to kick him to the moon? He couldn't decide if she'd truly been happy to see him or not. Initially she'd all but thrown herself at him, but only moments later she'd pulled back, hard.

He stepped into the warm interior and paused to suck in a breath. It had been a long haul to get here, no point in retreating now. Until today he'd never retreated—unless his life had been in danger. Or his buddy's.

His mouth soured. Now was not the time to be recalling that bleak day in hell. Fronting up to Charlie could never be as painful as dealing with what had happened to Rod. The man after whom he'd promised to name his first son, if and when he ever got around to settling down and raising kids. Some time around when he reached fifty.

Stepping along the wide hallway, he glanced at the framed black-and-white photos on the walls. Most of them featured Lake Taupo with the mountains in the background. They were very good. 'C Lang' was signed across the bottom-right corner. Charlie did photography? Darn, he knew so little about her.

He found her in the kitchen with the child. Definitely thinner than he remembered. Had pregnancy done that to her? Most women put on weight, didn't lose it. Could she have taken getting back into shape too seriously? An image of running along the beach in Honolulu with Charlie at his side sprang up and he smiled. Yes, Charlie had been a fitness fanatic. Had loved her sports almost more than anything else. Almost. Sex had been top of the pops. But that was a kind of sport too, she'd told him one day, a cheeky grin lighting up her face.

'What did John have to say?' the woman in question asked in a strained voice as she kept her back to him and supervised the little girl drinking juice. Most of the liquid made it into the child's mouth but the pink tee shirt had a yellow streak down the front.

The pranged cars. Of course. Focus, man. 'He seemed okay with it all.' Marshall tried for a nonchalant shrug to hide these oddball emotions charging around his head. He needn't have worried because Charlie continued focusing her attention elsewhere. He told her, 'I've phoned the rental company and they'll sort it out, including supplying me with another car.' His eyes were stuck on the child. She was so cute. Except for the eyes, she had her mother's colouring right down to the freckles on her button nose.

'Bet they loved that,' Charlie sniffed, and he knew she was crying.

Three long strides and he stood in front of her, reaching his fingers to trace the wet lines on her face. 'Hey, babe, don't cry. Sorry if I've upset you by turning up out of the blue. If you want me to disappear, I'll go. Pronto.'

Panic flared, widened those damp eyes that flicked from him to the child and back again. 'You can't go. Not yet.' She hiccupped through her tears and swiped at her face again.

Why the panic? Then he was holding her, wrapping his arms around those thin shoulders and tucking her up close to his big, warm body. Protecting her. From what? Himself? Hell, he hadn't even thought about taking her in his arms. It had just happened. And Charlie hadn't slapped him across the face and pulled away. He liked holding her. Liked feeling her small frame against his larger one, even if there was a frailty to her that hadn't been there before.

'Charlie?'

'Yes?' came the muffled reply against his chest.

'Why are you shaking?' Tremors had begun rocking through her. 'Why the tears?'

She said nothing.

Placing his hands on her waist, he tipped back a little to put some space between them. Hell, she was thin, bony even. Was she all right? 'Talk to me. Please. Tell me about you. About your daughter.'

Charlie's face whitened, and again panic flared in those haunting eyes. She nodded. 'Yes. Of course.'

What was going on here? Didn't she want him asking about her family? That seemed odd. What about her partner? Only one way to find out. 'You married now?'

Her head swung from side to side, that distinct unease still all over her demeanour. 'No. What about you?'

She wasn't going to change the subject that easily. 'Is this your house?'

'We share it with Dad. I grew up here. I do have a house in town, which I bought a couple of years ago, but it's rented out at the moment. Dad helps with looking after Aimee.' She drew a long breath and opened her mouth, and another torrent of words spilled out. 'We both work at a medical centre—'

Marshall placed a finger on her lips, felt an electric sizzle up his arm. 'Slow down, Charlie.' Under his hands the trembling continued. Because of him? Did his touch disturb her? Or was she afraid of something? He dropped his arms to his sides and stepped back, putting space between them. 'Are you all right?' he asked again. She'd better be. He couldn't bear it if something bad had happened to her.

Her chin ducked abruptly. 'I'm fine.' Then, 'I'm still getting over the shock of seeing you outside our house. Why were you driving away?'

Because I'm a prize idiot. 'Don't get the wrong idea here.' I'm not a stalker. 'I'd been parked outside for a few minutes, watching you and wondering if you'd welcome me or not. Then I saw your father walking around to the back of the house and got the wrong idea.'

'So you drove away.'

'I didn't want to give you any problems. We had an agreement back in Honolulu and obviously I've broken that.' Had to. Had needed to get over her by seeing her again. But already doubts were creeping in under his skin. Would he ever be able to get over Charlie?

'So if you hadn't gone all American and driven on

the wrong side of the road, I'd never have known you were here?' Anger laced her tone and those eyes fired up. 'You'd have gone away without a word?' she hissed, leaning closer.

'I thought I was doing the right thing by you.' Now *he* was on the back foot. What had just happened?

Her forefinger jabbed his chest. 'Do you have any idea how hard I've tried to find you?' Jab. 'Agreement or not?' Jab. 'I have spent…' jab '…untold hours on the computer, searching for you.' Jab. 'And you were driving away.' Then her anger disappeared as quickly as it had risen. Her chest rose and fell fast. 'Sorry. It's just that I wanted to find you and now you're here and I don't know how to tell you something important.'

Warning bells started blaring in his skull. Nothing Charlie said made any sense and yet he was on high alert. Incoming attack. Stepping back further, he leaned one shoulder against the wall and crossed his ankles, to all appearances totally at ease. But inside his head he was pulling up every scenario imaginable. Because something big was about to go down. Something very big.

Then Charlie glanced from him to the little girl. A sob broke across her lips.

And shocked realisation slammed into him. The green eyes should've warned him.

'Aimee's mine.'

CHAPTER FOUR

ALL THE AIR in Charlie's lungs whooshed out. Her arms instantly wrapped around her waist. And she stared, like her eyes were glued to Marshall's stunned face, watching and searching. *His* gaze, firmly fixed on Aimee, showed nothing of his thoughts. Not a hint.

Her heart crashed repeatedly against her ribs as fear and hope warred in her brain. Would he walk? Would he stay? At least stop long enough to hear the rest? Would he shout at her? Call her all sorts of names for not telling him, even when she'd tried so hard to get in touch? Or blame her for getting pregnant in the first place? The skin on her arms lifted in chilly bumps. Why had she not prepared for this moment? Yeah, right. Like how?

'Mum, mum.'

Charlie reluctantly dragged her eyes from Marshall and checked out her daughter. Their daughter. Oh, hell. Her stomach clenched. She clamped her hand over her mouth as nausea rose. This was so—so big. So difficult. Swallow. Swallow.

'Charlie? It's true, isn't it? I'm a father.' Those beautiful green eyes shifted their focus to her. Questions fired out at her.

Another swallow and she answered his first one.

'Yes.' The word whispered across her bottom lip. She swallowed, tried again. 'Yes, Aimee is your daughter. She…' Then the words locked into a lump at the back of her throat, refusing to budge.

'Holy Toledo.'

That was a good response. Wasn't it? It didn't sound bad. At least he was acting calm. So far. She managed, 'She was born a little over eight months after I got back from Honolulu.'

'You didn't have any way of contacting me.' A ton of regret darkened those words but no blame. Then, 'So this is why you've been trying to find me.'

'Yes.' He didn't need to know the rest yet. 'It's a lot to take in.'

'Where do I start?' He sounded completely bewildered. His bemused gaze flicked back and forth between Aimee and her.

At least he wanted to start. But wait until the shock completely wore off. It might be a different story then. Charlie turned to Aimee, who had her cup upside down, pointing in the general direction of her open mouth. Aimee. The love of her life. The reason she was in this situation. Warmth sneaked into Charlie. She never got tired of watching her daughter.

'Up, up.' Aimee's face began screwing up for an outburst.

Moving quickly, Charlie reached for a damp cloth to wipe some of the mess off Aimee's face before lifting her to hold her tightly. She wanted to hand Aimee to Marshall but for the life of her she couldn't. She froze, unable to make the move. Unable to share her daughter with this man. Their daughter, remember? Looking over the top of Aimee's head, her gaze clashed with

Marshall's intent one. Was this when he ran screaming from the house, never to be seen again? Admittedly he'd handled himself well so far but it had only been a few minutes since the truth had dawned on him.

His face softened from shock to awe. 'Charlie Lang, a mother. It suits you.' Then his gaze shifted infinitesimally, slowly cruised over Aimee. Looking for?

She said, 'She's got your eyes.'

'Yeah.'

'You want to hold her?'

His hands jammed into his pockets as he took a backward step.

Okay. Too soon. Shuffling sideways with her heavy bundle, she flicked the kettle on. 'I'll make that coffee I promised. How do you take it?' Her stomach would probably heave if she drank any but she had to do something other than hold Aimee, who'd gone very quiet and still. Twisting her neck, she saw Aimee studying the man in their kitchen.

'Black and strong.' Marshall was suddenly avoiding looking at either of them, apparently finding the view out the window far more interesting.

Aimee wriggled to be put down. Placing her carefully on her feet, Charlie watched as she tottered over to Marshall and stood staring up at this stranger. An important stranger, if all went well. Rubbing her hands up and down her arms, she wondered what to do if Marshall decided he didn't want anything to do with Aimee. Even if her health didn't let her down, every child was entitled to two parents.

The need to explain things gripped Charlie and she began talking fast. 'From the moment I found out I was pregnant I wanted you to have the opportunity to decide what role you'd have in your child's life.'

He turned back to face her, saying absolutely nothing. Thankfully his steady gaze didn't condemn her.

So she continued. 'I've spent a lot of time looking for you in between having Aimee and learning to be a good mum. I checked every known social network on the net. Then I started phoning M Hunters in various states.'

His eyes widened as he gave a grim smile. 'Truly?'

'You wouldn't believe how many there are in the US.' Too many. Her phone bills were horrendous some months. 'Marshall, I don't want anything from you. Not for me. Certainly nothing like money or other handouts. Because of an inheritance from my mother I'm comfortably off and can easily provide whatever my child needs as she grows up. But I do want you to know her. Aimee needs her father to be in her life in some capacity.' Her mouth was getting drier by the word, her tongue beginning to stick to the roof of her mouth.

Marshall's steady gaze unsettled her. What was going on in that head of his? If only he'd say something. Like what? *I'm thrilled to learn I've got a child. Let's play happy families and see how that goes. We know nothing about each other but our child will solve all the differences.*

Sounding good so far? Absolutely wonderful. If it wasn't completely fictitious.

Marshall watched the emotions scudding across Charlie's fragile-looking face as she babbled at him. He could read her like a neon sign. She was filled with the need to explain, to be fair and honest, and yet she was afraid he was going to skew everything for her and her little girl. That really stung despite knowing she was right on that score. But not in the way she imagined. She knew nothing about him. Had no idea he would make the worst father imaginable because of the upbringing he'd had. His fingers zipped across his head. What if he'd inherited his father's genes? No way was he going to find out. The stakes were too high for all of them.

Clearing his throat, he hurried to put her at ease. 'Charlie, whatever happens, however I decide to play this…' Play was the wrong word. He shrugged, temporarily out of the right words, then carried on. 'I will never try to take Aimee away from you. By that I mean I won't demand she lives with me six months of the year or anything equally hideous.'

She didn't relax. 'You would have a fight on your hands if you did.'

'I figured.' He tried for a smile, managed to paste something resembling one on his face. 'You could've picked a far better guy to be Aimee's dad.' If only he was more like his grandfather than his own father. A caring, tentative farmer, not a hard-nosed soldier and disciplinarian.

Her beautiful eyes widened. 'Come on. If I believed that I wouldn't have bothered looking for you.' Then she added with a hint of the fun-loving Charlie he'd once known, 'You're a wonderful man. Any girl would be proud to show you off on school sports day.'

'Sports day?' Gulp. 'You're years ahead of me, Charlie.' He was still trying to grapple with the fact he'd spawned this little kid currently shoving building blocks through juice in the middle of the floor. Kind of messy. Kind of cute. Slam. His heart squeezed. Hard. *She's mine? I did that? Helped make Aimee?* He dragged his

knuckles down his cheeks, digging in deep, checking
he was awake, if he was feeling something or this was a
dream. Everything was real. All too damned real. Spinning around, he charged for the door. He needed air,
needed to get out of Charlie's space. Needed to think
without seeing Charlie's concerns glittering out from
those tragic eyes.

Why did she look like that? He didn't remember seeing anything but laughter in her eyes and face before.
Guess last time had been all about fun. Today was about
consequences and reality.

Stumbling down the front steps, he charged down
the path, reining in the urge to run faster than he'd ever
run before. This situation was not going to go away.
Looking along the road, he saw the crunched-up vehicle
he'd driven down from Auckland. What a mess. Right
now New Zealand didn't seem to be agreeing with him.

Spinning around, he strode away in the opposite direction, trying to outwalk what he'd left at Charlie's
house. But she followed, in his head, as did that little
cutie named Aimee. They were probably never going
to leave him again. Even when he was on the other side
of the world, fighting battles, looking out for his com-
rades, those two females would be lurking in some corner of his mind. Gulp.

Since when did he let situations get the better of
him? He was trained to face adversity and deal with it.
Despite the sense of freefalling from a plane without
a parachute, he grinned. Or was it a grimace? In the
army they didn't teach you to deal with being told about
eighteen-month-old daughters.

But you're more than a soldier. You're a doctor. Doctors nurtured, cared, mended, saved.

Hadn't saved Rod.

He swore. Loud and badly. Stared up at the sky. 'What do you think about this, then, *buddy*? Huh? What the hell am I supposed to do now? Quit soldiering? Move down under to a tourist town with a big lake and a small population? Be a father?'

'Hey, watch out, mister,' a young voice yelled.

Marshall dropped his head, glared around. Hell, that had been close. 'Sorry, kid, didn't mean to do that,' he called after the boy on a bike. A horn tooted from behind him and he nearly leapt out of his skin. He had to get a grip. Standing in the middle of the road, shouting up at the heavens, was going to get him killed. Or locked up.

Waving an apology at the car's irate driver, he stepped off the road onto the grass verge that led down to the lake edge. Sinking down on his haunches, he studied the terrain. The choppy water didn't stop kids leaping and diving into the chilly depths. Beyond them sailboats and motorboats sped back and forth. On the shoreline scantily clad people laughed and chattered under sun umbrellas as they tried to cool off. All very innocuous. Summer fun, family time.

Two things he'd had next to none of, and then only with his grandparents. A rare wave of anger swept over him. He had missed out on things other kids took for granted. His parents had never taken him out for the day just to have fun. He sucked up the anger, swallowed it. Thought about Grampy and Granny. They'd had more than enough love to spare for the skinny kid who'd arrived on their doorstep every school break.

They'd been his mentors, and yet he lived by his father's role model. Always on the move, never stopping one place long enough to make friends or have a relationship that lasted longer than a couple of weeks. He'd met his only close friend in officer training camp and they'd been in the same unit ever since. Yeah, and look where that had gotten the guy. In a wooden box far too soon.

The same thing could happen to him any time. Active duty meant danger and the very real danger didn't take note of who was in the firing line. Rod had been one of the best and he'd still bought the big one.

Shuddering, Marshall asked himself how he could be a good father for Aimee. He'd be in and out of her life, never stopping long enough to go to that sports day Charlie had mentioned. It would be better if he told Charlie right from the get-go that she should find a decent man and settle down to raise Aimee properly, lovingly, knowing from day to day, week to week, that he'd always be coming home. Because she sure wasn't going to get that from him.

In the laundry directly off the kitchen Charlie mechanically folded clean washing and sorted it into piles. Where had Marshall charged off to? More importantly, was he coming back? Her heart slowed. That might've been the last time she'd ever see him. The only time Aimee saw her father, and unfortunately her wee girl had no idea who Marshall was to her.

But Marshall took responsibility very seriously. She'd seen that first hand while working with him in Honolulu. It wasn't something he switched on and off in different situations. It was as intrinsic to him as breathing. The only time she'd met his friend, Rod, in Honolulu he'd told her Marshall put looking out for his men before everything else, including his own safety.

Marshall hadn't said Aimee had nothing to do with him. When he'd declared, 'Aimee's mine,' without a doubt in his voice, the world had stopped moving. Round one to Marshall. Except there were plenty more hurdles to come. None of them would be easy. They had a long way to go towards making this shared parenthood work. If he came back.

He would. Her fingers reached for the tabletop, brushed the wooden surface lightly. Please.

Dad walked into the kitchen. 'Think it's probably about time for a cold beer. Wouldn't you agree, Marshall?'

'Can't say no to that,' came the deep rumble of the voice she'd been straining to hear for the last hour.

She sighed and dredged up a smile. This putting it out there seemed to work. Marshall had returned. Now the fireworks could start. Or maybe they wouldn't. She'd try to give him the time and space to absorb the startling news he'd never expected to hear.

'Hey.' A shadow fell across her.

Her tummy squeezed with longing when she looked up into the eyes that had been a part of her dreams for so long. Hunger flared for that fun they'd shared, for the uncomplicated nights when they'd explored each other's bodies, the simple pleasure of walking hand in hand along the beach to watch the sunset. Even a need tugged at her for that professional camaraderie when Marshall had mentored the intern fresh from medical school. But none of that had a place in this situation. 'Hey to you, too.'

'Sorry I charged off. I went down to the lake while

everything sank in.' He looked genuinely contrite. 'I hope you didn't think I was running away.'

She winced, went for the truth. 'I hoped you hadn't, but I did wonder if you'd disappeared from my life again.' Even she heard the sadness in her voice. 'It must've been a huge shock.'

His forefinger traced her bottom lip. 'One I hadn't prepared for, that's for sure. But I'm back and you have my undivided attention for the next day or two.'

'I can go with that.' More than she'd expected, less than she'd hoped for. She placed the neatly folded towel she'd been gripping against her chest on the pile in the basket and stood before Marshall, studying him. Butterflies spread their wings in her stomach, fluttering wildly as she noted the well-honed muscles of his upper arms.

She'd missed him. Two weeks of wild passion and she'd spent the intervening years thinking and dreaming about him, wondering how he was, where he'd gone, who he might be with. And now he stood before her, looking superb in his casual attire.

Leaning forward, she stretched up onto her toes and reached for his mouth with hers. When her lips touched his all those long months of yearning disappeared in a haze of heat. It was as though they'd never gone their separate ways, as if the intervening time had been a figment of her imagination. Her hands slid around his neck, pulled him closer so she could deepen her kiss and press her tongue to his mouth to slide it inside.

And then Marshall was hauling her up against his hard body, his hands splayed across her back as he held her to him. His lips claimed her mouth with a hunger that surprised and shocked her. Marshall had missed her, too. His tongue danced around hers. Her body melted into his, trying to become one with him.

She forgot everything except Marshall. His arms holding her, each one of his fingers pressing into her skin under her T-shirt like hot brands, his hard thighs that reached as high as her hips, that taut belly against her soft baby tummy. His hardening reaction to her.

'I'll take the beers outside to the veranda.'

Her father's quiet voice pierced her euphoria, returned her to normal quicker than anything else could've done. 'Thanks, Dad,' she managed to gasp.

Surprise radiated out of Marshall's eyes. 'Sorry. I got carried away. What will Brendon think of me?' Embarrassment coloured his cheeks as he let her gently down onto her feet then adjusted his jeans.

'He's pleased that you've made my day by turning up. He'll give you some slack.' Still reeling from the abrupt end to that electric kiss, Charlie raised a wobbly smile. She'd acted rashly, but Marshall did that to her.

'Your father knew about me?' His fingers rubbed at his eyelids.

A bubble of laughter rolled up her throat. 'It was only this morning Dad suggested I give up searching for a while, concentrate on—on other things. So I sort of agreed, and here you are. If I'd known you were going to turn up I'd have saved myself hours of trawling through web sites.'

'So Brendon's not going to send me on my way just yet?'

Dad would never do that unless he thought Marshall was bad for her and Aimee. 'Not a chance. Now, let's go and be social with him and get that beer into you.' Pulling the fridge door wide, she found some lemonade to fill a glass. After adding a squeeze of lemon juice, she led the way outside. 'Come and sit in the shade for a bit. Dad will crank up the barbecue soon and we'll cook you a Kiwi dinner.'

Marshall followed Charlie through the large villa, glancing into rooms they passed. The lounge room was enormous and tastefully decorated. The furniture was stylish yet comfortable. Everything appeared well maintained. Bet that took some doing in an old house like this one.

Stepping onto the veranda, he took the bottle of beer Brendon held out to him. 'Thanks.' At least there was no animosity in the other man's eyes. Certainly some curiosity. He supposed any father would want to check out the guy his daughter had taken a fancy to. God. How embarrassing to be caught necking only hours after catching up with Charlie.

'Take the weight off your legs.' Brendon indicated a chair.

Even though he'd have preferred to stand, having spent hours squashed up in the plane and then behind the steering-wheel of the car he'd wrecked, he did as he was told. No point in getting any further offside with the guy than he might already be, despite those friendly eyes. Charlie pulled up another chair beside his and plonked her cute butt down, careful not to spill her drink. He asked, 'You're not drinking wine these days?'

'Not since I found out I was pregnant.' Her glance was distant, as though he'd touched on something important. Like what? It had seemed an innocuous question. But how would he know? There was so much to learn about Charlie. Now that there was a child in the picture he couldn't walk away. So much for getting Charlie out of his system with a brief visit. If nothing else, Aimee had put paid to that theory. Fooling himself again. He wanted much more of Charlie, and Aimee.

He dug for another, maybe safer topic to chat about. 'This place is huge. You must rattle around inside. Or do you take in boarders?'

'Not likely, despite having five bedrooms and two lounges.' Charlie smiled over her glass, those aqua eyes bewitching him with their twinkle. 'Plenty of space for when we've had enough of each other.'

Brendon sat, stretched his legs out to the edge of the veranda. 'It's one of the original homesteads built more than ninety years ago. It belonged to Charlie's mother's family.'

Charlie added, 'Mum was born here. Then I was born here.'

'And now Aimee.' He looked around. Where was the little girl? His daughter. Holy Toledo. His daughter. His chest expanded with pride, even though he hadn't had anything to do with Aimee up until now.

'No.' Charlie chuckled. He'd forgotten how often she'd do that and how it had warmed his heart each time. 'Aimee was born down the road at the maternity hospital. I definitely didn't want a home birth.' She leaned forward and pointed under the trees. 'She's in the sandpit. Her favourite place at the moment. Long may that last.'

'Keeps her occupied while you get things done?'

'You've got it. I'm dreading the day she thinks tree-climbing is the best thing to do. There's a hut in that tree by the fence that I used to spend hours in.'

'She fell out and broke her arm once.' Brendon

grinned. 'That's what's bothering her about Aimee getting big enough to climb up there.'

He shuddered. 'I don't blame her. They're mighty tall trees. What are they?' His neck clicked as he tipped his head back to stare up at the odd trees.

'They're native fauna. That one's a rimu.' Charlie pointed to the one where the sandpit was. 'The flowering one is a pohutukawa and the big one in the far corner is a kauri. The wrong varieties to grow in town but every time Dad talks about cutting them down I get upset. It takes for ever to grow a kauri so big.'

'They must've been planted way back when this house was built by Charlie's great-grandfather. The land surrounding the house has been subdivided off over the years,' Brendon told him.

For the life of him Marshall could not imagine living in the same house his great-grandparents had. It was inconceivable. Even Grampy had only owned his farm for twenty years, and while it had been the one place on earth Marshall had hated to leave at the end of school holidays he still couldn't imagine living there week in, week out for years at a time. He shook his head.

'Charlie, haven't you ever wanted to move some place else? What about you, Brendon? I'm presuming you moved in when you married Charlie's mom.'

Two similar faces with the same piercing blue eyes stared back at him, amusement widening their generous mouths. 'Why would I?' they answered almost in unison.

'But there's a whole world out there.' He spread his hands, careful not to spill beer over the decking. 'Different homes, towns, people.'

'But this is home. Taupo is my birthplace. It's where

I went to school, learned to sail, met my best friends, where Mum's buried. This is where I want Aimee to grow up. She might not stay but I hope she'll come back from time to time.' Charlie looked bewildered. A cute frown formed between carefully styled eyebrows.

Alien. That's what her concept was. Totally alien. He leaned back in the chair and tipped the beer down his throat. Kiwi beer. Icy cold and tasty. Yeah, he could get to like this. Except he wasn't hanging around long enough to get used to anything.

Charlie was still watching him. 'Where did you grow up?'

'Everywhere and nowhere. I was an army brat, with two career soldiers for parents.' The next mouthful of beer soured on his tongue. It all sounded quite crappy compared to Charlie's life. But that's just how his life had been. Still was and probably always would be.

Look at this visit. Two days, maybe three in New Zealand before he flew back to the States and on to who knew where. Wherever his men went he went, making sure they were safe, or at least doing everything possible to keep them that way.

'That's terrible. I can't begin to imagine what that must've been like.' Her sweet mouth turned down, as though she was hurting for him, or the unhappy little boy he'd been.

Because she'd have guessed he had been unhappy. Not that he'd ever have admitted it, not back then, not now. But he'd known he'd been missing out on things, especially friendships, which was why he'd worked hard at being Mr Popularity at every school he'd attended. Trying to make the most of things all the time. 'I got to see plenty of new places.'

When the hurt entered her eyes he knew he'd been flippant. Had probably meant to be but equally he really didn't want to upset her. Charlie deserved better from him. 'It wasn't much fun,' he told her. 'But there was one constant in my life back then and that was school holidays with my grandparents. They took me in and gave me some stability until I was twelve.' Until the accident that had changed him for ever. Having to watch Granny suffer as they'd waited for help to arrive had set him on the path to becoming a doctor.

A childish shriek came from the direction of the sandpit and Charlie was up and off the veranda double quick. 'Hey, sweetheart.' She bent down at the edge of the pit and scooped Aimee up, plastering kisses over the scrunched-up little face. 'What's wrong? Did you drive the truck over your toes again?'

Aimee shook her head slowly from side to side and shoved a thumb in her mouth.

Gently removing the thumb to kiss it, Charlie peered down into the sand. 'Did Teddy fall off the truck?'

Aimee's head changed direction as she nodded agreement. Her gaze moved from her mother to Brendon. Then on to him. Those same eyes he had, as Granny had had. The moment they'd registered in his brain he'd known she was his. Not the tiniest of doubts. And while the reality had slammed through him he hadn't wanted to deny it. A strange sense of hope, of gladness, had taken over and spun him out.

Since when had he thought he wanted a child in his life? Never had, never should. This strange reaction had to be because his body clock was all out of whack after the long flight down here. But what if he could be a good dad? Not that it was likely with his pedigree.

Marshall's breath stalled in his throat. Those young eyes remained locked on him. He couldn't break the contact. Could Aimee read his mind? As if. She didn't yet grasp the concept of what a father was or did. Hell, he didn't want to disabuse her of any ideas Charlie might teach her about that, but he'd have to tell her the truth about his background one day soon.

Panic flared his nostrils, dried his mouth so that he had to pour some beer into it. But his bottle was empty.

'Here.' Brendon handed him another; icy cold and slick with condensation. 'Get that into you.' There was understanding in the man's eyes, in his voice.

'Thanks,' he croaked.

'Give yourself time.'

Didn't the guy get it? Did Charlie? He glanced in her direction, found her gaze fixed on him, too. Hell, everyone seemed to be keeping an eye on him, waiting for something from him. They weren't going to be happy. Despite learning about his appalling childhood of being hauled half across the country and back every year, they honestly thought he could do this. Could be a rock-solid father for Aimee. Damnation. He already had a whole troop of men to take care of.

Look at the three Langs. Completely at ease with their lifestyle and each other. Charlie and her father had a strong, loving connection that must've got them through a lot over the years, and would continue to do so long after he'd returned to duty. He didn't have that with either of his parents. He and Charlie? Chalk and cheese? Try the earth and the moon. That's how far apart they were, how different their lives were. They didn't have a hope in Hades of making this work.

CHAPTER FIVE

THE NEXT MORNING Charlie dressed with more care than she'd bothered with in forever. Zipping up her denim shorts, she muttered under her breath. She needed a belt to keep them up. Not fair. They'd fitted perfectly back when she'd first bought them at the market in Honolulu. Back before her treatment regime had burnt off all her body fat and then some.

Rummaging through the wardrobe, she found a near-new sleeveless blouse made in a soft cotton fabric and slipped it on. The bright reds and blues added some colour around her pale face. Not even spending time in the sun every day had tanned her skin to a healthy bronze this year. Would she ever look robust again? Would her strength come back if she worked out hard enough? She needed energy before she could work out. Even now, ten months after her last radiation treatment, there were days when walking to the letterbox was exhausting.

Her mouth twisted into a wry smile. Last night, when she'd announced she was off to bed at nine o'clock, Marshall had looked nearly as shocked as when he'd cottoned on to Aimee being his.

'You're what?' he'd blustered.

'Being a mum and a doctor wears me out,' she'd explained, once again avoiding the real issue.

Now, slipping into Aimee's room, she found the cot empty. She glanced at her watch to make sure she hadn't slept in. No, she'd got that right. Guess Dad had got up earlier than usual to get ready for his fishing trip.

No sound came from the kitchen but the front door was open so she headed in that direction, pulling up short the moment her feet hit the veranda. No way. She had to be hallucinating.

Marshall lay sprawled on the lawn while Aimee crawled over him, giggling when he tickled her. Marshall's total absorption in this simple game made her heart squeeze. This was what she wanted for her daughter. A father who played with her, who would take the time to do things for her and with her. There was wonder in Marshall's gaze, as though he couldn't believe he'd created this gorgeous tot.

Had he never thought about having a family of his own? From the little he'd mentioned yesterday about his childhood it probably wasn't at the top of his to-do list. Her heart squeezed painfully. She'd always thought she'd have children some time in her future. Children, as in more than one. It hurt to think that dream was over. Being grateful for having Aimee didn't always cut it. Her daughter would never have siblings. *She'd* never again feel a baby growing inside her body. It was damned hard to swallow at times.

Marshall looked up then and smiled that easy smile of his. 'Hey, you're looking good.' His gaze trawled over her.

'Thanks.' She blushed.

'Mum, mum. Play.' Aimee delivered a soft punch to Marshall's chin.

'Hey, small fry, watch it.' Marshall grinned and lifted Aimee up into the air above his head, rocking her gently as she shrieked with laughter.

The man was a natural. Aimee had obviously fallen for him already, appearing totally relaxed in his grasp. She'd definitely have made it known if she had any qualms. That had to be good.

'I hope it was okay to get Aimee up. She was chattering away to herself when I got up thinking about going for a run, so I figured I'd bring her out here and let you snooze a bit longer. Last night you looked so tired I thought you'd fall asleep on your feet.'

Charlie sat down on the steps. 'I was a bit zonked. Must've been the excitement of you turning up.'

'I'm losing my touch if you want to go to sleep when I'm around.' His smile turned into a grin, and set her heart racing wildly.

Her cheeks burned crimson as his gaze intensified, firing up memories of what they used to do in the evenings after work. She'd certainly never fallen asleep until the wee hours of the morning. 'Guess I'm out of practice,' she murmured.

'Really?' His grin stretched. 'I like that.'

'You're a bit cocky this morning.' She grinned back. Obviously he'd slept well. Sadly, not even Marshall's presence in her home had kept her awake for more than a few minutes last night. Sleep came far too easily these days. As for long, hot nights with Marshall, she doubted she'd last more than half an hour before nodding off.

A shiver ran up her back. A familiar pang of fear snatched at her previously happy mood. The uncertainty of her future seemed far worse now that Marshall was back in her life. He might be going away again but now that he'd met Aimee he'd keep in touch. He had to. Selfishly, that made her wish for more. She'd wanted to make contact for Aimee's sake, but now she knew she'd been lying to herself. She'd never got over him, had compared every man she'd dated since—all two of them—to him and had found them lacking in just about everything. Those two weeks had a lot to answer for, and not just her precious little girl.

'Charlie?' Marshall stood over her, Aimee in his arms. 'You okay? You've gone pale.'

I was pale before. 'Something stepped on my grave.' Ouch. She sucked a breath through clamped teeth. Wrong thing to say. There wouldn't be a grave for many years to come. Funny how she'd started to accept she just might make it, yet now with Marshall here on her patch the doubts and fears were creeping back in. Even more to lose than before? Did she want a future that had Marshall in it? Apart from as Aimee's dad?

Pushing up off the step, she reached to kiss Aimee on the cheek. 'Good morning, sweetheart.' And when Marshall leaned closer she rose onto her toes and kissed his cheek too. Except he moved and her lips found his. *Good morning, sweetheart.*

'Good morning, beautiful,' Marshall murmured against her mouth. 'You are a sight for sore eyes.'

'Mummy, hungry.'

Reluctantly pulling her lips away from that sensational mouth, she looked at her daughter. 'Hungry, eh?' Flicking Marshall a look, she asked, 'Have you been teaching her new words?'

He grinned. 'I tried for "Can I have lots of kisses?"'

but so far "hungry" is it.' Aimee wriggled to get down. Marshall obliged, carefully placing her on her feet, before straightening and draping an arm over Charlie's shoulders. 'Want me to cook breakfast? I do a mean piece of toast.'

Slapping her forehead with the palm of her hand, she groaned, 'How can I resist?'

'Morning, everyone.' Dad strolled out onto the veranda dressed in his lucky fishing trousers. Bending down, he plonked a noisy kiss on Aimee's forehead. 'Hello, poppet.'

'Hungry.'

'Well, that's a good thing because I'm about to cook up a storm. A bloke needs a hearty meal before he heads out on the lake to catch the family dinner.' Dad looked from her to Marshall. 'Ever been trout fishing, lad?'

'No. Tried salmon fishing in Canada once. Had a great time but didn't catch a thing.'

'I'll take you out some time. If you come back this way.' Talk about a loaded statement.

Charlie held her breath but Marshall shrugged it away with absolute ease. 'Sure. Want a hand with that breakfast?'

A totally noncommittal reply. She swallowed her disappointment. It was better this way than having him make promises he wouldn't keep once he'd had time to really think everything through.

'Can always use another pair of hands.' Dad seemed to accept Marshall's non-answer, and if anyone would be pushing him that would be Dad. This whole situation was unsettling for him too, worrying if she might pack up and head for the States so she and Aimee could be near Marshall. But Dad needn't worry. She wouldn't be doing that.

She smiled as she watched the men walk down the hall to the kitchen, Aimee tottering along behind. Amazing that Dad and Marshall appeared totally at ease with each other. Was Dad trying too hard to make Marshall feel welcome? She hoped not. She wanted Marshall to make up his own mind about what he was going to do. Anyway, he had an army career to get back to. A career that was unlikely to bring him anywhere near New Zealand.

Her heart sank. So much for being excited about having him around. This really was silly. She'd needed Marshall to know about Aimee, and now he did. The last thing even she expected was for him to give up his career. He might be a doctor but first and foremost he was a soldier. That had been abundantly clear in Honolulu when the call had come for him to report back to base earlier than originally expected. He'd immediately gone to the head of the ED and told the guy he was leaving. No asking if that suited, or could the department cope with being left in the lurch. The army and his men came first. And, she suspected, second and third.

'You're missing out on your run,' she muttered as she headed for the cupboards to get plates down.

'I'll go later. Maybe tomorrow you can come with me?'

Ouch. Once upon a time there had hardly been a morning she hadn't gone for a run or cycle first thing. 'I don't run any more.' The plates hit the bench with a bang.

'You don't?' Astonishment cracked through the air. 'Why not?'

'I had to stop in the last months of pregnancy and I've never got back to it.' Please don't ask any more.

'Charlie.' She felt his hand on her shoulder, turning her to face him. 'Am I missing something here?'

'I…' Swallow. 'You know what? I will go with you tomorrow but you'll have to go easy on me. Not try and race me home, as you always used to.' Hadn't she decided to start getting fit yesterday? No time like now to start. Hefting the plates, she headed for the door.

Marshall's eyes narrowed as she tried to pass him. He opened his mouth and she waited for the questions. But they never came. Slowly he leaned forward and kissed her lips lightly. 'It's a date.'

Marshall didn't know what Charlie was hiding from him but, sensing her unease, he'd let it drop. For now. He didn't have the right to interrogate her. Not until he'd spent more time with her. But tomorrow they'd go for a run and see if that didn't open up a line of conversation that might shed some light on the matter. Judging by Charlie's lack of strength, it would be a very short run. Had something gone horribly wrong during her pregnancy?

In the meantime, he'd concentrate on her father. He found it hard to make Brendon out. The guy made every effort to be friendly yet surely he had plenty of questions ready to fire at him. Taking the bacon and eggs the older man handed him, he said, 'I'll do my best to do what's right for Charlie and Aimee. I can promise you that.'

What I can't promise is not to hurt them. I know little about being a parent. Also, I will never ask Charlie to tie herself to me for the rest of her life. That would be a half-life. I'd hardly ever be around.

'I'm sure you will.'

That's it? The guy was playing with him. Had to be. 'You know nothing about me.' Neither did Charlie, come to that.

Brendon banged a pan on an element. 'You're right. I don't, but I trust Charlie's judgement.'

'That's it?' he repeated out loud. 'Come on. I can see you've got questions begging for answers. Fire away.' He pulled his back ramrod-straight, tightened his shoulders and faced the man down. At least he tried to but Brendon wasn't intimidated at all.

Shaking his head, Brendon asked, 'How do you like your eggs?'

Anger sped through his veins. What was this man about? Trying to scare him off in a weird, roundabout way? 'Charlie mentioned you'd suggested she give up looking for me. Would you prefer it if I hadn't got in touch at all?' Except not once, even when Brendon had seen them kissing, had this man indicated he had problems with his sudden appearance.

Crack. The fat sizzled as an egg slid into the pan. 'I've watched my daughter spend months trying to find you, only to be disappointed every day she failed. It was very important to her you know about Aimee. Now you do. So, no, lad, I am happy you've turned up.' Crack, another egg hit the fat. 'Can you throw some bread in the toaster? We'll eat outside on the veranda. The cutlery is in that top drawer.'

If Brendon had been thinking clearly he'd have remembered who had dried and put away the cutlery last night after their barbecue. Something was rattling him, something Marshall desperately wanted to know. But he couldn't offend Charlie's father by persisting with his questions. 'What does Aimee eat?'

'Toast and honey.' Brendon's stance relaxed.

Charlie breezed into the kitchen, her earlier unease gone. 'I could kill for a cup of tea. What about you, Marshall?' Switching on the kettle, she leaned back against the bench and folded her arms under her luscious breasts.

'Make that coffee and I'm in.' Trying to avoid staring, he turned to study the toaster, waiting for the toast to pop up. A hard-on now might change Brendon's attitude towards him. But his mind had other ideas, bringing up memories of what was under that bright blouse, of his hands holding her breasts, his thumbs rubbing the nipples until Charlie cried out with need.

The smoke alarm shrilled at the same time his phone vibrated in his back pocket. Black smoke streamed up from the toast he was supposedly watching. He jerked the plug from the wall and tipped the burnt bread into the sink, all the while listening to Charlie and Brendon going on about the American who couldn't even manage to cook a piece of toast.

Brendon reached for the 'off' button on the alarm, a smile lightening his face. 'Remind me not to ask you to cook anything again. Or drive a car.'

'Your dad is hopeless, sweetheart.' Charlie lifted Aimee into her arms, grinning like a cat that had just had a bowl of cream.

Dropping more bread into the toaster, he grinned back. 'Hopeless, am I?' Leaning over, he brushed a kiss over her lips. 'We'll see about that,' he whispered.

Blushing, she spun away. 'Didn't you just get a text?'

His grin faded as he read the message. 'Seems my flight's leaving early. Tonight at eight and I have to be at Whenuapai by seven. Damn.' He texted a reply and shoved the phone deep into his pocket. 'I'd better pick up that replacement rental car after breakfast.'

Charlie's face tightened as she turned away to make their drinks. Guess she hadn't wanted him leaving yet. They'd barely got past the Aimee disclosure and he was leaving. No doubt she had many things to tell him. Plenty more kisses to share? And no time. 'Why don't we walk into town later to get it? Take Aimee with us?' And talk as we go.

'Sounds like a plan,' she mumbled.

He started another lot of toast, this time keeping his eyes focused on it.

'Another scorcher of a day,' Marshall said as he pushed Aimee's stroller along the footpath.

'Hope Dad remembers his sun block. The number of times he's come home off the lake redder than a strawberry is unbelievable, considering he's a family doctor supposed to be warning his patients about the dangers of melanoma.'

'Did you become a doctor because your father was one?'

The things Marshall didn't know about her. 'In some ways I guess I did. I liked the way he helped people and could make them better. The community spirit of general practice also appealed. But I honestly can't remember a time I wasn't going to do medicine. At ten I thought surgeons were the best then at twelve I liked the idea of radiology. Pathology followed until Dad pointed out how isolated pathologists could be.'

'I can't quite see you sitting behind a microscope all day.'

'No, I'm definitely more of a people person and being a GP suits me, though I toyed with the idea of specialising in emergency medicine right up until I found out I was pregnant.'

'Did that have anything to do with your time in Honolulu?'

'You can wipe that cheeky grin off your face.' She playfully whacked his biceps and wished she could wrap her hand around it. 'Yes, you made the ED exciting for me.' When his grin stretched further she shook her head at him. 'Not the after-hours stuff back in our rooms but the nitty-gritty urgency of traumatised patients. I liked not knowing what was coming through the door in the next moment. I loved being tested again and again. It was stimulating.'

'So why change your mind because you were pregnant?'

'I wanted to have my baby in Taupo and there isn't a big hospital with a major emergency department here. Also, being a solo parent didn't faze me but I preferred to be near Dad. He brought me up on his own. I wanted him to be a part of Aimee's growing up.' Please leave it at that.

Of course he didn't. 'I looked this place up and saw that there's a major hospital down the road at Rotorua. Not too far away from your father.'

She'd spent too much time in Rotorua Hospital having treatment to ever want to work there. 'I considered it and flagged the idea.' So he hadn't just hitched a ride down to New Zealand on a whim. He'd done some research. Interesting. But how far should she go with what she told him? He was leaving in a few hours and she didn't know if he'd ever come back. Did he even need to know about her illness unless everything went pear-shaped?

'Are you a partner in the medical centre?' After looking along the road both ways, he edged the stroller over the kerb to cross the street.

'You're a natural at this kid stuff,' she teased, and laughed out loud at the stunned look on his face.

'You reckon? I've never taken a toddler for a walk in my life.' The stunned look became slightly smug and his chest puffed out a little.

'Hidden talents. Who'd have thought?' Then she pointed to a building further down the road. 'There's your rental company. And, no, I haven't taken a partnership but Dad's thinking about retiring soon and the other partners are keen for me to buy him out.'

She genuinely wanted to pay the going rate for Dad's share of the practice but so far hadn't been able to convince him of that idea. He kept telling her it was her inheritance and he didn't need the money anyway. 'We're also looking for another partner. Patient numbers are growing rapidly and it's hard to turn people away when they need our help.'

'I can understand that.' They'd reached the rental place. He stepped away from the stroller. 'I'll go and sort this car business out.'

She watched him saunter through the gleaming cars lined up facing the road. He walked with his back straight, his head high, shoulders back. Like a soldier. Her pathetic hint about another partner at the centre had been a waste of breath. Working there would be dull and monotonous for a man like Marshall.

Would he ever consider quitting the army and going into medicine full time? Doubtful. Even if he did return to civvie street it wouldn't be in New Zealand, and definitely not in a quiet town like Taupo. He was used to the excitement of war zones and the urgency of battlefield injuries, the variety of location and people. Taupo would never suit him.

Her stomach lurched. It had been pie-in-the-sky stuff to think they had a future together. She didn't even know if he liked her enough, let alone loved her. The fact he was her daughter's father wasn't grounds for marriage. Two weeks of hot sex and laughter in the sun weren't either.

How had she gone from talking about the medical centre to thinking about marriage? Because she loved him. Had always suspected that she'd fallen for him but with finding herself pregnant and then learning postpartum that she had cervical cancer her feelings for Marshall had been shoved into the too-hard basket. She hadn't wanted to deal with the heartbreak of knowing she loved a man who almost didn't exist.

But less than twenty-four hours since he'd crashed back into her world she knew from the bottom of her heart that this was the man she loved, would always love. And the worst of it was that she didn't know what to do about it. Tell him and he'd most likely leave town without giving her any contact details at all. That must not happen. The day might come when Aimee would need him, when he might have to step up as the sole parent.

Toot, toot.

'You going my way, lady?' Marshall pulled up beside her in an SUV, grinning like a loon.

'Depends what you've got to offer.'

'You've got a short memory.' He winked at her.

Her stomach tightened. Heat crept up her cheeks as she recalled fingers and a tongue on her skin and a hard body covering hers.

'Or maybe not, if that smoky look in your eyes is anything to go by.' Chuckling, he climbed out and undid the straps keeping Aimee in her stroller. 'Come on, girls, hop in. I'm taking you to a café for coffee and juice.' His brows almost met in the middle of his forehead. 'How do we strap Aimee safely into the seat? She's far too tiny.'

'The stroller very cleverly becomes a car seat and we thread the SUV's seat belt through those clips.' Within moments she had it all sorted and Aimee safe. Turning to Marshall, she suggested, 'We could drive out to Huka Falls. You may as well see something of Taupo before you leave, and there's a café there.'

His finger tilted her head up and those suck-her-in eyes locked with hers. 'I will be back, Charlie. I don't know when. It would be rash to make that sort of promise knowing the army as I do, but I will return.' He meant it. He really, really did. The truth, his honesty stared out at her.

It wasn't enough. Not nearly enough. She needed concrete dates for visits, not some vague idea that he'd return when it suited him or his superiors. But looking into his eyes, like peering into his soul, her breath stuck somewhere between her lungs and her lips, and she couldn't find the words to tell him what she needed.

Then her cellphone rang, shocking her back to the here and now of the rental company. Flipping the phone open, she saw it was Molly from the medical centre.

'Sorry, got to take this,' Charlie said to Marshall. 'Hey, what's up?' she asked the centre's receptionist.

'Emergency at the airport. A small plane with tandem skydivers on board crashed on take-off. The police are asking for any available doctors to proceed to the airport immediately. Can you go?'

'Yes. Hold on. I might have another doctor for you.' She looked at Marshall. 'There's been an accident and doctors are needed. Can you help? Under my guidance, of course, as you're not New Zealand registered.'

'What are we waiting for?' Marshall headed back round to the driver's door then changed his mind. 'Better for you to drive. That'll save time.'

Talking to Molly at the same time as slipping into the SUV, Charlie said, 'I'm on my way with another doctor. He'll have to work under supervision but I don't see a problem.'

'That's great. Where's your dad? I can't raise him.'

'He's out on the lake. I need to drop Aimee off with someone. I'm in town.'

'Got that covered. Gemma's here and says she'll meet you at the airport. She'll bring you a medical bag and take Aimee home.'

Charlie slammed the gear lever into 'Drive' and snapped her seat belt on. 'Let's go.'

CHAPTER SIX

THE RIDE TO the airport would've been exciting if Marshall hadn't been considering the injuries they'd find when they got there.

Obviously Charlie was too because she hissed through clenched teeth, 'Impact injuries mean spinal damage, ruptured organs and broken bones.'

'For starters.' Marshall grimaced. 'You're presuming there are survivors.'

'We wouldn't have been called if there weren't.'

'True. I wonder what altitude the plane reached before something went wrong. It would've been moving at maximum speed and could've spun into the ground nose first.' Goose-bumps rose on his arms. He knew exactly what that looked like. 'We had a plane crash on landing at my last posting in Afghanistan so I've some idea of what to expect.'

'How did you cope? Did you know any of the men on that plane?'

'Yes.' He stared out the windscreen but it was the injured bodies of his men he saw. He could hear Rod groaning, could see his shaking hands splayed across his leaking wound. Marshall closed his eyes, drew air deep into his lungs and focused inwards. If only he'd been able to save his buddy then he wouldn't have this guilt of failure weighing him down. It could've happened to him, and still could one day. He couldn't put Charlie and Aimee through what Rod's family had had to deal with.

Charlie's soft voice slowly broke through his dark thoughts. 'I wonder how many people were on board. Usually there's a maximum of six skydivers strapped together in pairs, and the pilot.'

Turning from staring outside to watching her, he asked, 'As the hospital here isn't a major one, what happens with the patients we attend?'

Indicating to turn left, Charlie slowed and turned into the airport grounds. 'Depending on the severity of the injuries, they'll be flown by helicopter to either Rotorua Hospital or Waikato Hospital up in Hamilton. Again, depending on the extent of injuries, one of us may have to accompany the patient or patients.'

A police car led them onto the grass perimeter. Ahead, black smoke spewed into the sky and fire trucks surrounded what had to be the wrecked plane. Ambulances were parked nearby, the back doors wide open as crews carried heavy packs of equipment towards the victims.

As Charlie pulled up beside the trucks she hauled in a deep breath and clenched her hands then loosened them. 'Here we go.' Shoving the door wide, she dropped to the ground and handed Aimee over to Gemma.

Jogging along beside her, Marshall took her free hand and squeezed it hard. 'You'll do fine. Once you get started, everything will slot into place. Just like you used to do in the ED.'

Then there was no more time to talk. They were at

the site of the crash. Tangled metal that no longer resembled an aircraft stuck up out of the ground from the small crater the impact had made. Bodies lay everywhere.

'Hey, Charlie. Glad you're here,' Joseph, a doctor from another medical centre in town, called to her. He crossed to them and shook Marshall's hand when she introduced the two men. She recognised the other doctor and a nurse already working with victims. 'I've been put in charge of the scene. We've triaged the poor devils who are lucky to be alive. Two dead. Four in a very bad way. We need to crack on.'

'Where do you want us? You understand that Marshall is an American army doctor without registration here?' She'd had Molly relay the information earlier.

Joseph nodded at Marshall. 'You're probably more qualified for this scenario than the rest of us. You two take that couple by the firemen. They're still strapped together in preparation for their dive.'

The male and female victims had been slammed into the ground, their bodies tangled together and bound by the parachute straps. Both were unconscious. 'Barely alive,' Charlie muttered, after finding very weak carotid pulses in both.

'Freeing them won't be easy,' Marshall muttered. 'We could cause more damage but there's no helping that. Let's start the ABCs.'

They dropped to their knees and began checking airways, breathing rates, pulses. Charlie automatically went for the young woman. At least she presumed the girl was young. Hard to tell with the facial injuries.

She looked around for one of the ambulance crew. 'Can we have two neck braces?' They'd need to put the braces on before trying to separate their patients and move them. She began a thorough examination of the woman, not easy when there was a man strapped to her back. 'Soft bone on the side of her skull, broken cheekbones.' Her hands moved down the neck, over her patient's arms. 'Broken right humerus, crushed ribs, palpable spleen.'

Marshall reported similar injuries in the places he could reach on his patient. With the help of two ambulance officers they placed the neck braces on, before supervising the firemen as they cut the straps and removed the parachute from the man's back.

'Slowly does it,' Marshall cautioned as the woman was placed carefully on a stretcher. Immediately Charlie began another check of the woman's vital signs. 'Blood pressure's dropping, resp rate's falling.' Suddenly there were no heartbeats. 'Cardiac arrest,' she yelled, and began CPR. Nodding at one of the ambulance officers, she gasped, 'Need an airway in place, attach a mask and bag. Someone get the defib.' Fifteen, sixteen, seventeen. She continued counting the compressions as the ambulance officer slipped the plastic airway into the patient's mouth and then strapped a mask over her face.

'Twenty-nine, thirty.' Charlie sat back, watched as the oxygen bag was squeezed twice. Leaning forward, she folded one hand over the other and began the next round of compressions while a paramedic placed the defib pads on the woman's now exposed chest.

'Stand back,' he ordered quietly but firmly.

Charlie stopped the compressions and moved away from her patient. She continued compressions when the electric shock did not restart the heart. Another shock, more compressions.

'I'm not giving up,' she muttered, more to herself than anyone else.

'I've got a pulse.' The paramedic sounded relieved.

She could relate to that. 'Right, let's finish the assessment and do what's necessary before sending this lady off to hospital. Where's Joseph?'

'Right here. Want to fly her to Waikato?'

'A.S.A.P.' Oh, hell. The monitors attached to the woman reading her heart rate gave a warning. 'Here we go again.' The blood loss from those internal injuries had to be huge, causing the heart to stop.

They got the woman's heart going again, gained large-bore IV access to give fluids for shock and made her ready for evacuation. The paramedics whisked her over to a waiting helicopter for her flight to Waikato Hospital's major trauma unit.

Charlie joined Marshall as he was splinting both his patient's legs. She held the cardboard splint while he strapped it tight enough to be effective without cutting off any blood supply.

'How're you doing?' she asked quietly.

'Like I'm not on holiday.' He flicked a grim smile. 'I thought you said Taupo was a quiet place.'

'Yeah, well, usually.' She looked across at the wreckage and shuddered. The impact had concertinaed the plane to a fraction of its original length. 'I've got to go with my patient.' Glancing across, she saw the ambulance crew loading the stretcher into the helicopter.

His mouth tightened. 'How will you get back from wherever you're going?'

'The pilot will wait while I hand over. I'll be away two hours max.' She glanced at her watch and her skin turned to ice. Two hours and Marshall would be gone.

They still had so much to talk about. She hadn't even got his contact details. Her teeth dug into her bottom lip as she stood up on surprisingly shaky legs.

'Charlie.' Joseph tapped her on the shoulder. 'Your flight's about to lift off.'

'I refuse to say goodbye, Marshall. Please call me as soon as you get back to the States.' Kissing her fingers, she touched Marshal's cheek and turned and ran fast. Towards the patient who needed all her skills, away from the man who owned her heart. Would she ever see him again?

Marshall drove carefully on State Highway One towards Auckland and his flight back to the States. He had covered nearly half the distance, and with every kilometre his heart grew heavier. He was leaving something very special behind. A wonderful family who'd welcomed him with open arms.

Hell, working together on those casualties had been like old times. Charlie's skills had improved no end despite not working in emergency medicine. Her confidence had grown a lot over the years.

Mindful of which side of the road he was on, he tried not to think about Charlie and their abrupt parting. Despite being used to the suddenness of changing circumstances in combat zones, he had not been prepared for the sudden departure of Charlie from his life only hours ago.

It was little more than twenty-four hours since he'd seen her for the first time in a long time. It had been like finding someone he hadn't known he'd lost until that moment—his other half. They'd fitted together instantly. There'd been no real awkwardness after the first few minutes. Not even the shock of learning about Aimee had driven a wedge between them or made him want to get away—except for a few brief, confused minutes.

Yet now he was on his way, leaving this country and his daughter and Charlie. Charlotte Lang. Her image had tormented him for years, colouring his dreams, unsettling his long-held beliefs. He'd truly thought he could come over here, spend a little time with her and walk away completely over what ailed him.

The oath that shot out of his mouth shocked even him, seasoned soldier that he was. He'd been a fool. Rod had warned him time and again that he was hooked but he'd disputed that, saying it wasn't possible to fall in love in two weeks. How could he love a woman he didn't know anything about apart from her stunning body and its fantastic reactions to his lovemaking?

But none of that mattered. He had to go. That's what he did, had always done. Moved on. It had never been a problem before. He'd never cared before. He had men depending on him back home so between here and Auckland he needed to pull on his army persona and start acting like the competent officer he was. He could definitely not behave like some lovelorn fool who was leaving behind the most wonderful woman he'd ever met and the sweet little girl he'd fathered. The only way to get through life without hurting others was to remain alone.

Hamilton. The road sign indicated he should carry on straight ahead.

Auckland. Turn right to bypass the city.

Marshall indicated a right-hand turn. He didn't need the delays that driving through a city would bring.

You didn't find out why deep sadness unexpectedly sneaked into Charlie's eyes at times.

Yeah, buddy, I hear you. Unfortunately it didn't work out. That plane crash took care of the last few hours I had with her.

Don't you want to know? Or is running away preferable to what Charlie might tell you?

Stop mucking with my head. I've got to concentrate on driving. These Kiwis aren't very forgiving motorists.

Excuses, excuses.

He wasn't running away. He didn't do that. The SUV slowed. He glanced at the dials on the dashboard. All normal. What was happening? He pressed down on the accelerator and the vehicle surged forward and maintained a steady one hundred kilometres an hour. Idiot. Why had he lifted his foot off the pedal? Slowing his departure?

The soft sensation he'd felt when Charlie had brushed her kissed fingertips over his cheek drifted through his mind. Charlie. They'd shared two kisses in these past hours. Kisses filled with hunger, longing, caring. Kisses that had held so much promise.

Pulling to the side of the road, he switched the engine off. He couldn't drive and deal with all this stuff going on in his head at the same time. So if he wasn't running, why leave? No one had ordered him to head back to Kansas today. The army had called and he'd jumped. A habit formed from following orders for too long. Orders designed to save a man's life in combat. Orders that took serious decision-making away if a man let it.

As you have.

'Damn it, Rod, can't you go and annoy someone else?' He slapped the steering-wheel. If he turned round and went back to Charlie, would she read too much into it? Expect more of him than he was prepared to give? His gut churned as fear of getting too involved reared up.

Reaching for the ignition, he hesitated. Withdrew his hand. Asked himself a scary question. 'What do I want to do? If I was free of the army, would I go back to Charlie without a thought?'

Hard to imagine being free of the army when it had been more of a family to him than his folks had. But it was an impersonal, unloving institution. This wasn't about getting out, only about returning to Charlie for a few more days.

Family. The word evoked things he'd missed out on and the hidden dreams that one day his parents might've remembered to acknowledge they'd had a son they loved. He'd spent his childhood trying to be noticed for the right reasons, but some things just didn't work out in life, no matter how hard a guy tried.

You could try to change. Make the most of this opportunity.

Opportunity. That was one word for what waited for him in Taupo. Commitment was another. Could he commit to being in Charlie and Aimee's lives from a distance? Stay safe for them? He wasn't going to know unless he tried. His hand wasn't as steady as it normally was when he reached for the ignition this time. A vision of Charlie filtered into his mind. She'd been awesome, the way she hadn't demanded anything of him for Aimee.

But it was her steady blue gaze that really got to him. Full of understanding, need and sadness. Occasionally tinged with laughter and something that shot straight to his heart and grabbed it. Love? Did Charlie love him? Not likely. But maybe she cared a lot about him. That was something he wasn't used to.

The engine turned over and he flicked on the indicator. When a break came in the traffic Marshall made a U-turn.

He wasn't finished with Charlie Lang. Not by a long shot.

Dad stuffed the trout with lemon zest and garlic then wrapped it in foil. 'That'll go on the barbecue shortly. Want a salad with it?'

Charlie nodded. 'Sure.' Like she cared. She doubted she'd taste a thing. Marshall had gone. At least he'd left an email address so she could contact him. Considering how much effort she'd put into trying to find an address, she should be grateful. She wasn't. Not at all. They hadn't talked through anything to do with Aimee. They hadn't talked at all.

'Charlotte.' Dad sat down at the kitchen table beside her.

When he called her Charlotte she knew she should listen, but today she didn't want to. What could Dad say that would make her feel any better? Raising one eyebrow, she grimaced.

'He promised me he wouldn't hurt you or Aimee.'

'Goes to show how much his promises mean, doesn't it?' She shoved her chair back and went to get a glass of water.

'I believed him. Still do. It wasn't Marshall's fault his flight was brought forward or that you had to fly to Waikato Hospital with your patient. Give him a break, love.'

Leaning back against the bench, she studied the inside of her glass. 'I can do that. But can I expect to see him again? I haven't told him everything. He needs to know why it's important he stays in touch.' She shouldn't have avoided the issue when she'd had the chance during their walk into town. But it had seemed too soon, a huge information dump when he had still been coming to terms with Aimee's existence.

'I don't believe you've seen or heard the last of him.'

'I only hope you're right.' She poured the water down her throat, hoping her father didn't see the threatening tears at the corners of her eyes. She'd stupidly admitted to herself that she loved Marshall and now she had to somehow forget that and get on with her life. The first time she'd done it, it had been hard enough. This time felt infinitely worse. They shared a child now. 'I'll take Aimee out to her paddling pool.' And try to gain some semblance of control over these feelings of despair.

Aimee loved water. So much so it worried Charlie at times. Smacking the water so that it splashed everywhere made Aimee burst into shrieks of laughter. Despite her mood, Charlie couldn't help smiling at her girl. 'Go for it, sweetheart.' She eased herself onto a garden chair by the small plastic pool.

'She's a water baby, just like her mom,' drawled a familiar American accent.

She shot off the chair so fast she tripped and would've fallen on her butt if Marshall hadn't caught her.

He laughed and said, 'You're obviously glad to see me.' And then he kissed her. Thoroughly. So that her muscles and bones liquefied. So that she forgot everything except the man whose arms were holding her upright, whose hard, lean body supported her. A bubble of desire and need and love rolled up her throat and burst across her lips to be caught in his mouth.

He pulled his mouth away enough to utter, 'God, Charlie, I've missed you,' and then went back to kissing her.

He'd missed her? Yes. A mental fist went up in the air. For more than two years? Or a few hours? Whatever. He was back. For how long? Did it matter when he'd made the effort to return? She slid her hands behind his neck and held on for all she was worth.

'Guess I should be getting the beers,' Dad growled from somewhere behind them.

Marshall slowly lifted his head, withdrawing that delicious mouth as though reluctant to stop kissing her. 'Yes, sir, that would be great.' And then he kissed her again, a quick kiss on her lips before putting her down on her feet. 'I like your dad.'

Dad probably felt a teeny bit smug right now, with Marshall's sudden reappearance. She asked, 'How far did you get?'

'The turn-off for Auckland outside Hamilton.'

'What happened? Did your flight get changed again?'

He took her hand and tugged her across to the lounger on the veranda where he sat and lifted her onto his lap, holding her there with an arm around her waist. He needn't have worried. She wasn't going anywhere.

'I bailed. Told the guys I'll find my own way back to the States later. If it's all right with you, I'd like to hang around and get to know my daughter.' Then he added, 'Actually, I'd like to get to know her mom even better.'

Warmth flooded her. Yes, this was what she'd hoped for. 'You can stay here.' He would, wouldn't he? It made sense.

His eyes narrowed. 'Are you sure that's a good idea? Hadn't you better check with Brendon first?'

'Check what with me?' Dad asked as he strolled out, two beers in one hand.

'Marshall's staying for two weeks and I said he could bunk down here.'

'I should think so.' Then he added, 'But don't let us pressure you, lad. You might find you want time to yourself.'

'Then I'll go for a run, or have a beer at the hotel. Thank you both. That's settled.'

Marshall had returned. That's all Charlie knew. And she was happy to accept that, to enjoy his company. At least she had time up her sleeve now. She could afford to give him some space. As long as they didn't share too many of those hot kisses. Otherwise all her good intentions would combust.

Now, there was a thought. Her smile felt smug even to her.

CHAPTER SEVEN

MONDAY MORNING AND the bedside alarm screeched into Charlie's sleep-soaked brain. Six o'clock. She jerked upright. Something wasn't right. Again Aimee hadn't woken her. She used the alarm clock as back-up.

Leaping out of bed, she threw her robe around her shoulders as she raced down the hall to Aimee's bedroom. What had happened? Was she okay? Her heart thudded hard against her ribs as she ran into the bedroom. She pulled up in a hurry. Aimee's cot was empty.

That had to be good. Didn't it? Had Marshall got Aimee up again? Back out in the hall Charlie strode fast to the kitchen. And slammed to a stop in the doorway.

Dressed in running shorts and a tight tee shirt, Marshall sat at the table with a mug of what looked like black coffee in one hand. Aimee bounced on his knee, held firmly in place with his other hand. The smile beaming out at Aimee from her father stopped Charlie's heart. Filled with awe and happiness and care—or was that love?—his mouth curved into the sweetest smile she'd ever seen and his eyes glowed with emotion. He really had no problem accepting Aimee was his child. He'd embraced the concept, not once questioning if she was sure.

She opened her mouth to say something but the words stuck in her throat. Never in all the months of searching for this man had she believed he'd fall for his daughter so easily, so quickly.

'Look who's woken up.' Marshall spoke to Aimee but his eyes had focused on Charlie. 'Aimee was a wee bit grizzly so I figured it would be okay to get her up. But by the look on your face, I guess I did wrong.'

'Not at all.' She drew breath to get her emotions under control. No point giving him any clues as to how she felt about him yet. If ever. Now he was getting the hang of being a parent he might start thinking of wanting more kids, which would lead to even more problems. Her heart squeezed. She'd love more of Marshall's babies. Gulp. Concentrate on what they were talking about, not the impossible.

On an indrawn breath she said, 'Aimee usually wakes me up, so when the alarm went off I thought something had happened to her.' Her mild panic sounded stupid, even over the top, now. Trying for a nonchalant shrug, she crossed to the hot kettle and flicked the switch to make tea. Then she plopped a kiss on Aimee's grinning face. 'Morning, sweetheart.'

'Do I get one?'

'Sure.' She leaned closer, kissed Marshall's stubbly chin. 'Morning.'

The hand that had been holding his mug now gripped her arm and held her in place while his mouth reached for hers. 'We can do better than that.' And then he was kissing her. Again. This was getting to be a habit. A habit she enjoyed.

Aimee grabbed a handful of Charlie's hair and pulled hard. 'Mum, mum.'

'Ouch.' She stepped back a pace. 'Careful, little one. Mummy's head hurts when you do that.' Her scalp had been tender since the day her hair had fallen out due to the chemo. Blinking rapidly, she turned away from Marshall's all-seeing gaze and concentrated on making tea.

When she sat at the table with her drink, she'd got her emotions in order again. 'You're an early riser,' she commented to Marshall.

'Like to go for a run before it gets too hot.' He jiggled Aimee on his knees and was rewarded with giggles. 'But I got sidetracked this morning.'

'I can understand that. She's always been a great time-waster. But if you want to go out you can put her down. We'll be showering as soon as I've had my tea. Aimee usually joins me.' It was the fastest and easiest way to get her girl washed.

Marshall's face lit up. 'A family affair.'

Her cheeks heated up. 'You needn't think you're joining us.'

He scowled exaggeratedly and held a hand over his heart. 'Ow, she wounds so easily.'

'Go on with you. I'm still getting used to you being here. I'm certainly not ready for anything more intimate yet.'

'Yet? So there's a possibility? If I behave?' His grin turned wicked. As did the glint in his eyes.

'You don't know how to behave.'

'Is that so? Talk about a challenge.' His grin only widened. Any further and he was in danger of splitting the corners of that delectable mouth she so enjoyed kissing.

'Go for your run. I haven't got time to sit around talking nonsense at this hour of the day. I've got to get ready for work.'

He wiggled his eyebrows at her. 'Nonsense? Did you hear that, Aimee? Your mom's a hard woman. Take it from me.' Then his face settled back to near normal. 'Have you got time to join me on the run?'

Yes, she did but was she up to it? 'I'll be too slow.'

'Let's give it a shot. We can turn back any time you've had enough.' Definitely a challenge twinkling out at her.

In the past she'd have taken him up on it, but now, after everything she'd been through? 'I'll be turning back. You can keep pounding the pavement for your usual time. I'll tell Dad.'

'What time do you leave for work?'

'A little after eight. Aimee goes with me. We've got a crèche at the centre for staff families, as well as for patients' children so they can have a more relaxed consultation.'

'Exactly how little after eight?'

She shrugged. 'Five, ten minutes, maybe more. I go when I'm ready.'

Annoyance battled with bewilderment in his face. 'What time do you start work, then?'

'When I get there.' She chuckled as it dawned on her what Marshall's problem was. 'At the medical centre we aren't regimented. It's not a standing order to arrive exactly at eight-thirty. As long as we're there on time for our first appointments at nine no one has any concerns. I like to spend half an hour or so looking up test results that have come in overnight, check who I'm seeing and going over their medical histories. But if I don't have time before the day gets under way it's not the end of the world. I do those things as I go.' Draining her mug, she stood and reached for Aimee. 'Come on, little one. Let's find Granddad.'

'But working to a strict timetable saves a lot of wasted time and many mistakes.' Marshall also stood and gathered up their mugs, placing them in the sink.

'Sounds too stifling for me.'

'It works for the armed forces. There'd be no end of problems if we weren't so controlled. Imagine telling the men to draw arms and have them doing it as it suited them.' He shook his head. 'Impossible.'

She smiled at his serious countenance. 'Although there are times when it feels like it, the medical centre is not a war zone.'

'I guess.' Then he relaxed and his heart-wrenching smile returned. 'You might even have a point. Yesterday at the airport it was amazing how everyone worked together without anyone issuing constant directions. People knew what had to be done and got on with it, helping each other, giving the patients the utmost in care.'

The smile turned wry. 'I had to bite my tongue a couple of times when I was about to yell an order only to find whatever I thought needed doing was already being done. It wasn't my place to say anything, but it wouldn't have stopped me.'

No surprise there. 'There's more than one way of getting the best out of people.' She headed for the door. 'Sorry, but I haven't got time to sit around talking all morning. I'm going for a run.'

'Are you sure you're up to this?' Worry glinted out of Dad's eyes. 'Running's hard on the body when you're not used to it.'

'I'll only do about four or five k's. If that.'

'I don't know.'

'I'll be fine. Promise.' Dad had become overprotective. Who could blame him? He'd lost his beloved wife to cancer and lived in terror of losing her. But she couldn't go on not trying to get back to being the fit person she'd once been.

The sun mightn't be up to speed in its intensity but the morning was still hot. The sweat poured off Marshall as he pounded the footpath down to the lake. Glancing sideways, he got a shock to find Charlie hadn't kept up with him. Slowing to jog on the spot, he waited for her to catch up. 'You were serious about being out of practice.'

Her chest rose and fell rapidly. 'Yes,' she gasped. 'I'll turn back now.' Her disappointment was obvious.

Stopping his jogging completely, Marshall took her hand and began walking along the path. 'Deep breaths.' When her fingers curled around his hand, warmth stole through him and settled around his heart. 'You did fine for your first time out in a while.' He doubted they'd come as far as she'd hoped but he wouldn't put a dampener on her attempt. 'Want to walk or run home?'

'Definitely walk. I can't believe how hard that was. To think I used to run for an hour and not feel too bad. You have no idea how angry that makes me feel.'

'So why didn't you get back into running once Aimee was born?'

'Long story.' Tugging her hand free, she added, 'Talk to you later. I'll be late if I don't get a move on.'

'I'll come with you.'

Her hand came up in a stop signal. 'No way. Carry on. I'll see you soon.' And she turned for home.

He wanted to go with her and demand an explanation because he got the impression there was a lot she hadn't told him yet. A long story she'd said, with sadness creeping into her voice and eyes. Pushing her might get the answers he craved but could also make her tetchy with him. So he'd continue his run and try to talk to her later.

Anyway, he needed the exercise. Nothing like a hard run to loosen his muscles and get him ready for the day. Not that he knew how he'd fill in the hours until Charlie came home from the medical centre.

Unless he offered to take care of Aimee for a while. Get to know his little girl. She fascinated him, so cute and small. He could take photos. Mom and Dad might like to see them. Yeah, right. If they hadn't had time for him it was very unlikely they'd be bothered about Aimee. Especially as she lived halfway round the world from their usual haunts.

They'd be the losers. Not him. Even if he didn't become a regular feature in his child's life he'd make sure she knew he loved her. Like how? Emails, computer video calls, phone calls when she was older, birthday and Christmas presents. It didn't sound like enough. Would he have been satisfied with that when he'd been growing up? Hell, he'd got the presents and phone calls and, no, he hadn't been at all happy.

Marshall shivered. Balancing this parenting lark with his army life wasn't going to be easy. It didn't help that he lived in a different country from Charlie and Aimee. Would Charlie consider moving to the States? Not fair to ask her. She'd be lonely and miss her support network of Brendon and friends. Besides, she had her career here, was set up for life really.

He increased his pace, trying to outrun his thoughts, and for a while he succeeded. Finally he turned for home. Damn. Turned for Charlie's home. They were sucking him in with their kindness, openness and honesty. No pressure about what he wanted to do now he knew he was a dad. Nothing like that at all. Just make himself at home and go with the flow. So alien for him. Yet he kind of liked it. Could even get used to it.

At the gate into the large section where Charlie's home stood he flicked the childproof lock and walked through as though he'd always done this. As if coming home to a wonderful woman and his child was normal.

Hell, turn around and run away, fast. But no. His feet kept moving in the direction of the front door. He'd shower and have breakfast before taking over looking after Aimee for a while. How hard could that be?

Charlie laughed fit to bust. 'I think you'll have to try a more hands-on approach.'

Marshall looked from Aimee to her and back again, confusion gleaming in his eyes. 'Hands on?'

Slipping the strap of her laptop case over her shoulder, she reached for the car keys hanging on the hook just inside the kitchen door. Still laughing, she told him, 'You can't insist that Aimee goes pee pee. Learning to use the potty is still a bit of a mystery to her.'

'Truly?' He looked stunned.

She couldn't help adding, 'She's not an army recruit. You have to take her to the bathroom, remove her pants and sit her down on the pot.'

'You don't think I can do this, do you?' The smile returned but didn't quite reach his eyes. He was seeing this as a challenge. Not good for either him or Aimee.

Stepping over to him, she placed a hand on his arm, squeezed gently. 'I would never leave my daughter with someone I didn't believe capable of caring for her. Not even her father.'

He glowered at her. 'You're trying to con me, babe.'

'Yep. Totally.' Up on tiptoe she planted a kiss on his now clean-shaven chin. 'See you both later at the centre.' As she strode away she added quietly, 'All clean and tidy with big smiles on your faces.'

'I heard that.' Marshall stood at the kitchen door, Aimee on his hip. 'You are so in for a surprise, Charlotte Lang.'

She hoped so. Waving her hand over her shoulder in his direction, she headed outside. Another glorious day and Marshall was here. Still here. He'd shocked her when he'd returned last night. Not to mention warming her from the bottom of her stomach right through to her heart. He certainly didn't shy away from responsibilities, even those he'd had dumped on him only the day before.

It felt weird going into work without Aimee accompanying her. But within minutes of parking at the back of the building she'd explained to the girl running the crèche that Aimee would be in later and quickly became absorbed in laboratory results and radiology findings. Aimee and Marshall were firmly at the back of her mind by the time she read an abnormal mammogram result for a patient of hers. Keisha Harris was in her mid-thirties and had two gorgeous boys she adored. She'd gone to school with Charlie, been in the same netball team, gone out clubbing with the same friends.

And now she might have the same bloody disease. If further tests came back positive then, despite a different part of Keisha's body being affected, it would still disrupt Keisha's life as badly as it had hers.

With a heavy heart Charlie picked up the phone and dialled Keisha's home number. When the answering-machine picked up she went to ask Molly, 'Do you know if Keisha's working during the school holidays? I need to speak to her.' As soon as possible.

'She and Toby have taken the boys to Phuket for two weeks. I think they're due home at the end of the week.'

'I'll leave a message on her phone that hopefully won't cause alarm.' What were the chances of that? She had to make Keisha aware she needed to get in touch fairly quickly. The radiology centre had probably left a message recalling Keisha for further X-rays. There wasn't any point in disrupting the family's holiday, though. One week wouldn't make any difference and they might as well make the most of their fun time because the next few weeks were going to be tough while Keisha underwent tests and waited for results.

Molly told her, 'Your first patient's here.'

Charlie dealt with prescription renewals, a sprained ankle and a mildly depressed teen before Mrs Withers slipped into her room, complaining of chest pains. With Gemma's help Charlie ran tests and promptly called an ambulance to take their patient to hospital.

Next six-year-old Josh Donaldson bounced in, every bit of exposed skin covered with what looked like hives. Scratching like mad at his arms, he grizzled, 'I don't like these bumps. They sting and make me stay awake at night.'

'I don't blame you for not liking them.' Charlie studied his red, puffy skin. 'What did he have to eat before these started appearing?' she asked his mother, Vicki.

His mum looked distressed at the thought she'd fed her son something he might be allergic to. 'Nothing out of the ordinary. Chicken sandwiches, ice cream and peaches. He's never shown a reaction to any food before.'

Charlie smiled across at Vicki. 'Being a mother

doesn't get any easier, does it? Every time I think I'm making headway with Aimee she tosses up something different for me to deal with.' So far health issues hadn't been a problem, but she crossed her fingers anyway. 'She's started climbing everything in sight.' Which wasn't good when there was a road outside the front gate.

'I know exactly what you mean. It's like a minefield. I thought that once Josh was old enough to go to school he wouldn't be having any problems. Shows how much I know.' Vicki ran her hand lovingly over her son's head.

Charlie turned to the boy. 'Josh, where were you playing yesterday?'

'Dad took us to the river for a swim.' Scratch, scratch. 'I saw an eel and my sister cried when she slipped on the rocks.' He grinned, with no sympathy for little Karla whatsoever.

'No sand flies? Bees? Wasps?' When the boy shook his head she continued, 'I'll arrange for an allergy test to be done by one of our nurses. It will take about an hour. And I'll give you some cream to take the itch and heat out of those bumps.'

Josh asked, 'Can Gemma do it? I like her best.'

'I'm sure she can.'

Vicki and Josh disappeared back to Reception to make an appointment with Gemma.

Charlie went in search of her next patient and bumped into her father in the hall. 'Why are you here so early?'

His eyes lit up. 'I've been replaced at home. My breakfast was waiting when I came out of my room. Aimee was in her highchair, firing pieces of toast around the kitchen and quite happy to be waited on by Marshall, who looked as though being out on a recce with his troop would be a whole lot easier than dealing with an eighteen-month-old.'

She chuckled. 'Wish I'd been a fly on the wall.'

'Can't you at least pretend to feel sorry for him?'

Pressing her lips together, she shook her head. 'Nope. It's good for him.'

'You're a hard woman, Charlotte Lang.'

'Wonder where I learned that?' She walked into the waiting room and looked around the patients. 'Kathy, come on through.'

By eleven Charlie was more than ready for a coffee and biscuit. As her previous patient disappeared Gemma stepped through the door, her eyes wide and bulging.

'I thought the Greeks had it sussed when it came to male gods. But I'm telling you, there's a hunk out in Reception, holding Aimee, who puts all those statues to shame.'

And that's with his clothes on. Charlie's stomach tightened as she smiled. 'Am I right in thinking he might be about six-three, broad shoulders tapering down to slim hips, buzz-cut hairstyle and a face to get lost in?'

'That's the one. Aimee's plastered all over him as though she's never going to let him go.'

Charlie's smile slipped. That could be a problem. 'I'd better go and rescue her. Or should that be him?'

Gemma laughed. 'Charlie, you've been hiding out on me. I know you said Aimee's dad was one of a kind, but I never got an inkling just how wow he really is.'

'Dribbling doesn't suit you.' Running a hand over her hair, she slipped around her desk, excitement fizzing along her veins. It hadn't been three hours since she'd last seen Marshall but it was impossible to deny the need crawling through her. To see him, kiss him, touch him. Oops. Hold on. She was at work.

'Hey, did Marshall come right out and say he was Aimee's father? To everyone?'

Gemma stood blocking the doorway, a wide smile on her face. 'Yes, he did. Looked quite pleased with himself, too. He's gone through to the kitchen with Brendon to meet everyone. Your man seems to be getting on well with your dad.'

Her man? If only. 'They do get on, but I think Dad's working on buttering him up for a long-term plan that will work for both Aimee and me.'

'Sounds like Brendon, always thinking ahead.'

'That reminds me. Dad thinks you're pretty good, too. I just wanted to say if you're interested in getting close to him, go for it. I heartily approve.' Good-natured, sweet-hearted, happy-go-lucky Gemma would be perfect for Dad.

Gemma. Someone she owed so much to. She'd spent hours sitting with her as she'd puked her stomach dry after rounds of chemo. It was Gemma who'd gone shopping for wigs with her, and had laughed until she'd cried when a wig had got whipped off her head as she'd ducked under a low-hanging branch one day. Gemma had held her hand and listened to all her fears for Aimee and Dad. Gemma, fifteen years older than her and yet the best friend she'd ever had.

Gemma's hug enveloped her. 'Didn't think you'd mind. Now, go and claim that hunk out in the kitchen before one of the other females in this building hustles him away.'

CHAPTER EIGHT

EARLY TUESDAY MORNING Charlie got dressed in her running gear. 'I can't believe how much my muscles ache,' she grumbled as she jogged beside Marshall. 'It's going to take weeks to get fit.'

'Toughen up.' He nudged her gently and when she flipped her head up he was grinning at her.

'Easy for you to say.' She glanced at his long legs, which were eating up the metres no problem at all. One stride of his equalled almost two of hers. 'I've got an idea. Tomorrow I'll ride my bike while you run. Then we'll see who's fastest.'

His laughter made her happy and caused him to lose his breathing pattern. She laughed in return when he had to stop to sort his lungs out and she got a little way ahead. Not for long, though.

'Going my way?' He waved as he raced past.

Her lungs were hurting and her legs protesting. Wishing she could take up the challenge, she wheezed out, 'I'm heading home. See you later.'

He turned and ran backwards for a moment. 'I'll bring lunch in to work.'

'We'll go down to the lake.'

A little after midday Charlie swallowed a mouthful of panini filled with salad and chicken and asked Marshall,

'What did you find to talk about to the other doctors all afternoon yesterday?'

'Medical stuff. You'd be surprised what other doctors want to know about the trauma cases I deal with out in the field.' Marshall chewed a blade of grass and gazed out over the sparkling wavelets the light breeze was churning up on the lake. 'I don't give a lot of detail but I guess it seems exciting compared to the routine of a clinic. What they don't get is that there are days I'd happily swap places. At least most of your patients won't have lost a limb or have holes blasted in their torsos by random gunfire.'

Charlie put her food aside, suddenly not hungry. 'How do you deal with that all the time?' Marshall rarely talked about his medical duties.

'I try to think about the guys I'm helping and put the rest aside.'

'Like that works.' Disappointment at being fobbed off grabbed at her. He'd finally said something personal and then backed away the moment she'd picked up on it.

He turned a grim face to her. 'Not a bit.'

She gasped at the raw pain in his eyes. 'Marshall?' she whispered, as she wrapped her hand around his much larger one. Small tremors shook him. His skin felt clammy and cold. His chest rose and fell on short breaths.

'It doesn't matter,' he croaked.

'Yeah, it does.' She looked around at Aimee, playing happily with the stones at the edge of the bank. 'Tell me,' she said.

His hand turned to cover hers, his grip intense. 'You remember Rod? My best buddy?' When she nodded he continued in a low voice, 'Two months after we left

Hawaii we were in Afghanistan.' His Adam's apple bobbed. 'A plane carrying half my troop crashed at the end of the runway. Rod didn't make it. I tried everything I could to save him. Finally put him on the casualty flight out to Germany. I never saw him again.'

What could she say? Nothing that would help. She knew how hard people tried to make you feel better with words when your world had imploded. Words that usually just didn't work, didn't soothe or cure. She tightened her hold on his hand and leaned her head against his shoulder. 'I'm sorry.'

'Me, too.' His tongue slicked across his bottom lip. 'The worst of it? He knew he'd be dead before he got home so he wanted to stay on base with me. But I insisted he went, hoping beyond belief that he'd somehow make it to see his wife and boys. Who knows? Maybe I could've saved him. Or at least held his hand and talked with him.' His voice trailed off. His eyes were focused somewhere thousands of kilometres away, seeing something she'd never see.

'You're blaming yourself for something you couldn't prevent.'

'I mightn't have been flying that damned plane but I should've been able to hold him together long enough to get to a major hospital.'

'In another country.'

'It's why I became a doctor. To save people.' His voice sounded clogged with tears.

'You're the man who once told me we can't save them all.' Charlie rubbed her fingers back and forth across his hand.

'I should've been able to save my closest friend.'

'We can't save them all,' she repeated quietly yet

firmly. He mustn't go on blaming himself. This could destroy him if he let it. Lifting her head, she kissed his neck, his cheek, his lips.

Marshall gripped Charlie's hand, held on. Her lips were soft, sweet, caring. Touching him deep inside somewhere around his heart. Warming the cold place locked in there, no matter how many months had gone by since Rod had been loaded onto that flight.

Her touch was totally in contrast to the harsh reality of his life, of what he'd told her. Why the hell had he spilled his guts? It was the last thing he should be saying. He didn't do heart-to-heart stuff. Never had, never would. Except that's exactly what he'd just done.

A stone banged against his knee and rolled down his leg to his foot. Aimee stood on his other side, holding out her empty hand, grinning that cute grin that got to him every time. 'Hey, my girl, come here.' Wrapping his free arm around her, he tucked his daughter in against his side. Aimee on one side, Charlie on the other. The perfect picture, a family portrait. Alien. And the reason he had to keep surviving in the next place the army posted him to. And the next. And the next.

He'd be gone by the end of next week and he didn't have a clue when he'd be able to get to Taupo again. Charlie would be hurt. But not half as much as she would be if she thought they had a future together and then he got himself killed. He'd do what he could for Aimee, mostly the small stuff. But a full-on, day-by-day commitment? Not likely. These two were better off without him.

Charlie didn't sleep much that night. Tossing and turning, throwing the bedcovers off because she was too hot, pulling them back when the sweat on her skin chilled. Every time she closed her eyes she saw the anguish on Marshall's face, heard the pain in his voice as he'd talked about Rod.

Used to him always laughing and joking, she'd been shocked that he'd opened up at all. But she'd also been grateful because it meant they might be able to forge a deeper friendship, something strong enough to carry them through the months and years ahead.

Forget that she loved him. Yeah, right. Like how? Okay, her love wasn't going to vaporise or leave her in peace, but she had to take her time with that. First things first. Give Marshall the space to fall in love with his daughter. Because no matter that her own heart was his, Aimee had to take precedence.

The morning finally dawned, rays of sun sneaking around the edges of her blinds just after five. Long before Aimee cried out or the alarm beeped, she crawled out of bed. A cool shower might wake her up and refresh her head, which felt full of cotton wool. Sodden, heavy cotton wool.

'Hey, you look like something the dog buried.' Marshall stood outside his bedroom door, watching as she shuffled along the hall yawning so hard her jaw ached. 'Didn't sleep?'

Shaking her head, she pushed the bathroom door wide. 'Too hot.'

Those all-seeing eyes bored into her, filled with concern. 'You're not worrying about anything, are you, Charlie?'

Only how I'm going to get through the day on very little shut-eye, how Aimee will react when you leave us, how I'll cope if you don't stay in touch. 'Thinking about one of my patients.'

She lied because now wasn't the time to tell him the truth. He would hate it if she put pressure on him, asked him exactly what he thought he might do about seeing Aimee occasionally. Or more often. Then there was the biggie. Would he sign papers accepting responsibility for Aimee in the worst-case scenario? Hopefully the untruth wasn't glittering out at him from her tired eyes. She'd have looked away but it was as though his gaze had locked onto hers, keeping her in place.

Annoyance flickered over his face. 'Really?'

Had he guessed she'd fibbed? Or did he want her to have been worried about the situation after all? Guilt gripped her. Everything seemed too hard this early in the day. She needed a shower, a mug of tea and something to dull the pounding behind her eyes.

'Going for a run?' she asked, in a vain attempt to move him away, to stop that questioning look searing her.

'Shortly. You joining me?'

'I should, I know, but...' She didn't have the energy. Plain and simple.

'Go have a shower and I'll put the kettle on for you before I go. You do look exhausted.'

His thoughtfulness only ramped up her guilt. He mightn't know for sure why she got so tired but he was prepared to help her out. 'Thank you.'

As she stripped off her nightgown and waited for the water to warm, she stared in the mirror, trying to see what Marshall might see when he looked at her. Nothing like the happy doctor he'd had a short fling with, that's for sure. Did he wonder where that woman had gone? He'd probably put the dark shadows staining her upper cheeks and the short and curly, easy-to-handle hair all down to motherhood.

Soaping the night's sweat off her skin, she smiled despite the weariness dragging at her muscles. Marshall looked as delectable as ever, as sexy as any hot-blooded woman could imagine. During the night, whenever she woke up, her thoughts immediately went to him, sleeping three rooms down from her.

The temptation to go and slip into bed with him was huge, but she managed to hold onto a thread of reason, knowing it was the wrong thing to do at this stage. They'd never get to talk and plan for the future if they went back to that steamy sex life that had produced Aimee in the first place.

But how long would she be able to hold out? What would she do if Marshall made a serious pass at her? Her body warmed at the thought of it, an ache of need centring at the apex of her legs.

It isn't going to happen, Charlie. It mustn't.

Sluicing the soap from her belly her hands paused over her hysterectomy scar. No more babies. That hurt. Hurt even more now that Marshall had come back into the picture. She didn't have the right to ask him to forego having more children.

Leaning her aching head against the glass wall of the shower, she fought the urge to have a damned good howl. Which only went to show how tired she was. She didn't do tears, remember?

Marshall watched the bathroom door close behind Charlie. Her feet were dragging this morning. What was with all this tiredness? Motherhood and a demanding career were obviously taking their toll on her, but he still had the feeling he was missing something. Like what?

He filled the kettle, got out the cereal she liked, sliced up some fruit into a small bowl, and set everything at her place at the table. He enjoyed doing little things for her. Made him feel as though he was contributing to the family. His family. Whether he lived with Charlie or not, he now had a family of his own. Aimee Hunter-Lang was his family and by association so was Charlie.

Goddamn, Charlie had stunned him when she'd shown him Aimee's birth certificate. His name had stood out. Hunter. Okay, Hunter-Lang, but he was more than happy with that. Thrilled, if the truth be known. He'd never planned on having kids. But he'd become a father without knowing it, without being hauled up to the line and made to decide, and, damn it—he liked it. That should surprise him, scare him away. But it didn't. Unfortunately. Because he really needed to put space between himself and those two females dominating his mind, his time and just about everything he did at the moment.

It was time to start talking to Charlie. Really talking. Because he might like it that he was a dad but nothing had changed. He still had to go away, might not be back for up to a year, and then only for a few days at a time. And Charlie needed to understand that.

A loud cry erupted from down the hallway in the vicinity of Aimee's room. 'Coming, my girl.' He grinned. His daughter didn't do delicate, or shy, or quiet. Everything about her was full on. Just like her dad. Like her mum had been.

'Morning, Marshall.' Brendon stood outside Aimee's room, looking from him to his granddaughter inside.

Guilt hit Marshall. Brendon probably did the morning routine with Aimee and since he'd arrived the guy hadn't got a look-in. 'I'll go and make you a coffee.'

'Don't be silly, lad. Your daughter wants up.' Brendon slapped his shoulder lightly as he passed him. 'I'm over wet nappies.'

Nappies. 'What's wrong with calling them diapers?' He grinned at this man who was so generous, not only with his home but with his heart.

He got an exaggerated eye-roll in reply.

Laughing, he went to swing Aimee out of the cot and kiss her on each cheek, blowing raspberries in between. The giggles she let rip were all the reward he required. Turning to head to the kitchen, he paused to scan the hundreds of photos covering one wall. Aimee, from the moment she'd been born to the present. Charlie had already put up one of him holding her.

'I'll add more of you soon.' Charlie leaned in the doorway, a small smile lightening those heavy eyes.

She reached up to kiss Aimee. 'Morning, sweetheart.' Tickling her tummy got more giggles.

The breath stuck in Marshall's throat. By the simple act of reaching out to her daughter Charlie had let go the front of her satin robe, exposing her cleavage and giving him a partial view of her beautiful breasts. Full, lush and damned tempting. His mouth dried. She might be tiny but she was perfectly endowed. He could remember the weight of her breasts in his hands, could hear the catch in her breath as he fingered her nipples, the groan escaping her lips as the desire built to an inferno inside her.

'Mum, mum.' Aimee kicked and wriggled, thankfully diverting his licentious thoughts back to more prosaic needs.

But her movements didn't cool his racing blood or knock down the instant hard-on the sight of those breasts had fuelled. Now what? He couldn't turn his back on Charlie, neither could he adjust his shorts to hide the bulge without drawing attention to himself.

The wriggling bundle in his arms was trying to get down. Bending, he placed Aimee carefully on the floor and said to Charlie, 'Your breakfast is ready. The tea might be getting cold.'

'Right. I'll get dressed. Oh…' Her gaze dropped to her front and she quickly pulled the robe closed over those thought-diverting breasts. 'I—I won't be long.'

He watched her cute butt as she all but ran to her bedroom. The satin slipped and slid, accentuating the curves that led to her legs. Legs he remembered waking up and finding entangled with his most mornings they'd been together. Always smooth, soft and yet firm, perfectly suntanned. Athletic. Sensational. Sexy as hell.

The groan that tore from his throat was filled with raw need. How long could he last without touching her, without feeling her naked body pressed against his? Without her sprawled across him after mind-numbing sex? How had he managed to stay in his own bed every night, knowing she was just down the hall?

So much for deflating his hard-on. It was bigger than ever. A cold shower might fix it. Or a solid, knee-slamming, gut-busting run. With a hard-on? Yes, damn it.

'Aimee, go and see Mummy. I'm going out.'

'Me come.'

'Not this time. Charlie,' he called, 'I'm heading out for a run. You okay with Aimee?'

'Sure.' And there she was, scooping Aimee up into her arms, avoiding looking at him. She'd dressed super-fast. Her blouse was skew, with the buttons lined up incorrectly. 'Let's have some breakfast, sweetheart. Morning, Dad.'

Brendon stood at the end of the hall. 'Morning, love.'

Great. Now he had to get out of the house without either of them noticing his predicament. He turned for the front door, in a hurry to get out of there.

As he closed the door he heard Brendon saying, 'I'm going fishing on Saturday on the Tongariro River, staying over for the night at Billy's shack.'

Up the ante, why don't you? Marshall's shoes slapped the pavement as he headed for the lake. *Charlie and I alone in the house all damned night?* Knowing Brendon slept at the far end of the house had been about the only thing keeping him from knocking on Charlie's door most nights. He hadn't been able to bring himself to abuse the man's hospitality in that way.

He paused at the kerb, looked left, then right. Damn, got it wrong again. Looked right, then left and shot across the road to the path wending around the lake edge. The lake was calm this morning, as it often was until the afternoon breeze struck. At the far end, miles away, mountains rose into the pale blue of the morning sky. No denying the raw beauty of this place.

His heart ached. For the beauty. For Charlie. For the fact he had to leave at the end of next week. The army and his men awaited him.

Amazing. Charlie grinned. Once again Marshall had put her favourite breakfast together while she'd been in the shower after their run. He'd returned home with her this morning, not bothering with going further. 'I could get used to this.'

'Don't get your hopes up too high.' Dad grounded her fast.

'You don't think he'll come back to visit again?' Her heart sank. The truth was that she didn't either, but she couldn't help hoping. He was obviously still attracted to her. That had been monumentally obvious the other morning. But so far he hadn't acted on that attraction.

Dad buttered his toast. 'I'm sure he'll visit. Often.' The raspberry jam went on thickly. 'I just don't want you getting hurt. Marshall will do the right thing by you and Aimee. But I'm not sure that means making your breakfast every morning for the next fifty years.'

'You're talking commitment.' The cereal crunched between her teeth. 'I always knew that would be a difficulty, but I can't complain. I've got what I set out to find. If Marshall changes his mind about more involvement then that's a plus.'

Despite her tiredness, she suddenly felt free of all the worries of the last two years. Free of the need to try and make Marshall see things from her point of view. If commitment wasn't on his agenda, so be it. She'd find another way to make it work for Aimee. What that would be she didn't have a clue. But he was here for at least another week. Surely something would come to mind in that time.

Why had he come to see her? He hadn't known he had a child with her so it had to be because he'd had good memories of their time together. Had he thought they might pick up where they'd left off for a short while? A long, low sigh slipped over her bottom lip. Now, there was a thought. She'd love nothing more than to share a few hot nights under the sheet with him. But it wasn't going to happen.

She still had to tell Marshall about her dodgy health. It hung over her like a stormcloud. Swallowing the last of her breakfast, she pushed back from the table. Today was Friday, and then there was the weekend. Who knew what they might get to talk about then? But first she had a day of patients to see to. And tonight it was her turn to cook dinner.

At last. Charlie's car turned into the drive. She was well over an hour late home, which was unusual. Marshall's heart stopped its panicked beating and his brain deleted the horrific scenes he'd conjured up.

He opened her door and drank in the sight of her. 'Hey, you coming out to play?'

'Sure. I missed you at lunch. But I heard you were very busy with the boating-accident victims.'

'Yeah.' His grin vanished. 'When I was walking your way I saw a crowd on the beach and went to investigate. The moment I knew there were injured people out on the lake I volunteered to help. There were kids involved.' His voice hitched with anger. 'Two weren't wearing flotation jackets. How can parents be so careless?' He certainly wouldn't put Aimee's life at risk like that.

Charlie passed him a bag of groceries from the passenger seat before clambering out of the car. 'The national water safety council has an ongoing battle with that every summer. They swamp the television programmes with ads about wearing lifejackets, target the worst offenders, and yet our drowning statistics are appalling.'

Marshall nodded. 'This is very much a water-orientated country. I guess that explains some of the higher figures. But to let your kids out on a boat without any thought to their safety is beyond me. Why are people so careless with their kids' lives?' He shook his head at the stupidity of it.

'Which is why Aimee's already started swimming lessons and there's a miniature lifejacket hanging up in the shed alongside mine.' Charlie gave him a knowing grin. 'You're acting like a responsible dad.'

'I feel like one. How cool's that?' He grinned right back. Damn, but she was cute when she thought she'd bested him.

She changed the subject. Typical. 'Joseph says you were great out there today. Impressed the hell out of him.'

'Good to know. That's twice I've been able to help out. Seems I can be a doctor anywhere, not just on the battlefield.' He felt surprisingly good about that. Food for thought.

Her eye-roll was lopsided and made him laugh. Draping his free arm around her shoulders, he tugged her close. 'You and I are having a night out. All by ourselves. Dinner at Camper's. I believe they do a damned fine meal.'

She stumbled, quickly recovered. 'What about Aimee?' What happened to asking me?

'Brendon's happy to look after her. He's got to get his fishing tackle ready and cook a pie or something for lunch tomorrow.'

Her chuckle warmed him. 'Dad's fishing gear is always ready.'

'Yeah, I kind of figured that, but I'm not going to turn him down when he offers to babysit so I can take you out for some one-on-one time. So, my lovely, how about you take yourself inside for a long, relaxing shower or bath? Then dress in something gorgeous and we'll hit the town.' Excitement twirled in his belly. A night out with Charlie. Bring it on.

CHAPTER NINE

MARSHALL STARED AT the apparition floating down the hall towards him. A cloud of pink and yellow balanced on dangerously high heels. A hint of frangipani tickled his nose, bringing back memories of nights on the beach in Honolulu. The biggest, sweetest smile he'd ever seen split Charlie's face.

He could not speak. The roof could've fallen on his head and he wouldn't have got a word out. Charlotte was the most beautiful woman he'd ever seen, had ever had the good fortune to meet and touch, to kiss and laugh with. Holy Toledo.

'Marshall? Is something wrong?' The hesitancy in her voice mobilised him.

Two strides and he reached for her hands. Her fingers curled around his. 'No.' A swallow. 'Nothing.'

Her eyes scrunched up, her brow creased. 'I can change if my dress is all wrong. I'm so not used to dressing up these days.'

Now he got the hang of talking. 'Don't you dare. You look sensational. You took my breath away, that's all.' That's all? It was huge. He didn't usually stop breathing for anyone, let alone a woman. But Charlie was something else. If he ever fell in love it would have to be with someone exactly like her.

Relief battled with laughter in her eyes as she relaxed. 'Thank goodness for that. For a moment there I thought I'd have to wear my best pair of jeans.'

'Want to say goodnight to Aimee and your dad?' He had to get out of there, get Charlie to himself. He'd come to Taupo with the vague idea of spending time with her, and so he had, but he'd been sharing her all the time. Tonight was his. Theirs.

The waiter showed them to their table at the window, where they had a bird's-eye view of Huka Falls. Marshall had gone all out to find the best restaurant around. Charlie felt even more special, and determined to be fun and witty. And to stay awake—at least long enough to have dessert.

'This is lovely,' she murmured as she sank onto the chair he held out for her, having just nudged the waiter aside none too gently.

Then he further upset the young man by shifting his setting around so that he sat beside her and not opposite. 'I want to see the view too.'

The way his voice caressed her, she wondered exactly which view he meant. Though if he'd wanted to stare at her all night, he wouldn't have shifted, would he? Then his shoulder settled against hers and his hip touched hers and she smothered a sigh of pleasure. When his hand engulfed hers she smiled directly at him. 'Are we eating one-handed? Rice or mashed spuds maybe?'

His grin warmed her through and through. 'I've missed you. I want to be with you. It's been great staying at your house, getting to know you and your family, but tonight I want you for myself. All of you.'

Gulp. So they were to have an interesting, exciting evening, were they? Bring it on. Heat trickled along her veins, warming her from head to toe. She loved being treated like someone very special. It boosted her flagging ego, made her feel completely feminine again. 'I think I'll have a glass of champagne tonight.' Her strict regime of no alcohol could go to blazes. For tonight at least. She'd spent too long worrying about the possibilities of getting sick again. It was time to let her hair down and have fun. Pity she didn't have that long hair Marshall had known before.

'Atta girl. Let's celebrate being together again after far too long apart.'

She could do that. And when a bottle of very good champagne appeared on their table almost immediately, she smiled. 'So you'd already ordered?'

'Yep. I remembered how much you used to enjoy drinking this stuff so hoped I could entice you into partaking tonight. I'm surprised that you don't drink wine at all now.'

So she couldn't relax completely. There was no way she'd spoil tonight with her sorry tale. 'The moment I suspected I was pregnant I gave up anything remotely alcoholic. Then I breastfed Aimee for a while. Guess I've never really bothered since.' She raised her glass and toasted him. 'To you. Thanks for turning up out of the blue. You have no idea how much that meant.'

The rim of Marshall's glass tapped hers very carefully. 'The pleasure's all mine. I really had missed you and during this last deployment found myself thinking about you more and more. Besides, I wanted to know how your medical career was going since I had some input in it.' His lips seemed big and full against the delicate glass. Lips that could turn her body on with a single kiss. 'I'm glad I followed up on those instincts.'

'How often have you been deployed overseas since we were in Honolulu?'

'Twice.' When the gleam faded in his eyes she wished her question back. Marshall also had issues best left alone tonight.

Quickly changing the subject, she said, 'Tell me about your grandparents and their farm. Didn't you say you went there for school holidays?' It must've been the right thing to say because the tension she'd begun to feel in the hand holding hers backed off. She turned a little so she could watch all his facial expressions. There'd never be enough time just to absorb them, drink in this man who had her heart in his care.

'You'd have loved Grampy and Gran. They were so loving and sharing, like you and your father. I always put on a right performance when it was time to go back to whichever base my parents were at after my stays with them. I never understood why I couldn't just go to their local school.'

'So you went to a lot of schools?'

'Oh, yes. Too many. Not like you, eh?' His hand squeezed hers. 'What is it like, living in the same place all the time?'

That was easy. 'I don't know anything different. Apart from Mum's death, I had a truly happy child-hood. I learned to sail on the lake and can catch a trout on a spinner.' She grinned when his eyebrows rose. 'There were week-long school trips to the mountains for skiing and day trips to Rotorua and the mud pools.'

'You sound like a travel brochure.'

The champagne bubbles burst on her tongue. 'That's divine. How could I have managed not to have this for two years?' She saw the waiter hovering and added, 'Guess we'd better order our meal.'

'What's the hurry?' Marshall picked up his menu.

I turn into a pumpkin at nine o'clock. 'I'm hungry.'

Charlie ordered steak, medium-rare, and mushrooms, while Marshall went for the lamb rack. 'Should try what this country's famous for.'

'Have you told any of your family about Aimee yet?' she asked quietly a little while later.

'No. I'd talk to you before I did that.'

She stared at him. 'You don't get it, do you?' Hadn't he picked up on any of her vibes? 'If I hadn't wanted you and your family's involvement with Aimee I would've sent you packing the moment you stepped through the front gate.'

As the waiter placed their meals before them Marshall kissed her cheek. 'Sometimes I get it wrong when it comes to knowing you.'

'We don't know much about each other at all.' But for her it had been love at first sight.

They talked and ate and enjoyed the wine for the next hour. Marshall was reticent about his army career and his parents. Charlie avoided her illness completely, fudging over those months when she'd been going through treatment. He raved on about the farm in Montana and how he'd learned to ride horses when he was nine. She spoke of her girlfriends and all the pranks they'd got up to as teenagers, and how she hoped Aimee would have such good friends as she grew up.

'Are any of those friends still living here?' he asked as he reached for the dessert menu.

'Jacqui's a teacher at the local high school, and Lisa is a radiologist up the road at Waikato Hospital. It's hard to see a lot of each other with our careers and families getting first dibs on our time. But twice a year we go away to a spa for a girls-only weekend.'

Marshall dropped his chin into his palm. He looked so sexy. Those come-to-bed eyes twinkled at her, making her toes curl with desire. How had she managed to stay out of his bed all week? 'Spare me. I can hear the three of you now, talking non-stop for the whole weekend.' Then he grinned at her. 'I'm having the strawberries. You?'

'Same,' she muttered around a sudden yawn. At least she'd made it until now for the first one. Hopefully she'd be okay for the rest of their meal. Shouldn't have had the champagne. Hurriedly covering her mouth as another yawn ripped through her, she forced herself to focus on the menu. 'Strong black coffee, too.'

Marshall squashed a flare of disappointment when Charlie yawned for a third time. They'd made it to nine o'clock before her tiredness had won out. He'd been hoping that a change of environment, a romantic dinner for two and just relaxing and talking might've kept her alert for longer. But seemed he was wrong. She was fading fast. Leaning close, he kissed her cheek. Then the corner of her sweet mouth. Then her lips. She tasted of champagne and mushrooms.

'Come on. Let's go home.' Standing, he lifted her up against him, kissing the top of her head softly. That exotic fragrance wove around him again. So Charlie. So erotic.

But Charlie sat back down. 'No. We've ordered dessert and coffee. I'd like to enjoy them.' Her eyes were wide as she stared up at him, as though she was deliberately holding them open while her brain was trying to make her go to sleep. 'Please.'

'Am I allowed to carry you out of here later?' His grin was forced.

Glancing around the nearly full restaurant, Charlie laughed. 'That'd be entertaining.'

'That's a yes, then.' He slid back onto his chair and pulled it closer to her. To feel her thigh against his gave him a sense of belonging. Yet he never wanted to belong to someone, not even Charlie. That would mean living with her whenever he wasn't on active duty, which he could handle, even enjoy.

But he never wanted see the light go out in her eyes as he packed to go away for months on end. He knew the hurt and anger and sense of abandonment that went with that look. Because he'd felt it, seen it in his own eyes every time his parents had headed out, leaving him behind.

Her elbow jogged him. 'Where have you gone?' she asked as she tried to hide another yawn.

'I'm right here, babe.' She shouldn't be so tired all the time. About to ask about it, he stopped, swallowed the words. They were having a good time. Why spoil it? But he would be talking to her later. Maybe making an appointment for her with one of her partners at the medical centre.

Thankfully the desserts and coffee arrived and they went back to chatting about everyday things.

Marshall didn't have to carry Charlie out of the restaurant but he did carry her up the path and through the

front door of her house. She was unbelievably light in
his arms. Her eyelids had drooped shut, her eyelashes
dark on her pale cheeks. Not even the light dusting of
make-up had given colour to her face. With her head
lolling against his shoulder, he felt incredibly protective of her. Wanted to look out for her. Knew he'd do
anything to keep her safe. And happy. Anything except
quitting the army and letting his men down. Even that
was beginning to feel odd.

'Have a good time?' Brendon asked from the kitchen
doorway. 'Charlie didn't make it all the way, then?'
Sadness darkened his eyes as he followed them down
the hall to Charlie's bedroom. 'Shame, when she was
so excited about going out. It's been so long since she
dated.' Ducking around them, he headed for the bed
and pulled back the covers.

So Charlie hadn't been dating. Didn't make a lot of
sense. She was attractive, gorgeous and very friendly.
Having a toddler wouldn't prevent most hot-blooded
men from wanting to spend time with her. 'We had
a fabulous meal. Perfect setting for spending special
time together.'

He placed Charlie on the bed, pulled up the sheet
and tucked it under her chin. Standing back, he gazed
down at the beautiful woman who'd somehow managed to snag his heart when he'd thought he'd had it
well and truly locked away. Goddamn it, he loved her.
No denying it. He loved her. For the way she just accepted him. For how she made no demands on him and
didn't ask what he was going to do about his daughter.
Love meant protecting. It meant making sure Charlie
and Aimee got what was best for them.

Brendon cleared his throat. 'If it's all right with you,

I thought I'd head away tonight. Bill and I like to be on the river before sun-up and he's already gone down to the shack.'

Twisting his head, he met the keen gaze of Charlie's dad. This man was on the same page as him. Wanted only the best for his daughter and granddaughter. And yet he was leaving Marshall alone with them for the weekend. Didn't he know what would most likely transpire? Then he saw the understanding, the acknowledgement of his daughter's needs in the man's eyes. 'Of course it's okay. Just bring me back a trout to taste, won't you?'

'Then I'll be off.' Brendon leaned down and kissed his daughter's cheek. 'Goodnight, sweetheart.' When he stood up he was blinking hard.

What the hell? 'Brendon?'

The guy turned for the hall, waving a hand over his shoulder. 'See you Sunday night.' Then the front door closed, and moments later Brendon's car pulled out onto the road, the sound of the engine fading into the night.

Marshall went through the house, locking up and turning off lights. Was Brendon afraid he was going to take his girls away to the States? The man's big heart wouldn't stop them going if that's what Charlie wanted, even though it would break him apart. If only the guy had said something, he'd have reassured him that wasn't going to happen.

He had no intention of bundling Charlie and Aimee up and dragging them off to another country where they knew no one and would be left to fend for themselves for months at a time. He might like the army but Charlie living on base? After growing up here with family and friends all around? It would never work. Not to mention being totally unfair.

He checked on Aimee and grinned to see her lying on her back with her teddy clutched tightly against her. How had he managed to father something so gorgeous that his heart hurt? She was a cracker of a kid. A Kiwi kid. He kind of liked that.

Now what? He was feeling antsy. His night had been cut short. There'd been no particular plans for after dinner but Charlie falling asleep on him hadn't featured either. His grin was self-deprecatory. So he'd been a boring date? Not if the way she'd cuddled in close to him had been a clue. That small, hot body had seemed to fold into his shape. No denying he'd hoped they might've got hotter than just touching.

It was time he found out what was going on with Charlie and why she had so little energy. He needed to know, wanted to help her if at all possible.

With a glass of bourbon in one hand and the bottle in the other, he returned to her bedroom and removed the workclothes she'd dumped earlier on the recliner chair in the corner. Pulling it out from the wall, he toed off his shoes and stretched out on the leather. The comfortable chair sucked him in, made him relax as he sipped his drink and watched over Charlie. He suspected he'd be there all night.

Not a problem. There'd been many nights in his life when he'd been on duty, watching out for something, someone. Tonight Charlie came under his scrutiny, and if she so much as whimpered in her sleep he'd be there for her. Not quite the way he'd thought he'd be spending nights with her when he'd hopped on that flight down to Auckland.

Strange how sitting here made him feel quite happy. True, he'd love nothing more than to slip into bed and make love to her, bring her to the peak of ecstasy and hear her cry out before entering her. But that hot and fast relationship they'd had two years ago had morphed into something that touched him more than physically. Talk about complicating things.

He sipped his drink and tried not to think about how he'd deal with this new feeling for Charlie when he flew out of the country.

Charlie rolled over. Sweat ran between her breasts. Her hand slid over her damp neck, then further down. Huh? She was still wearing her dress. Why hadn't she undressed before going to bed?

Sitting up, she pushed the sheet off and reached for the bedside light switch. A golden glow filled the dark room from the low-wattage bulb. The air in her lungs leaked out as she stared across at the nursing chair, where she'd spent many hours feeding Aimee. Correction, stared at the man sprawled over it. Marshall's long legs spread off the end; his arms hung on either side, with his hands brushing the carpet. And the cutest little snore ricocheted around the room.

Now she remembered—dinner. She'd fed strawberries to Marshall, one at a time. He'd licked her fingers every time he'd taken another berry, sending slicks of heat up her fingers, her arms and throughout her body, making her crave his touch. For a while she'd believed she was in heaven and that she'd manage to stay awake for a few more hours to enjoy what was so obviously going to be a very exciting night in Marshall's arms.

A rueful glance down at her dress. She'd let this

wonderful man down. She remembered walking out of the restaurant clutching his arm, but the rest was a blank. No memory of the drive home, of coming inside or getting into bed. Marshall must've put her to bed. And now look at him. Sound asleep in her room. Had he been waiting, hoping she'd wake up so they could finish their evening in the way they'd been headed?

There was nothing to stop them having a good time now. A wicked sense of mischief teased her. Why not wake Marshall up and lead him to bed? Her bed. Or start undressing him, kissing any bare flesh that appeared. That would arouse him in more ways than one.

Carefully, quietly, she slipped out of bed and removed her dress. Thought briefly about pulling on a negligee, decided against it. The black lace panties and matching bra she wore were about as sexy as it was possible for her to get. The stretch marks on her breasts and belly gave her a moment of panic. The scar from her hysterectomy stood out, ugly against her pale skin. He'd notice, want an explanation. A sure passion-killer.

Tonight was not the time to tell him about that. A smear of make-up might help and she could turn the light off as soon as they were in bed.

Moments later she tiptoed across the room and knelt between Marshall's legs, her breath catching in her throat as she marvelled at his toned body. Even covered with a shirt and trousers, there was no denying the strength of his body or the very male bump shaping the front of his trousers. So close she only had to lean slightly one way or the other and she'd be touching him.

Her fingers were trembling as she reached for the buckle of his belt. She didn't want him to wake up immediately, would prefer to gradually undress him and enjoy each little exposure. Slowly, slowly she fed the end of the belt out of the buckle. Then started inching the zip down, one notch at a time over that bump. Her heart rate shot through the roof. Her fingers jerked the zip down the final centimetres. Desire raced along her veins, heating her rapidly all over, pooling at her centre.

She hadn't known this need, this feeling of urgency since Honolulu. Since this man had taken her to bed and taught her more about sex and loving than she'd believed possible. He'd woken her up in many ways, ruined her for any other man.

A sudden movement and her hand was pinned down. Marshall's hand gripped hers, his fingers splayed as he pressed his growing erection into her palm. His other hand grasped the back of her head and began to draw her close.

'Stop,' she croaked. And when he still pulled her closer she said loudly, 'Stop, Marshall.'

The hand on her head dropped away. The other didn't. He tried to sit up but she was impeding him. Good. This was her show. They'd do things her way.

Looking up, she caught him watching her, eyes wide with lust, tongue tracking those full lips she loved to kiss. When he made to move again she shook her head and pushed him back into the chair. 'Wait.'

Returning her hands to his trousers, she finished unzipping them, all caution gone. She spread the opening wide and scooped into his boxers and lifted his weight into her palm, surrounded his hard length with her other hand. The throbbing erection felt like silk against her sliding fingers.

'Charlie. Oh, God.'

Leaning close, her mouth found him, her tongue

licked and stroked, and the desire in her body ramped higher and higher until she shook with the need for him inside her.

His fingers wove through her hair, gripping as he held her head. His body strained in the chair, pushing up at her. His breathing was fast and hot, his thighs tense as he tightened them against her.

Then he reached for her shoulders and lifted her up. 'No, Charlie, you first.' The words were hoarse with need.

Scrambling to her feet, she tore her panties off and straddled him. As she hovered above him, her sex throbbing with need, she shook her head. 'No, Marshall. Together.'

He caught her waist. 'Condom. In my trouser pocket. Right side.'

So he *had* been hoping for this. She grinned and pushed into the pocket to find the small foil pack. Not that she'd get pregnant. He'd taught her to put one on with alacrity and finesse, and the moves came back in an instant. His passionate groan told her she'd got it right.

His hand found her wet centre, his fingers touched and caressed. She gritted her teeth, felt her neck cord as she fought to keep control, and reached for him again. This was their night. They had to share, to come at the same time. And then it was too late. She lost the battle as wave after wave of liquid need rocked through her, tightening her muscles and thrumming each and every nerve ending in her body.

She almost screamed. 'Marshall.'

His mouth quickly covered hers, took the next

scream. His tongue danced with hers. Those lips held hers. And still she rocked with the power of her orgasm.

Slowly, slowly it dissipated and her heart rate returned to something resembling normal as she laid her head against his chest. 'You cheated,' she whispered.

'Lady, I never go first.' Then he pushed up against her, his penis finding her opening immediately.

Lowering herself onto him, Charlie met his thrusts as they became more urgent. Her hands gripped his shoulders as she rode him equally hard and fast. And his name filled the room as she came again. Their world closed around them as they found release, and then they were slumped together, their bodies melding into one another.

Finally, maybe hours later but most likely minutes, they both moved. Charlie lifted herself off Marshall. He caught her hand, tugged her back. His mouth covered hers with a kiss. A kiss that deepened until she thought she'd explode with need. Shaking, she pulled away. This time she tugged his hand and headed for her bed.

'Lady, any time you want to wake me up, feel free to go about it that exact same way.' Marshall climbed into bed and wrapped her in his arms.

'Any time, huh?' She grinned and reached to switch off the light.

He caught her hand, effectively stopping her. 'I want to look at you. It's been so long and my memories need a recharge.'

Huddling her shoulders, she snatched her hand back and tucked her arms under her breasts. Biting down on the flare of panic again clawing its way through her, she told him, 'I've got stretch marks now. I'd prefer you to remember me without those.' How lame could she get?

He knew she didn't have hang-ups about her looks or body. But that had been then, this was now.

Beside her he leaned back against the headboard. 'Okay, Charlie. What's going on?' His tone was light and caring but there was steel running through it. There'd be no fobbing him off this time. 'Why do you always go to bed almost before the sun sets? Why did you all but fall asleep at the restaurant? Why don't you want me to see your beautiful body? I remember the Charlie who danced naked for me in my apartment.'

Here it was. The moment of truth. 'I...' Her mouth closed. She took a big breath and shuffled around so that she could see his face. She wanted to know exactly what he thought the moment he learned what had happened. She needed to know if he'd be around for Aimee. Now.

'I've had a hysterectomy.' His eyes widened. She held up her hand before he could say anything. 'I won't be having any more babies. Like you and I, Aimee's an only child.'

'Nothing wrong in that. I've managed without siblings. So have you.' His eyes bored into her. 'So why the operation? Something to do with Aimee's birth?'

If only. 'Eight weeks after Aimee was born I went for a routine check-up with my obstetrician and she discovered a growth on my womb. It was malignant.'

'Hell, Charlie.' Shock slammed into him, his face tightening, his eyes popping. 'Tell me you're okay now. Please.'

'As far as anyone can say, yes, my prognosis is good.' She shuddered. 'But sometimes I fear for the future. It's a black cloud hovering over me.'

'It must've been hell. Are you sure you're okay? You're not hiding anything from me?'

'I can show you the medical reports if that'll help.'
But those hadn't taken all her fears away so she understood Marshall's need for reassurance.

'Oh, babe, I wish I'd known. I really do. You
shouldn't have had to go through that on your own.'
He reached for her, wrapped those strong arms around
her and held on. 'I know Brendon was there, but…' His
chin touched the top of her head. 'I don't know what I'd
have done but I'd have been here for you.'

'I know you would've. That's why I kept looking
for you.' She could stay tucked up in his arms for ever,
feeling his strength, his tenderness, but they'd started
this conversation. She wanted it finished.

Leaning back in his arms to see his face, she continued, 'My mum died of cervical cancer when I was
seven. I was lucky. I have the greatest dad on the planet.
He was always there for me as I grew up, and though
I missed my mother I never felt lost or lonely. I'm sure
I've disappointed him at times. When I came home
pregnant he took that in his stride. My cancer was a
huge shock for him, a rerun of when Mum got ill, but
he's never once let me down.'

'In the short time I've been here I've seen how good
he is, how strong his love is for you and Aimee.' Marshall straightened against the headboard, his eyes locking with hers. 'This is why you spent so much time
trying to find me. If something goes wrong, you want
the same for Aimee as you've had from Brendon.'

He saw straight to the truth every time. She didn't
have to hit him over the head to make him understand.
This was one of the things she loved about him. He
could be brutally honest but he always got it. 'Yes. If
anything happens to me, Aimee would need you in her

life. She has to have one parent at least. Like I did. I need to know you'll look out for her.'

A cloud formed in his gaze. Setting her aside, he swung his legs over the edge of the bed and dropped his head in his hands. For a long time he said nothing, and she sat still, watching and waiting, knowing whatever he said wasn't going to be what she hoped for.

Finally he lifted his head and turned desperate eyes on her. 'I hear you. I even understand you. But, Charlie, I'm nothing like Brendon. It's not in my make-up.'

Talk about brutally honest. Her heart sank. He'd hinted at his past and she'd wondered if that might affect how he'd react to this situation. But to not even think about it beyond a few minutes—which surely hadn't given him time to think of the whole situation, not just his part in it—bowled her flat. 'You've been fantastic with Aimee all week. Playing with her, dressing and feeding her, being endlessly patient. Yet now you're pulling back from a chance to see if we can make it work.'

Standing, he crossed the room, flicked the curtain open and raised the window so he could lean out, his arms braced wide, his head bowed. 'I had a hard upbringing. Dad ruled with his fists. What if I'm the same?'

'Have you ever hit anyone?' She reckoned she knew the answer already.

'No.'

Exactly. 'You're a strong, tough man, Marshall, but you're not a hard one. Nothing's changed. I would trust you with Aimee any day.'

His shoulders stiffened, his back straightened and he turned to look at her. 'Thank you.' His gaze locked with hers and it was as though he was searching right inside her. Then, 'Did you ever want to find me for us? Or was it all about our child?'

Her heart slowed. Where was this going? 'I watched you walk away in Honolulu and I ached from the need to chase you down the road to beg you to stay in touch, to come and see me when you had the time.' She swallowed around a lump that suddenly clogged her throat.

'I knew you didn't want any long-term relationship but I'd have sold my soul to have another week with you. A month even.' Her gaze remained fixed on him. 'So, yes, I wanted to find you. For me. For us. And, heaven knows, I tried. Even when I suspected you'd be angry if I did make contact.'

'I'd never be angry with you.'

'You confused me by leaving your email address in my pocket and then having my emails bounce back.'

'At the time I believed you were better off without me. I still do.' Marshall slowly leaned back against the window ledge, folded his arms across that expansive chest. 'But...' He paused. 'Those weeks were something special, weren't they? Wild and crazy, fun and exciting. Yeah, very special.'

'Is that why you came to see me?'

'I haven't been able to get you out of my head. It's like we haven't finished what we started. At the end of my last posting I headed home thinking I'd be able to put you into perspective once I was in familiar surroundings and no longer trying to distract myself as I listened to gunfire in the middle of the night.'

'Didn't work, huh?' She tried for a smile, failed badly. 'So you came for another fling. Or a continuation of the old one.' The bitterness in her voice disgusted her. She didn't usually act like this, yet her tongue was like a runaway train. 'I'm surprised you stayed when you learned I had a child. Hardly the excitement you were looking for.'

Crossing the room, he gripped her elbows and hauled her up off the bed to hold her as his eyes poured out his anger and his hurt. 'Stop it, Charlie. I don't deserve that any more than you deserve what's happened to you. I got a shock when I realised Aimee was mine. Who wouldn't? But I stayed. I'm still here. And I'll always be in contact. For Aimee. For you. No matter what the future brings. That's my promise to you.'

Then he kissed her. Hungrily. As though he hadn't had a woman for a very long time. As if he'd been waiting for her and the sex they'd just shared hadn't even begun to fill a void within him. His hands slid over her arms, over her back, her tummy, cupped her breasts.

Pulling her mouth away from his demanding lips, she murmured, 'I'm sorry. That was selfish of me.' When he leaned close again she put a finger on his lips. 'I like the fact you'll stay in touch. Hopefully, my health will keep improving and we won't need to revisit this discussion.' Then she returned to kissing him. She could give him time to take in this latest information. Her heart might be squeezing with anguish at the thought of Marshall leaving but that was nothing new.

As her body cried out its need for his she gave herself up to the moment. Plenty of time to deal with the debilitating pain of letting him go after he'd gone.

CHAPTER TEN

CHARLIE SAT ON the veranda, overseeing Aimee playing in her paddling pool. At the barbecue Marshall was cleaning up after the lunch he'd cooked for them.

'What are you smiling about?' He dumped dirty paper towels in the rubbish bin.

'Just thinking how this time last week Dad told me to stop searching for you and see what the universe brought.' Her smile widened. 'Weird.'

'A troop carrier brought me, not the universe.' He parked his delectable butt on the top step and tipped his head back to look up at her. 'But, hey, who's checking?'

'I promise not to watch the sky too often after you've gone.' She kept the smile on her face despite the sadness threatening to break through.

His big hand covered her knee. 'I've put all my contact addresses and numbers on your laptop, as you asked. Feel free to call or email any time. I will answer. Might be late if we're out on patrol, but I'll get to it as soon as possible.'

'Thanks.' It was good to know he'd be contactable. Which had been all she'd wanted—at first. Now, having admitted she loved Marshall, she wished for so much more. But did she really want him here with her if his heart was elsewhere? Yes. No. Not really. She had six days left to enjoy his company. Why waste them being miserable? 'Shall we take a picnic tea out to Acaia Bay later?'

The hand on her knee squeezed lightly and his eyes lit up. 'Sounds like a good idea.' Glancing across at Aimee, he grimaced. 'She seems full of energy this afternoon. More than usual. Must know I've got plans for her mother when she goes to sleep.'

An afternoon in the sack with Marshall. She couldn't think of a better way to spend the hours. Except Aimee was busy jumping up and down, intent on making the biggest splashes possible. 'Funny how she seems to know when I want her to go down on time.'

'If not energy then she'll run out of water shortly.' Marshall grinned and leaned up on his elbow to kiss her. 'I could put a wee hole in the bottom of the pool to hurry things up.'

Her elbow caught him in the shoulder. 'Shame on you, Marshall Hunter.'

The sound of car doors banging reached her from the other side of the fence. Please, don't be coming here. Not that she was expecting anyone. Then the gate opened and four people streamed through. 'Keisha and Toby.' And their boys. She shivered. The afternoon had just turned grey.

'The woman you mentioned with the breast lump?' Marshall stood and held his hand out to her.

'Yes. Can't say I'm too surprised. If I'd got that message I'd want to know what's going on. But it's not going to be easy.' Letting him tug her to her feet, she stepped down to greet the couple trudging up her path. 'Hey, you're home.' She stated the obvious, letting them set the tone for the meeting.

'Got into Auckland last night and drove down today.' Toby stood irresolute, one arm around Keisha's waist. 'I'm sorry we've barged in but…' His voice petered out.

Reaching a hand out to Keisha, who stood like a rabbit caught in headlights, Charlie said, 'It's okay. I understand what you're going through.' More than most.

Keisha gripped her hard, nearly breaking the bones in her fingers. 'Is it…?' Swallow. 'Does this mean I've got…?' Another swallow. The word was hard to say, and Charlie knew that once Keisha did utter it then it became all too real.

Charlie looked directly at Keisha. 'We don't know what your mammogram means yet. Come inside and we'll talk.'

Marshall stepped up beside her. Held his hand out to Toby. 'I'm Marshall Hunter, Charlie's friend. Want me to keep your boys occupied while you talk with Charlie? There's a football in the shed.'

Toby shook his hand in return. 'Would you? That's good of you. Calib, Zac, this is Mr Hunter. You're to go with him while Mum and I talk to Dr Lang, okay.'

'Sure,' Calib answered. 'Can Aimee play, too?'

Giving Marshall a grateful peck on the chin, Charlie whispered, 'Thank you. I owe you.'

'We'll make up for lost time tonight,' he whispered back, and planted a big kiss on her lips. No subtlety, then.

Turning to the upset couple, she indicated that they follow her inside. Keisha's eyes were on stalks as she agreed. Once inside she gasped, 'Is he really just a friend? That'd be a waste.'

So much for doctor-patient boundaries. Sometimes Taupo seemed even smaller than it actually was. She understood Keisha was deliberately delaying the conversation to come. So, 'Marshall is Aimee's father.' No secret there. The man had made sure everyone at the medical centre knew, which meant hundreds of others were now aware of the fact, too. 'I'll make some coffee.'

She filled the coffee percolator and sat her guests down at the table. 'How was Phuket? You've all got great suntans.'

Keisha answered. 'We had a fabulous time. Right up until the moment we got home and heard the messages.' She seemed stunned and yet simultaneously thinking about many things.

Toby added, 'We had to come see you. No way could we wait until Monday.'

'It's truly all right,' she tried to reassure the distressed couple, at the same time knowing exactly what they were going through. The shock, the fear and the many unanswerable questions. All very debilitating. Dropping onto a chair, she placed her elbows on the table and her chin in her hands. 'Keisha, your mammogram shows an abnormality. There's a dense spot in your breast, like a lump. At the moment no one can say for sure what it is.'

The other woman's face whitened. Toby took her hand and held on tight. Suspecting and knowing were miles apart. And at this point they hadn't had confirmation that Keisha did have cancer.

Charlie continued quietly, 'The radiology centre has left you a message, too.'

Keisha nodded. 'I have to make an appointment for

another mammogram. She said something about the X-rays of one breast not being very clear.'

'That's standard practice. The woman phoning is not a doctor so can't tell you anything about your X-ray results.' The coffee percolator made sucking sounds and she got up to turn it off. 'Considering you were away, I thought it best we make you an appointment. Eleven o'clock on Monday. You can change the time if that doesn't suit.'

'We'll be there,' Toby growled.

'The radiologist will give you an ultrasound scan. He'll also take a tiny sample from the lump to send to the laboratory. Until he gets the results of that there's nothing you can do.'

'Except worry ourselves sick.' Keisha leaned against her husband, her fingers now interlaced tightly in her lap. 'How long will it take for the results to come back?'

'A few days. I won't deny that'll be hard.' Absolutely terrifying, if the truth be known. They wouldn't get much sleep over those days. 'If you want to talk about anything in that time, phone me. Or drop in. I really don't mind.'

Gleeful shouts had them all turning to look out the window. Marshall had the boys kicking the ball at one end of the lawn while Aimee tottered around them in her wet swimsuit, laughing and chasing the ball.

'He's good with kids, your man,' Toby said.

'It's all very new to him, this fatherhood stuff.' He'd taken to Aimee like cheese to crackers. But try telling Marshall that.

Keisha watched them, her hungry gaze flicking from Calib to Zac, Calib to Zac. Tears gathered in her eyes. 'My boys. Will they be all right? If…?'

'Don't go there.' Yeah, right. Like she hadn't? The moment she'd heard she had to have tests done she'd panicked and had spent every waking hour—which had been most of the days and nights leading up to getting her results—making numerous and varied plans for Aimee if the worst happened.

Keisha turned big, sorrow-filled eyes on her. 'Yeah, right,' she echoed unwittingly. 'How did you manage…' she wiggled her fingers in the air '…not to go there?'

'I didn't. It's a very scary time.' The not knowing had eaten away at her, as it did with anyone facing the same horrendous situation. 'I suggest you try to take things one day at a time. You couldn't have got an appointment any sooner. The lab will do their best to have answers quickly. They always do in these cases.'

'I have to say it, Charlie.' The woman drew a deep breath and spat it out. 'Cancer.'

Toby blanched at his wife's sudden directness. 'Keisha, sweetheart…'

'No, Toby, I'm saying it as it is. I have to. At the moment that's what we're looking at. This time next week we might be dancing in the street and celebrating a good result.' Her voice lowered. 'Or I might be baking and filling the freezer with meals for you to give the boys while I'm in hospital.'

Charlie dredged up a smile. 'Why do women always start trying to sort out their family in times like this? That seems to be their first concern.'

'Guess it's the nurturing instinct in us.' Her bottom lip trembled and Charlie reached across to squeeze her hand. Nothing she could say would make this go away.

Then a loud shriek from outside had Charlie leaping out of her chair. 'Aimee?' Loud sobs followed that she recognised as Aimee hurting, intermingled with a deep male voice talking lovingly.

'Sorry, but I've got to go and see to Aimee.'

Toby's words stopped her. 'But Aimee's dad's with her.'

'He isn't used to comforting her when she's hurt or upset.'

'Give him a moment. Seems to me he's doing his best.' Toby stared her down. 'Come on, Doc, let him show Aimee who he is to her.'

Slowly she inched back down onto the chair. 'You're right. But I want to be there for Aimee.'

Keisha nodded. 'That nurturing thing. But Toby's right. If Marshall hasn't had much to do with kids, and especially with his daughter, then he's doing really well. It's gone quiet out there.'

Charlie blinked. 'So it has.' Pride swelled in her chest. Marshall was a fantastic dad. If only she could get him to see that, to believe it.

Marshall watched Toby gently help Keisha into the car and close the door with a soft click. 'Poor bastard. He doesn't have a clue what to do other than be right beside his wife every moment.'

Charlie grimaced. 'Not much either of them can do right now. The waiting is horrible. They'll be wondering if Keisha is going to die, if she'll live and see her boys grow up, if she even has cancer or not. They'll make plans for the boys in case the worst happens and then change them every five minutes.'

His heart thudded in his chest. Charlie was speaking from experience. If only he hadn't changed his email address he'd have been here for her. Yeah—if the army had given him leave. 'How long did you have to wait to find out your results?'

'Ten days. Felt like ten years. I hardly slept that whole time. Spent hours just watching Aimee in her basinet, drinking in as much about her as possible. She was so tiny and vulnerable and I didn't know how long I'd be there for her.' Her voice caught and she slapped the back of her hand over her cheek.

Wrapping an arm around her shoulders, he hauled her up against him. 'But you are here, and the future's looking good. Aimee's happy, and lucky to have the best mom ever.' He kissed the top of her head. 'You made it, Charlie. Hang onto that and try to let the past go.'

She sniffed against his shirt. 'I'm trying, believe me. But having to tell Keisha she might have cancer threw me. I thought I'd manage but it seems I haven't completely put it all behind me.'

'You're strong and getting stronger by the day.' He put her away from him enough to be able to see her face. 'Promise to let me know any time you feel you can't manage. I can't make up for not knowing but I can be sure to talk with you any time you're worried. Okay?'

Her teeth left an indentation on her bottom lip as she nodded. 'Okay. That would be good.' She didn't look overly convinced, though.

Hours later Marshall tucked a strand of Charlie's hair behind her ear as she slept, curled up against him in her bed. He hadn't had more than a catnap through the night, afraid to miss any moment holding Charlie to him. What she'd told him about her cancer had cut him deep. How had she coped with all the worry and fear it had brought while trying to look after a baby? At least she'd had Brendon but Keisha was way better off having Toby with her at this time.

His hand fisted. If only he'd known. If only he hadn't deleted his address. If only a whole bunch of things. But nothing could be changed except what he did for the future. He had to stay in touch with Charlie, no matter what.

Seeing the first hint of sunlight creeping around the edge of the curtains, he grimaced. Friday. Tomorrow— well, tomorrow was his last day here.

He'd spent as much time as he could with Aimee during the past two weeks, which had been pretty much all of it. Being with Charlie hadn't come as easily. She had a job to do. She'd pointed out that asking for time off when she'd already taken months over the previous year and a half didn't sit easily with her.

The reason for that time off terrified him. Was Charlie really going to make it? She had to. No argument. Aimee needed her. It was sad that there'd be no siblings for his girl but not the worst thing to come out of this. Charlie had all the love she needed from her father and it would be similar for Aimee. But cancer? Showed how little he had to do with everyday medicine if he hadn't recognised her gauntness and lack of energy for what it was. He still didn't want to think about Charlie and cancer in the same sentence. But there'd be plenty of nights ahead when he wouldn't be able to avoid it.

Since learning what was behind her exhaustion, he'd wanted to do even more for her. But mostly, every night when she'd crawled into bed, exhausted as usual, he'd followed and held her as she'd fallen into that first deep sleep. He'd lain awake, hearing every breath she'd taken, feeling the rise and fall of her breasts against his arm, absorbing her warmth and scent. Trying to pass his strength on to her.

About an hour later she'd wake up suddenly, her eyes wide and excited, her lips searching for his mouth, her hand pushing down his body until she encountered the hard result of him holding her so close.

They'd made love, sometimes so slowly and exquisitely it hurt him inside where his heart lay. At other times their passion and need had driven them wild with excitement and they'd had to restrain themselves from crying out loud enough to be heard throughout the house.

Afterwards Charlie usually fell back into such a deep sleep it was as though she was unconscious, and he'd return to holding her. He loved her more and more every day. Falling asleep and missing a single moment of Charlie in his arms was not possible. Time was precious—and running out fast.

His ticket for his flight out of Auckland on Saturday night was tucked out of sight in a pocket of his pack but hiding it hadn't changed the fact. He was leaving. Going back to the States. And the army. Walking away from this wonderful, gutsy woman. Leaving his daughter behind because this was the best place for her. The days were jerking along, sometimes whizzing by, sometimes crawling so slowly he had to keep checking his watch to make sure he hadn't got the time wrong.

The slow times were when Charlie wasn't with him. At times he resented her patients and then hated himself for that selfish emotion. She was doing one hell of a balancing act, juggling Aimee's needs, her patients' requirements, her father and him. All while she was so goddamned exhausted. Yet every night she went to bed with a wicked gleam in those deep blue eyes. Every morning she woke up with enthusiasm and laughter on her lips.

No doubt about it. He would miss her like crazy. So much for coming and working her out of his system. She'd managed to completely infiltrate every cell of his body. She would never leave him in peace now. Even when he was halfway round the world in some alien place, putting broken soldiers back together in the makeshift hospitals they used.

Charlie would be his guardian angel, there to escape to in the middle of the night when he couldn't sleep for thinking about the next day's duties.

Maybe that was a load of crap and he just had to accept he loved her but wasn't going to do a damned thing about it for fear of hurting her.

Saturday. Charlie stared at the dent left by Marshall's head on the pillow beside hers. He'd made love to her as the sun had come up. Tender, yet gripping love that had spoken of the things he couldn't say to her. He did care about her, maybe came close to loving her. She'd felt that in his touches, his kisses, the times they'd spent talking, or when they'd just sat watching their daughter.

He was leaving her.

When he'd climbed out of bed to go for a run there had been tears in his eyes. She'd reached for him but he'd avoided her outstretched fingers. 'If I get back into bed with you, chances are I'll never leave.'

Yeah, well, what was wrong with that? Her heart squeezed with need as he slipped out of the room. Honest to a fault, he'd never hidden the fact he couldn't stay. Tears slid from the corners of her eyes and tracked down to her ears, on further to soak into her pillow. She let them come, though she should be fighting them. She'd allow herself this one moment of self-pity then she'd get up and go on with her life.

But first she had to get through the remainder of the day until Marshall hopped into his rental vehicle and drove away. Smudging tears across her face, she sat up. There were two ways to do this. She could go around with a dark heart all day and make everyone miserable, and probably make Marshall glad to be escaping.

Or they could celebrate the fact they'd found each other again and that Aimee now had her father in her life, albeit mostly via the ether.

She tossed the sheet off and her feet hit the floor. Pulling a drawer open, she chose a top with shoestring straps in a sky-blue colour that highlighted her eyes. From her wardrobe she took a short denim skirt that emphasised her slim legs and hugged the curves of her backside. A black G-string and a very lacy push-up bra went onto the bed beside the other clothes. Marshall might not get to see the underwear but she'd feel more feminine for wearing it. And he'd certainly get an eyeful of what he was leaving behind when she waltzed out to the kitchen dressed in that skirt and top. She wasn't going down without a fight.

She got the eyeful bit right. Marshall was leaning against the bench, pouring water down his gasping throat, when she hit the kitchen nearly an hour later, her hair washed and styled, her face lightly made up. He spluttered water down the front of his tee shirt and his eyes bugged out. Coughing and wiping his mouth with the back of his hand, he stared at her.

Then his mouth lifted into a grin and his eyes filled

with a wicked gleam. 'Hey, Charlie, you look fabulous. You've gone all out this morning.'

So he'd caught onto her ploy. Good. At least he'd remember her as a sexy woman and not just a tired mother and doctor. 'Thought we'd have the full works this morning. A brunch rather than breakfast. Bacon, eggs, sausages, mushrooms, tomatoes.'

Dad walked in as she was talking. 'We could pop a bottle of bubbles, too. There's one in the other fridge.'

She wasn't celebrating Marshall leaving. But, then again, she was going all out to make a lasting memory. 'Great idea, Dad. I'll chop up the peaches, apricots, strawberries and raspberries I got at the roadside stall yesterday for a fruit salad.'

Marshall continued leaning against the bench. His legs not capable of holding him up any more? Had she finally knocked the stuffing out of him? He did look a bit stunned. Had expected her to stand around sniffling all day, had he? She had news for him. She wasn't going to show him how much this hurt. That would come later, in the middle of the night when he filled her head and prevented her from sleeping.

Nudging Marshall in the waist, she reached for the kettle. 'Out of the way, big boy. I've got heaps to do and I can't start without that first cup of tea inside me.'

His legs did work. Just. He stumbled sideways, leaned against the stove. 'Ah, right. What can I do to help with this banquet?'

Dad beat her to answering. 'Get out of those shorts and shirt first. Then there's Aimee to see to. Later you can help me cook this mountain of food on the barbecue.' His voice went up a notch and he looked away, but not before she saw the distress in his eyes.

She nearly canned the whole idea right then. They might be fooling themselves they were going to have a blast today, but everyone was hurting. But as she opened her mouth, Marshall spoke.

'Sounds like we've got ourselves a plan. Thanks, both of you.' And he disappeared quick-smart out of the room.

Charlie stared after him until Dad draped an arm over her shoulders. 'He's no happier than you, my girl.'

'So why go?'

'He belongs to the army. Not us.' His hand squeezed her arm gently before he stepped away.

Dad's understanding got in the way of her determination not to let her emotions go on the rampage. Sniffing hard, she made the tea, squeezing the teabag until it nearly split, stirring in the milk until liquid spun over the side of the mug. Sniff, sniff. Clang. The teaspoon hit the bottom of the sink.

'Mummy, I got up.' Aimee wrapped her arms around Charlie's knees.

'Hey.' Reaching down, she lifted up her baby. 'How did you get up all by yourself? Bet Daddy helped you.'

'I caught her climbing out of the cot.' Marshall grinned from the doorway, his eyes full of pride. 'You're going to have to put her in a bed any day now, little monkey that she is.'

Hugging Aimee tightly, Charlie managed a smile for him. 'Wonder where she gets that from.'

'Don't look at me. No monkeys in my family. Until now.' And once again he headed away, this time hopefully going to the bathroom.

Once again Marshall found himself clearing up after the barbecue. It had become his job since he'd arrived.

It was almost as if, by having allocated jobs, it meant he had a place in this family. Something new for him. Different from being ordered to do something in the army. Or in his parents' house. This was about sharing the chores and doing things for those he cared about. And who cared about him.

Charlie was putting Aimee down for her afternoon nap. He'd held his girl on his knees throughout brunch, had kicked a ball around the yard with her afterwards, with Charlie egging them on from the sidelines, and he'd kissed her goodbye. His heart had come near to breaking then. But going away was the right thing to do. One day Aimee—and Charlie—would thank him for this. One day they'd understand. He hoped. Because right now he sure as hell didn't.

One-thirty. Nearly time to hit the road. Brendon had gone into his shed a few minutes ago. He'd go and see the guy, try to let him know how much he meant to him.

Brendon stood at his workbench, viciously sandpapering a wooden table. Marshall wondered if the older man was mentally attacking him as he worked.

Clearing his throat, he spoke above the rasping sound of Brendon's work. 'I want to thank you for everything you've done for me. Especially for the way you've welcomed me into your home.'

The sanding continued as the fingers gripping the sanding block whitened. 'You're welcome. Any time.'

In other words, he was meant to come back. Swallowing the sour taste in his mouth, he continued. 'I truly appreciate that.' Not that he'd be back in a hurry. He'd decided that would only complicate things and give Charlie reason to hope for more from him.

The sanding block clunked down on the bench and

Brendon clapped the dust off his hands. 'Right.' He glanced around the shed's interior, his gaze finally settling on a small catamaran stashed in a corner, cobwebs attaching the yacht to the wall. 'I caught her struggling to haul that outside a couple of months ago, adamant she was going sailing.'

'It's chained to a peg in the floor.' He'd known they'd end up talking about Charlie. Unavoidable.

'Broke my heart to see her unable to do something that a couple of years ago was easier than falling off a bike for her.' Brendon's voice sounded hollow. 'I chained the damned thing up so she couldn't try again.' His head rolled from side to side. 'My girl used to be so strong.'

And you're afraid she won't ever regain that strength.

He wouldn't even think about that. 'I see her as very strong mentally. She never wavers. Always looking out for Aimee, her patients. Refuses to let the cancer set her back.' If it dared to come back it was in for a hell of a battle from Charlie.

'You are right, lad. She is strong. I only hope she's strong *enough*. The next weeks are going to be hard for her.'

A perfect shot. Straight at his heart. Marshall winced. Couldn't blame the man for putting his daughter's case. 'I have to go, Brendon. There is no other option.'

'Keep moving? That the army way, lad? Or your way?'

'It's the only way I know how to live, how to be me.' Except now that way of life seemed odd from where he stood.

From the doorway came, 'That's a copout.' Charlie's hands were firmly on her hips. 'You fall back on that excuse for everything. You've been conditioned to think

like that. Yes, it is the army way. No, you don't have to
live like that. You can make a life that suits you and get
what you want from it.'

'Maybe I have.' The path of least resistance. Yeah,
even he could see that. 'But there is no getting away
from the fact that I have to follow orders, which means
going wherever I'm told.' He could tell the army to stick
the next contract due to be signed in a few weeks, but
then what? Could he become a GP in a small town?
He'd still be helping people, caring for their families.

Brendon slipped past Charlie and headed outside.
No fond farewell, then. He couldn't blame the guy. He
was hurting his girl.

Charlie came inside and approached him, her eyes
brimming with need, love and earnestness. 'Well, here's
my way. I love you, Marshall. I love you with all my
heart and then some. Have done since that first day in
the ED when you teased me about my funny accent.'
She stepped close, rose up on her toes and kissed him
hard on the mouth.

His arms rose almost of their own volition to wrap
around her. Pushing his tongue between her lips, he
tasted her mouth, felt his knees weaken. God, it would
be so easy to stay. To pretend he didn't have commitments elsewhere. To pretend it would all work out—
that he'd be a great dad, a wonderful husband and turn
into a settled doctor living in small-town New Zealand.

It took every last ounce of his strength to put Charlie aside. 'Nothing's going to change because of what
you've revealed, Charlie. I still won't be around for you.'

Her eyes glittered with anger. 'Don't you get it yet?
Having you some of the time is better than never. Loving you means letting you be the person you are, not

trying to change you into someone else, not tying you down in one place. I understand that would be the quickest way to turn our relationship sour.'

Tempting. So bloody tempting. To stop in one place occasionally. To have special time out with Charlie and Aimee, to be the partner and parent and still have his army career with the duty that was his rod.

So damned unfair on them. He could see it now. Aimee crying every time he left, begging him to stay one more night, to take her to school the next day. It would be him all over again. Except he'd be the one going away.

Air hissed through his teeth. 'You deserve better than that. You can and should have the whole enchilada. So should Aimee. I'm going home, Charlie.' Home? A cold, lonely barrack room. Home.

'Sure.' Her hurt blinked out at him, cutting him to the heart.

He continued relentlessly, trying to ignore the pain in her face that reflected what crunched inside him. 'You need to find a good, kind man who'll love and cherish you, who'll come home to you at the end of the day and sit down with a glass of wine to talk about what you've done. A man who'll take Aimee to school sports.'

The colour drained from Charlie's cheeks at that reminder of what she'd wanted for him. He had to make her see he was right. 'A man who'll take you on vacation, be there to teach Aimee things. A man totally unlike me.' His lungs were struggling to inhale. His blood had slowed to the point he was in danger of collapsing.

He wanted to haul her into his arms and tell her he'd made a mistake, that he didn't mean a word of it and that he'd stay. Except he knew himself too well, knew he couldn't. So he wasn't finished. 'Find yourself a man who'll see you into old age, Charlie.'

Her voice sounded like it came through a gag. Her eyes leaked tears. But her shoulders were drawn back tight and her chin pointed at him. 'You're wrong, Marshall. I don't need anyone to take care of me. What my heart needs is you as and when I can have you. Nothing more, nothing less.'

Reaching his hands to her shoulders, he felt the tension in her muscles, the tremors racking her body. Leaning down, he kissed her forehead then her lips. 'Take care, Charlie.' *Goodbye, my love.* And he strode away with a resolution he didn't feel.

Hamilton. The road sign indicated to continue straight ahead.

Auckland. Turn right to bypass the city.

Marshall blinked. 'Here already?' He hadn't noticed a thing as he'd driven up from Taupo, his mind firmly fixed back with two beautiful females.

Indicating to turn right, he turned onto the road leading to Auckland and his trip back Stateside. No stopping today, no turning around and going back to Charlie.

He swallowed hard, trying to dislodge the blockage in his throat. Failed miserably. The vehicle surged forward until he lifted his foot from the accelerator. 'Careful. Trying to outrun that love and sadness in Charlie's eyes isn't going to work. She's a part of you for ever, Marshall.'

Yeah, maybe, but that didn't mean he had to put her heart in jeopardy. He loved her beyond reason but how did he know that love would last through everything life tossed up? Could he guarantee he'd always be there for Charlie in heart and mind, if not in body? No, he couldn't. Despite the sense of belonging to her family that had quickly overtaken him these past weeks, it scared him to think they'd rely on him to always come through for them.

He'd failed Rod, hadn't he? Rod had been the closest thing to a brother he'd ever had. The pain and guilt over losing him hadn't diminished at all.

He turned onto the motorway. The international airport was getting closer by the second.

Charlie had been through enough. He couldn't ask her to face more heartache. And he couldn't expect his little girl to get to know him and then face the devastation of losing him, like Rod's kids had.

Those two boys had been completely lost and bewildered as they'd waited for Daddy to come home from yet another mission. It had taken a long time for them to finally understand that Rod was never coming home. And it had thrown them completely. Karen had told him how little Johnny wet the bed every night while his older brother had taken to lashing out at his friends at school. Only now was counselling starting to show some signs of working to improve the situation.

He didn't want that for Aimee.

Or Charlie. There were no guarantees with his life in the army. End of.

His heart clenched so hard he feared he was having a cardiac event. He was, just not a medical one. Pulling to the side of the road, he opened the door and dragged in a lungful of fresh air, waited for the pain to ebb. Knew it would never, ever go away completely.

CHAPTER ELEVEN

THREE WEEKS LATER Charlie clicked onto patient files prior to seeing her first patient for the day. Notes from Keisha's surgeon caught her attention. Keisha had had a full mastectomy. Treatment would start in six weeks' time. Concern slipped under Charlie's skin, raised the hairs on the back of her neck.

She'd hoped fervently that this wouldn't be the case. An image of those two beautiful boys kicking a ball around the front lawn with Marshall sneaked into her head. Aged seven and eight, they were so young to be facing this. Some kids didn't get a fair shot at childhood.

Like Aimee. She mightn't have known what had been going on with her mother but she'd missed out on lots. The breastfeeding had stopped. There'd been many nights when her grandfather had put her to bed because her mother had been too ill to do something so simple and vital. Charlie sighed.

Aimee didn't appear any the worse for her rocky start in life. She had yet to meet a happier, more well-adjusted little girl. Whether that was due to Aimee's nature or her loving grandfather, Charlie didn't know but she was very grateful. And now, with Marshall on the periphery of their lives, things had to be even better—for Aimee, at least.

Gemma placed a cappuccino in front of her. 'How're you doing?' She dropped into the nearest patient's chair and sipped her latte.

No need to ask what she meant. 'Absolutely fabulous. Aimee's talking non-stop—' about her father '—and loves sleeping in a bed because that means she can get out and come find me whenever it suits her. Dad's fishing regularly for the first time since I got sick and seems to be really enjoying it. But, then, you'd know that.'

Gemma's mouth lifted into a smile.

'Work's humming with more patients than I know what to do with.' She locked eyes with her friend, determined to brazen this out.

'And Charlie? How's she doing?' Gemma stared her down.

Terribly. There didn't seem to be a cure for broken hearts. Being a doctor, she should be able to come up with something to remedy what ailed her but so far that had been a big fail. 'I'm running between five and six k's a day now.' And it's boring on my own.

'Still haven't heard from Marshall?'

'Only occasional emails, which tell me next to nothing about what he's doing.' Twenty-three days since he'd left. Not that she was counting. 'Aimee will forget who he is soon.' He'd promised to stay in touch. Foolishly she'd believed that meant regular phone calls or computer video calls, something where Aimee could see or hear him. Emails didn't cut it with her.

'And Charlie will pretend she's forgotten him.'

'I miss him so much it hurts physically.' So much for being strong.

Admitting she loved him hadn't softened the intensity of her feelings for him or about his disappearance. If anything, her emotions were stronger, more focused. As if admitting her love had painted the world a whole new colour—glowing golden when he'd been here, dull grey now he'd gone. 'Unfortunately he's in my head all the time. There's no let-up. But I can't get angry at him. I always knew he'd leave and I'd have to love him from afar.'

Gemma stood up and tossed her empty paper cup in the bin. 'Give him time. I can't believe he's gone for good. His love for you and Aimee came through in everything he did. He might not realise how he feels yet, but he'll get there.'

'You've been reading too many romance stories.' Or talking to Dad. Her despair was obvious even to her. Charlie shrugged. So what? It hurt. Beyond belief. 'Even if he does work that out, he's not giving up his army career for anyone. He doesn't do settled down.' Draining her coffee, she also aimed her paper cup for the bin. It went in. First thing to go right that morning.

Stop feeling sorry for yourself. Get the day started and put all this Marshall stuff aside for a while. Take Aimee swimming at the pool after work.

'Who's your first patient?' Gemma asked, obviously finished with Marshall for a while.

Relieved, Charlie smiled. 'Faye Burnside and her baby. Can you give Ryan his shots after I've seen them?' Smoothing down her skirt, Charlie followed the nurse out to the waiting room.

'Faye, come through. How's your wee man?' She picked up the heavy day bag the young woman had left beside the chair and swung it at her side as she walked to her consulting room. Definitely getting fitter. A few weeks ago she'd have struggled to lift the darned thing.

'Ryan's only waking twice for feeding during the night now. Thank goodness. I thought he'd never get used to sleeping for more than a couple of hours at a time.' Faye sank onto the chair Gemma had recently vacated. 'To think I used to be able to party all night and get up to go to work the next morning.'

'You weren't doing that seven nights a week for weeks on end.'

Charlie smiled as she took Ryan from Faye. 'Hey, gorgeous. You still being a good boy?' Jiggling him in her arms brought memories of Aimee at this age flooding into her mind and whipping up another storm of emotions. The amazing sense of achievement that her body could produce someone so perfect and precious. The instant love, the need to protect. Being a mother was indescribable. Longing for another baby hit hard.

Get over yourself. You're with patients. Not to mention there won't be any more babies. But— No. No more babies. Be happy with the healthy child you have.

Faye interrupted her selfish mental monologue. 'Can you look at Ryan's tummy? Sometimes a bump comes up just below his ribs.'

'Of course. Any other things you're concerned about?' Charlie didn't mind asking new mothers about their worries. Better to clear them up than have mums stressing needlessly. 'I know I had plenty of questions when Aimee was this little. Being a doctor meant diddly squat.'

Faye grinned as she took Ryan to undress him for Charlie to examine. 'Not at the moment. I have bugged the Plunket nurses with loads of questions. They're so patient, answering everything like I'm not crazy. It was one of them who said I should show you Ryan's tummy.'

'That's what they're there for.' New Zealand's Plunket Society had been around for ever, helping mothers with their newborns.

'There. Do you see that?' Faye gently touched a raised area below her son's ribs.

Charlie carefully palpated the area. 'I think Ryan has a small hernia, which is easily repaired with minor surgery.'

Faye gasped. 'No way. Surgery? But he's so little.'

'Hernias are quite common with infants and the procedure is straightforward.' She'd have been terrified if Aimee had had to have the op done, despite knowing the lack of risk involved.

'Faye, I'll refer you to a surgeon who's excellent with babies. He'll decide if Ryan needs surgery or if he'll take a wait-and-see approach. You really mustn't worry.' Like Faye would take the slightest bit of notice to those words of wisdom. She certainly wouldn't have if this had been Aimee. 'Sorry. Silly thing to say. I'll print out some information for you to take home and read. Show it to your partner, too.'

Faye's face had turned pale as she snapped together the studs down the front of Ryan's romper suit. Lifting him into her arms, she hugged him desperately. 'But he's so happy, doesn't cry like he's in pain or anything.'

'That's because he's not. Sit down for a few minutes. Ask anything that pops into your head.' Charlie answered numerous questions while searching on her computer for medical information and quickly found the relevant notes on infant hernias to print out.

'Here you go. And here's a referral to the surgeon in

Rotorua. I'll get Molly to phone through for an appointment while you're here. The sooner Ryan sees him the sooner you can stop worrying.'

'Will we have to wait months for an appointment?' Faye's hand soothed Ryan's back, even though he was the least distressed person in the room.

Shaking her head, Charlie reassured her. 'I imagine you'll see him within a week. Seriously, while this isn't something you wanted to happen, you mustn't get too wound up about it. I bet if you ask at your postnatal group you'll find other mums who've dealt with the same condition and they'll be able to tell you the same as I am. Ryan's going to be fine.'

She escorted Faye to Reception and arranged for Molly to make the appointment. Glancing at the timetable, she turned to the waiting area. 'Beau, come through to the surgical room.'

A twenty-three-year-old man lumbered to his feet, dwarfing everyone around him. 'Sure, Doctor. How are you today?'

Grinning up at him, she replied, 'I'm supposed to ask that.'

'I know.' He grinned back at her. 'How many of these little suckers are you cutting out of me today?'

'Three.'

'Bet you don't let your little girl out in the sun without layers of sun block on.' Beau had a history of basal cell carcinoma. Two had been removed in previous years and now he opted to have anything remotely abnormal removed before it got too big. While non-malignant, the carcinomas would never go away without medical intervention.

'I smother her from top to toe. So much she's prob-

ably going to be vitamin D deficient instead.' Hard to
get a balance. Too much sun was bad, too little wasn't
great either. Just like everything else, steering a middle course often seemed like juggling a bucketful of
balls all at once.

Marshall sat in Karen's kitchen, his hands playing with
an empty beer bottle. 'Man, it's hot.'

'Hotter than New Zealand?' Karen grinned.

'It was toasty but nothing like this.' He should never
have told her about Charlie, but one night two months
ago when he'd been to see her after returning from Afghanistan she'd been so down about Rod's death he'd
filled in the silences by talking about anything that had
come into his head. As Charlie was always in his head,
that's who he'd talked about. Today he'd already let slip
that he'd flown over to New Zealand to see her.

Karen looked over the rim of her wine glass at him.
'How was Charlie?'

Hot. Sexy. Loving. Wise. And wishing for far too
much from him. 'Surprised to see me.' Angry with him,
pleased with him, and very disappointed. No surprise
there. He'd walked away with a very heavy heart. Now a
shaft of jealousy crawled through his gut at the thought
of her following through on his stunning piece of advice to find another guy.

'In a good way?' Karen wasn't letting up.

'Yep.' Then the words he'd been holding back, telling the news he'd wanted to share with someone since
he'd got back to the States, spewed out. 'We have a
daughter. Aimee. Eighteen months old and the cutest
little girl I've ever met.' And he missed her as much as

her mother. Pulling out his phone, he showed photos of Aimee and Charlie.

Karen's eyes stuck out as if they were on stalks. Her mouth curled into a soft smile. 'Wow, what a little cutie. Got her daddy's eyes.' The smile widened. 'I'm guessing that's Charlie. She's beautiful, too. When do I get to meet them, huh? Are they coming over here?'

'What's this? A quiz show?' Why had he opened his goddamned mouth? Shoving his chair back, he headed for the trash to dump the bottle.

'You bet it is. If Rod was here you'd be spilling the beans to him.' Her voice caught, and twisted his heart at the same time. Her brave face had been all for show.

Spinning around, he crossed to lift her into a gentle hug. 'Take it easy.' With a soft squeeze he sat her back on her chair and circled the table. He wanted that smile back on her face before he left, no matter how fragile it appeared.

'Charlie and Aimee are not coming here. And I'm not moving to New Zealand. You know how it is with the army sending me all over the show. Hardly fair on Charlie, is it?'

'She said that?' Strength was returning to Karen's voice.

'No. I didn't give her the chance. We're not going down that path. It's too hard on everyone. Imagine how bewildering it would be for a little girl. She'd no sooner start to get to know me than I'd be off again.'

'Better than not knowing you at all.'

'Charlie will find someone else, a guy who can be a regular dad to Aimee.' His gut clenched painfully. Another man raising his kid? Didn't seem right from here. Neither did he feel ecstatic about another guy sharing

Charlie's bed. But what was a guy supposed to do if he wanted to protect those he loved?

Karen locked gazes with him. 'I don't believe I'm hearing this. What's happened to you? Leave your brain in Afghanistan? Lose your nerve between battles? Come on, Marshall, you're shirking your duty, never mind your heart.'

'Not fair. You know where my duty lies.' When her eyebrows rose he hurriedly continued before she could say anything else disturbing. 'Charlie lives in the house where she was born. The only time she's left Taupo was to train as a doctor. She works in the same medical centre as her father. Me.' He stabbed his chest with a thumb. 'The longest I've lived in the same place is fifteen months. We are completely incompatible.'

His tongue had got away from him again. It had been happening far too often since he'd returned from New Zealand and that woman who seemed to have stolen his heart and tipped his world upside down.

'Never took you for a scaredy-cat.' Karen gripped his hand. 'I've lost my husband and lover, my kids have lost their father, but we will always remember him and know the love he shared with us. Did you know Rod had decided not to sign up again? He wanted to put us before the army. He believed in us, saw the army had many men, and that we only had him.'

She blinked. 'Marshall, what's staying in the army because of your perceived guilt over his death going to achieve? Nothing. You've got to stop blaming yourself for his death. He wouldn't hold you responsible.'

'He never told me he was getting out.' Rod's timing had sucked. He'd nearly made it. A shiver ran up Marshall's spine. For Rod? Or himself and those he loved?

Had he got it all wrong? Did his men need *him* or would any competent officer suffice? Certainly no one could take his place as father to Aimee, no matter what he'd told Charlie. No man could love Charlie as much as he did. But to walk away from his long-held beliefs, his guilt and start over?

Karen withdrew her hand. 'I'm sorry. You've come visiting, and I appreciate that more than you'll ever know. But I see you missing out on so much. Don't you want to be with someone you love, someone who loves you back so completely you wonder how you survived before you met her?'

Time to get on the road. 'Thanks for lunch, Karen. Call me if there's anything you or the kids need, okay?' He plonked a light kiss on her cheek. 'Say hi to the boys for me.' And he took his leave before she could throw any more offbeat ideas at him.

But her words followed him down the path. To love someone that much? He did love Charlie. That much. It was his love for her that kept him away. He was saving her from heartbreak. But it also hurt that he hadn't been there for her through the most terrible time of her life. He might have a duty to his men but the one to Charlie and Aimee was bigger.

What did he really want out of life? He'd never made plans for his future past what he did now. Maybe he should be thinking about it.

Back in his motel room he stared at his laptop. Would Charlie mind if he gave her and Aimee an internet call? Why wouldn't she? She'd said she loved him. Suddenly he knew that if Taupo was only a few hours away he'd hop a plane right now, go and see her, hug her small frame to his. But the people he cared about most were at the other end of the world, where they belonged.

And he missed them.

The screen came up and his finger hovered over the internet icon. Click. Click off. Charlie could be at work, or busy bathing Aimee. If he wanted to call her he needed to arrange a time with her.

Her number was on his cellphone. A simple text would sort out that problem.

Charlie came back so quickly he had to wonder if she'd been waiting three weeks to hear from him. Which made him feel bad. She was at home, available any time, but the sooner the better if he wanted to see Aimee.

Click. As he waited for the connection he rummaged through the small fridge for a beer, twisted the top off, gulped a mouthful.

And then they were there, filling his laptop screen with their smiles and chatter. He stared at Charlie, drinking in the wonderful sight. God, she was beautiful. That crooked smile, those teary eyes filled his heart with tenderness and need.

'Hey.' Aimee's shriek filled the sterile room he stood in with wonder and love and warm fuzzies. Her arms waved at him and her cute face filled the whole screen as she leaned close to the computer. 'Hello, Daddy.'

The beer bottle slid out of his fingers and crashed to the floor. Daddy. As beer spilled across the vinyl he stood transfixed. Daddy. Aimee had called him Daddy for the first time ever. In his chest his heart didn't seem to know what it should be doing. Thumping, squeezing, racing, aching.

'Daddy,' his daughter shouted, her face puckering up at his lack of response.

Swallowing the sudden blockage in his throat, he croaked, 'Hello, Aimee.' Huh? That was it? Your daughter calls you Daddy for the first time and you say, 'Hello Aimee'? What's wrong with you, man?

'Marshall?' The voice of reason washed over him, and Charlie's concerned face slid into the picture next to Aimee's grinning one. 'You okay?'

Of course he wasn't okay. Who would be? Had Charlie set him up? Taught Aimee to use the D word to knock him off his feet? Somehow he didn't think so. She hadn't used dirty tactics before so why would she start now?

Dropping onto a chair, he grunted, 'I'm good. How's everything with you? Not working too hard, I hope.'

Disappointment—or was it annoyance?—altered her voice, made it edgy. 'No more than usual. I took Aimee to the public swimming pool tonight. She's a little seal, flipping all over the place. We can go to the tepid pools when summer's over.' Charlie's face was serious, not at all excited as it usually was when she was talking about Aimee.

He'd done that to her. He swore silently, then gathered his strength. 'Aimee? Can you hear me?'

His daughter's eyes lit up. 'Daddy? Where are you?'

'I'm a long way away, sweetheart.' Too damned far away. Bloody miles and miles. Even if he wanted to kiss her goodnight, he couldn't. 'Did you like swimming in the big pool?'

'Yes, Daddy.' Another ear-piercing shriek.

As Aimee chattered on excitedly he watched every nuance of expression on Charlie's face. Something was wrong. She blinked too often. Her cheeks were stained red, like she'd been crying. The skin beneath her eyes was swollen.

He wanted to cut across Aimee's chatter to ask what was up but understood he had to wait.

When Aimee finally got bored with talking to the computer she got down and headed away without a backward glance, and he felt a moment of disappointment despite needing to talk to her mother.

Charlie surprised him with, 'There's a chance we might be getting another partner at the centre. A doctor from South Africa has made enquiries and hopes to come and talk to us all next month.'

Marshall sat up straighter.

Charlie continued. 'She seems very keen. Wants to move to a small town rather than a city.'

It was as though a door had slammed in his face. That partnership had been offered to him. Didn't matter that he'd turned it down. 'Brendon will be pleased if she buys in. Give him plenty of time to go fishing then.'

'We'll be eating trout every day of the week.' Her smile didn't override the sadness darkening her eyes.

'Charlie? You're not keen on this South African doctor?'

She shrugged. 'Won't know until I meet her. Sorry, but I've got to put Aimee to bed.' Charlie started to push away from the table her laptop was on.

'Wait. You've been crying. Why?' Why wasn't he there with her? 'Talk to me, babe.'

At first he thought she'd shut down on him but slowly she returned to her chair. 'Keisha's results came back today.'

His blood ran cold. 'That bad?' He pictured that lovely woman who'd come to see Charlie while he'd been there. A person didn't have to be in a war zone for a grenade to be lobbed at them.

Charlie's head dipped. 'Yeah. It's aggressive. The treatment starts very soon and will be tough on her.' Her lips trembled and she began blinking back tears. 'Those poor little boys, Marshall. They need their mum. They're too little to be facing this.'

And Charlie needed someone to hold her, a shoulder to let all the pain out on. Because although she would be hurting for Keisha and her family, Charlie was also reliving her own pain and fear from her own cancer experience, and possibly for the loss of her mother.

'Babe,' he whispered as he put his hand on the screen. 'Put your hand on mine, Charlie. I'm sending my love. You know I love you, right? You can deal with this. We can deal with it. I'm here for you.' Yeah, and he should be *there* for her.

Her eyes met his as her hand touched her screen. 'Thank you.' Her voice shook. 'Maybe I'm not cut out for doctoring in my home town. It's harder than in a hospital where the patients aren't people I went to school with, sailed or cycled with.'

'You do a fabulous job. I bet Keisha would prefer you as her GP right now than anyone else.' He always felt a kinship with the men he treated in the army. He knew them, their families and what they were hoping for.

Just like a GP.

Her smile was wobbly but it was a smile. 'Yeah, you might be right.'

'Of course I'm right.' He grinned. 'Who wants to talk about something as serious as this with a doctor they don't know well?'

'Keisha knows I've been through it so she's asking some hard questions.'

'You've got the answers for her. You won't be saying things that are blatantly untrue.' His grin wavered. He mightn't have been injured in war but he certainly understood the fear of being taken out by a sharpshooter.

He and Charlie weren't that different in their careers. Could he swap location? Change his uniform for an open-necked shirt and slacks? Get weekends off even?

Because he owed Charlie his allegiance more than he owed it to the army. *Thank you, Karen.*

In the background Aimee squealed. Charlie looked disappointed. 'I'd better go. Teddy's spilled his dinner and is in danger of being stuffed into the dishwasher. Can we do this again? Soon?'

'How about tomorrow?' He didn't want her to go. Could have talked to her all night. Tomorrow—a full twenty-four hours away. How could he wait that long?

'Tomorrow's good. I haven't heard anything about what you've been up to yet. Love you.' She blew him a kiss and was gone. Leaving Marshall staring at a photo of Charlie and Aimee on his screen. His heart was heavy. Aimee had called him Daddy. And Charlie was hurting, needed lots of TLC.

Charlie tucked Aimee into bed and kissed her chubby cheeks. 'Goodnight, sweetheart.'

'Where's Daddy? I want him here.'

Her heart clenched so hard it hurt, took her breath away so she couldn't answer immediately. You and me both, her brain screamed. Never once in the last few days when Aimee had learned to say Daddy had Charlie anticipated that question. Aimee was too small to understand much, but it seemed that even she knew her father should be here with her. 'Daddy lives a long way away and can only come to see you when he's not working.'

'Okay, Mummy.' Aimee snuggled down under the light cover, a yawn creasing her face.

'Goodnight, darling.' Another kiss and she crept out of the room, pulling the door closed behind her. Already asking where her father was. What would she be asking by the time she started school?

Pulling on a light jersey, she headed for the kitchen to make a cup of tea before going outside to sit on the veranda in the cooler evening air. The endless clicking sound of cicadas had quieted as the day turned into night. In the distance cars roared along the main road into town. Overhead a plane was on its final approach for the airport. Otherwise the evening was quiet.

So Marshall had called on the internet. Talking to him about Keisha had made her feel better. He seemed to understand her, knew what to say. Damn, she missed him. Would give anything to be able to cuddle up with him.

Dad strolled out and sat on the lounger beside her. 'Progress?'

She couldn't help sighing. 'Who would know? Every day I hoped he'd phone or call me. Every night I've gone to bed angry that he hadn't. Yet now? I should be happy, pleased he got in touch.' The tea was hot on her tongue. 'Yet the more I get, the more I want.'

'Could be you were expecting too much too soon.'

How come Dad always stuck up for the guy? She snapped at him, 'I wasn't hanging out for a proposal.'

'No, love, I'm sure you weren't. But you might've been hoping for more of a connection to his life.' His reasonable tone incensed her, which in turn made her feel terrible. None of this was Dad's fault.

Blinking hard, she strived for a softer tone. 'Marshall made it very clear I'm never going to get that. But I can't stop wishing for it. I love him, Dad.' Where had all these tears come from?

'Even a blind fool could see that.'

'I told him before he left. I don't know what I thought I'd achieve but it seemed important that he knew.' She set the mug on the boards to cool. 'How can he can ignore that?' Marshall loved her, too. Who or what had hurt him so badly that he truly believed he would be wrong for her and Aimee? Right now, if she had the answer to that, she'd want to strangle that person. Or persons.

'Be patient, Charlotte. Your health's good, and your energy's coming back. Aimee's got you. You wanted to find Marshall so he'd be there for Aimee if anything happened. You've achieved that.'

She'd wanted to find him because she loved him.

Dad added, 'A little over five weeks ago Marshall didn't know he had a child, didn't consider he had other options about how to live his life. He's a man who thinks things through. He doesn't act rashly.'

At least Dad hadn't told her to put it out there and wait to see what happened. She stood up. 'Thanks, Dad, but even I know Marshall is never going to come and live here. I've been fooling myself to even wish he might.'

'You could move to the States.'

'No way. Leave my home, my job? Leave you? Never.' The words shot out of her mouth like bullets. 'No, Dad. No.' Her foot stamped hard on the veranda.

'No.' She'd have preferred putting it out there to this suggestion.

'Just a thought.'

'Not a very good one.' Her dad was the most sensible, grounded person she knew. He didn't have random thoughts. So where had this come from? Did he really believe that her taking his granddaughter to live in another country was a good idea? Or was he being his usual selfless self? Guilt stabbed her. Could it be that he wanted to finally have a life that didn't revolve around looking out for her?

'Dad, you're the best father any girl could wish for. But I can stand on my own two feet now. You need to do some of those things on your dream list.'

She'd even accept the South African doctor if it meant Dad could have a life. The dream of Marshall buying into the medical centre would be over. But she'd still live in this house she'd known all her life, and bring Aimee up as a Kiwi kid at the same schools she'd attended. Insular? Too much so? Was she as afraid of making changes as Marshall? Perhaps she was. That needed some thought.

Unfortunately Dad hadn't finished. 'America is only twelve hours away by plane.'

'Drop it, Dad.'

But later, lying in bed, she couldn't let the crazy idea go. Why not move to another country? She'd enjoyed her time in Hawaii. That had been for a few months. Not a lifetime. It was hard to imagine living somewhere else and making plans for the future that didn't involve her home town. How could she walk away from people she'd known all her life? But Marshall would be there for her, with her. Some of the time anyway. He'd be a part of those plans. He could share raising Aimee, really be a part of her life, instead of dropping in occasionally via the internet.

Charlie held up a finger in front of her face. She loved Marshall with all her heart. He was the only man she ever wanted to be with.

A second finger went up. Marshall was Aimee's dad. They should be together.

The third finger. Marshall loved her.

Fourth point. She could be a doctor anywhere. There'd be some legalities, but nothing insurmountable.

Fifth point. There wasn't one. Definitely not a positive one.

Could she move away from all she knew for the man she loved?

Her fingers folded into a fist and her hand dropped to her tummy. Marshall would never agree to this madcap idea anyway.

CHAPTER TWELVE

MARSHALL PULLED THE SUV over to the kerb on the left and hauled on the handbrake. At least he'd made it without any incidents involving other vehicles. Glancing further along the road, he grinned to see John's newly panel-beaten and painted work vehicle parked in the same spot it had been the day he'd pranged it.

'Bet if John knew I might breeze by he'd have parked it in his driveway.'

Using his shoulder to shove the door open, he climbed out to stand, hands on hips, staring around him. His heart hammered against his ribs. His mouth dried while his eyes moistened. There hadn't been a night since he'd left he hadn't thought of this place. If he'd been a romantic kind of guy he'd have said he'd left his heart in Taupo that day. Not anywhere in Taupo but right at this address, this house that begged to be filled with kids and laughter, with happy adults and fun times around the barbecue with friends.

Looking over at the house Charlie had grown up in, he noted the windows and front door weren't wide open as they had been in January. April here was cooler. Driving down from Auckland he'd noted that the trees were beginning to change colour as autumn sent out its first chilly tentacles. Though not the trees in Charlie's yard. They were evergreens. Solid native trees the likes of which he'd never seen before coming here.

The paddling pool had disappeared. No one sat on the veranda, though the lounger still remained in its place. Charlie must be inside because her car was parked on the other side of the closed gate. He didn't know if he was pleased or disappointed she wasn't in the same place she'd been that first day he'd turned up.

He'd come to talk to her, to tell her his plans for the future. So why was he suddenly shaking? He was doing the right thing. He was doing what he wanted, needed to do. Until now he'd believed Charlie might be pleased with his decision. Yet standing on the road outside her house, he felt an alien fear. What if she'd decided she was better off without him? Worse, could she have already met another man?

No. She'd told him she loved him. Charlie wouldn't be replacing him that easily or quickly. From what he'd seen of her and Aimee and Brendon, love in the Lang family was for ever. He just had to expand his horizons and allow this family into his heart.

Too late, mate. They're already there. Which is why you're taking this enormous risk.

That, and because life wasn't worth much without these people in it.

'Daddy.' The sweetest young voice on the planet shrieked from somewhere behind the fence. His stomach crunched, his heart played a weird tattoo against his ribs. And his mouth lifted from grim to happy. He stepped across the road.

Another shriek, louder still. 'Daddy's here. Lift me up.'

* * *

From the flowerbed where she was planting daffodil bulbs Charlie jerked back on her heels so fast her neck cricked. 'Aimee?' She couldn't have seen Marshall. He was in Kansas. 'Aimee, come here.' Away from strangers. Away from the disappointment that was sure to follow when she realised that her daddy had not suddenly appeared.

Ever since the day she'd called Marshall Daddy as they'd talked on the computer Aimee had been talking about Daddy, looking for him in cupboards and under beds. It had broken Charlie's heart to see the tears well up every time Aimee came to her and said, 'Daddy's gone away.'

She looked around the empty lawn. 'Aimee, where are you?'

'Hello, Charlie.'

Her heart stopped. 'Marshall?' she squeaked. That deep, velvety voice sounded like his. Her gaze lifted slowly, fearful of finding a stranger looking down at her. The thighs filling out those tight jeans seemed familiar, the narrow hips, the broad chest stretching a light woollen jersey. She swallowed hard. And lifted her chin enough to see the face belonging to this body. Green eyes glittered down at her, a hesitant smile caught at her, and a hand reached down for hers.

'Marshall?' she whispered, as she placed her soil-stained hand into that firm grasp.

With a gentle tug from Marshall she stood upright, balancing precariously on her toes, drinking in the sight before her. Words had deserted her. Her world was tipping all over the place. The only vision filling her hungry eyes was the man who'd owned her head space for weeks. Could this be a mirage? The hand holding hers felt real; solid, strong, warm, right. The eyes holding a steady gaze were real. The arm gripping Aimee like he'd never, ever let her go was real.

'Marshall.' Her voice came out low and quiet. 'You came.' But for how long?

'Couldn't stay away another moment.' His smile slipped. 'I'm sorry it took so long for the truth to hit me. I really believed I could walk away and let you get on with finding a better life. How dumb was that?'

'About as dumb as me thinking I could let you go without putting up a fight.'

His free arm went around her shoulders, pulling her close to him. 'I've missed you both. You have no idea how much.'

Oh, yes, she did, but who was she to argue? She'd been going crazy with the need to see him. 'I have to kiss you to know I'm not dreaming.'

'Can't argue with that.' As his head came down closer and closer to hers a familiar tension wound through her, a hot tautness that had everything to do with recognition. Her body knew this man. A kiss wasn't going to change a thing. But, still, a girl had to kiss her man when he came home, didn't she?

Then Marshall pulled back. His steady gaze locked with hers. 'This is for ever, Charlie. I've left the army, packed up my few belongings and shipped them out here. I've even made enquiries about registering with the New Zealand Medical Council.'

Her tongue stuck to the roof of her mouth, preventing her saying anything, so she nodded, waiting for him to go on.

'It isn't going to be easy. I've never stopped in one

place long enough to see two Christmases in a row. I don't know what it's like to treat the same patients month in, month out, to become involved with them and their families.' He sucked in air. 'And I certainly have no idea about living in a loving family. But I want to give it my absolute best shot.'

'Then it will work out just fine.'

'You know I love you, don't you?' A hint of uncertainty underscored his question.

Tapping her chest, she smiled. 'Right in here I feel your love all the time.' Reaching up on tiptoe again, she said against his mouth, 'And now for that kiss.'

His lips brushed hers and then he pulled back again. 'One more thing.' This was getting to be an annoying habit of his.

She gave him a mock glare. 'This had better be good, Marshall Hunter. A girl can only wait so long for a kiss.'

His mouth twitched like he was holding in a laugh. 'You'll get all the kisses you want once you answer my next question.' Juggling Aimee on his hip, he used his other hand to brush a strand of hair off her cheek. 'Charlotte Lang, will you marry me, be my lifelong partner and keep me grounded? Share the raising of our daughter with me?'

Doubt suddenly rose in her, dwarfing the hope in her heart. 'What about having more children?' His frown creased his forehead and when his mouth opened to answer her she raced on. 'I can't have any more babies. Ever. Have you thought about that?'

The frown disappeared, and his gorgeous mouth curved into a sensational, toe-curling smile. 'Babe, you and Aimee are all I need. You'll both be running rings around me as it is. I don't need any other children to make me happy. I've already got everything I could ever want.'

For the life of her she couldn't move. Her legs had turned all jellylike and her body felt weightless. Warmth flowed through her, touching every corner, knocking out the chills. Marshall wanted her, wanted to be with her, for ever.

'In case your hearing has got bad these past weeks, I'll repeat myself. Charlie Lang, will you do me the honour of marrying me?'

Whipping her hand out from his fingers, she gripped his arm and held on. Marry Marshall? 'Yes, yes, yes, and yes.' He had asked four things of her, hadn't he? 'Yes, Marshall, my love and my lover and the father of my child, I will become Mrs Charlie Hunter.' Stretching up, she begged, 'Now can I have that kiss?'

Some kisses were made in heaven. This one had been brewing since the day they'd met in the ED in Honolulu, and had only just reached its full potential. It had the right blend of love and desire and commitment and dedication. It spoke of their future—together. It was all about love.

* * * * *

CHANGED BY
HIS SON'S SMILE

BY
ROBIN GIANNA

Published in Great Britain 2014
by Mills & Boon, an imprint of Harlequin (UK) Limited,
Eton House, 18-24 Paradise Road, Richmond, Surrey, TW9 1SR

© Robin Gianakopoulos 2014

ISBN: 978 0 263 90740 7

Harlequin (UK) Limited's policy is to use papers that are natural,
renewable and recyclable products and made from wood grown in
sustainable forests. The logging and manufacturing processes conform
to the legal environmental regulations of the country of origin.

Printed and bound in Spain
by Blackprint CPI, Barcelona

Dear Reader

When I decided to write a Medical Romance™ set in an exotic place Benin, West Africa, was an easy choice. I could still see the gripping photographs my husband had taken when he worked in a mission hospital there some years ago, and enjoyed hearing his account of the months he was there. It was interesting learning more about Benin and thinking about the kinds of people who dedicate their lives to medical work there and elsewhere.

My story's hero is Dr Chase Bowen, who grew up in mission hospitals and is now dedicated to his patients and to the work he considers his calling. Because he knows from experience that it isn't safe for non-native children in the countries where he works, Chase believes having a family of his own isn't an option. Until Dr Danielle Sheridan returns to his life, bringing with her the son he didn't know he had.

Danielle believed she was doing the best thing for her son, keeping him a secret, since Chase had made it clear he never wanted children. Now that Chase knows, can they make a new relationship work with the challenges of their careers and fears? Chase wants marriage, but Dani isn't convinced. Then a terrifying event challenges them both.

I hope you enjoy reading CHANGED BY HIS SON'S SMILE as much as I enjoyed writing it!

Robin Gianna

**CHANGED BY HIS SON'S SMILE
is Robin Gianna's debut title!**

Dedication

To George, my own doctor hero husband.
Thank you for supporting me in my writing dream,
for answering my endless medical questions, and for
putting up with the piles of books and pens and papers
and Post-it® notes that clutter our house. I love you.

Acknowledgments

For me, it takes a village to write a Medical Romance™!

Many thanks to:

Kevin Hackett, MD and Betsy Hackett, RN, DSN, for
tolerating my frantic phone calls and hugely assisting me.
SO appreciate the awesome scene, Kevin!

My lovely sister-in-law, Trish Connor, MD,
for her great ideas and help.

Critique partner, writer friend, and pediatric emergency
physician Meta Carroll, MD, for double-checking scenes
for accuracy. You're wonderful!

The many writer friends I can't begin to thank enough,
especially Sheri, Natalie, Susan and Margaret. Without
you, my bootstraps might still be laying on the floor.

My agent, Cori Deyoe of 3 Seas Literary Agency,
for her tireless assistance with everything.

CHAPTER ONE

THE POOR WOMAN might not be able to have more babies, but at least she wasn't dead.

Chase Bowen's patient stared at him with worry etched on her face as she slowly awakened from surgery.

He leaned closer, giving her a reassuring smile. "It's okay now. You're going to be fine," Chase said in Fon, the most common language in The Republic of Benin, West Africa. If she didn't understand, he'd try again in French.

She nodded, and the deep, warm gratitude in her gaze filled his chest with an intense gratitude of his own. Times like these strengthened his appreciation for the life he had. He couldn't imagine doing anything else.

Chase understood why, despite their family tragedy, his parents still spent their lives doctoring the neediest of humankind.

"Her vital signs are all normal, Dr. Bowen," the nurse anesthetist said. "Thank God. I've never seen hemoglobin as rock bottom as hers."

"Yeah. Ten more minutes and it probably would've been too late."

He pressed his fingers to her pulse once more and

took a deep breath of satisfaction. Ectopic pregnancy from pelvic inflammatory scarring was all too frequent in this part of the world, with polygamy and the diseases that came with that culture being commonplace. He'd feared this was one of the patients who wouldn't make it.

There'd been too many close calls lately, and Chase tried to think what else they could do about that. Their group had an ongoing grass-roots approach, trying to encourage patients to come in before their conditions were critical. But people weren't used to relying on modern medicine to heal them. Not to mention that patients sometimes had to walk miles just to get there.

"Will there be more babies?" the woman whispered.

He couldn't tell if the fear in her voice was because she wanted more children, or because she didn't want to go through such an ordeal again.

"We had to close off the tube that had the baby in it," he said, gentling his voice. "But you still have another tube, so you can probably conceive another baby, if you want one."

Whether she was fertile or not, Chase didn't know. But the children she did have still had their mother. He squeezed her hand and smiled. "Your little ones who came with you looked pretty worried. Soon you'll be strong enough to go home, and they'll be very happy to have their *maman* again."

A smile touched her lips as her eyelids drifted shut. Chase left her in the capable hands of the nurse anesthetist and stripped off his gown to head outside. Moist heat wrapped around him like a soft, cottony glove as he stepped from the air-conditioned cement-block building that made do as the clinic and O.R. for the local arm of Global Physicians Coalition.

Dusk still kept that particular inch of sub-Saharan West Africa bathed in low light at nine-thirty p.m., and he didn't bother to pull his penlight from his pocket. The generators would be turned off soon, and the growl of his stomach reminded him he hadn't eaten a thing since lunch. Finding dinner in the dark was a crap shoot, so a quick trip to the kitchen had to happen before the lights went out.

He strode around the corner of the building and nearly plowed down Trent Dalton.

"Whoa, you off to save another life?" Trent said, stumbling a few steps. "I heard your patient's sister calling you '*mon héros.*' I'm jealous."

"I'm pretty sure you've been called a hero once or twice, deserved or not," Chase said.

"Not by such a pretty young thing. I recall it coming from an elderly man, which didn't stroke my needy ego quite as much."

Chase snorted. "Well, thank the Lord the pregnant sister was my patient instead of yours. Your ego would explode if it got any bigger."

"I'm confident, not egotistical," Trent said, slapping Chase on the back. "Let's see what there is to eat. I've gotta get some food before I have to scrounge for a coconut by the side of the road."

"With any luck, Spud still has something in there for us."

"No chance of that. He left a while ago to pick up the new doc who just arrived from the States."

Spud wasn't even here? Chase's stomach growled louder as he realized the chances of finding anything halfway decent to eat was looking less likely by the minute.

The place would doubtless fall apart without Spud Jones, the go-to guy who cooked, ordered all the supplies, transported everyone everywhere and pretty much ran the place.

"How come I didn't know there was a new doc coming?" Chase said as they walked toward the main building.

"Well, if you weren't wrapped up in your own little world, maybe you'd enjoy more of the gossip around here."

"Do you know who he is?"

"Not a he. A she. A very pretty she, according to Spud," Trent said. "Thank God. As a constant companion, you're not only the wrong gender, you're dull as hell. We're overdue for some new female beauty to spice things up around here."

"We? You mean you," Chase said with a grin. "There's a reason Dr. Trent Dalton is known as the Coalition Casanova."

"Hey, all work and no play makes life all work." His light blue eyes twinkled. "She's coming to finally get electronic clinic records set up on all the kids. I can't wait to offer my suggestions and assistance."

Chase laughed. As they neared the building, the sight of a Land Rover heading their way came into view within a cloud of dust on the road. Chances were good he'd worked with the new doctor before. The Global Physicians Coalition was a fairly small group, and most were great people. Medical workers who saw mission work as a calling, not just an occupation.

The sound of the Land Rover's engine choked to a

stop just out of sight in front of the building, and Trent turned to him with a smile of pure mischief. "And here's my latest conquest arriving now. What a lucky lady."

Trent took off towards the front doors and Chase followed more slowly, shaking his head with an exasperated smile. One of these days Trent's way of charming the pants off women then leaving them flat with a smile and a wave was going to catch up with him. Not that his own record with females was much better.

"*Bon soir*, lovely lady. Welcome to paradise."

Trent's voice drifted across the air, along with Spud's chuckle and a few more words from Trent that Chase didn't catch.

Feminine laughter froze Chase in mid-step. A bubbly, joyous sound so distinctive, so familiar, so rapturous that his breath caught, knowing it couldn't be her. Knowing he shouldn't want it to be her. Knowing that he'd blown it all to hell when he'd last seen her anyway.

Without intent or permission, his feet headed towards the sound and the headlights of the dusty Land Rover. Shadowy figures stood next to it, and he could see Trent taking the new arrival's bulky shoulder bag from her. Spud was obviously introducing the two, with Trent giving her his usual too-familiar embrace.

Chase had to fight the sudden urge to run forward, yank Trent loose, and tell him to keep his hands off.

He hadn't needed to see the curly blonde halo glowing in the twilight to know it was her. To see that beautiful, crazy hair pulled into the messy ponytail that was so right for the woman who owned it. A visual representation of impulsive, exuberant, unforgettable Danielle Sheridan.

Chase stared at her across the short expanse of earth,

his heart beating erratically as though he'd suddenly developed atrial fibrillation.

He'd always figured they'd run into one another again someday on some job somewhere in the world. But he hadn't figured on it stopping his heart and shortening his breath. Three years was a long time. Too long to still be affected this way, and he didn't want to think about what that meant.

She was dressed in her usual garb—khaki shorts that showed off her toned legs and a slim-fitting green T-shirt that didn't attempt to hide her slender curves. In the process of positioning another bag on her shoulder, it seemed she felt his gaze and lifted her head. Their eyes met, and the vibrant, iridescent blue of hers shone through the near darkness, stabbing straight into his gut.

Her big smile faded and her expression froze. A look flickered across her face that didn't seem to be just a reflection of what he was feeling. The feeling that it would've been better if they hadn't been stuck working together again. Bringing back memories of hot passion and cold goodbyes.

No, it was more than that. The same shock he felt was accompanied by very obvious dismay. Horror, even. No happy reunion happening here, he guessed. Obviously, the way they'd parted three years ago had not left her with warm and fuzzy feelings toward him. Or even cool and aloof ones.

"Chase! Come meet your new cohort in crime," Spud said.

He moved closer to the car on legs suddenly gone leaden. Dani's heart-shaped face wore an expression of near panic. She bent down to peer into the backseat of the Land Rover then bobbed back up, their eyes meeting again.

"Danielle, this is Dr. Chase Bowen," Spud said as he heaved her duffle. "Chase, Dr. Danielle Sheridan."

"Dani and I have met," Chase said. And wasn't that an absurd understatement? They'd worked together for over a year in Honduras. The same year they'd made love nearly every day. Within warm waterfalls, on green mountain meadows, in sagging bunk beds.

The year Dani had told him she wanted to make it permanent, to have a family with him. For very good reasons, a family couldn't happen for Chase, and he'd told her so. The next day she'd left the compound.

All those intense and mixed-up memories hung in the air between them, strangely intimate despite the presence of Trent and Spud. Suddenly in motion, she surprised him by moving fast, stepping around the hood of the car in a near jog straight towards him, thrusting her hand into his in a brusque, not-very-Dani-like way.

"Chase. It's been a while. How've you been?"

Her polite tone sounded strained, and he'd barely squeezed her soft hand before she yanked it loose.

"Good. I've been good." Maybe not so good. As he stared into the blue of her eyes, he remembered how much he'd missed her when she'd left. More than missed her sunny smile, her sweet face, her beautiful body.

But he'd known it had been best for both of them. If a family was what she wanted, she should marry a guy rooted in the States. No point in connecting herself to a wandering medic who wouldn't have the least idea how to stay within the confines of a white picket fence.

Apparently, though, she hadn't found husband and father material, because here she was in Africa. The woman who had burrowed under his skin like a guinea worm, and he had a bad feeling that her arrival would start that persistent itch all over again.

"Dani," Spud called from across the car, "I'm going to take your duffle to your quarters, then be back to help you get—"

"Great, thanks," Dani interrupted brightly. "I appreciate it."

She turned back to Chase, and he noted the trapped, almost scared look in her eyes. Was the thought of having to work with him again that horrible?

"I thought the GPC website said you were in Senegal," Dani said. "Are you…staying here?"

"No, just stopped in for a little day tour of the area."

The twist of her lips showed she got his sarcasm loud and clear. What, she hoped he was about to grab a cab and head to the next tourist destination? He couldn't remember Dani ever saying dumb things before. In fact, she was one of the smartest pediatricians he'd had the opportunity to work with over the years. One of the smartest docs, period.

"Well. I…" Her voice faded away and she licked her lips. Sexy, full lips he'd loved to kiss. Tempting lips that had been one of the first things he'd noticed about her when they'd first met.

"So-o-o," Trent said, looking at Dani, then Chase, then back at Dani again with raised brows. "Chase and I were about to have a late dinner and a beer. Are you hungry?"

"No, thanks, I had snacks in the car. You two go on and eat, I'm sure you're starved after a long day of clinic and surgeries." She put on a bright and very fake smile. "I'll get the low-down on the routine around here tomorrow. Right now I'm just going to have Spud show me my room and get settled in. Bye."

She walked back to the other side of the Land Rover and then just stood there, hovering, practically willing them to leave. Well, if she wanted to act all weird about the two of them being thrown together again, that was fine by him.

"Come on," he said to Trent as he moved towards the kitchen. While his appetite had somehow evaporated, a beer sounded damned good.

"Mommy!"

The sound of a muffled little voice floated across the sultry air, and Chase again found himself stopping dead. He slowly turned to see Dani leaning into the back of the Land Rover. To watch, stunned, as she pulled a small child out through the open door and perched him on her hip.

Guess he'd been wrong about her finding husband and father material. And pretty damned fast after she'd left.

"Mommy, are we there yet?" The sleepy, sweet-faced boy of about two and a half wrapped his arms around her neck and pressed his cheek to her shoulder. A boy who didn't have blue eyes and crazy, curly blond hair like the woman holding him.

No, he had dark hair that was straight, waving just a bit at the ends. A little over-long, it brushed across eyebrows that framed brown eyes fringed with thick, dark lashes. A boy who looked exactly like the photos Chase's mother had hauled all around the world and propped up in every one of the places they'd lived. Photos of him and his brother when they were toddlers.

Impossible.

But as he stared at the child then slowly lifted his gaze to Dani's, the obvious truth choked off his breath and smacked him like a sledgehammer to the skull. He didn't have to do the math or see the resemblance. The expression in her eyes and on her face told him everything.

He had a son. A child she hadn't bothered to tell him about. A child she had the nerve, the stupidity to take on a medical mission to a developing country. Something he was adamantly against...and for good reason.

"I guess...we need to talk," Dani said, glancing down at the child in her arms. She looked back at Chase with a mix of guilt, frustration and resignation flitting across her face. "But let's...let's do it tomorrow. I'm beat, and I need to get Andrew settled in, get him something to eat."

"Andrew." The name came slowly from his lips. It couldn't be a coincidence that Andrew was his own middle name. Anger began to burn in his gut. Hot, scorching anger that overwhelmed the shock and disbelief that had momentarily paralyzed him. She'd named the boy after him, but hadn't thought it necessary to even let him know the kid existed?

"No, Dani." It took every ounce of self-control to keep his voice fairly even, to not shout out the fury roaring through his blood and pounding in his head. "I'm thinking a conversation is in order right this second. One more damned minute is too long, even though you thought three years wasn't long enough."

"Chase, I—"

"Okay, here's the plan," Trent said, stepping forward and placing his hand on Chase's shoulder. "I'll take Andrew to the kitchen, if he'll let me. Spud and I'll rustle up some food. You two catch up and meet us in the kitchen in a few."

Trent reached for the boy with one of his famously charming smiles. Andrew smiled back but still clung to Dani's neck like a liana vine.

"It's okay, Drew," Dani said in a soothing voice as she stroked the dark hair from the child's forehead. "Dr. Trent is going to get you something yummy to eat, and Mommy will be right there in just a minute."

"Believe it or not, Drew, I bet we can find some ice cream. And I also bet you like candy. The kids we treat here sure do."

The doubtful little frown that had formed a crease between the child's brows lifted. Apparently he had a sweet tooth, as he untwined his arms from Dani and leaned towards Trent.

"And you know what else? It's going to be like a campout in the kitchen, 'coz the lights are going out soon and we'll have lanterns instead. Pretty cool, huh?"

Andrew nodded and grinned, his worries apparently soothed by the sweet adventure Trent promised.

Trent kept talking as he walked away with the child, but Chase no longer listened. He focused entirely on the woman in front of him. The deceiving, lying woman he'd never have dreamed would keep such an important thing a secret from him.

"I want to hear it from your lips. Is Andrew my son?" He knew, *knew* the answer deep in his gut but wanted to hear it just the same.

"Yes." She reached out to rest her palm against his biceps. "Chase, I want you to understand—"

He pushed her hand from his arm. "I understand just fine. I understand that you lied to me. That you thought it would be okay to let him grow up without a father. That you brought *my son* to *Africa*, not caring at all about the risks to him. What is wrong with you that you would do all that?"

The guilt and defensiveness in her posture and expression faded into her own anger, sparking off her in waves.

"You didn't want a family, remember? When I told you I wanted to marry, for us to have a family together, you said a baby was the last thing you would ever want. So, what, I should have said, 'Gosh, that's unfortunate because I'm pregnant'? The last thing *I* would ever want is for my child to know his father would consider him a huge mistake. So I left."

"*Planning* to have a child is a completely different thing from this and you know it." How could she not have realized he'd always honor his responsibilities? He'd done that every damned day of his life and wasn't about to stop now. "What were you going to do when he was old enough to ask about his father? Did it never occur to you that if his dad wasn't around to be a part of his life, he'd feel that anyway? That he'd think his father didn't love him? Didn't want him?"

"I…I don't know." Her shoulders slumped and she looked at the ground. "I just… I know what it's like to have a father consider you a burden, and I didn't want that for him. I thought I could love him enough for both of us."

The sadness, the pain in her posture stole some of his anger, and he forced himself into a calmer state, to take a mental step back. To try to see it all from her perspective.

He *had* been adamant that children wouldn't,

couldn't, fit into his life, ever. He'd learned long ago how dangerous it could be for non-native children in the countries where he worked. Where his parents worked. He couldn't take that risk.

So when she'd proposed marriage and a family, he'd practically laughed. Now, knowing the real situation, he didn't want to remember his cold response that had left no room for conversation or compromise.

No wonder she'd left.

She lifted her gaze to his, her eyes moist. "I'm sorry. I should have told you."

"Yes. You should have told me." He heaved in a deep breath then slowly expelled it. "But I guess I can understand why you didn't."

"So." She gave him a shadow of her usual sunny smile. "We're here. You know. He's still young enough that he won't think anything of being told you're his daddy. My contract here is for eight months, so you'll have a nice amount of time to spend with him."

Did she honestly think he was going to spend a few months with the boy and leave it completely up to her how—and where—his son was raised?

"Yes, I will. Because I accept your marriage proposal."

CHAPTER TWO

"Excuse me?" Dani asked, sure she must have heard wrong.

"Your marriage proposal. I accept."

"My marriage proposal?" Astonished, she searched the deep brown of Chase's eyes for a sign that he was kidding, but the golden flecks in them glinted with determination. "You can't be serious."

"I assure you I've never been more serious."

"We haven't even seen each other for three years!"

"We were good together then. And we have a child who bonds us together now. So I accept your offer of marriage."

The intensely serious expression on his face subdued the nervous laugh that nearly bubbled from her throat. Chase had always been stubborn and tenacious about anything important to him, and that obviously hadn't changed. She tried for a joking tone. "I'm pretty sure a marriage proposal has a statute of limitations. Definitely less than three years. The offer no longer stands."

"Damn it, Dani, I get it that it's been a long time." He raked his hand through his hair. "That maybe it seems like a crazy idea. But you have to admit that all of this is crazy. That we have a child together is…crazy."

"I understand this is a shock, that we have things to figure out." Three years had passed, but she still clearly remembered how shaken she'd been when she'd realized she was pregnant. Chase obviously felt that way now. Maybe even more, since Andrew was now here in the flesh. "But you must know that marriage is an extreme solution."

"Hey, it was your idea to begin with, remember? You've persuaded me." A slight smile tilted his mouth. "Besides, it's not extreme. A child should have two parents. Don't you care about Andrew's well-being?"

Now, there was an insulting question. Why did he think she'd left in the first place? "Lots of children are raised by unmarried parents. He'll know you're his father. We'll work out an agreement so you can spend plenty of time with him. But you and I don't even know each other any more."

Yet, as she said the words, it felt like a lie. She looked at the familiar planes of his ruggedly handsome face and the years since she'd left Honduras faded away, as though they'd never been apart. As though she should just reach for his hand to stroll to the kitchen, fingers entwined. Put together a meal and eat by candlelight as they so often had, sometimes finishing and sometimes finding themselves teasing and laughing and very distracted from all thoughts of food.

A powerful wave of all those memories swept through her with both pain and longing. Memories of what had felt like endless days of perfection and happiness. Both ridiculous and dangerous, because there was good reason why a relationship between them hadn't been made for the long haul.

Perhaps he sensed the jumbled confusion of her emotions as his features softened as he spoke, his lips no longer flattened into a hard line. "I'm the same man you proposed to three years ago."

"Are you?" Apparently his memory of that proposal was different from hers. "Then you're the same man who didn't want kids, ever. Who said your life as a mission doctor was not just what you did but who you were, and children didn't fit into that life. Well, I have a child so you're obviously not the right husband for me."

His expression hardened again, his jaw jutting mulishly. "Except your child is *my* child, which changes things. I'm willing to compromise. To adjust my schedule to be with the two of you in the States part of the year."

"Well, that's big of you. Except I have commitments to work outside the States, too." For a man with amazing empathy for his patients, he could be incredibly dense and self-absorbed. "We should just sit down, look at our schedules for after the eight months I'm here and see if we can often work near enough to one another that you can see Drew when you have time off."

"I will not have my son living with the kinds of dangers Africa and other places expose him to."

"You grew up living all over the world and you turned out just fine." More than fine. From the moment she'd met him she'd known he was different. Compassionate and giving. Funny and irreverent. Book smart and street smart.

The most fascinating man she'd ever known.

The unyielding intensity in his eyes clouded for a moment before he flicked her a look filled with cool determination. "I repeat—my son needs to grow up safe in the States until he's older. Getting married is the most logical course of action. We figure out how to make our medical careers work with you anchored in the U.S. and me working there part of the year. Then we bring him on missions when he's an older teen."

"Well, now you've touched on my heart's desire. A marriage founded on a logical course of action." She laughed in sheer disbelief and to hide the tiny bruising of hurt she should no longer feel. "You've got it all figured out, and you haven't even spent one minute with him. Or with me. So, I repeat—I'm not marrying you."

Frustration and anger narrowed his gaze before he turned and strode a short distance away to stare at the dark outline of the horizon, fisting his hands at his hips, his broad shoulders stiff. In spite of the tension simmering between them, she found herself riveted by the sight of his tall, strong body silhouetted in the twilight. The body she'd always thought looked like it should belong to a star athlete, not a doctor.

She tried to shake off the vivid memories that bombarded her, including how much she'd loved touching all those hard muscles covered in smooth skin. All the memories of how crazy she'd been about him, period. Three light-hearted years ago the differences they now faced hadn't existed. Serious differences in how Andrew should be raised, and she still had no proof that Chase wouldn't be as resentful in his reluctant role as father as her own parent had been.

Now that Chase would be involved in Andrew's life, she had to make sure her son never felt the barbed sting of being unwanted.

Tearing her gaze from his stiff and motionless form, she turned to find Andrew and get him settled in. Chase must have heard her movement as he suddenly spun and strode purposefully towards her.

The fierce intensity in his dark eyes sent an alarm clanging in her brain. What was coming next she didn't know, but her instincts warned her to get ready for it. He closed the inches between them and grasped her waist in his strong hands, tugging her tightly against his hard body.

A squeak of surprise popped from her lips as the breath squeezed from her lungs.

This she was definitely not ready for.

His thick, dark lashes were half-lowered over his brown eyes, and her heart pounded at the way he looked at her. With determined purpose and simmering passion.

"I remember a little about your heart and your desire." His warm breath feathered across her mouth. "I remember how good it was between us. How good it can be again."

She pressed her hands against his firm chest but didn't manage to put an inch between them. Her heart thumped with both alarm and ridiculous excitement. "It's been three years. Too long to just take up where we left off."

"Not so long that I don't remember where you like to be kissed."

Surprise turned to shock when he lowered his head to touch his lips to the sensitive spot beneath her earlobe, slowly sliding them to the hollow of her throat, his voice vibrating against her skin. "How you like to be kissed."

"Chase, stop." A delicious shiver snaked its way down her body before he lifted his head to stare into her eyes. "We—"

His mouth dropped to hers and, despite the part of her brain protesting that a kiss between them just complicated things, her eyes slid closed. The soft warmth of his lips sent her spiraling back to all the times they'd sneaked kisses between patients, celebrating successful outcomes, or held each other in wordless comfort when a patient had been lost. To all the times they'd tramped in the mountains and made love anywhere that had seemed inviting.

Apparently, her hands had their own memories, slipping up his chest to cup the back of his neck, his soft hair tickling her fingers. *He's right.* The vague thought flitted through her head as his wide palm slid between her shoulder blades, pressing her body closer as he deepened the kiss. It had been very, very good between them. Until it hadn't been.

Through her sensual fog the thought helped her remember what a strategic man Chase could be. That this wasn't unchecked, remembered passion but a calculated effort to weaken her resolve, to have her give in to his marriage demand.

She broke the kiss. "This isn't a good idea."

"Yes, it is." His warm mouth caressed her jaw. "I've missed you. I think you've missed me, too."

"Why would I miss being dragged out of bed to do calisthenics at six a.m.?" The words came out annoyingly breathy.

"But you missed being dragged into bed for another kind of exercise."

His mouth again covered hers, sweet and insistent and drugging. One hand slipped down her hip and cupped her bottom, pulling her close against his hardened body.

He'd always teased her about how she couldn't resist his touch, his kiss. A pathetically hungry little sound filled her throat as she sank in deeper, doing a very good job proving he'd been right.

But that was before, her sanity whispered.

Yanking her mouth determinedly from his, she dragged in a deep, quivering breath. "This won't work. I know your devious strategies too well."

His lips curved and his dark eyes sparked with liquid gold. "I think you're wrong. I think it's working." He lifted one hand to press his fingers to her throat. "Your pulse is tachycardic and your breath is all choppy. Both clear indications of sexual desire."

"Thanks for the physiology lesson." She shoved hard at his chest to put a few inches between them and felt his own heart pounding beneath her hands. At least she wasn't the only one feeling the heat. "But memories of good sex do not make a relationship. And definitely not a marriage."

"So we make new memories." His big hands cupped her face as his mouth joined hers again, and for a brief moment she just couldn't resist. Softening, yielding to the seductive, soft heat of his kiss, to the feel of his thumbs feathering across her cheekbones, until her brain yelled his words of three years ago. That, despite what he said now, marriage and a family were the last things he ever wanted.

She couldn't let him see the pathetic weakness for him that obviously still lurked inside her. She had to stay strong for Andrew.

The thought gave her the will to pull away completely and shake the thick haze from her brain, ignoring the hot tingle of her lips. "This is not a good idea," she said again, more firmly this time. "Our…relationship…needs to be based on logic, just like you said. None of this to muddy things up."

"You used to like things muddied up."

The teasing half-smile and glint in his eyes made her want to kiss him and wallop him all at the same time. "I need to rescue Trent. You can meet Andrew, but I don't want to tell him about…you…tonight. Let him spend a little time with you first."

"So long as you understand this conversation isn't over."

Conversation? Was that what they'd been having? "I'd forgotten what a prince complex you have, bossing everyone around."

She headed in the direction Trent and Andrew had disappeared, relieved to be back on stable ground without the confusion of his touch, his kiss. Then realized she hadn't a clue where they'd gone. "Where is the kitchen anyway?"

Chase strode forward with the loose, athletic stride she'd always enjoyed. As though he was in no hurry to get where he was going but still covered the ground with remarkable speed.

"This way."

His warm palm pressed her lower back again as he pulled a penlight from his pocket, shining it on the ground in front of her. "Watch your step. Rocks sometimes appear as though they rolled there themselves."

As they walked in the starlight, the whole thing felt surreal. The heat of his hand on her back, the timbre of his voice, the same small, worn penlight illuminating the dusty path. As though the years hadn't passed and they were back in Honduras again, feeling close and connected. She stared fixedly at the uneven path, determined to resist the gravitational pull that was Chase Bowen.

Chase shoved open a door and slipped his arm around her waist, tucking her close to his side as he led her down a short hallway. Quickly, she shook off his touch.

"Stop," she hissed. "Drew needs to get to know you without your hands all over me."

"Sorry. It's so nice to touch you again, I keep forgetting." He raised his palms to the sky, the picture of innocent surrender, and she again had the urge to punch the man who obviously knew all too well how easily he could mess with her equilibrium.

Several camp lights dully lit the room, showing Drew sitting at a high metal table, his legs dangling from a tall stool. The low light didn't hide the melted ice cream covering the child's face from the tip of his nose down, dripping from his chin.

"Hi, Mommy!" He flashed her a wide grin and raised the soggy cone as if in a toast, chocolate oozing between his fingers. "Dis ice cream is good!"

"I can see that." She nearly laughed at the guilty look on Trent's face as Drew began to lap all around the cone, sending rivulets down his arm to his elbow.

"I'll clean him up." Trent waved his hand towards Drew, looking a little helpless. "Didn't see the point of it until he was done."

"Don't worry, making messes is what Drew does best," she said, giving Trent a reassuring smile. "Right, honey?"

"Wight!" Drew shoved his mouth into the cone, and the softened ice cream globbed onto the table. He promptly dropped his face to slurp it straight from the flat metal surface then swirled his tongue, making circles in the melty chocolate.

"Okay, no licking the table." Chase probably thought she'd never taught the boy manners. Hastily, she walked over to lift his wet, sticky chin with her palm. "Finish your cone, then we'll find out where we're sleeping. And you'd better do it quick, 'coz it's about to become all cream without the ice part."

"You know, Drew," Chase said in a jocular tone that sounded a little forced, "when you stick your tongue out like that, you look like a lizard. We have big ones around here. Maybe tomorrow we'll look for one."

Drew's eyes lit and he paused his licking to look up at Chase. "Lizards?"

"Yep. Maybe we'll catch one to keep for a day or two. Find bugs to feed it." Chase moved from the sink with two wet cloths in his hands. His thick shoulder pressed against Dani's as he efficiently wiped the chocolaty table with one cloth then handed it to Trent, whose expression was a comical combination of amusement and disgust.

Chase lifted the other cloth to Drew's mouth, his gaze suddenly riveted on the little boy's face. *Their* baby's face. Still cupping Drew's chin in her hand, Dani stared at Chase. Every emotion crossed his face that she'd long imagined might be there if he knew about his son. Within the shadowy light she imagined that through all those mixed emotions it wasn't horror that shone through but joy. Or was that just wishful thinking?

Her breath caught, remembering how many times in the past two and a half years she'd thought about what this moment might be like. After the miracle of Drew as a newborn and when he'd cried through the night. When he'd first smiled. Crawled. Run.

Her throat closed and she fought back silly tears that stung the backs of her eyes as Chase lifted his gaze to hers, wonder filling his.

The sound of Trent clearing his throat broke the strange spell that seemed to have frozen the moment in time.

"I'm going to head to my room, you three. See you in the a.m.," Trent said, smiling at Drew.

Heat filled Dani's face. "I appreciate you getting him the ice cream. I don't think there's much doubt he enjoyed it."

"Yeah, thanks, Trent." Chase and he exchanged a look and a nod before Trent took off, and Dani could see the two of them were good friends. Something that often happened when working in the GPC community, but not always. Occasionally personalities just didn't mesh and a strictly professional relationship became the best outcome.

Then there were those rare times that an intimate relationship took over your whole world.

"I think this one's done, Lizard-Boy," Chase said, taking what remained of the soggy cone and tossing it in the trash. He took over the clean-up with an efficiency that implied he'd had dozens of children in his life, wiping Drew's hands then pulling Dani's hand from her son's chin, about to take care of his gooey face, too.

The frown on Drew's face as he stared at the stranger washing his face while his mother stood motionless snapped her out of her stupor.

She tugged the cloth from Chase's hand and took

over. "I'm not sure if you ate the cone, or the cone ate you," she said lightly. She rinsed it again, along with her own sticky hand, before dabbing at the last spots on Drew's face.

"Dat's enough, Mommy." Drew yanked his head away as she tried for one last swipe of his chin.

Spud poked his head into the kitchen. "Everything's ready, if you are, Dani. Tomorrow Ruth is coming to meet both of you and take care of Drew while we give you the low-down around here."

"Great. Thanks." She lifted Drew onto her hip and turned to Chase, inhaling a fortifying breath. "We'll see you tomorrow."

"Yes." His gaze lingered on Drew. When he finally looked at Dani, his eyes were hooded and his expression serious. "Tomorrow will be a big day."

Dani awoke to a cool draft, and she realized Drew was in the process of yanking off her bed sheet.

"Hey, you, that's not nice. I'm sleeping."

No way could it be morning already. She pulled the covers back to her chin but Drew tugged harder.

"Get up. I hungry."

She peeled open one eye. From the crack visible between the curtains, it looked like the sun had barely risen above the horizon. "It's too early to be hungry."

"Uh-uh. My tummy monsters are growling."

Even through her sleep-dulled senses Dani had to smile. Drew loved the idea of feeding the "monsters" that growled in his stomach. "What color monster's in there today?"

"Blue. And green. Wif big teeth."

He tugged again. Dani sighed and gave up on the idea

of more sleep. Doubtless both their body clocks were off, and no wonder. Sleeping on a plane was something she never managed to do well, but Drew had conked out both on the plane and in the car, and she'd been amazed he'd slept at all once he'd got into bed.

"All right. Let's see what there is to eat."

She threw on some clothes but left Drew in his Spiderman pajamas. It took a minute to remember which door led to the kitchen, and she hesitated in the hallway. Getting it wrong and ending up in someone's bedroom was an embarrassment she didn't need. Cautiously, she cracked open the door, relieved to see a refrigerator instead of a sexy, sleeping Chase Bowen.

"Let's see what your monster wants," she said, pushing the door wide as she nudged Drew inside. To her surprise, Trent was sitting at the table, sipping coffee and reading.

"When I took this job, no one told me the hours here were dawn to dusk," Dani joked as she plopped Drew onto the same stool he'd sat on the night before.

"Spud's a slave driver, I tell you," Trent said with an exaggerated sigh. "Actually, I just finished up an emergency surgery. Clinic hours don't usually start until nine. Coffee?"

He started to get up, but she waved her hand when she spied the percolator on the counter. "Thanks, I'll grab it myself." Last night, the darkness had obscured most of the kitchen, but this morning showed it to be big and functional, if a bit utilitarian.

"So, do you and Chase share a room?" As soon as the words left her mouth she wondered why in the world she'd asked. She stared into her cup as she poured, heat filling her face at the look of impassive assessment Trent gave her in response.

"No. The medical workers used to stay with families nearby, but they built the sleeping quarters you're in a couple years ago, with small rooms for everyone."

"Oh. Can you tell me where there's oatmeal or something for Drew?"

"Top cupboard on the left. Spud fixes breakfast around eight. Chase runs every morning." He leaned his back against the table and sipped his coffee. "But you probably know that."

She did know. The man was a physical fitness nut. "How long have you worked with Chase?"

"We've worked together in the Philippines and Ghana. Been here a year. Both our commissions are up, but we're hanging around until there are other surgeons here and we get new assignments."

Did that mean Chase might not be here long? A sharp pang of dismay stabbed at her, which was both ridiculous and disturbing. Shouldn't she feel relief instead? It would be so much better for Drew if Chase moved on before the two got too close.

"Mommy, I need food," Drew said, fidgeting on his stool.

Lord, she had to be sure this whole mess didn't distract her from the work she'd come to Africa to do. If she couldn't even get Drew's breakfast going, she was in serious trouble.

In a sign that their new, temporary home was practically made for her and Drew, two of his favorite foods sat in the cupboard. Dani microwaved the apple-flavored oatmeal and opened a box of raisins.

Trent got up and pulled some construction paper and

crayons from a drawer to place them in front of Drew, poking a finger at his pajama top. "While your mom gets your breakfast, how about drawing me a picture of Spiderman climbing a wall?"

Wow, the man sure knew kids, and she wondered what Trent's story was. Just as she was about to ask, he beat her to the questions.

"So, obviously you and Chase go back a while. Where did you meet?"

"Honduras." Back then, her expectations for mission work had been so starry-eyed and naive. And the last thing she'd expected was to meet a hunky, dynamic doctor who'd knocked her socks off. Among other things.

Apparently, Trent expected more than a one-word answer, looking at her speculatively. It was pretty clear he wondered if her arrival was bad for Chase. Her stomach twisted. Who knew if this situation they were in was good or bad for any of them?

"I'd just finished my pediatric residency and wanted to do something important for a while," she said, tucking raisins into the steamy oatmeal to make a smiley face. "Go where kids don't get the kind of medical care we have at home."

She didn't add that she'd stayed months after her contract was up because she hadn't been ready to say goodbye. Knew she'd never be ready. Until she was forced to be.

She slid Drew's artwork aside to make room for his breakfast. He picked the raisins out one at a time and shoved them in his mouth. "He can't see now! I ate his eyes!"

A smile touched Trent's face as he watched Drew

dig into his breakfast, but when he turned to Dani, his expression cooled.

"So, why didn't you tell Chase? Frankly, I think that's pretty lame."

She gulped her coffee to swallow the burning ache in her chest that was anger and remorse combined. Who was he to judge her without knowing Chase's attitude? Without knowing she'd had to protect her baby? Without knowing how hard it had been to leave the man she'd fallen crazy in love with?

"Listen, I—"

The kitchen door swung open and the man in question walked in, which immediately sent her pulse hammering at the thought of what lay ahead of them. Telling Drew, and what his reaction would be when he learned Chase was his daddy. What demands Chase might or might not make in being a part of his son's life. How it all could be balanced without Drew getting hurt.

Chase filled the doorway, sweat glistening on his tanned arms and face, spikes of dark hair sticking to his neck. A faded gray T-shirt damply clung to his broad chest, his running shorts exposing his strong calves and thighs. His brows rose as he paused in mid-stride, wiping his forehead with the sleeve of his shirt.

"What is this, a sunrise party? Not used to seeing anyone in here this early."

She tore her gaze from his sexy body to focus on wiping Drew's chin. "Andrew needed food more than he needed sleep. Guess we're not on West Africa time yet."

Chase grabbed a bottle of cold water from the fridge and took a big swig as he leaned his hip against the counter, his attention fixed on Drew. Dani found herself staring as he swallowed. As his tongue licked droplets of water from his lips.

Quickly, she glanced away and swallowed hard herself. Why couldn't she just concentrate on the serious issues that lay between them, instead of wanting to grab him and sip that water from his lips herself?

Toughening up was clearly essential, and she braved another look at him, sternly reminding herself they'd been apart way longer than they'd been together. His demeanor seemed relaxed, but she could sense the undercurrent of tension in the set of his shoulders, the tightness in his jaw. Obviously, he felt as anxious about their upcoming revelation to Drew as she did.

Trent stood. "Think I'll get in a catnap before the clinic opens."

"Don't worry about getting to the clinic at nine. I can't take how cranky you get when you're tired," Chase said.

"Better than being cranky all the time, like you," Trent said, slapping Chase on the back. "See you all later."

The kitchen seemed to become suffocatingly small as Chase stepped so close to Dani that his shoulder brushed hers. His expression told her clearly that it was showtime, and her pulse rocketed.

Why did she feel so petrified? At least a thousand times since he'd been born, she'd thought about how or if or when she'd tell Drew about his daddy. He was still practically a baby after all. Like she'd said last night, he probably wouldn't think anything of it.

But as she looked at her little boy, the words stuck in her throat. She turned to Chase, and he seemed to sense all the crazy emotions whirling through her. The intensity on his face relaxed, his deep brown eyes softened, and he slipped his arm around her shoulders.

"I promise you it will be okay," he said, dropping a kiss on her forehead. "No. Way better than okay. So stop worrying."

She nodded. No point in telling him she'd been worrying since before Drew had been born, and couldn't just turn it off now. But deep inside she somehow knew that, even though he hadn't wanted a child, Chase would never say and do the hurtful things her own father had.

Chase released her shoulders and pulled two stools on either side of Drew's before propping himself on one and gesturing to Dani to sit on the other. She sank onto the stool and hoped her smile covered up how her stomach churned and her heart pounded.

She wiped the last of his breakfast from Drew's hands and face and slid his bowl aside. "Drew, you know Mommy brought you to Africa so I could work with children here. But I brought you here for another reason, too."

Okay, so that was a total lie, and the twist of Chase's lips showed her he was still ticked about not knowing about Drew. But she was going with it anyway, darn it.

"And that reason is…because…" She gulped and struggled with the next words. "Dr. Chase here is, um…"

She was making a complete mess of this. Drew looked at her quizzically and she cleared her throat, trying to unstick the words that seemed lodged in there.

Chase made an impatient sound and leaned forward. "What your mom is trying to say is that I'm really happy to finally meet you and be with you because—"

The door to the kitchen swung wide and Spud strode

in with hurricane force. "A truck plowed down two kids walking to school. One's pretty beat up. I have them in pre-op now."

Chase straightened and briefly looked conflicted before becoming all business. He stood, downed the last of his water and looked at Drew, then focused on Dani, his expression hardened with frustration. "We'll talk later."

Spud turned to her. "Ruth is on her way to take care of Andrew," he said. "I'll show you the facility and the clinic schedule after he's settled in."

"I want to help with the injured children as soon as she gets here," Dani said. She wasn't about to let the drama with Chase interfere with her reason for being here in the first place, and caring for sick and injured children was a big part of that reason.

Spud inclined his head and left. Chase paused a moment next to Drew and seemed to hesitate before crouching down next to him.

Dani's heart pinched as she saw the usually decisive expression on Chase's face replaced by a peculiar mix of uncertainty, determination and worry.

"Later today, how about you and your mom and I go look for those lizards?"

"'K." Drew beamed at Chase before grabbing his crayons to scribble on his Spiderman artwork.

Chase strode to the door, stopping to give Dani a look that brooked no argument. "Plan on a little trek this afternoon."

CHAPTER THREE

WITH DREW HAPPILY playing under the watchful eye of a gentle local woman, Ruth, Dani hurried to the prep room Spud directed her to.

The room, only about fifteen feet by twenty or so, echoed with the whimpers of a child. The harsh, fluorescent light seemed to bounce off the white cinder-block walls, magnifying the horror of one child's injuries.

Chase was leaning over the boy as he lay on a gurney, speaking soothingly in some language she'd never heard as he focused on the child's leg. She'd almost forgotten how Chase simply radiated strength, calm, and utter competence when caring for his patients. The boy nodded and hiccupped as he took deep breaths, an expression of trust on his face despite the fear and pain etched there.

Dani looked at the boy's leg and nearly showed her reaction to his injury, but caught herself just in time. Jaggedly broken, the child's femur protruded through the flesh of his thigh. Gravel and twigs and who-knew-what were embedded in the swollen wound. His lower leg was badly scraped and lacerated and full of road debris too, and his forehead had a gash that obviously required suturing.

The other child, at first glance anyway, seemed to have suffered less severe injuries.

She looked to be about eight years old. Her wounds would need suturing, too, and before that a thorough cleaning. A woman, presumably her mother, sat with her, tenderly wiping her scrapes and cuts with damp cotton pads.

"What do you need me to do first?" Dani asked. She'd probably be stitching up the girl but, as bad as the boy's injuries looked, Chase might need her help first.

"Get a peripheral IV going in the boy. His name's Apollo. Give him morphine so I can irrigate and set the leg. Then you can wash out his sister's cuts, scrub with soap and stitch her up. I have her mom putting a lidocaine-epinephrine cocktail on her to numb the skin."

Dani noted how worried the mother looked, and had to applaud her for her calm and efficient ministrations. A cloth that looked like it might have been the boy's shirt lay soaked with blood on the floor next to her, which, at a guess, she'd used to try to stop the bleeding. The mother's clothes were covered in blood too, and Dani's throat tightened in sympathy. The poor woman had sure been through one terrible morning.

"Where are the IVs kept? And the irrigation and suture kits?" If only she'd had just an hour to get acquainted with the layout of the place. Right now, she felt like the newbie she was, and hated her inadequacy when both patients needed help fast.

"IVs are in the top right cupboard. The key to the drug drawer is in my scrub pocket."

She stepped over to Chase, and he straightened to give her access to his chest pocket. As she slipped her hand inside, feeling his hard pectoral through the fabric, their eyes met. The moment took her rushing back to Honduras, to all the times just like these, as though they had been yesterday instead of three years ago. To all the memories of working together as a team. To all the times he'd proved what an accomplished surgeon he was.

Heart fluttering a little, she slipped the key from his pocket, trying to focus on the present situation and not his hunkiness quotient. She turned and gathered the morphine and IV materials and came back to the whimpering boy, wanting to ease his pain quickly.

"Tell him he'll feel a little pinch then I'm going to put a straw in his hand that'll make his leg hurt less," she said, concentrating on getting the IV going fast.

"Damn," Chase said.

She looked up and saw him shaking his head. "What?"

"I'd forgotten how good you are at that. One stick and, *bam*, the IV's in. I don't think he even felt it."

His voice and expression were filled with admiration, which made her feel absurdly pleased. "Thanks."

He leaned closer. "He's lucky you're here."

"And he's lucky to have you to put his leg back together."

He smiled and she smiled back, her breath catching at how ridiculously handsome the man looked when his eyes were all fudgy brown and warm and his lips teasingly curved.

"The little girl's going to get the world's most meticulous stitcher-upper, too," Chase said, still smiling as he tweezed out lingering pieces of gravel from Apollo's wound. "I remember a button you sewed so tightly on my shirt I couldn't get it through the little hole any more."

"Well, I only did it for you because, considering you're a surgeon, you're really bad at sewing on buttons."

His eyes crinkled at the corners as they met hers again, and her heart skipped a beat, darn it all. With the IV in place, the boy's eyes drooped as the morphine took effect. Chase placed an X-ray plate under the boy's calf, then rolled a machine across the room, positioning its C-arm over his shin, obviously suspecting, as she did, that it also might be broken.

"Is the X-ray tech coming soon?"

"No X-ray tech. Honduras was loaded with staff compared to this place. I'll get this film developing before I work on the compound fracture."

Wow. Hard to believe they had to take and develop the X-rays. "I'll get started with the girl. Where's irrigation?"

He nodded toward the wide, low sink. "Faucet. The secret to pollution is dilution. It's the best we have."

Her eyes widened. "Seriously? I stick her wounds under the faucet?"

"Attach the hose. We've found it provides more force than the turkey basters we use on less polluted wounds. It's how I'm going to get him cleaned up now that he's had pain meds. You're not in Kansas any more, Toto. Be right back." With a wink, he left with the X-ray cartridge in his hand.

Dani grabbed a pair of sterile gloves from a box attached to the wall and rolled a stool from under the counter to sit next to the gurney. She smiled at the wide-eyed girl and her mother.

If only she spoke their language, or even a little French. The girl looked scared but wasn't shedding a single tear. Hopefully, when the local nurse arrived, she could interpret for Dani. Or Chase would. One of the many amazing things about the darned man was all the languages he could speak fluently or partially. He had a true gift for it, while Dani hated the fact that it had never come easily to her.

"I'm going to wash—*laver*—her cuts to get all the gravel and nasty stuff out of there." Lord, was that the only French word she could come up with?

The mother seemed to understand, though, nodding gravely. Dani rolled the gurney to the low sink and couldn't believe she had to stick the child's various extremities practically inside it, scrubbing with good old antiseptic soap to clean out the debris. Thank goodness the numbing solution seemed to be working pretty well, as the scrubbing didn't seem to hurt her patient too badly.

"You're being very brave," she told the little girl, who gave her a shy smile in return, though she probably didn't understand the words.

The mother helped with the washing, and Dani thought about how her own perspective had changed since she'd had Drew. When she had been in med school, and then when she'd become a doctor, she'd thought she'd got it. But now she truly understood how terrifying it must be to have your child seriously injured or ill.

When Chase returned, Dani had finished prepping the girl and helped him get the boy's wounds washed out. Not an easy task, because tiny bits of gravel seemed determined to stay embedded in his flesh.

Thank heavens the morphine made the situation tolerable for the child.

"You want me to stitch this big lac on his head, or do you want to do it after I work on his leg?" Chase asked, then grinned. "Or maybe we should call in the plastic surgeon."

"Funny. I'm as good as any plastic surgeon anyway. Tell his mom he'll be as handsome as ever when I'm done."

Chase chatted with the mother as they laid the boy back on the gurney, and the woman managed a smile, her lips trembling and tears filling her eyes for a moment.

"I haven't seen anything like this since Honduras," Dani said quietly to Chase as they got the patient comfortable and increased his morphine drip in preparation for setting the leg. "Been in a suburban practice where the bad stuff goes to the ER. The roughest stuff I dealt with was ear infections."

"So you're sorry you came?"

"No." She shook her head and gave him a crooked smile. "Even though you're here, I'd almost forgotten how much we're needed in places like this."

"Except you shouldn't have brought Drew. Which we'll be talking about." His expression hardened.

Oh, right. Those deep, dark issues they had to deal with separate from what they were doing now.

Yes, Chase was a great surgeon and good man, but she had to remember why she'd left in the first place. Because he didn't want a child. And she wasn't about to let him bully her into doing things his way and only his way, without regard for how it would affect Drew.

Glad to be able to put some physical distance between them to go with the emotional distance that had suddenly appeared, she stepped away to stitch the girl's cuts.

"I'm taking him into the OR to set the bone and put a transverse pin in the distal femur," Chase said, wheeling the gurney to the swinging door that led to the operating room. "If Trent comes down, tell him I'm just going to splint it and put drains in for now, until the swelling goes down. When the nurse anesthetist gets here, tell her to grab the X-rays and come in."

He stopped to place his hand on the mother's shoulder, speaking to her in the soothing, warm tones that always reassured patients and family and had been known to weaken Dani's knees. From now on, though, when it came to Chase, she had to be sure her knees, and every other part of her, stayed strong.

"Once you heal, it's going to take a while to get your leg strong again. But I promise we'll help you with exercises for that, and you'll be playing soccer again in no time." Chase smiled at the boy, now in a hospital bed with a trapeze apparatus connected to his leg with a counterweight, which had to feel really miserable in the hot, un-air-conditioned hospital ward.

Lucky, really, that it wasn't a whole lot worse, with bad internal injuries. Barring some hard-to-control infection, he'd eventually be running again. Damned drunk driver apparently hadn't even seen the poor kids. Chase's lips tightened.

As Chase suspected, in addition to the compound fracture, the boy's tibia had been broken too, and he'd put a cast on it before finally getting him set up in bed. It would be damned uncomfortable for the kid, but would keep the bones immobile so he could begin to heal.

"Nice work, Dr. Sheridan," he said to Dani as he looked closely at the boy's forehead, which she'd nearly finished stitching. Dani looked up at him from her sitting position next to the bed, a light glow of perspiration on her beautiful face. Her blue, blue eyes smiled at him in a way that made him want to pick up where they'd left off the night before. If they'd been alone, he would have. Convincing her to marry him was a pleasure he looked forward to. Except he needed to stop thinking about all the ways he planned to accomplish that before everyone in the room knew where his thoughts had travelled.

He could tell Dani already did. "I've always appreciated the superior techniques you implement for everything you do," he said, giving her a wicked grin.

Her smile faded and her fair skin turned deeply pink, and she quickly turned to finish working on the boy's forehead. He nearly laughed, pleased at how easily he could still rattle her.

The nasty gash was now a thin red line within the tiny stitches Dani was currently tying off. If anything, she'd gotten even better at it than when they'd been in Honduras. Even back then he'd been amazed at her talent for leaving only the smallest scar.

"Tell him he looks very handsome and rugged, like a pirate," she said, smiling at the boy. "His friends will be jealous."

Chase translated and the kid managed a small smile, but his mother laughed, the sound full of relief. She'd been fanning the child practically non-stop with a home-made fan, trying to keep him comfortable in the stifling heat of the room and to ward off pesky flies that always found their way into the hospital ward, regardless of everyone's efforts to keep them out.

They'd set Apollo's sister up in the bed next to him, though she didn't really need to stay in for observation. Their mother, though, would be bringing food in for her son and sleeping next to him on the floor to help care for him, so it made sense to keep the little girl here too, as the bed was available.

"We'll be putting a new cast on his whole leg some time after the swelling goes down, but for now we'll be keeping him comfortable with some pain medicine," he said to the mother. "I'll be back later to check on him."

He tipped his neck from side to side to release the kinks that always tightened there after a long procedure. With everything they could do for the kids finished for now, he felt suddenly anxious to find Drew and tell him the truth. He gathered up Dani's suture kit. "Ready to go, Doctor?"

"Not really," she mumbled under her breath as she stripped off her gloves.

She looked up at him as she stood, her face full of the same uncertainty and anxiety that had been there earlier. Why was she so worried about telling their son that he was the boy's father? If she didn't look so sweet and vulnerable, he'd be insulted.

Sure, he'd said he didn't want kids, but that had been before he'd known it was already moot.

She'd see how good it would be. He'd reassure her, romance her, be a good dad to Drew, and she'd realize that everything would be okay. His mood lifted, became downright buoyant, and he tugged at one of the crazy blonde curls that had escaped from her ponytail.

Last night when he'd kissed her, she hadn't been able

to hide that she still wanted him the way he wanted her. She'd come round. Marry him. He'd find a good job for her in the States where he could work sometimes, too, and Drew would be safe.

Yeah, it was a good plan. He knew he could make it happen.

He tugged another curl.

"You know, you're like a second-grader sometimes," she said, pulling her head away with a frown. "Next, you'll be putting a frog down my shirt."

"No. A lizard." He folded her soft hand into his. "Let's find Drew."

CHAPTER FOUR

"THIS LOOKS LIKE a good lizard spot." Chase maneuvered the Land Rover off the dusty road and around some scrub towards a grouping of rocks.

"I can't believe you're really planning on catching one," Dani said, shaking her head. "I know you have quick reflexes, but I think even you are a little slower than a lizard. And if you do catch one, it'll probably bite you."

"Watch and learn." He grinned at Dani but the smile she gave in return was very half-hearted, and shadows touched the blue of her eyes. He stuffed down his impatience to tell Drew and get it over with so she'd relax and see what a great dad he was going to be. So she'd get over her illogical attitude and say yes to marrying him.

Chase stopped the vehicle by the rocks, which would hopefully prove to be a good hiding place for the reptiles. Not that the primary reason for coming out this afternoon was really about lizards. But he wanted Drew to like him and remembered how much fun he'd had searching for lizards and various other creatures with his own dad and brother.

"Spud packed an old blanket we can use as a sort of tablecloth on the rock," Chase said. He turned to the child sitting in the car seat in the back. Every time he looked at the boy the wonder and worry over having a child slammed him in the chest all over again. "How about a snack, Drew? Then we'll go hunting."

"I'll get the picnic bag Spud put together for us," Dani said.

He watched Dani slide from the front seat, enjoying the view of her perfect, sexy behind in her khaki shorts. Her lean, toned legs. She opened the back door and unlatched their son from his car seat.

His son. Such a crazy word to think. To have rolling from his lips when he'd been alone and tried out how it would feel to say it. *My son.* But none of it was as strange as how normal it felt to look at the child and know Drew was his. To feel the strong tug of emotion that pulled at his heart for the sweet-faced boy he barely knew.

If Drew wouldn't have balked at it, Chase would've taken his son from the seat himself and carried him to stand tall on the biggest rock where they planned to enjoy a picnic before going lizard hunting. Now that he knew about Drew, it felt oddly natural to be a father, and that itself seemed more than surprising.

During his run this morning, he'd found himself thinking of all the things he wanted to do with Drew. All the things he'd loved as a kid. All the things his own father had shared with him, taught him. Except so many of those things stemmed from having lived in other places and cultures around the world. He'd have to figure out which of those things they'd be able to do together in the States, where Drew belonged.

While he'd never been particularly comfortable in the U.S., he was more than willing to work there part of the year to spend time with his child and his wife.

Seeing them every day while he was there would make it worthwhile. And with global communications being what they were these days, it would be easy to stay in touch, even close, when he worked missions.

He knew in his bones it would work out fine for everyone. His family.

Chase grabbed the blanket from the back of the car, along with a wooden box he'd brought for any lizards they'd manage to catch.

The savannah stretched for as far as they could see to the hilly horizon, with scruffy trees here and there amid lush grasses and brown scrub. He headed to a nice, flat rock perfect for a picnic and began to lay the blanket across it.

"Let me help." A few soft, blonde curls that had escaped Dani's ponytail fell across her cheek as she leaned over the rock. He wanted to drop the corner he was holding and feel them wrapped around his finger. Tickle the shell of her ear as he tucked them there. Bring her mouth to his.

She doesn't like it when you push. He grabbed one end of the fabric and together they smoothed it across the rock. Or attempted to smooth it, with Drew scrabbling across the rock on all fours looking a bit like a crab and bunching up the blanket until Dani grabbed him up and swung him in circles.

"We can't eat with you messing up the blanket, silly."

"I a lizard!" Drew protested as Dani set him on his feet and kissed the top of his head.

"I know. And I have yummy bugs to feed you if you sit on the rock like a good reptile."

"Okay. I like bugs." Drew quickly climbed onto the rock and sat, comically sticking out his tongue and giggling.

Chase and Dani both chuckled. The kid was so damned cute. He and Dani reached for the food bag at the same time, and her eyes met and locked with his. For a moment they just stared at one another, and Chase nearly reached for her, wanting to kiss away the worry behind her smile and whatever other emotions he saw flickering in their blue depths. The beautiful blue he'd seen so many times in his dreams after she'd left Honduras.

He gave up resisting and lifted his hand to cup her cheek, placing a quick, gentle kiss on her soft lips. "Why so gloomy? The Dani I remember was full of sass and saw everything as an adventure. Not a worrywart," he said. "You've been adventuring with Drew alone. All I want is to jump in and join you."

She gave him a twisted smile and shook her head. "Maybe today. But what about tomorrow? What about next year, when you're who-knows-where and have forgotten all about us?"

What a damned insulting thing to say. As though he'd ever forget all about them. "If you'll just—"

"I want my bugs!" Drew began lizard-walking again, sticking out his tongue and tangling the blanket.

"Okay, lizard-boy. Let's see what's in here." Chase huffed out a frustrated breath at both her attitude and his apparent inability to just shut up about the subject for one minute.

Except he knew why he'd opened his mouth. He'd wanted to wipe that worry from her face. Wanted to see the sunny, vibrant Dani again. But pushing her was the wrong approach, and he knew it. Showing her his commitment to making a marriage and family work was the way to convince her, not with words. Not by getting irritated with her doubts, which he supposed he couldn't blame her for having.

He pulled out the grilled chicken on sticks that Spud always made and looked to see what else was in the bag. "Here are the best-tasting bugs in Benin," Chase said, pulling a box of raisins from the sack. Drew sat back on his haunches and opened his mouth. They began a comical game, with Chase tossing the raisins into Drew's mouth and the child slurping up any that fell onto the blanket.

"Okay, you two. Even lizards need more substantial food than bugs," Dani said.

She put the rest of the picnic on metal plates. "What's this stuff?" she asked, lifting the foil from a plastic bowl to expose soft, lumpy, brown and beige discs.

"Those are *akara*," Chase said. "Fried fritters made from black-eyed peas. They're kind of ugly but they're good."

Dani handed one to Drew as she assembled a few other things on the child's plate. Holding it in both hands, he took a big bite then promptly spit it out right onto the blanket, leaving his tongue hanging from his mouth with a comical look of anguish on his face. "Cookie yucky!"

Chase didn't want Drew to think they were laughing at his distress, and tried to keep his face from showing how hilarious the poor kid's expression was. "Sorry, buddy. That's not a cookie. Guess we should have made that clearer."

"Poor Drew. Have a drink to wash it down." Dani handed him a water bottle and wiped up the food. Apparently she wasn't too worried about Drew being offended, as a laugh bubbled from her lips, and the sound of her amusement stole Chase's breath. He looked at the curve of her sexy lips and the sparkle in her beautiful eyes, beyond relieved that she was finally more relaxed and happy.

He'd always loved her laugh, her smile, her sense of humor. Kissing that laughing mouth was almost as high on his agenda as telling Drew that he was his father, but he reminded himself he had to go slowly.

But not too slowly. Who knew when his next assignment would come through? The thought of having to leave before Dani believed in their relationship again scared the hell out of him.

After they'd eaten, Chase grasped Dani's hand to let her know the time had come to tell Drew, together. Instantly, a grim expression replaced the soft happiness on her face of just a moment ago, and he shoved down the disappointment he felt at the transformation. What had he ever done to make her look at him like that?

"Andrew." The child stopped banging a stick against the rock and looked up at him expectantly. Chase figured he should take the lead in this, as he had a feeling Dani would be as tongue-tied as she'd been earlier if he left it all up to her. "This morning your mom was telling you she brought you to Africa for two reasons. Besides helping kids here, she wanted you to meet me. And I really wanted to meet you."

He looked at her and the worry—damn it, he'd even call it torment—in her eyes made him pause. Did she need to be the one to say it?

"Yes, Drew." Her voice sounded strained and her grip on his hand tightened. "I'm so happy because, believe it or not, you finally get to meet your daddy. Dr. Chase is your daddy. Isn't that great?"

To Chase's shock, her lips quivered and fat tears filled her eyes and spilled over. She quickly swiped them away, but not before they hit him hard in the gut.

Dani wasn't an over-emotional woman, crying over any little thing. That she was moved to tears now showed him what he hadn't even thought about. How hard all this had been on her, no doubt from the beginning. Being pregnant with Drew, alone. Giving birth to him, alone. Raising him, alone.

Painful guilt swamped him. No, he hadn't known about Drew. But he should have been more intuitive when she'd proposed to him, damn it. And it had been his words that had driven her to secrecy.

He wrapped his arm around her shoulders and pulled her close, kissing her salty cheek and giving her a smile he hoped would show her that her solitary hardship was over. That, even when she was in the States while he worked elsewhere, she would never be truly alone.

He looked at Drew, whose head was tipped to one side, his big brown eyes studying Chase. "Your mom told me you're the best boy in the whole world, and I'm incredibly lucky to be your dad. I'm really happy to get to spend time with you now."

Drew looked at his mother then jumped off the rock to start banging the stick on it again. "I thought maybe Mr. Matt was gonna be my daddy."

Mr. Matt? Chase stiffened and his arm dropped from Dani's shoulder. Was Dani involved with someone? His brain froze. Why hadn't he even thought to wonder? Or ask?

A short, uncomfortable laugh left Dani's lips. "Mr. Matt is just a friend. Dr. Chase is your daddy, and I think he'd like it if you called him that."

"Yes, I'd like that, Drew." He only half heard himself speak. What the hell was he going to do if Dani was in love with someone else? A strange sensation gripped his heart that was panic and anger combined. They had a son together, and she belonged to him. It would be over Chase's dead body if another man tried to claim her. Tried to make decisions that affected Drew. That affected where his son lived and who he lived with.

"'K." Drew smiled then shrieked. "A lizard! Look!"

The boy ran, chasing a tiny lizard through and around the rocks, and Chase turned to Dani, trying to speak past the tightness gripping his throat and squeezing his chest.

"What the hell? Do you have a boyfriend?"

"What do you mean, 'What the hell?'" Dani said, frowning. "You act like you and I were still together. In case you've forgotten, we'd both moved on with our lives until yesterday."

The primitive possessiveness that roared through his blood shocked him in its intensity. "You can tell this Mr. Matt to get lost. That you're getting married."

She looked at him like she thought he was crazy. Which was fine, because he suddenly felt a little crazy. She made him crazy.

"I'm pretty sure I already told you I'm not marrying you. Can't you just stop with the full court press and get to know Drew? Like I said, we'll work out a solution where you can spend time with him each year."

"Are you—?" Chase realized he was practically shouting and lowered his voice. "Are you in love with this guy?"

"My feelings for Matt are irrelevant. What is relevant is figuring out how to make sure Drew knows he's important to you. That he's not just some in-the-way, annoying afterthought in your life."

He grasped her shoulders in his hands and pulled her close. "You know, I'm getting damned tired of you implying I'm going to be a deadbeat, rotten, selfish father. I've known Drew barely one day, but if you don't think I'd throw myself in front of a truck for him, you don't know me at all."

She drew a deep breath, and stared at him searchingly as she slowly released it. "Okay. I'm sorry. Let's… let's just enjoy the day with Drew. We'll figure out the rest later."

Jealousy and frustration wouldn't let him agree. He glanced over at Drew to see him occupied, enthusiastically poking his stick into a crack in a rock. "Is this Matt guy the reason you won't agree to marry me?"

"No. I won't marry you for all the reasons I've already said. I believe two people should get married because they want to live together and be together and love one another. Not so you can call the shots or because it's a logical course of action."

There was damned well nothing logical about the way he was feeling. Nothing very mature or sophisticated either. He wanted to throw her over his shoulder and make her his right then and there. Then he wanted to find this Matt guy and punch him in the face. But since he couldn't do either of those things, he settled for the one thing he could do.

He pulled her tightly against him and kissed her. Without finesse. Without thoughts of reminding her what they'd had three years ago. He kissed her with the anger and fear and uncertainty that pummeled his heart. He kissed her with the release of a deep and pent-up hunger for her he hadn't even realized was there until she'd come back into his life.

Her palms pushed against his chest and she pulled her mouth from his. She stared at him, both confusion and desire swimming in her eyes. The memories of past kisses, of yesterday and of three years ago, crackled between them. Her breath mingled with his. Her clean, sweet scent enveloped him. And there was no way he could keep from taking her mouth with his again.

This time her palms swept up his chest, her cool fingers slid across his nape. A low moan sounded deep in her throat, and he tasted the same wild desire on her tongue that surged through every nerve in his body. He cupped the back of her head, tangling his fingers in her thick hair, wanting to release her ponytail and feel those crazy curls slide across his skin.

The anger, the jealousy that had shoved him headlong into the kiss faded. Replaced by the warm and heady craving that had always burned between them. The taste of her, filled with a soul-deep passion and the promise of intimate pleasures only she could give.

He let his hand wander, cupping her bottom and pressing her against him. Her heat sent his thigh nudging between her legs and he felt her respond by rubbing against him, a sweet murmur of pleasure vibrating from her lips to his.

"Mommy! I catched the lizard! I catched it!"

They pulled apart, and he was sure he wore the same shocked and slightly horrified expression she did. Both their chests were heaving with rapid breaths, and she lifted shaking fingers to her lips as she turned towards Drew.

Damn. Chase scrubbed his hand across his face.

He'd like to think he would have remembered Drew was there. That he wouldn't have put his hand up her shirt or down her pants or any of the many things he'd been about to do. But he had to grimly admit that he'd been so far gone, he just might have done any and all of it anyway.

He'd have to be more careful. Remember there were three of them now, not just him and Dani. Of course, she'd goaded him into it with the whole thing about her refusal to marry him. Her damned boyfriend.

But with that thought came a smile of grim satisfaction. If Dani thought she was in love with this Matt guy, the spontaneous combustion they'd just shared had surely proved her wrong. The way it had always been between them, from the very first weeks they'd met.

"Chase!"

Dani's slightly panicky voice had him quickly heading to her and Drew.

"Chase, are you sure these things don't bite? I think you should drop it, Drew. Now."

"No. It mine." The boy's chin jutted mulishly. "Daddy said we could catch some."

Daddy. To hear Drew call him that in such a natural way, like they hadn't met just yesterday, was inconceivable yet wonderful, and the tight band constricting his chest eased slightly.

The boy's stubby little fingers grasped the tail of a lizard no bigger than a mouse as it writhed to get loose. He had to chuckle at the triumph on Drew's face and the distaste on Dani's.

"A master lizard-catcher. Like father, like son." Yeah, the boy was a true Bowen. If only his brother was here to share the moment.

The thought brought his enjoyment down a notch, at the same time reinforcing exactly why he was adamant that Drew grow up in the U.S. He reached for the wooden box he'd found at the compound. "Here, Drew, I brought this to put it in. We can only keep it for a day then we'll let it go so it stays healthy. Okay?"

"Okay." Drew dropped it into the box, a huge grin on his face. "I a good lizard-hunter, aren't I?"

"The best." Chase's heart filled with something powerful and unfamiliar as he looked at the boy's adorable little face, lit with the kind of joy unique to children. Drew's smile was blinding. The boy might look like him, but that beautiful smile was all Dani.

He lifted his gaze to Dani's and their eyes locked in a wordless connection. So many emotions flickered in her eyes. Wariness, apprehension, anxiety. Warring with the remnants of their intoxicating kiss. His gaze dropped to her full lips, still moist, and it was all he could do not to grab her and start what they hadn't been able to finish.

He forced himself to step back and give her the breathing room, the time she'd asked for. Waiting wasn't one of the things he was best at, but he'd try. With maybe just a little nudge to shorten the wait.

"So, is there any chance you and Dad can make it down here?" Finally, his mother had returned his call. Chase had begun to wonder if something was wrong, or if they'd left Senegal and hadn't told him, with sketchy cell service somewhere remote.

"We'd love to see you, honey. It so happens we have a few days off," his mother's voice said in his ear. "But it's usually me trying to get us together, not you. Anything going on?"

"Actually, yes." He paced in his room, still undecided whether he should tell them about Drew over the phone or just let them meet him.

"Well? Are you going to tell me or keep me in suspense?"

He wasn't sure exactly what to say but decided he should just let them know so they'd be prepared. "I want you to meet your grandson. Andrew. He's two and a half and cute as can be."

There was a long silence, and Chase could just picture his mother's stunned expression. Probably similar to his when he'd first seen the boy who looked exactly like him and his brother.

"Are you there?" he asked.

"Yes. It's just that I thought you said I have a grandson. A grandson?"

Her voice rose in pitch, and Chase was pretty sure it was with excitement. Of course she'd be excited. Both his parents loved children and knew he'd always said he'd never have kids. Most likely, this was a dream-come-true for her.

"Yes. I just found out… It's kind of a long story. But Drew's mother is here with me, and we're getting married soon." True, she hadn't yet agreed to that. But if he had to move mountains, she would. And having his parents come was another step towards convincing her. They'd love Dani and Drew, and she'd love them, too. It would give her a chance to see how good they'd be as a family.

"Oh, Chase, I can't believe it!" His mother laughed, and obviously pulled her mouth from the phone as she spoke to his dad. "Phil! Phil, we have a grandson! Get on the internet and book a flight to Benin right now."

Chase grinned. He'd had a feeling his mom would drop everything to meet Drew.

"Let me know when you're going to get here, and I'll try to pick you up from the airport. Or Spud will, if I can't get away."

"Okay. Oh, goodness, I can't wait to get there. I'm off to pack. Bye."

She hung up without even waiting for a response, and the disturbing feelings he'd had ever since he'd heard about this Matt character eased a little. Not only would his mom and dad embrace his son and hopefully soon-to-be wife, he'd recruit them to emphasize to Dani how important it was to keep Drew in the U.S. until he was older. Maybe she'd listen to two experienced mission doctors who happened to be Drew's grandparents in a way she wasn't currently listening to him.

The little nudge named Evelyn Bowen was on her way.

CHAPTER FIVE

WITH CHASE MYSTERIOUSLY gone somewhere, Dani sat in the empty clinic room and tried to focus on the sketchy and incomplete care and immunization records. She was working to get them organized and into the laptop computer she'd brought from the States—fairly unsuccessfully, since she kept wondering where Chase had gone. Kept thinking about the charm he'd been intent on oozing nonstop since yesterday when they'd told Drew that Chase was his daddy.

Kept reliving the feel of his stolen kisses against her cheek or the side of her neck whenever they were together, his fingertips sliding across the skin of her arms. How had she not known her arms were an erogenous zone?

They probably weren't, unless it was Chase touching her. She couldn't help but respond to his teasing caress, the curve of his lips, the sensual promise in the chocolaty depths of his eyes.

She huffed out a frustrated breath. Why, oh, why did she have such a hard time steeling herself against the man's sexual energy and tempting persuasion?

She'd been relieved at how easily Drew had accepted that Chase was his daddy. But, of course, she'd known he was so young he wouldn't have many questions about it. She'd hoped they could tell Drew then ease into a new relationship as two parents living separate lives, with the best interests of their child the only personal connection between them.

But what happened instead? She'd fallen into his embrace, into his kiss, with barely one second of resistance. Her cheeks burned with embarrassment. Especially because his kiss certainly hadn't been full of tenderness. It had been full of anger and possessiveness, no doubt because Drew had mentioned Matt and a competitive man like Chase wouldn't just shrug at something like that.

No, she had a feeling that had just added more fuel to the hot fire already burning within Chase about the two of them getting married.

Matt was the first man she'd dated since Chase, since leaving Honduras to go back to the States to work and start a new life there with Drew. Having a man in her life hadn't been on her to-do list. But Matt had seemed so easygoing, so harmless, really, that she'd finally given in to going out with him a few times the month before she'd left for Benin. He'd been happy to include Drew in several excursions and had been pleasant to spend time with.

Kissing him had been pleasant, too. Pleasant, but not knee-weakening. Not breathtaking. Not so mesmerizing that she'd forget everything except how his mouth tasted and her heart pounded and how much she wanted to get naked and intimate the way she had when Chase had kissed her. So all-consuming that she'd lost all thought about anything but the way he'd made her feel.

And that was bad. In so many ways. More than bad

that she hadn't spared one thought about Drew seeing them devouring one another and rubbing their bodies together. Her face burned all over again at the thought, even though Drew was too young to think much of it, even if he'd noticed.

It was bad because she had to keep her focus. She had to resist the intense, overpowering attraction she'd felt for Chase since practically the first moment she'd met him and which clearly hadn't gone away with time and distance.

As she'd told him before, great sex wasn't a reason to get married. Neither was a feeling of obligation on Chase's part. Or a need to control their lives. If she ever did marry, she wanted it to be because her husband loved her more than anything. Wanted to be with her more than anything. Believed she was every bit as important to him as his work.

And that obviously just wasn't true with Chase.

Love had nothing to do with him wanting marriage, and she shoved away the deep stab of pain that knowledge caused. His reasoning that she and Drew should stay in the States while he lived his life the way he always had, or close to it, just wasn't enough. Not for her and not for Drew.

Working with underprivileged people around the world was important to her, especially after she'd seen all the need in Honduras. She had her career plan all worked out, where she'd be employed in the U.S. for two years, spend nine months abroad, then head back to the States for two more years. And giving Drew exposure to other cultures couldn't be anything but good for him.

Not to mention that, if Chase was still going to live all over the world, it made no sense to get married and pretend they were a family the years they lived in the U.S. Didn't he see that Drew would always know he wasn't as important to his dad as his job? But if they weren't married, Drew would accept that his parents were no longer together, and would understand why his dad lived somewhere else.

She believed Chase when he said he wanted to be part of Drew's life. It would probably work out okay if he saw Drew several times a year for a few weeks each time. After all, they lived in a global world now. With phone calls and video chats online, being close to one another shouldn't be too hard.

What a tangled mess. But she was here to do a job, not think endlessly about the problems. She stared at the scribbled index cards, and wondered why some of the previous doctors and nurses had even bothered to record the unreadable notes.

"Dani, are you in here?"

"Yes." She absolutely wouldn't ask Chase where he'd gone. For all she knew, he'd been seeing a woman. And it was none of her business.

Chase strode into the room, looking so good in jeans and a pale yellow polo shirt that showed off his tanned skin and dark hair and eyes that she caught herself staring. She pulled her gaze back to the cards, typing what she could into the computer.

"Making progress?" he asked, leaning over her to look at her work, resting his palm between her shoulder blades.

"Not much. I can't even read most of them. We're just going to have to start with new records of children as we see them." She stared fixedly at her work. "I'd like to talk with you about ways we can get parents to bring their kids in for checks."

"It's not easy. A lot of folks don't have transportation, so they only come when there's a serious problem. Some believe Vodun will keep their children from getting sick."

"Vodun?"

"Voodoo. The word translates as 'spirit.'" His hand slid up her back to cup the back of her neck, his breath whispering across her cheek. "We'll talk about all that when we go into the field soon to do immunizations in various villages."

His mouth dropped to caress the skin beneath her earlobe, which sent a delicious shiver across her throat until she jerked her head away.

"You know, back home that would be considered sexual harassment. Don't make me contact the GPC to lodge a complaint."

"You think a tiny kiss is sexual harassment?" His low laugh vibrated against her skin. "I can think of lots more ways to harass you sexually. If you ask nicely."

"You're ridiculous." She shook her head, feeling slightly dizzy. She should be annoyed, but instead had to desperately will herself to be tough and strong against the seductive temptation of his lips. "In case you haven't noticed, I'm trying to work here. Leave me alone. Seriously."

To her surprise and relief, he straightened and his warm hand left her nape. "Take a break from that for a minute. Ruth and Drew need you to come outside."

"Why?" She swiveled to look at him. He had an odd expression on his face, slightly amused and clearly anticipatory. Obviously nothing was wrong and her curiosity was piqued, in spite of herself.

"You'll see. Come on."

He grasped her hand and she rose from the chair, tugging her hand from his as she followed him out the clinic doors.

As they approached the small enclosure that served as a playground for patients' children and siblings, she could see Drew scooting around on a plastic ride-on toy train that hadn't been there earlier, a wide grin on his face. And two people standing next to him with equally ecstatic expressions.

Who...?

"Toot-toot! Toot-toot!" Drew exclaimed, scuffing his shoes in the dirt as he rode.

Chase put his arm across Dani's shoulders before they stepped inside the gate of the wooden fence. "Mom and Dad, I'd like you to meet Dr. Danielle Sheridan. Dani, my parents, Drs. Philip and Evelyn Bowen."

His parents. Drew's grandparents. Stunned, Dani smiled and reached to shake Chase's father's hand. "It's nice to meet you." Nice and shocking. They just popped in for a quick trip to Benin to meet Drew?

About to shake Evelyn's hand, the woman gave her a warm embrace instead. "It's so delightful to meet you, dear. And our Andrew is so adorable. Precious! I can't believe how he looks just like Chase did at that age. You have no idea how happy you've made us."

Our Andrew. The words put a funny little flutter of joy in Dani's chest. She had to smile at the lovely woman's greeting and obvious sincerity. How wonderful that Andrew had grandparents who would clearly want to be a part of his life. Her own mother lived pretty far from where Dani had gotten a job and, as a nurse, worked a lot of hours. Not the kind of grandmother who would be baking cookies and babysitting.

Then again, neither were the Drs. Bowen, working in mission hospitals around the world. Nonetheless, it was nice.

"I'm…surprised you're here," Dani said, giving Chase a look he couldn't misinterpret. He responded with a grin that showed no guilty feelings at all about his subterfuge. "Where do you live?"

"We're working in Senegal right now. Benin's a pretty quick airplane ride from there, really." The woman clasped her hands together, her eyes sparkling. "When Chase told us about Drew and you, we were over the moon. We brought the little train and a few other gifts. I hope that's okay?"

"Of course." Dani smiled. "But I can't tell if he likes it or not, can you?"

They all chuckled, as it was more than obvious he loved it. Scooting around, toot-tooting endlessly and grinning.

"They'd barely taken it from the box before he jumped on it," Chase said as he watched Drew, his gaze soft with a hint of pride. "He's going to be riding a bike in no time."

"We're happy he likes it," Phil said. "I'm especially pleased because if he didn't, I have a feeling Evelyn and I would be heading straight to another store to look for something else, even if we had to fly to Cotonou. I kept having to remind her we were bringing everything on a plane, she had so much stuff."

"It's a grandparents' prerogative to buy their grandchildren presents," Evelyn said, an indulgent smile on her face as she watched Drew. "Especially the very first one."

First one? She couldn't know Chase's attitude about having children if she thought there would ever be more.

That thought led Dani in a nasty and very uncomfortable direction it hadn't gone before, making her stiffen. What if Chase did marry someday? What kind of woman would be stepmother to Drew? Just thinking about it made her stomach twist. She reminded herself he'd be working in remote places around the world, so Drew wouldn't be around a stepmother much anyway, but didn't succeed in ridding herself of a slightly sick feeling in her gut.

Evelyn turned her attention to Dani. "I hear there's to be a wedding soon. Have you decided on a date?"

What? One look at Chase proved he really had told his parents they were getting married. How arrogant could the man be? He had an infuriatingly smug smile on his face, and an expression that said he couldn't wait to see how she'd react to his mother's question.

"A wedding? I hadn't heard about one. Is it someone I know?" She kept her voice light, her expression bland, but knew Chase could see the challenge in her gaze. So he thought this was one big chess game? He'd forgotten she'd learned to play from him.

His parents looked at one another then at Chase, obviously confused. "Chase said—"

"I said we were getting married. I didn't say Dani had agreed yet," Chase said smoothly, with a look that said, *Answer that.* "But wouldn't it be great to make it happen some time when you could be here to share it with us? Please help me convince her how nice it would be to celebrate our marriage as a family."

Damn the man. He'd certainly played his turn well, with both his parents staring at her with bemused expressions.

"Chase and I just recently met up again," she said, trying to figure out exactly what to say. It was a battle to keep from narrowing her eyes and scowling at Chase for putting her in such an awkward position. Though she was pretty sure that, even if they didn't know the details of her relationship with Chase, his parents knew how babies were made. "I don't feel we know each other well enough again to consider something as important as marriage."

Both his parents looked back at Chase, and Dani felt a slightly hysterical desire to laugh, thinking they looked like they were watching a tennis match.

"All I want is for the three of us to be a family, and I'm sure you'd agree that's the best thing for Drew. But Dani's being difficult." Chase rocked back on his heels, his hands in his jeans pockets. "It's hard to believe, because any woman would be lucky to put my ring on her finger, right, Mom?"

That smile continued to play about his lips. He'd always been good at that delicate combination of joking humor while making a very serious point.

Dani looked at Evelyn, figuring that, as his mother, she doubtless agreed he was an awesome catch for any woman.

"Dr. Bowen, I..." Dani began, not even sure what she was going to say.

"Please, call me Evelyn." She reached to squeeze Dani's arm. "Pay no attention to Chase's heavy-handed attempts at manipulation. I'm surprised, really, at his clumsiness. From the time he was little, he could get whatever he wanted without anyone even knowing he was leading them there."

Astonished at his mother's words, Dani was also more than amused at the surprised and outraged expression on Chase's face.

"What the hell?" He folded his arms across his chest. "You don't think Dani should marry me? What about Drew? What about us being a family?"

"Don't drag your father and me into this." His mother held up her hand. "Obviously, there's some reason you didn't even know about Drew until now. While we'd love to welcome Dani as our daughter-in-law, you two will have to figure all this out on your own. As long as I get to play doting grandmother to our darling baby, I'm happy."

Phil chuckled. "And I have a feeling that 'doting' will be an understatement."

Evelyn grasped Phil's hand and they walked over to stand on either side of Drew, forming a bridge with their arms. "Drive through the tunnel, engineer Andrew. But watch out, there might be a landslide and it could collapse on you," Phil said.

Drew shrieked in delight as he drove around their legs and through the "tunnel," ending up trapped as their arms surrounded him.

As she watched them, Dani's heart filled with how lovely Chase's parents were and how lucky Drew was that they wanted to be a part of his life, even though their time together would doubtless be infrequent.

"I can't believe this," Chase said.

She looked at his disgusted scowl and knew he wasn't talking about his parents' game with Drew. "Is this finally the proof you need that you should get over the unpleasant controlling streak you have? Even your mother thinks so."

"She didn't say I'm controlling. And I'm not."

He stepped close and she was glad his parents were here. Surely Chase wouldn't touch her and kiss her and make her feel all weak and out of control while they were around.

"But convincing?" His mouth came close to her ear, and he smelled so good, like fresh soap and aftershave and him, that it was all she could do not to turn her head for a kiss anyway. "Convincing you will be a pleasure."

He backed off a few inches, and the promise in his dark eyes told her resistance would be tough going. But she could do it. She *would* do it. To protect Drew and to protect her own heart.

"Lunch, everybody!" Spud bellowed from the door.

Drew jumped off the plastic train, knocking it over onto its side, and ran to Dani. He flung one arm around Dani's leg and wrapped the other around Chase's. "I hungry! Daddy, will you feed me more bugs?"

"You bet. I've got some big, fat ones picked out just for you." Chase lifted his gaze to Dani. His eyes turned from soft and smiling to hard and cool in an instant. "Drew, at least, knows we're already connected, no matter what you want to believe." He reached down to lift Drew into his arms, kissing his round cheek before settling the child against his shoulder like he'd been doing it fo rever.

The image of father and son, of their brown eyes and thick dark hair so like the other, along with the tender expressions on his parents' faces, gave Dani another pang of guilt. But she reminded herself she hadn't really robbed all of them of two and a half years of togetherness. Chase and his parents would have been living who knew where in the world without her and Drew anyway.

"Whatever Spud made, it'll be good," Chase said, his head tipped against Drew's for a moment before he looked at his parents. "Then we'll make a plan for the rest of your visit with your grandson."

CHAPTER SIX

"To think you've always hassled me about my smooth moves when you're the true master," Trent said as he and Chase pulled off their gloves and gowns after surgery and headed toward the hospital corridor.

"What smooth moves?"

"Getting your parents to come and gush over Drew and put the pressure on Dani. Brilliant." Trent grinned. "Except, of course, that my moves work and yours are a pathetic failure."

"Glad you think it's funny," Chase said, still stunned at his parents' reaction to Dani not wanting to marry him. He'd been so sure his mother would have seemed, at the very least, disappointed. And with Dani's eyes looking so soft and tender as she'd watched them with Drew, he had been positive a little pressure from them would have been a big help toward his goal.

"I still can't believe they didn't back me up. Even threw me under the bus completely when they said it was between the two of us and didn't care whether we got married or not."

"I never thought I'd hear you say you wished you had more interference from outside forces in your life." Trent chuckled. "Seems to me you always complain when any-body at GPC sticks their nose in your business."

"Interference wasn't what I had in mind. Coercion was what I had in mind. Helping Dani see what's ob-viously the best solution here." No, the interference he was worried about might come in the form of a jerk named Matt he didn't even know. Except the guy was halfway across the world, while he had Dani with him, and there was some old saying about possession being nine-tenths of the law. He planned to take full advan-tage of it.

"You have no clue about women," Trent said, shak-ing his head. "The harder you push, the faster she'll run. Show her what a great dad you'll be to Drew and give her time."

"There might not be much time. Who knows how soon you and I'll be relocated?"

"True. But you've got to relax a little instead of bug-ging her to death. Let her remember why you two were together in the first place. Lord knows, I can't figure out why, but a lot of women do like you."

"I'm just trying to remind her what we had before." Seemed to have worked, for a moment at least, both times he'd kissed her. Just thinking of the feel of her mouth on his, her sweet body pressed close, made his body start to react all over again.

"Then lay off and play hard to get. I guarantee she'll start thinking of your old times in Honduras and come back for more. Women are perverse like that."

"I'm beginning to see why your relationships with women last a nanosecond." Part of Chase wanted to laugh, but Trent's words did make him pause. Could giving Dani a day or two to take the lead be the answer to speeding things up? Just the thought of heading to his next job without his ring on her finger filled him with cold anxiety. Especially with "Mr. Matt" waiting in the wings, four thousand miles away or not.

"Trust me. She won't be able to figure out why you're suddenly not touching her and annoying her all the time. It'll drive her crazy and she'll want to jump your bones. Then she'll say yes, and you can get married." He slapped Chase's shoulder and grinned. "We'll get three weeks off before we start our new jobs. Plenty of time for a honeymoon. I bet your parents would love to have Drew stay with them up in Senegal while you and Dani go somewhere alone. You'd better start deciding where."

The thought of a week or two alone with Dani shortened Chase's breath and sent his thoughts down the erotic path they persisted in going. Not good, because he and Trent had just entered the hospital to do rounds on patients.

A halo of curly blonde hair immediately caught his attention. Dani moved her stethoscope here and there on a child's chest, and while he couldn't really see her expression, he knew it would be intent and focused.

As though she could feel him looking at her, heart-stopping blue eyes lifted to him, and for a moment they stared at one another across the room. She seemed so far away and yet not, as though they were touching one another, breathing one another's breaths, sharing one another's thoughts, despite the expanse between them.

Trent leaned closer and in an undertone said, "Yeah, she's crazy about you. Take my advice, and I'll call the preacher." With an unholy grin he headed towards one of his patients.

Chase inhaled a deep, mind-clearing breath. Why not give Trent's method a try? What he'd been doing the past few days hadn't seemed to convince her, that was for damned sure.

He joined Dani as she checked on her patient to find out what she thought of the child's condition. She smiled at the boy before turning to Chase. "His lungs seem to be clear today. I think it's fine for him to go home tomorrow. Will you tell him?"

The boy grinned at the good news and pumped his arms in the air victoriously. Dani joined him, smiling brightly, mirroring his fists pumps with her own as she exclaimed, "Yahoo!"

The boy laughed, and Chase marveled at her cheerful exuberance. From the very first moment he'd met her he'd noticed that whenever she walked into a room, worries cleared, people smiled, and the rise in energy seemed palpable. His own energy included.

He turned to Dani. "I'm about to check on Apollo. Want to join me?"

Her beautiful eyes smiled at him. "Yes. I was waiting for you."

He liked the sound of that. More than liked it, and wished it was true in more ways than for work. Like in her room at night. In her life, for ever.

It was all he could do not to clasp her face between his palms and give her a soft kiss. He turned away and walked toward Apollo's bed.

The boy's mother had gone somewhere for the moment, with the blankets she used as she slept on the floor carefully folded and stacked. Apollo looked uncomfortable with the apparatus holding his leg in traction to keep the bones aligned, and his expression reflected his misery. He touched the child's forehead with the backs of his fingers, and it felt thankfully cool. No fever was a good sign.

"Does your leg hurt?" he asked. They'd kept him on painkillers, but sometimes it just wasn't enough. "Is the traction rubbing against you anywhere?"

The child shook his head then turned his attention to Dani as she stopped at the other side of the bed. And who could blame him for wanting to look at her? He himself could look at her all day and night, and never tire of her sweet face and vivacious smile.

"The nurses tell me he's eating and drinking okay, so that's good," Dani said to Chase. She examined the stitches in Apollo's forehead closely, then put her stethoscope in her ears and pressed the bell of it to his chest.

Chase studied the pin he'd placed in the bone as it protruded from the boy's skin. Thank God it wasn't bleeding and didn't show signs of infection. The boy was lucky. "Your leg looks good. Pretty soon we'll change the cast to cover your whole leg, okay?"

Apollo nodded, still looking miserable, poor kid. Chase wished he could hurry the process, but controlling the pain was the best he could do for now.

"Vous avez...un coeur...très fort," Dani said haltingly to Apollo.

Chase had to grin at her accent, which was pretty bad, but he gave her credit for trying. "She's right," he said in Fon, in case the boy wasn't adept at French. "You do have a very strong heart. And your leg will be strong again, too. I promise."

"You'll be getting better every day, and that should make you smile." Dani placed her fingers gently on the corners of Apollo's mouth and tipped them up, and he gave her a small, real smile in response. "Maybe we need to find a way to help you remember that smiling and laughing will make you heal even faster."

She picked up the homemade fly swatter fan, composed of a dowel rod with cardboard taped to it. She pulled a marker from her pocket and drew a smiley face on it before turning it to fan Apollo.

"Don't worry, be happy," she began to sing in her sweet voice. And then, in typical Dani style, she began cutely bobbing from side to side, smiling her dazzling smile.

"Don't worry, be happy." She waved the smiley-face fan and twirled around. Between singing, she coaxed, "Come on, sing with me! Don't worry, be happy."

The child attempted a feeble version of the song then laughed for the first time that day, looking starstruck.

Probably the same expression he wore when he was around her, Chase thought. He watched her slim figure dance around, looked at the sparkling blue of her eyes, and thought about the moment he'd first met her. How she'd stopped him in his tracks for a second look. And a third. Gorgeous and adorable didn't begin to cover the impact she made on everyone the second she walked in a room with that blinding smile.

At that moment Apollo's mother arrived, and beamed at Dani and her dancing and singing. Chase reassured her on the boy's progress, and Apollo turned to his mother, looking much more cheerful than when they'd first examined him. The child spoke to her in Fon, and she smiled and nodded, looking warmly at Dani and thanking her.

"What did he say?" Dani asked.

"He says he likes the pretty doctor. But that's no

surprise." He wanted to say how much he liked the pretty doctor too, but remembered he was supposed to be playing hard to get. Though that seemed kind of stupid, like he was in middle school. But he was going to give it a try, damn it.

Dani turned a bit pink. "Tell him I like him too. And that I'm glad he's starting to feel better."

After Chase did as she asked, she handed the fan to Apollo, patted his shoulder and moved to their next patient. Chase followed and focused on being all business. Just a colleague, not her former lover. Not the man who wanted to marry her and become her current lover as soon as possible. When they finished rounds, they headed back to the housing compound.

"Is it okay with you if I spend some time with Drew and my parents before we hand him back to you tonight?"

She looked surprised. "I... Sure. You don't want me there, too?"

He shrugged nonchalantly, proud of his acting skills. Yes, he wanted her there but, no, he wouldn't show it. "I just figured you'd like some time to yourself for a change. We'll play with him for a while then bring him in for dinner. Sound okay?"

"Sure," she said again, a slight frown on her face.

Cautious optimism bloomed at the confusion on her face as she clearly wondered why he wasn't touching and teasing her as he had been before. Damn it, maybe he *had* let his worry and frustration push him to come on too strongly.

Maybe Trent's idea was a good one after all.

CHAPTER SEVEN

"Got everything?" Chase asked.

"I think so." Mentally, she reviewed her supply list as she looked inside her backpack. Vaccines, syringes, antibiotics, blood-sugar monitor. "Did you say there's a blood-pressure cuff already there?"

"Yeah. We keep a lockbox in the building with various things in it. Otoscope, flashlight, and a small pharmacy for drugs that don't need to be refrigerated." He threw the strap of his battered doctor's bag over his shoulder, lifted up a small box that held more of the supplies Dani carried in her backpack and headed out the door of the clinic.

She followed, refusing to notice his flexing triceps and wide, strong shoulders beneath the white polo shirt he wore. The sky was an iron gray but even without the scorching sun the air rested hot and heavy against her skin.

"You don't think it will be too much for your parents to watch Drew all day? Maybe Ruth should come give them a break."

"Are you kidding?" Chase rolled a dusty motorcycle from beneath an overhang. "They were practically rubbing their hands together with glee at the prospect of having him to themselves."

"All right, then, I won't worry. Though you already know that when he's on the go, he's like a rubber-band-powered balsa-wood plane. He keeps going until he conks out."

"Yeah. He's a lot of fun."

The indulgent smile on his face was filled with pride. Why had he been so adamant he didn't want children? It was so obvious he already adored their little boy.

"I'm sorry about having to ride the motorcycle," Chase said. He slipped the box into a bigger container attached to the bike. "I usually go alone, and didn't think to talk to Spud about the car. Didn't know he needed to get supplies today."

"In case you don't remember, we rode all over Honduras on a bike like this." As soon as she'd said it, she wished she hadn't. Memories of Honduras weren't something she wanted to think about. Memories of her body pressed against his as they'd ridden to an off-site clinic like they were today, or when they'd had a day off to spend together and find a great hiking spot. A great lovemaking spot.

Dani shook her head to dispel the thoughts. It should be easy to forget how close they'd been back then. For some reason Chase had stopped the constant touching and teasing and tiny stolen kisses he'd been assailing her with. Surely he didn't really think she'd report him for sexual harassment?

Chase swung his leg over the bike's seat and curled his fingers around the handlebar grips, turning to look at her. "This village is only about a half-hour ride. But I warn you," he said, his teeth showing white in his smile, "the road can be rough at times. So hang on tight."

"Got it." Sitting on the back of the bike, she slipped her arms around him, her fingers curling into his taut middle.

"Ready?"

"Ready." Actually, she wasn't ready at all. Not ready for the feel of her breasts pressed against his hard body. The sensual feel of her groin pressed against his backside. The clean, masculine scent of his neck filling her nostrils.

He opened the throttle and the motorcycle took off down the dirt road. Soon there was nothing visible but groves of trees here and there and lining the bumpy road, the occasional car or truck passing them, and scooters and motorcycles often carrying as many as four and even five people. Bumps in the hard earth jammed her body against Chase and she threaded her fingers together against his sternum to keep from bouncing right off.

"You okay?" Chase shouted over the engine, glancing over his shoulder at her.

"Yes." Except for that urge she kept feeling to slip her hands beneath his shirt to feel the smooth skin she knew was right there, like she'd used to. The urge to touch more private parts as she had in Honduras when they'd been riding together, making Chase laugh and accuse her of trying to make him crash the bike. Then quickly finding the best place to enjoy finishing what she'd started.

Her own body part that she currently had pressed hard against Chase's rear began to tingle at the memories and she wished she could loosen her grip on Chase's middle to smack herself.

She had to stop thinking about their past and focus on the future. On her job. She was here to work and now to establish the framework they'd agree on regarding Drew. A second broken heart over Chase she didn't need, and the future he envisioned for them would mean exactly that.

Finally, the wide and desolate savannah showed signs of habitation. Small rectangular structures made of mud-baked walls, some with thatched roofs and others covered with corrugated steel, were scattered here and there. Happy, smiling children, many naked or wearing only colorful bottoms and beaded jewelry, played in the dirt or worked with their mothers, hanging laundry or grinding some kind of food in large vessels. A group of men and boys, their hands covered in wet, orange mud, were building a new house. As she and Chase rode by, the men waved and shouted, grinning with pride at their work.

Chase stopped the bike next to a small, worn, cinder-block building with an open doorway and windows. When he turned off the engine, the sudden silence was a relief, with the sound of the breeze in the trees and children laughing the only things to be heard.

Dani slipped off the bike and Chase followed. "Did GPC have this place built for a clinic?" she asked.

"No. I'm told some other group built it to be a school but had to abandon the project. We use it on the first of each month so folks who aren't from this village will know when we're coming, too."

An odd stack of stones and other things atop what looked like a mud sculpture caught her eye. Nestled beneath a nearby tree, there were chains and beaded necklaces looped around the entire thing. "What's that?" she asked, pointing.

"A fetish. It's like a talisman. Voodoo to keep away bad spirits."

"Really?" She walked closer to examine it. "Does all this stuff have a special meaning?"

"I don't know about that one in particular, but it's animism. Belief that everyday objects have souls that will help and protect you."

"Do their beliefs make it hard to get people to come to the clinic, if they think the voodoo will keep them healthy and safe?"

"Sometimes. Like anywhere, it depends on the person." Chase pulled the supply box from the motorcycle and stepped towards the door. "About two hundred people live in this village, and we get quite a few from elsewhere. I think they appreciate knowing we'll be here, and rely on modern medicine more than they used to because of it. Which makes it worthwhile to come."

Dani followed him into the little building, the darkness taking a minute to get used to after the comparatively bright daylight. The single room was certainly sparsely furnished, with only a rickety-looking examination cot, a small table, and a few old chairs inside.

"So they don't use voodoo to treat illnesses?"

"They do. Sakpata is the Vodun god for illness and healing, and many call on him and offer sacrifices when someone is sick. Priests also use healing herbs." He organized the supplies on the little table. "Vodun is an official religion in Benin, and a lot of people who are Christian or Muslim still use voodoo elements in their lives, especially when somebody's sick."

"So are you going to have someone make a little doll of me and stick it with pins to make me marry you?" She meant it as a joke, but then had to ask herself why she'd brought up the subject of marriage when he hadn't mentioned it all day.

"Don't I wish there was some way to make you agree to marry me." His lips twisted into a rueful smile. "Unfortunately, the dolls and pins thing is mostly Hollywood. While there is some black magic, it's not a significant part of voodoo. It's really about belief in ancestry and calling on the spirits to help with their lives. Peace and prosperity."

"Well, shoot, that's too bad. I was just thinking about the list of people I might want dolls made of."

"Sorry. Except not really, because I'm probably on your list." Chase stepped over to the locked box and pulled out a stethoscope, blood-pressure cuff, and some drugs to bring back to the table. "You'd be amazed by some of the fetishes, though. Hippo's feet and pig genitalia and even dog and monkey heads." He grinned. "In bigger towns there are voodoo festivals worth seeing. Drew would probably like all the colorful clothes and dancing."

"I bet he would. Maybe we could find a day to go to one." She smiled then looked out the door. Nobody seemed to be heading their way. "So now what? Do you go round people up and bring them in?"

"Round them up?" He smacked his palm against his forehead. "Darn, I forgot my lasso."

"You know what I mean." She placed her hand on his thick shoulder and gave him a little shove. "Let them know we're here."

Her vision had become used to the low light, and

she could see the curve of his lips and the little crinkles in the corners of his eyes before he gave a low laugh.

"I'm sure they saw us." He reached out to tuck loose strands of her hair behind her ears, of which there were many after their ride. As he curled one strand around his finger, his smile faded, replaced by something in his gaze that sent her heart thumping. "No way they could miss the beautiful blonde as she rode into town."

His finger travelled down her jaw and she found herself standing motionless, staring into his eyes, holding her breath. His hand dropped to his side and he turned away to briskly finish organizing the supplies.

"As people arrive, you can take care of the children and I'll look at the adults. I'll translate when you need me to. I have the records for the kids we've immunized here since I've been in Benin."

The shift in his demeanor was startling. What had happened to the Chase of yesterday who doubtless would have taken advantage of them being alone and kissed her breathless? Or, at the very least, continued with the flirting he was so good at?

She'd been sure she didn't want that from him. But when he'd turned away, suddenly all business, the traitorous part of her that had been thinking about sex during their entire motorcycle ride wanted to grab him and kiss him instead. Wanted to feel that silky skin covering hard muscle she'd been itching to touch the whole time her arms had been wrapped around him.

She mentally thrashed herself and pulled her own supplies from the backpack. Apparently her libido, which had come to life since seeing him again, wasn't up on the fact that her sensible brain wanted to keep their relationship platonic.

As if by voodoo, the first patients suddenly appeared at the doorway and the next hours were filled with basic examinations and immunizations, distribution of drugs for various problems, medicine to rid children of intestinal worms—which were apparently common here, as they had been in Honduras—and topical or oral antibiotics for the occasional infected wound.

Communicating with the children and their parents was surprisingly easy, with hand gestures working pretty well and Chase translating over his shoulder for the rest.

After being concerned at first that they'd have few patients, Dani couldn't believe the line of children, standing three and four deep, waiting for their shots. After being so frustrated at the sorry state of the immunization records they had, she was more than pleased at how much she'd be able to add to the database after today.

What a great feeling to know that coming here could make such a difference in the health of these kids. More than once during the day she smiled at Chase and his return smile was filled with a sense of connection, the same understanding of exactly what each was feeling that they'd shared long ago.

By late in the afternoon the line had dwindled to just a few stragglers. The work left Dani feeling both tired and energized at their accomplishments.

"How long do you usually stay?" she asked Chase as she cleaned her hands with antiseptic and looked at the few people remaining outside. "Do you hang around until there's nobody waiting?"

"It depends. Obviously, at some point you just need to shut it down, especially when it gets dark early. Believe me, you don't want to be riding home on a motor-cycle after the sun sets. It's not common to be robbed, but it does happen." He grinned at her. "And the last time I rode on all those rough potholes without being able to see, I was more convinced I might not live an-other day than the time I walked across a frayed rope bridge over the Amazon in a windstorm."

Now, there was a image. Dani laughed. "Then let's be sure to wrap it up before then. We don't want to or-phan Drew."

The thought squashed her amusement. In her will she'd listed her own mother as guardian to Drew if any-thing ever happened to her. But her mother was alone, and tremendously busy. Now that Chase was involved in Drew's life, should they make other arrangements?

"You know, we should talk about that, unlikely as it is, as we figure out our future arrangements with re-gard to Drew," she said. "If something happened to me, I figured my mother should take him. But maybe your parents would be a better choice."

Chase's expression turned fierce. "No. That's not a good option. Nothing's going to happen to us."

"But we—"

Distraught shouting interrupted her thought as a man pushed his way through the few people standing in line and burst through the doorway.

CHAPTER EIGHT

CHASE STEPPED OVER to him, speaking in an authoritative yet calming voice that seemed to help the man get himself under control. Dani wished she knew what was going on, but it was clearly something that would need their attention. The man spoke fast with frantic gestures, and the frown and concern on Chase's face grew more pronounced.

Chase spoke to Dani as he shoved some items in his medical bag and flung the strap over his shoulder. "I need to go with him. He lives about half a mile away, so I'm going to take the bike to get there fast. I'll tell the last in line we'll come back next week so you can put stuff away and lock up the drugs as quickly as possible. Someone can show you where I am. You'll have to walk, but I think I might need you there."

"What's wrong?"

"His wife's in labor and something's not right. She's bleeding and in abnormal, extereme pain—the midwife doesn't know what to do. Assuming we have a live infant, your expertise may help."

He spoke quickly to a man in line, who nodded. "This man will show you where she is."

"Okay." She'd barely uttered the words before Chase

left with the worried husband, and the sound of the motorcycle engine came to her just moments later.

Dani quickly stashed the medical supplies and pharmaceuticals in the lock box then followed the man Chase had asked to guide her through the village.

A rusty bike leaned against the wall of the clinic building and to her surprise he gestured for her to get on it. While it would be great to get there faster than it would take to walk, it wouldn't help to ride it if she had no idea where she was going.

The man cleared up that question when he straddled the bike himself while still gesturing for her to get on the battered seat. Precariously perching herself on it, she placed her hands on the man's shoulders and he pedaled off.

At first their wobbling movement was so slow she ground her teeth in frustration. They'd never get there at this rate, and an increasingly disturbing feeling fluttered in her stomach that the situation just might be dire.

Thankfully, the guy seemed to get the hang of pedaling standing up with her weight behind him, as they picked up speed on the bumpy dirt path, passing a hodgepodge of straw huts and mud houses.

The sound of a woman's moans and cries made the skin over her skull tighten and the bike stopped outside a hut that seemed larger than several others nearby.

She jumped off the bike. "Chase?"

"In here."

She followed his grim voice and stopped just inside the doorway, stunned at the scene. The writhing and moaning woman in labor lay on a pad on the floor that had at one time been some yellowish color but was now stained red with the blood that was literally everywhere. All over the poor woman's lower body. The dirt floor. The midwife, crouched beside her and holding her hand. Chase.

"What's wrong?" Her heart tripped in her chest. "What can I do?"

"Placental abruption. You can see the pain she's in, and her abdomen is rock-hard." He finished swabbing the woman's belly with antiseptic wipes and drew some drug into a needle. "Got to do an emergency C-section. I'm about to give her a local anesthetic, which is the best I can do here. Then we've got to get that baby out."

She crouched next to him. "Tell me what to do."

"Get my knife out of my bag. The ball suction to clear the baby's mouth and nose. The ambu-bag. Then get ready, because when I pull the baby out I'm handing it to you and praying like hell."

She grabbed the bag and went through its contents to find what he needed. She snapped on a pair of gloves and grabbed some antiseptic wipes to clean the knife.

Chase injected the woman's stomach in multiple locations until there was nothing left in the syringe, then tossed it aside to take the knife from Dani.

"Are you going to do a low, transverse incision?" She had a feeling the usual C-section standard wouldn't apply here in this hut, with the poor woman likely bleeding to death.

"No. We'll be damned lucky if a vertical gets the baby out in time."

With a steady hand Chase made a single, smooth slice through the skin beginning at the woman's umbilicus down to her pelvis, exposing the hard, enlarged uterus within the cavity. Chase looked briefly at Dani, his jaw tense. "Ready?"

She nodded and prepared herself for fast action. Adrenaline surged through her veins as she knew the infant had probably lost its oxygen connection to its mother and would need immediate help to breathe on its own. If it was still alive.

Chase began the second incision through the uterus itself, exposing the infant. He reached into the womb and carefully lifted the baby out, using his fingers to wipe the baby boy's tiny face and body gently to remove the tangle of clotted-off blood vessels that had torn and lead to the abruption.

"Here." He passed the motionless baby to Dani and began scooping out the loosened placenta from the mother's uterus. "I've got to get her bleeding stopped or we'll lose her."

The infant was dark purple, his lips nearly black from lack of oxygen. Dani quickly used the bulb suction to clear the amniotic fluid, mucus, and black meconium from his mouth, nose, and throat, but he still didn't breathe.

Heart pounding, she attached the smallest mask to the ambu-bag then placed the mask over the baby's nose and mouth. She slowly and evenly squeezed the bulb, praying the air would inflate the baby's lungs.

After what seemed an eternity a shudder finally shook his tiny body. He coughed and drew in several gasping breaths before weakly crying out. His little arms and legs started jerking around and as his cries grew stronger, Dani sagged with relief.

She grabbed one of the stacked cloths the midwife must have put by the mother and quickly wiped the baby down. Getting him dryer and warmer was critical to keeping him from going into shock.

Satisfied that he was now warm enough, she grasped the umbilical cord and milked it gently, trying to get every drop of the cord blood into the baby's body. She then cut the cord and clamped it off.

Looking into the baby's little face, she saw he was no longer crying, his eyes wide as he saw the world for the first time, and it filled her heart with elation. "We did it! We did it!" she said, turning to Chase.

"Good. Give him to the midwife and get me another clamp."

His tone and expression were tight, controlled as he worked to sew the woman's uterus, and Dani's jubilation faded as she switched her focus from the infant to his mother.

The woman was speaking between moans, looking at her baby, but blood still flowed from her body. Such a frightening quantity that Dani knew they had very little time.

She quickly stood to pass the baby to the midwife then grabbed a clamp from his bag. She kneeled next to him again, heart racing. Why was the woman still bleeding? It looked like he'd already tied off the big uterine veins and stitched the uterus itself.

"What's wrong, Chase?"

He shook his head. "Uterus can't seem to naturally clamp down and stop the flow. Check her pulse."

Dani pressed her fingers to the woman's wrist and stared at her watch. "One-forty," she said, dismayed. Clearly, the woman's pulse was rocketing to compensate for her blood volume loss.

He worked several more minutes in silence. "Damn it!" Fiercely intense, he turned to look at Dani. "Get me the garbage bag that's in the motorcycle box and the sponges and gauze in there. Hurry."

She ran to grab what he asked for, wondering what he could possibly have planned but not about to ask with the situation so dire. As she hurried back into the hut she heard him barking orders and the few other women in the room ran off.

Blood literally dripping from his hands and arms, he grimly took the garbage bag from Dani. He slipped his hands inside the bag and began to ease it into the woman's belly cavity.

"What in the world are you doing?" In her astonishment the question just burst from her lips.

"Packing the belly. Like a big internal bandage. It's her only chance. I'll stuff it with the sponges and strips of cloth the women are getting. Tamp it down and apply pressure to stop the bleeding. Pray like hell."

He grabbed the sponges and gauze and stuffed them inside the garbage bag. Then he yanked off his own bloody shirt and rapidly tore it into small strips before stuffing them, too, into the bag. The women returned with cloth strips and he shoved them inside before pressing on it all with his hands.

He kept the pressure on the woman's belly for long minutes before lifting his gaze to Dani. With blood spattered across his face and naked torso, his eyes looked harshly intense. "Check her vitals again."

She quickly took the woman's pulse, and her heart tripped. "One-fifteen. It's working!"

She doubted they'd get it down to a normal reading of seventy, but at least it was heading in the right direction.

"Call Spud. Tell him to get a car here stat to take her

to our hospital. We can't transfuse there, but if we pump her with fluids, it should be enough."

She stepped outside the hut to call Spud, and when she returned she saw that Chase was stitching the woman's belly closed with the filled garbage bag still inside.

"So, you leave it in there until she clots well enough? Then take it out?" Dani had never seen such a thing. Never even heard of it. Amazement and awe swept through her at Chase's incredible knowledge and skill.

"Belly-packing is battlefield medicine." He continued his steady, even stitches to completely close the incision except for the very top of the garbage bag, which was still exposed. The plastic extended outside the woman's body as he stitched around it. "Eventually, we'll be able to pull the sponges and cloth out piece by piece, then the empty bag, and hopefully not have to open her up again."

The woman started speaking again in barely a whisper. In spite of what she'd been through, she extended her arms towards the midwife. Holding her new, tiny son close to her breast, she kissed his head and managed a weak smile.

Dani's throat filled and tears stung her eyes. Chase had done this. He'd somehow, miraculously, saved this woman's life. Her baby hadn't lost his mother.

Chase spoke to the women who'd fetched the strips of cloth, and they brought several pads and put them beneath the patient's legs. Obviously, Chase was concerned about her going into shock before they got her to the hospital.

The women brought some water and, silently, Chase stripped off his gloves and washed the blood off his chest and arms as best he could, with Dani following suit. Spud arrived with a nurse from the hospital, and they carried the woman and her baby to the car and drove off.

Other than quick instructions to Spud and the nurse, Chase had barely spoken for fifteen minutes. Standing next to the motorcycle after they'd packed everything up, Dani touched his arm.

"That was amazing. I've never seen anything like it. You should be very proud of what you did today."

He didn't respond, just looked at her. She couldn't decipher the emotion on his face exactly but it definitely wasn't triumph, which was what she thought he'd be feeling. It seemed more like despair.

He reached for her, grasping her shoulders, and slowly pulled her against his bare chest, which was still sprinkled with dried blood. His lips touched her forehead, lingered, until he stepped back to mount the bike.

Chase was quiet the entire ride back to the GPC compound. Not that there could be much conversation over the loud engine, but on the way to the village he'd managed to throw the occasional comment or observation over his shoulder. Probably the low light made it even more important that he concentrate on avoiding precarious ruts and potholes.

This time her arms were wrapped around a naked torso, and she had to control the constant urge to press her palms to his skin, slide them across the soft hair on his chest, down to the hard corrugated muscle of his stomach. Distracting him while driving in the near dark was definitely not a good idea.

After they'd unpacked the items they hadn't used and returned them to the clinic, Chase seemed remote, preoccupied. "I'm going to go clean up. See you and Drew at dinner."

"Okay." She didn't know what to think of his demeanor. Distance. The lack of touching and flirting earlier that day. And for the past forty-five minutes he'd spoken to her as though they were strangers.

Annoyed with herself at the hurt she felt because of the sudden change in him, she decided to check on Drew before she, too, washed off all the road dirt and changed her bloody clothes. She knew the Bowens had Drew, but had no idea exactly where they were. She turned to find out and felt a hand close over her forearm.

"Do you have pictures of Drew when he was first born? When he was a baby?"

"Of course. Though I don't know how many I have with me. Some on my laptop and a few on my phone."

"I'd like to see them."

Why did he appear so oddly somber? How could he not be elated that fate had sent them to the village that day? "You know, you did just save two lives today. I'm surprised you aren't exhilarated." She certainly had been, until his seriousness had tempered it.

"We saved their lives together." He placed his hand on her cheek. "And three years ago we made a life together."

His eyes were now darkly intense, and she tried to decipher the jumble of emotions there, all mixed up with his somber demeanor and the grim lines around his mouth. He almost looked… Could the word be vulnerable? She searched his face and realized, stunned, that was exactly the word. Never would she have guessed the *über*-talented, ultra-confident Chase Bowen could ever look or feel vulnerable in any way. No matter what the circumstances, he always seemed…invincible.

"Yes, we did," Dani said softly. "And I can see you're as proud of him as I am. I'll find what photos I can and show them to you after dinner."

He nodded and turned to walk to his room, leaving her staring at his back and asking herself if she really knew him as well as she thought she did.

She went to find Drew, and had to wonder. In her infatuation with Chase, with his obvious strengths that had dazzled her so, had she never taken time to look inside at the rest of the man? At all facets of him and his life and what had shaped him to become the person he was today?

Chase was her son's father. They might not be spending much time together in the future, but the emotion on Chase's face tonight proved she needed to understand better what made the man tick.

CHAPTER NINE

CHASE LAY ON his bed, his hair still wet from his shower, and stared at the cracked ceiling. He hoped everyone went ahead and started dinner—he and Dani had arrived back much later than they'd expected as it was. But he needed a few more minutes to deal with the overwhelming feelings that had unexpectedly swamped him after the birth of the baby that afternoon.

Damn it, he'd never wanted this. Never wanted to be susceptible to the same kind of pain he'd felt when his brother had died. Never wanted to feel vulnerable to his whole universe being crushed in an instant.

But when he'd brought that baby into the world, the moment had taken away his breath.

In his career he'd delivered more babies than he could possibly guess at. Had always appreciated the miracle of birth, the joy of the mother, the pride of the father. Had enjoyed gently passing a healthy infant to suckle at its mother's breast, and sympathized with the loss when a baby hadn't made it.

Never had it felt personal. Until today. The first baby he'd delivered since he'd found out he had a child of his own. Seeing the baby's tiny body, hearing his first cries, watching him looking with wide eyes at the world for the very first time had clutched at his heart like nothing before.

And the mother. She'd suffered so much with the baby's birth and yet, barely escaping death and in tremendous pain, she'd smiled through it all when she'd first seen her son.

He'd missed that with Drew. Missed being there to help Dani. And he hated that he'd never even thought to ask her if it had been an easy birth or a hard one. Even with all the modern technology in the U.S., not all babies were born without complications.

He scrubbed his hands over his face. He never wanted to feel the cold terror for Dani and Drew that had gripped him as he'd worked with mother and infant today. The sudden fear that if something happened to either of them, his entire world would be ripped to pieces. How did people cope with that? Did they just refuse to see the dangers? The risks?

Inhaling a shaky breath, he swung his legs off the bed and sat up. The past couldn't be changed. Andrew had been conceived and born healthy and he was the most beautiful child Chase had ever seen. And Dani was a very special woman. An incredible woman.

He'd do whatever he had to do to keep both of them safe.

As he stepped through the doorway of the kitchen, it looked like everyone had finished eating but Dani. The scene was much livelier than usual, the room filled with Spud, Trent, Dani, his parents, and Drew, who obviously enjoyed being the center of everyone's attention. Laughter at his antics bounced off the walls of the room, but Dani's big smile faded as he walked in, her blue gaze seeming contemplative.

He hoped like hell she hadn't sensed how disturbed he'd felt. He also hoped he had all those feelings under control.

"Daddy!" Drew grinned and raised his arms toward Chase, his fingers gooey with mashed yams.

Chase's chest felt peculiarly heavy and light at the same time. He couldn't believe how quickly Drew had accepted him as his dad. How he wanted to be held by him. To be played with by him. He had to swallow hard to shove down the emotions that had swamped him earlier.

"Hey, lizard-boy. What have you been up to today?" He grabbed a wet towel, partly to give himself something to do, and wiped Drew's hands before sitting next to him.

"Your mother and I showed him the technique for shinnying up a palm tree today," Phil said. "He's a natural. Even better than you when you were that age."

"Yes," Evelyn agreed with a proud smile. "He made it up at least three feet. With us spotting, of course. Pretty soon he'll be getting all the way up to grab a coconut or two."

"Little did I know this was a Bowen family tradition," Dani said with a smile. "When Chase first showed off how he could climb a coconut tree, I thought it was just a macho thing he did to impress women."

"It worked, didn't it?" Chase asked. He conjured up a smile and took a swallow of beer, hoping it would help him relax and feel more normal. Last thing he wanted was to have anyone guess at his feelings. Or, worse, ask.

"A few of the places we lived actually had palm-tree climbing contests. Chase and his brother even won occasionally," his mother said.

Chase stiffened and glanced at Dani. He'd never mentioned Brady to her. Or to Trent or Spud, for that matter. What were the chances they wouldn't ask questions?

"Chase has a brother?" Dani looked questioningly from his mother to him, her eyebrows raised.

Obviously, no chance. Chase gritted his teeth. The last thing he wanted to talk about was Brady. Not ever and especially not today.

"Had." Evelyn's eyes shadowed. "He—"

"Dani said she'd find some pictures of Andrew when he was a baby," Chase interrupted. He wasn't hungry anyway, and stood to gather empty plates, with Spud following suit. "I know you two proud grandparents want to see them as much as I do."

Dani looked at him for a long moment before speaking. "Yes. I had more downloaded than I realized."

She stood to retrieve her computer from a kitchen shelf, and Chase drew a deep breath of relief. Not that she wouldn't ask again, but at least he'd be prepared to give the most basic account possible, without his parents around to embellish it, before changing the subject.

Everyone crowded around as Dani gave a slide show on her laptop. Drew had been so damned cute as a baby, with a shock of dark hair sticking up around his head, his brown eyes wide, his cheeks round and pink. Sitting on the floor amid a pile of blocks, a big grin showing just a few teeth, drool dripping from the corners of his mouth like a bulldog. She even had a video of him crawling up to the hearth in her little house, pulling himself to his feet then yanking to the floor the houseplant perched there, scattering dirt everywhere.

It was a hell of a thing that he'd missed it all.

Amid the laughing and *aww*s echoing in the kitchen, and Drew's delight at his photos, Chase found himself looking at Dani between nearly every picture. The love and tenderness in her eyes as she looked at the captured moments in time. Not so very different from the expression on her enchanting face when they'd shared so many intimate moments in Honduras.

Her smiling gaze met his more than once, warm and close, and he almost blurted out the words right there in front of everyone. Almost asked why she was being so stubborn about marrying him when they had this beautiful child between them. The closeness they'd shared before and could share again. Why? Did she still honestly not believe him, or trust him, when he promised they could make it work? Was it her feelings for that Matt guy?

"That's it, I'm afraid." Dani shut her laptop with a smile at Drew. "I need to remember to take more pictures while we're here in Benin. You seem to grow bigger every day."

"The good news there is that Drew has grandparents with a very nice camera who now have a new favorite subject," Phil said. "We've taken so many of him it's a good thing I brought an extra memory card. Too bad we have to leave in a couple days."

"Perhaps you and Dani can bring Drew to Senegal," Evelyn said to Chase. "How much longer are you here in Benin?"

"Not sure." He wasn't about to go into that potential problem right now. He didn't know if Dani knew he'd be leaving soon, and the last thing he wanted to give her was another reason to think they shouldn't make things permanent between them.

Drew yawned, and Chase grabbed the excuse to get out of there. "Looks like a certain tree-climbing monkey needs to go to bed," he said, lifting him into his arms. Drew snaked his arms around Chase's neck and he held the child's little body close. Would he ever stop feeling the amazement, the joy that nearly hurt at having this little guy in his life?

"I a lizard, not a monkey," Drew said with another yawn.

His eyelids drooped and Chase headed for the door then stopped to look at Dani. He realized he didn't know Drew's bedtime routine, and that had to change. "You coming?"

She nodded, saying her goodnights to everyone before following him down the hall to her room.

"I'll get him ready. You don't have to stay," Dani said as she pulled Drew's Spiderman pajamas from a drawer.

"I want to know what's involved in getting him ready for bed," Chase said. He gently sat a half-asleep Drew on the edge of the bed and took the pajamas from Dani. Afraid the child would conk out before he'd even had a chance to change him, Chase quickly pulled Drew's little striped shirt over his head and finished getting him into his PJs.

"We usually read a book after using the bathroom, but I don't think he's going to stay awake for that tonight," Dani said as she put Drew's discarded clothes away.

Together, they took him down the hall to take care of bathroom necessities before tucking him into bed.

"'Night, Daddy," he said, lifting his sweet face for a kiss.

"'Night, Drew. Sleep tight."

Drew did the same with Dani, and as Chase watched her soft lips brush their child's cheek, saw her slender fingers tuck her unruly hair behind her ears, saw her tempting round behind as she bent over, he knew he couldn't play the hard-to-get game any longer. Not just because it hadn't seemed to work, he thought wryly.

He had to touch her. Had to kiss those soft lips. Had to satisfy the desire, the longing he'd barely been able to contain since she'd first arrived. Since he'd first seen her silhouetted in the sub-Saharan twilight.

He needed her tonight, and could only hope she'd give in to the feelings he knew they'd both shared, remembered, since finding one another again. Let him show her what she meant to him. Let him show her how good their future could be.

She straightened and stepped closer to Chase in the small room. "He's already sound asleep," she said with a smile. "Your parents wore him out. Or he wore them out. They've obviously had a wonderful day. Thank you."

"For…?"

"For bringing them here. For Drew getting to know them. He hardly has any family and yours is…special."

Her luminous eyes looked up at him, held him, and he closed the gap between them. He pulled her close, hoping she wouldn't resist, object. "Not as special as you. No one is as special as you."

Then he kissed her. Slowly. Softly. Not wanting to push, to rush, to insist. He wanted her to want the same thing he wanted. For them to join together and make love in a way that made everything else fade away. All the worries, the fears he'd felt earlier buried beneath the kind of passion only she had ever inspired in him.

She tasted faintly of coffee and vitality and Dani, and she kissed him back with the same slow tenderness he gave her. So different from the spontaneous combustion of their previous kisses. The kisses he fed her, that she gave in return, were full of a quietly blossoming heat. Slowly weakening him as they strengthened his need.

Her hands tentatively swept over his chest and shoulders to cup the back of his head, her tongue in a languid dance with his. He pulled her tightly against him, loving the feel of her soft curves molded perfectly to his body. Made for him.

She broke the kiss. "You are the most confusing man."

"Not true." He brushed her lips with his because he couldn't stand even a moment's distance. "There's nothing confusing about what I want right now."

He kissed her again, and her sigh of pleasure nearly had him forgetting about gently coaxing. Nearly had him lifting her to the bed and yanking off their clothes to tangle their bodies together, to feel every inch of her skin next to his.

She pulled her mouth away with a little gasping breath. "A couple of days ago you wouldn't stop touching and kissing me then all day today you acted like we barely knew one another."

"So it did work." He pressed his mouth below her ear. Tasted her soft throat. Breathed in her sweet, distinctive scent.

"What worked?"

"I was playing hard to get. Trent told me to. Said you'd want to jump my bones."

She gave a breathy laugh. "I swear, boys never grow up, do they?"

"So, do you?" He slipped his hands up her ribs, let one wander higher. "Want to jump my bones?"

Her lips curved, but she shook her head. "I don't think that's a good idea. We have…issues to resolve without making things harder."

"Except something's already harder."

She chuckled, her eyes twinkling, and he knew he could look into the amazing blue of them for ever. He kissed her again, hoping to make her forget about any and all issues and just feel.

Surely she could sense, through his kiss, what she meant to him. That she wouldn't stop and pull away and end the beauty of the moment before it began. That she could feel what she did to him through the pounding of his heart and the shortness of his breath.

Dani pulled her mouth from his and untwined her hands from behind his neck. She stepped out of his hold, and Chase tried to control the frustration that had him wanting to grab her and refuse to let her go. "Dani—"

"Shh." She pressed her fingers to his lips then slid their warmth down his arm to grasp his hand. "Your room is close by, right? Let's go there. We'll hear Drew if he wakes up."

Relief practically weakened his knees. Or, more likely, he thought with a smile, they'd already been weakened by her. "Come on."

Dragging her behind him, Chase could hear her practically running as he strode the short distance down the hall to his room, but slowing down wasn't an option. He'd barely shut and locked the door behind them before he grabbed her again.

This time the kisses didn't start out sweet and slow. He found himself in a rush, his mouth taking hers with a fierceness and possessiveness he couldn't seem to control. His hands slid over her bottom, up her sides to her belly and breasts, further until he cradled her head. He released her ponytail, and the tangle of her hair curling around his hands took him back to the first time he'd kissed her, when those ringlets had captured his fingers and refused to let go.

"I've always loved your crazy curls," he said. "Love the way it feels, tickling my skin."

"Well, if you really love it…" Her soft fingers slipped up his ribs and he shivered as she pulled his shirt over his head. She leaned forward and nuzzled his neck, her wild hair caressing his shoulders, and he couldn't control a groan.

"I love your hair, too," she said. Her hands traveled back up his chest before she buried her fingers in his hair, pulling his mouth down to hers for a deep kiss. "It's like thick silk. Drew's lucky he has your hair and not mine."

Her lips were curved and her eyes were full of the same desire that surged through his every cell. "I can't agree," he said. "But arguing with you isn't on our agenda right now. Getting both of us naked is."

He tugged off her shirt then reached for the button on her shorts before desperation seemed to grab both of them at the same time and every garment was quickly shed until both stood naked in front of each other.

His breath caught in his throat. Three years since he'd seen her beautiful body. Three years without enjoying her small, perfect breasts. The curve of her waist, her slim hips and legs, the blonde curls covering the bliss between them. Three years without touching and tasting every inch of her soft, ivory skin, and suddenly he couldn't wait one more second to join with her.

He reached for her at the same time she reached for him, and they practically fell onto his bed with a bounce.

Her breasts grazed his chest and he dipped his head to take one pink nipple into his mouth. With his eyes closed, tasting first one taut tip then the other, he could imagine they'd been together just yesterday, without the three years of distance between them. He could hope, as his lips traveled over her flat abdomen, that she had missed him as much as he'd missed her. He could believe, as his fingers explored the moist juncture of her thighs, as he breathed in the scent of her, as he listened to her moans of pleasure, that she was already his, for ever.

"Chase." As she gasped his name, her hands tugged at his head, his arms, his torso.

He rose to lie above her and she opened her arms and body to him, a beckoning smile on her beautiful lips.

"You said your goal was to make me want to jump your bones." Her voice vibrated against his chest. "You've succeeded. So do it."

She held him close, wriggling beneath him, trying to position herself in a way that left him no option for staying strong and enjoying her body for a whole lot longer.

He managed a short laugh. "And you call me bossy." He wanted to kiss that smiling mouth of hers, but wanted to watch her, too. He slipped inside her heat, and was glad he could see her eyes, her lips. See her desire, her pleasure. Knowing he gave it to her.

He wanted, more than anything, to give her pleasure. He wanted to make this moment last, to show her he would give her everything. To assuage whatever worries she had about them staying together for ever.

As they moved, he tried to take it slowly. To draw out the distinctive rhythm the two of them had always shared. But the little sounds she kept making, the way she kissed him, the way she wrapped her legs around him and drew him in drove him out of his mind.

He couldn't last much longer. He reached between them to touch her most sensitive place as they moved together, and was rewarded as she closed her eyes and uttered his name. Saw the release on her beautiful face as he let himself fall with her.

The quiet room was filled with the sound of their breathing as they lay there, skin to skin. He buried his face in the sweetly scented spirals of her hair, stroking his hand slowly up her side to cup her soft breast.

He smiled. After what they'd just shared, even stubborn Dani couldn't deny they belonged together.

Neither seemed to want to move, and they lay there for long minutes, skin to warm skin. Until her hands shoved at his shoulders and he managed to lift himself off her and roll to one side. With his fingers splayed across her stomach, he finally caught his breath.

"If I didn't know better, I'd think I didn't have any bones left for you to jump," he said, kissing her arm.

"I have to check on Drew."

She struggled to get up and Chase swung his legs off the bed to give her room. Then, shocked, he saw the expression on her face.

It wasn't full of blissful afterglow, the way he knew his had been. It was sad and worried. Distant.

What the hell had happened?

"Dani." He reached for her hand, but she shook him off, grabbed up her clothes and quickly put them on.

"I'm sorry." Her voice was tight, controlled, so unlike the Dani he used to know as she struggled with the button on her shorts. "This was…a mistake. We shouldn't have complicated an already complicated problem."

Chase tamped down a surge of anger at her words. "You're the one making it a complicated problem. To me, there's no problem at all."

"Our…making love…doesn't change anything. Doesn't solve the problem of you wanting us to be married and act like we're a normal family while you live halfway across the world."

"Damn it, Dani." He grasped her arm and halted her progress in getting on her shoes. "We *can* be a normal family. How many people travel on business while their spouse keeps things going at home? It's the same thing."

She pulled her arm loose and slipped on her sandals. "It's not the same thing. Do I have to keep saying it over and over? Seeing you just a few months a year, Drew would wonder why your work is more important than he is."

"I'd make sure he knows he's the most important thing in my life. That you both are." He wanted to shake her. How could she still put up this damned wall between them after what they'd just shared?

She shoved her glorious curls from her face and finally looked him in the eye. He saw the same despair and anxiety that had been there from the minute she'd arrived in Benin, and didn't know what the hell to do about it. Hadn't he given her every reason to trust him? Why could she not see what was so very clear?

He tried to reach for her, but she stepped to the door,

shaking her head. "I need to check on Drew," she said again. "And I need to think. About you and me and my own mission work and Drew. I'll...see you tomorrow."

As the door clicked behind her, he nearly dropped down onto the bed in frustrated defeat.

After what they'd shared, he'd been sure he'd won her tonight. And didn't know what the hell his next move should be.

CHAPTER TEN

CHASE WALKED INTO the kitchen after his run and work-out to make coffee for Dani. An extra five miles had cleared his head and brought renewed optimism. Surely, after last night, she'd dreamed of him the way he'd dreamed of her. Relived every achingly sweet moment in her arms and body.

He'd hated feeling so shaken and disturbed last night before dinner. Not a feeling he was used to, and defi-nitely a feeling he didn't like. But making love with Dani had calmed him, soothed him, deep within his soul, and he wanted that again. And again.

Hopefully, she was over whatever had prompted her doubts and regrets and quick exit last night. And if she wasn't over it, he had a plan to get her over it.

His plan was to take a cup of coffee to her room, awaken her with a kiss then, assuming Drew was still asleep, kiss her and touch her and convince her that a morning shower together was the perfect way to start the day. Just thinking about kissing her soft lips and soaping her every delicate curve had him breathing faster.

Maybe he should just forget about waiting for the coffee to brew and head in there that minute. Except the woman was addicted to her morning coffee, and the gesture would probably soften her up and help him get what he wanted. Her, naked, wet, and slippery against his equally naked, wet, and slippery body.

Reminded yet again of what they had together. Why they belonged together.

Despite the uncertainty of his plan, he had to chuckle, thinking about how irritated she used to get when he dragged her out of bed early in the morning to do push-ups and sit-ups with him. A cup of coffee under her nose, though, always seemed to bring down her annoyance and bring up that sunny smile that had him starting the day with a smile of his own.

Drumming his fingers against the countertop as he listened to the coffee perk, he spotted yesterday's mail in a small pile. After being gone all day then preoccupied afterwards, he hadn't looked at it. A good distraction from his currently surging libido.

He shuffled through the envelopes then stopped cold when he spotted one addressed to him with the GPC logo and return address. The back of his neck tightened and he had a bad, bad feeling he knew what it was.

He ripped open the envelope and unfolded the letter. It didn't take more than a quick skim of its contents to see he'd been right.

Damn it! Half crumpling the letter, he pressed both palms to the countertop.

Panama. His new assignment. One more week here, three weeks off, then Central America.

What the hell should he do now?

No way was he heading to Panama before Dani became his wife. Even if he stayed here for the three weeks' vacation, she'd have plenty of work to do with the two new surgeons arriving to replace him and Trent. Unless she was willing to share her room and single bed, which she apparently wasn't ready to do, he'd have to find another place to stay. Acquire his own car or scooter to get around.

He straightened. Those were easy things to accomplish. The hard part was convincing Dani that marriage between them was best all round. The way they'd burned up the sheets last night should have shown her they still had what they'd shared in Honduras and had her saying yes right then.

Damn it to hell. Could GPC have possibly sent him farther away? It couldn't have been the Congo, or someplace close where he could fairly easily hop a plane to see her and Drew?

No, it had to be literally halfway across the world from Dani.

Without a guarantee that he could charm and cajole her into marriage before he had to leave, he couldn't afford to just hope absence would make the heart grow fonder, or however that stupid old saying went. More likely it would be out of sight, out of mind, and she'd end up back with Matt in less than eight months, leaving *him* in the cold and with no influence at all about what mission trips she might head to in the future with their son in tow.

An icy hollow formed in his chest at the thought of never again holding her or kissing her. Maybe even having to see her with some other man when he visited Drew.

No. Not happening.

Various solutions spun through his mind until he struck one that seemed viable. He'd been with GPC a long time. Year-round, unlike a lot of docs. And his parents had worked for them at least thirty years. Surely all that gave him some clout.

In a few hours, when the GPC offices opened, he'd make a phone call. Tell his old buddy Mike Hardy that Dani and her son needed a change of assignment from Benin, and to find someone to replace her. That she needed to join him in Panama for the duration of her contract commitment.

He sucked in a calming breath and nodded. Yeah. It could work. Somehow he'd get the folks at the GPC to keep mum on why she was being reassigned with him. Come up with a good reason she'd believe.

The kitchen door swung open and he jumped as he turned to see who it was.

Trent. A breath of relief whooshed from his lungs.

"What are you up to?" Trent asked, eyebrows raised. "You look like you just robbed the GPC piggy bank. Shake out your pockets so I can see if there's more than a buck fifty in there."

Thank God it wasn't Dani, because if Trent was getting guilty vibes from him, she'd be sure to suspect he was up to something. She'd always had a sixth sense when it came to what he was thinking and feeling.

"Just wondering how I can snitch that fancy watch you bought in Switzerland before you head to your next assignment." Chase threw out a grin he hoped was convincing. The last thing he wanted was another lecture from Trent on how to deal with Dani. On playing hard to get or letting things unfold as they would or whatever the hell he came up with next. "So, where are they sending you?"

"Eastern India. West Bengal, to be exact." Trent

grabbed a cup and poured the coffee Chase hadn't noticed had finished brewing. "How about you?"

"Panama." Just the word made his stomach churn.

Trent sipped his coffee and gave him a measuring look. "So, now what?"

Chase didn't pretend to not know what he meant. "Not sure. I'm thinking I'll call Mike at GPC and have Dani reassigned with me."

Trent nearly spit out his coffee as he choked. "Reassigned with you?" He burst out laughing. "Oh, man, I want to be in the room when she finds out you're moving her halfway across the world without even asking."

"None of this is funny." Chase gritted his teeth. "I can't go all the way to Panama without things tied up between us. Or anywhere else, for that matter. And since it's not looking like that's going to happen in a few weeks, the logical solution is for her to come with me."

"You are so delusional." Trent shook his head. "Do you really think Dani would want to marry a guy who's so controlling that he first demands marriage and then, when she says no, manipulates the whole world so things will turn out the way he wants them to?"

"This has nothing to do with being controlling." Why the hell did everyone keep accusing him of that? "This has to do with making the best decision and getting married because of Drew."

"*Your* best decision. Which isn't necessarily *her* best decision."

"What, you think I'd be a lousy husband? Thanks a hell of a lot." Surprise and anger burned in his chest. "You know, I'm damned tired of my friends and family turning on me this way. I try to do right by my own son and all I get is a raft of crap over it." He grabbed a glass of orange juice and downed it in one gulp. "I'm calling the GPC. And once Dani and I are married and happy, there's no way she'll be mad about moving with me."

Trent looked at him steadily before he gave a small shrug. "You know her better than I do. And I honestly wish you the best of luck because, of course, I know you'd be good to her and Drew. But I think you're making a mistake if you don't talk to her first."

The sound of squeaking hinges preceded Dani as she came into the kitchen. Absently, Chase recognized the anticipation in her eyes—it was her I-smell-coffee look. Her pleased expression morphed into a frown as she looked first at Chase then at Trent then back at Chase, a question in her blue eyes.

"You two fighting about something?"

"No." Chase stalked over to Dani, placed his hand behind her head and gave her a hard kiss. To show Trent and her and himself that she belonged to him—would belong to him for ever—no matter what the obstacles. No matter how stubborn she was.

Her shocked eyes widened and she opened her mouth to speak but Chase had had enough talking for one morning. He dropped his hand. "I'm going to check on Drew before I take a shower." He knew his voice was tight, barely controlled, but it was better than yelling at both of them, which was what he wanted to do. "See you in the clinic."

"See, that wasn't so bad, was it?" Dani rubbed the arm of the little girl she'd just immunized and smiled, holding out a sheet of the stickers she'd brought from the States for the girl to choose from. The child's dark eyes lit up at a sparkly fairy, and she carefully stuck it to the big index card Dani gave her.

With any luck, the children's families would pay attention and bring both the child and the card back when her next shots were due. Of course, they didn't have calendars so they would doubtless have trouble remembering exactly when they should return. And, sadly, most couldn't even read. But the double system, with Dani having the information entered into the laptop, too, just might help keep track of their care better than before. If and when they showed up again.

Spud and the local nurses had gone into different communities to let people know they'd be doing immunizations all week, and it seemed to have worked pretty well. Trent had the day off, but she and Chase managed the substantial turnout.

Dani was surprised and thrilled with the slow but steady stream of children that arrived, some on bicycles, some on scooters, some on foot. One entire family showed up in a rickety horse-drawn cart, and Chase had teased her again about not being in Kansas any more, as it was apparently a common occurrence.

Dani smiled at the next child in line and, for at least the fiftieth time that day, found herself momentarily distracted by Chase standing ten feet across the room. Her gaze catching on his profile as he listened with his stethoscope. Staring at the strong muscles in his arms, his big gentle hands as they moved over a patient's body. The creases in the corners of his eyes as he caught her looking and gave her a knowing smile that showed he, too, was remembering last night.

This was exactly why she'd practically run from the room. Chase was a dangerous drug she wasn't sure she should keep taking. Bringing a euphoria that made her want to forget about anything but the scent of his skin, the delicious feel of his heavy body atop hers, the mind-blowing pleasure only he had ever given her.

She just might have been able to resist his magnetic pull. Stayed strong despite the way her pulse tripped and her breathing suspended every time he touched or teased her. But watching his amazing work yesterday had filled her with awe. Not that she'd forgotten what he did every day. What miracles he could accomplish when a situation demanded it.

But seeing how disturbed he'd obviously felt after the difficult birth of the baby and nearly losing the mother, combined with the admiration that had filled her heart, had touched the healer in her.

It seemed obvious he must have been thinking about Drew and how blessed they both were that their son had been born without complications. Asking to see pictures of Drew as a baby and toddler must mean he'd been painfully thinking about having missed those years.

She hadn't made a conscious decision to give in to her desire to be with him. But when she'd seen the haunted look in his eyes, she'd wanted to make it all better. To bring back the normally tough and confident Dr. Chase Bowen who never showed the vulnerability that had so surprised her.

Even now there was tenseness about his mouth and eyes. Edginess that had been there when he'd given her that hard kiss in the kitchen right in front of Trent. Like he had been staking his claim.

She dragged her attention back to the child she was about to immunize. The bad news was that their love-making had done more than momentarily take the strain from Chase's face. It had touched the wound deep in her heart she'd thought had healed and scarred over. The wound she absolutely did not want ripped open again.

But apparently her self-protective mechanism wasn't working quite right, because she couldn't stop thinking about what they'd shared last night. Couldn't stop thinking about how wonderful and special and overwhelming it had been, and how she wanted it again.

Which was very, very dangerous.

You'd think she'd never made love to him before. Hadn't spent an entire year exploring every inch of Chase's body in every possible location.

Disgusted with herself for thinking about every inch of his body for the hundredth time that day, Dani finished the little girl's immunizations. She looked around the room and saw Chase locking some drugs in the drawer.

He must have felt her gaze on him because his brown eyes met hers. "Need some help?" Chase asked.

She turned back to her work table, smiling at a little boy now ready for his shots. "A back rub would be nice. I feel like my spine is frozen in a permanently bent position."

And wasn't that kind of invitation a totally stupid thing to say? She gulped and focused on making the boy feel at ease as she poked him with a needle. Suddenly, right next to her, Chase placed his hands on her shoulders, gently kneading, lowering his head next to hers. "I'm very good at the kind of doctoring where we find a new position for your back. I can make it feel all better."

The sensual promise in his voice took her right back to last night, suspending her breath and making her heart flutter. The boy she'd just immunized left with his stickered card clutched to his chest and she glanced up at Chase. At the curve of his lips. At his eyes, smoldering and dark. And somehow shadowed, too, with something else she couldn't figure out. Worry? She'd thought that was her domain.

"How's that feel? Better?"

"Yes. Good. Thanks, that's enough." She stood and stepped to a cupboard, gulping in oxygen not infused with Chase's scent.

Why, oh, why did her body and mind so want to get physical with him again, instead of listening to logic? But it was more than obvious it would take very little persuasion on his part to start what they'd had last night all over again.

And why not? that traitorous part of her brain whispered. Just like last night, she was finding it harder and harder to come up with a good reason why she couldn't just enjoy the unbelievable way he made her feel. To give herself up to it until he left.

Until he left. How she'd feel then, she had no clue. Tough as it had been leaving him three years ago, she'd survived it. Even managed to stop thinking about him constantly. Stopped wondering where he was and what he was doing and who he was doing it with.

But this time would be different, and that knowledge brought heaviness to her chest and a painful stab to her soul.

This time, because they had Drew to share, she'd be in contact with him. Know all that she hadn't known before, including if he had a serious relationship with someone else. That most definitely would not be a good feeling, but she'd have to toughen up and deal with it. The question was, would making love with him or not

making love with him while they were here together
make it any less painful in the future?

Was it worth the risk to her heart to fall headlong into
the heady, emotional crevasse that was Chase Bowen?
A crevasse she'd foolishly thought three years ago that
he'd fallen into along with her?

Through the doorway the sun glowed low in the sky
and the tall man walking in seemed to bring a sweep of
muggy heat along with him. He wore a cylinder-shaped
striped hat and a bright and colorful tunic completely
at odds with the grim exhaustion etched on his face. A
boy of about fourteen followed him. Nearly expression-
less except for his deeply somber eyes, he had a length
of equally bright fabric wrapped around his shoulders
and arms like a cape.

Chase stepped over to them and spoke to the man,
who turned to the boy with a single nod. Like an unveil-
ing, the child slipped the fabric from his arms.

Dani's breath stopped and she stared in disbelief.
She'd thought Apollo had had a terrible injury? This
was something straight out of a horror movie.

CHAPTER ELEVEN

Two LONG BARE bones stuck out below the child's elbow from what was left of his arm. The normal soft tissue abruptly ended, with the skin black and mummified.

Dani could hardly believe what she was seeing. Her chest constricted at what unimaginable pain the boy had to have suffered over what must have been weeks, or even longer. Clearly his hand had completely rotted off and left behind what they were staring at.

Dani lifted her gaze to Chase's. His expression was carefully neutral as he asked questions of the father and the boy. But his dark eyes held grave despair.

"Okay." Chase's chest rose and fell in a deep breath as he turned those eyes to Dani. "I don't have to tell you we have to remove what's left of his arm. I'll take it off above the elbow. You'll have to act as my assistant. If you don't want to, we can have them spend the night and I'll have Trent or the nurse help me tomorrow."

"Of course I'll assist." Did he think she couldn't handle the tough stuff? She'd feel insulted if the situation wasn't so awful.

"Let's get him set up in the OR. I'll scrub then get him anesthetized."

With a few quick words to the father he laid his hand

gently on the boy's back and guided him through the doors to the OR. Dani tried to give a reassuring smile to the man, reaching out to touch his forearm, trying to let him know it would be okay, but the man's expression didn't change.

The ache in her chest intensified, imagining what not only the boy but his parents, too, had been through with this. Why, oh, why hadn't they come in sooner? It was a miracle that infection hadn't killed the child.

As she entered the room, she was struck by the stoic expression on the boy's face. Just lying there, quiet and still, looking at her and Chase with serious, deep brown eyes. Not upset. Not even grim. Just accepting of this horrible thing that had happened to him, which would affect him for the rest of his life. She swallowed down tears and busied herself getting the surgical equipment together.

Chase put the boy under sedation with some antiquated-looking equipment. "I've never seen a machine like this," Dani said, both because she wondered about it and to distract her from what was about to happen. "Does it ever fail?"

"It looks like hell, I know. But it's reliable and safe, believe it or not. A hospital in Cotonou donated it."

Dani watched Chase prep the skin above the boy's elbow, waiting for him to tell her the story about the child. When he said nothing, she had to ask. "Did they tell you what happened? Why they waited so long to come in?"

"This kind of thing happens way too often." Chase picked up the knife. "He fell from a tree. They live over sixty kilometers away, with no easy way to get here."

Dani thought about Drew learning to shinny up the

palm tree, at the climbing competitions Evelyn and Phil had told her about, and her heart stopped. "If kids fall from trees all the time, why do parents allow it? Why did *you* do it?"

"They're not climbing for fun. They're gathering leaves for their livestock. During the drought that can follow the rainy season, there isn't enough food to feed the animals. After a long time working in the trees, they get careless or just lose their footing."

Chase seemed fiercely focused on making a circumferential, fish-mouth incision above the child's elbow to leave plenty of skin and flesh to fold beneath what would end up being the stump of his arm. Dani noted the tightness of his lips, his jaws clamped together, and knew that, no matter how many times he'd seen these kinds of horrific things, he never got used to it. Never just took it in his stride but felt deep empathy for all the people born without the privileges so many others took for granted.

She suddenly saw what she hadn't completely understood before. Why he'd said this wasn't just what he did but who he was.

He had been born into this life. Accomplished more in a year to help people on this earth than most did in a lifetime. And she again felt overwhelmed with the admiration and respect she'd felt yesterday. Had felt in Honduras when she'd seen the lives he'd changed.

From the moment she'd met him, she knew he was like no one she'd met before. And with painful clarity, she understood even more what a nearly insurmountable situation yawned between them. His work was his life, and while he wanted to be a good father, he'd never be able to be that unless they lived together. He didn't want Drew anywhere but the U.S., but she, too, wanted to make at least a small contribution to people like this young boy. So where did that leave them?

There was no good answer. Marriage? Leaving her alone and Drew wondering why his dad didn't want to live with them? No marriage? Leaving them even more distant from one another? Dear Lord, she just didn't know.

Chase clamped off the artery and vein then reached for the bone saw. As he sawed through the humerus she clenched her teeth at the horrific sound and thought of her own son. Wanted to know more about why the family had waited until the situation was this bad.

"Why didn't they come in sooner?"

"I told you. They live far away. Just spent two days walking here. Obviously, it was a compound fracture, and the local healer tried splinting it and called on the spirit Sakpata to help him heal. They probably thought it would be okay. But I'm sure it was full of debris just like Apollo's and got infected."

He set aside the bone that would never again be a part of the child. With heavy sadness weighing in her chest, she pressed sponges against the opening to soak up blood and fluids. "But they must have seen that it wasn't getting better. I can't even imagine what it must have looked like."

"Don't judge them. Don't impose your Western views on the life they have to live here." His voice was fierce as he clamped off the artery and vein and began to sew the fish-mouth incision back together over the stump. "They didn't know what to think. Thought maybe it was healing, part of Sakpata's plan when his hand turned from pink to purple to black."

He leaned more closely over the gaping, raw flesh, carefully stitching the tissue. "But, as you can tell, there was superficial dry gangrene of the exposed tissue. He must have a good immune system, which sealed the gangrene off in the junction between the wound and the rest of his arm. Kept him alive. By the time his hand was mummified and hanging on by just the neurofiber bundle, they knew it was too late."

"My God," she whispered, and tears stung her eyes again. It was hard to even process what the child had gone through.

Chase glanced at her, and his grim expression softened slightly. "Please don't cry. It doesn't accomplish a damned thing. These people are tough and used to challenges we can't even imagine. To absolute hell being handed to them on a platter."

A tear spilled over and Dani lifted her shoulder to swipe it away. "I'm not as hardened as you are to all this."

"I hope I'm not hardened." He laughed without any humor in the sound at all. "I'm just determined. Determined to get more doctors and nurses in places like this. Determined to get more funding. And as much as you might not understand his parents letting this happen, I give the father huge credit for bringing him in now. I've seen people who lived with something this bad for years that was never addressed by modern medicine."

She looked at him, at the intensity in his eyes as he worked. "If more doctors are needed here, why are you so determined that I take Drew to live in the States? Why wouldn't you just want us to stay here? For me to work alongside you?" Wasn't that the obvious solution?

He claimed to want her to marry him. At least that way they'd be together as a family.

"Didn't you just hear me say it can be hell in a place like this? Drew doesn't belong here. Not until he's an adult."

"It's not the same thing for him as it is for the people who live here. Obviously, he wouldn't be exposed to the same problems."

"To some of them he would." His anger seemed to ratchet higher, practically radiating from him as he pinned her with a ferocious gaze. "He cannot and will not live in developing countries. Period. Now, are you going to just stand there or are you going to help?"

Sheesh. "Yes, Dr. Bowen." She couldn't remember him ever being this domineering and cranky before. Must be the stress of this poor boy's injury compounded by the stress of their personal situation.

She grabbed thin suture material and handed it to Chase to finish tying off the artery and vein, then continued to sponge out the blood as he worked. There was clearly no talking to the man once his mind was made up, and now wasn't the right time anyway. Though, so far, there hadn't seemed to be any right time to come up with a solution they could agree on.

"While I finish the ligation of the artery and the stitching, you can pull together the sterile cotton dressing and elastic wrap."

When it was over, all that was left of the child's arm was a stump neatly rounded in a compression dressing. Dani wondered if he'd be relieved at no longer looking at his own bones, or if the final loss of his arm would grieve him, too.

Her heart squeezed. As Chase had said, the boy had

been handed hell and, unlike in the U.S., would probably never have a prosthesis that would give him a usable
limb. Her own mom had always told her to remember
that life wasn't fair, and wasn't that the truth? Next
time she felt like complaining about something, she'd
step back and picture this boy's arm and his tragically
stoic expression.

They settled the boy into a bed, and Chase told the
father they could stay for three days until it was time
to change the dressing.

"Usually, we'd just send him home tomorrow and
have them come back to have the dressing changed in a
few days, as we're pretty full up in the hospital," Chase
said as they headed out the doors to find Drew. "But I
bet they wouldn't come back, because they live so far
away. We can't risk infection."

Dani nodded, and they continued walking, not saying anything. His expression was still grim and she
wasn't sure if it was because of the boy or their conversation about Drew or both. She felt emotionally spent
from the whole experience and, really, what more was
there to say?

"I forgot to tell you," Chase said, shoving his hands
in his pockets as they walked side by side. "Mom has a
bee in her bonnet about going to some hotel in Parakou
that a friend of theirs owns before they leave. It's about
thirty kilometers from here. Wants to have lunch there.
I guess there's a nice pool too, and as we have tomorrow off, she wants us to take Drew swimming. Is that
okay with you?"

"Drew doesn't know how to swim. He's only two."
Climbing trees and swimming with the child barely out
of diapers? What was with this family?

"Two and a half," he said, his expression lightening in a slight smile. "I'll teach him. The sooner he learns, the better."

"I assume you won't just throw him in the deep end and tell him to flap his arms and kick?"

"Don't worry. I'll show him the basic moves before I send him off the diving board."

"Chase!" She stared at him then frowned as he chuckled. He'd always delighted in teasing her, and too often she fell for it.

He put his arm around her shoulders. "I promise not to scare him. We'll just have fun. He won't learn how to be really safe in the water for a while, but it's a first step."

Apparently his anger with her had cooled, as he touched his warm lips to her temple, lingering there for a moment, sending a tingle across her cheek and down her neck. "If it works out, we could probably take him to the hotel weekly, even though Mom and Dad will be gone."

She looked into his deep brown eyes and wanted to ask the question hanging between them. What was going to happen when he was gone, too?

"Sure. Sounds fun. I'd like to see more of the countryside. And another city."

"Good." He stopped walking, and since his arm was around her she stopped, too. He used his free hand to cup her cheek and gave her a soft kiss she should have stepped away from. Should have prevented from quickly morphing into something hotter, needier.

His tongue slipped inside her mouth and the taste of him was so delicious, so overwhelming she couldn't resist. One tiny taste. One more minute. One more time.

On their own, her arms wrapped around his waist and held tight as he moved his hands down her body, firm and sure and insistent. One large palm cupped her behind as his other hand slipped beneath her shirt, caressing her skin, making her gasp as he pulled her close against his hardened body.

His lips separated a whisper from hers, his breath quick against her moist skin. "Dani." His mouth covered hers again, slanted to deepen it, intensify the taste and feel of his kiss, and the heat between them became so scorching she was sure she just might combust right there outside the building.

He tore his mouth from hers, his eyes passion-glazed and nearly black as he stared at her. "How about that back rub? Like now, and naked?"

Now and naked sounded very, very good, but the moment without his lips on hers gave her enough time to gather a tiny semblance of sanity. A second to protect her heart. "I just…don't know if that's a good idea. I admit last night was wonderful. But I'm afraid it just makes things more…confusing."

She pulled out of his arms completely, regretting no longer having his arms around her, his fingers touching her skin, his mouth igniting hers. But her brain told her she should stay strong. Wouldn't having sex, being together again intimately, just lead to heartache?

For a moment he didn't speak, and she wasn't sure what emotions flickered across his face. Frustration? Contemplation? Agreement? She was surprised he didn't reach for her again, and quickly turned to continue into the building before something else happened that might put her yet again under his spell. Again weaken her resolve.

"Dani—"

"Let's not talk about any of this right now." She kept going, counting the steps to the door. Maybe it was cowardly, but she needed a minute to regroup. Some time to get her breath back and her heart back into a normal rhythm. Some time to figure out the confusing messages her brain and body kept sending through every nerve. "After your parents leave, we'll sit down together and discuss options. When we make some decisions, I promise to be reasonable."

He grasped her arm and stopped her progress, turning her to him. His gaze no longer passionate or angry, he looked beyond serious. "Reasonable is marrying the man who cares about you and our son. Reasonable is planning our future together. I don't get what's not obvious about that."

"Because I don't want to be married to someone who doesn't live with me. I don't want Drew to wonder why his father's work is more important to him than he is." *I don't want to be hurt again.* "Why don't you understand that?"

"Dani." He cupped her face in his hands, and the tender and sincere expression on his face gripped her heart. "I promise I'll be with you as much as I can. I've already talked with the GPC and asked about eight-month assignments. I admit it'll be hard for me to adjust to working in the States some, but I'm willing to do it. For Drew and for you. What more can I say and do to convince you it will work out?"

Maybe the words *I love you*? She wanted to say it aloud—nearly did—but bit the inside of her cheek just in time. She'd refused to even think about that being part of the equation. Until last night. Until they'd practically set the bed on fire and her along with it. Their time together brought back every single memory of the intense physical and emotional intimacy they'd shared in Honduras.

True, he had told her he loved her back in Honduras. Once or twice had uttered those three little, wonderful-to-hear words.

Then he'd turned her down flat when she'd asked him to marry her, saying he just wasn't the marrying kind. Knowing that he only wanted to marry her now because of Drew still pained her more than she wanted to admit.

Was she able to be in the kind of marriage he was offering? Would it be okay for Drew? Could she convince Chase how important it was to her to spend at least some time doing mission work? After a few years, would Chase feel a need to work full time outside the U.S. again, leaving them alone almost all year?

She didn't know. And all the uncertainty weighed heavily in her chest. All the questions spun in circles in her mind.

"Like I said last night, I need time to think." She tried hard to ignore the delicious feel of his thumb gently sliding across her cheekbone, his breath touching her skin. "I've asked you before, and I'm asking again. Please stop pushing for an answer. Let's let…things unfold…. as they will. Without you confusing me with your hot kisses."

"Since you think my kisses are hot," he said, a smile finally touching his lips, "and you asked nicely, I'll be good. For how long I can't say, but I'll try."

He touched his mouth to hers, light and quick, and the, oh, so brief touch still made her feel weak. His five o'clock shadow gently abraded her cheek as he whispered in her ear, "If you change your mind tonight, though, you know where my bed is."

CHAPTER TWELVE

"EAT UP YOUR breakfast so we can get going," Dani told Drew as he fidgeted on the kitchen stool, just poking at his oatmeal. "I've already got your swimsuit and everything packed. We're waiting for you."

"I ready to go."

"Not until you eat." Her cellphone rang and she pulled it from her pocket, wondering who could be calling.

"Dr. Sheridan here." She touched Drew's hand, mimed him eating, then jabbed her finger at his bowl.

"Hello, Dr. Sheridan, this is Colleen Mason from GPC. How are you?"

"Fine. How can I help you?" She picked up Drew's spoon and poked oatmeal in his mouth, to his frowning annoyance.

"I'm Director Mike Hardy's assistant. I wanted to let you know that your request for a transfer to Panama has been granted, and we have arranged for a replacement for you in Benin. You'll start four weeks from today. Would you like for me to make all your travel arrangements?"

"I'm sorry, there must be some mistake. I didn't ask for a transfer to Panama."

"This is Dr. Danielle Sheridan? Currently in Benin?"

"Yes." What a weird error. "But I'm scheduled to stay here for eight months, and I only arrived a week ago."

"Well, I'm confused now. I'll have to check with Mike, but it was my understanding that you're scheduled to relocate with Dr. Bowen at the same time he goes to work in Panama."

Her breath backed up in her lungs and she nearly dropped her phone. "Dr. Chase Bowen? Is he moving to Panama?"

"Yes. The same date I have you scheduled to go."

Shock and anger welled up in her chest and threatened to choke her. It didn't take a genius to realize this was no mistake. That this was the work of a certain master manipulator determined to have everything his way and make decisions for her, and to heck with talking to her about it beforehand.

She could barely catch her breath to speak. "Well, I'm afraid this is a mistake. I have no intention of moving to Panama. Let me speak with Dr. Bowen and I'll call you back."

"All right. And I'll speak with Mike, too, to see what the mix-up is. Thanks."

Normally, Dani was pretty easygoing and couldn't remember ever feeling quite like this. Her whole body shook and her head tingled with fury. "Eat your food, Drew. I'll be right back."

She stalked towards the door but before she could push it open to go find the controlling man and let him have it, the jerk in question walked in.

"The car's packed up. Are you—?"

She flattened both hands against his chest and gave him a shove. "Who do you think you are?"

His eyes widened and his brows rose practically to his hairline. "What?"

Her jaw clenched, she glanced back at Drew to see him finally eating, and grabbed Chase's arm. She pulled him into the hall and had to rein in her desire to pummel him with her fists just to release the wild anger welling within her.

"You're moving to Panama." She dragged in a breath so she could speak past the pounding of her heart. "You didn't even tell me. And you didn't even ask what I thought about moving there and working there with you. You just decided Drew and I should go and that's that?"

The surprise on his face settled into grim seriousness. "Okay. I get it that you're upset. Let me explain."

"There's no explanation necessary. It's pretty obvious what you think."

Her anger morphed into a different emotion, and she found herself swallowing a huge lump in her throat and the tears that threatened to accompany it.

Now she knew. Knew how she'd feel when he moved away. And it was so much worse, so much more painful than she'd expected. As she stared at his face, she knew without a doubt she'd miss him horribly. Even more than when she'd left Honduras, though she would never have dreamed that was possible.

And Drew. Drew would miss the daddy he'd so easily embraced and now loved to be with. What she'd feared and dreaded all along.

But moving with him? What would that solve?

Nothing. It would just delay the inevitable. She and Drew would move back to the States when her contract was up, but Chase wouldn't. It was as simple and wretched as that.

"I'm not moving to Panama with you. I'm not moving anywhere with you."

He grasped her arms and narrowed his eyes, his voice tight. "Listen. Panama is safer for Drew than Africa. And it would give us almost eight more months together, for you to think about us. For you to see we belong together. I'm not leaving here without this resolved between us."

"Then don't leave." She tipped her chin and stared at him. The man she knew never backed down from a challenge. "Stay here. Tell the GPC you're taking a leave of absence."

"I can't do that." Now he too was angry, his brows deeply furrowed over fierce brown eyes. "I have a contract with them. I have work to do."

"Well, so do I." She tried to shake free of his grip, but he held her tight. "This is why—"

"Is our baby ready to go?"

Evelyn's cheerful voice came down the hall with her and Phil, but both of them stopped short near the kitchen door.

"I'm sorry." Chase's parents looked at them with obvious uneasiness. "Are we…still on for today? Would you like us to take Drew by ourselves?"

"No. We're coming." Chase released Dani's arms and his chest rose and fell as his expression cooled into stone. "Where's Drew?"

"Eating. I'm sure he's done."

Without another word she stepped into the kitchen to gather up her son and his gear. Drew deserved a nice day with his grandparents, who were leaving tomorrow, and his daddy, who was leaving very soon. Before they went back to life as it had been. Back to just the two of them.

* * *

So much for worrying about Drew maybe being intimidated by the swimming pool. Dani sat with Evelyn at an ornate wrought iron table and watched her son splash with delight in the warm, crystal-clear water.

Drew's silliness and his grandparents' laughter at everything he did and said had made the drive to the hotel bearable. Had given Dani time to cool off, toughen up, and accept that Chase was leaving. To swallow that pain. To even forgive his audacity at trying to get them moved with him, because he thought, in his twisted sort of way, that it would have given them more time together. How could she really be angry about that?

No, her anger had proved to be as fleeting as their relationship had been. And she was left with only bleak resignation weighing heavily on the depths of her soul.

Chase stood in the shallow end of the pool, holding their son's little body with both hands around his ribs while Phil tossed him a plastic ball, and she had to admit the child looked practically ready to do breaststroke.

Breaststroke. An unfortunate name for a swimming position that made her think, with an ache in her heart, about their time together last night. Since he was leaving, she figured she deserved to stare at Chase's half-naked body. To imprint it one last time upon her memory.

She'd had her turn in the pool with Drew before they'd taken a break for lunch. Twists of both pain and pleasure had knotted her stomach as Chase had watched her swim with Drew. With his eyelids low, his gaze had been filled with the same emotions swirling through her now. A heightened sensual awareness tempered by frustration and dejection.

After having chlorine repeatedly stinging her eyes, she'd been more than happy to hand Drew over to Chase, quickly moving across the tiled floor because having her damp body brushing against his skin was torture. Thankfully, the hotel gift shop had a white terrycloth swimsuit cover-up she could buy, as she wasn't about to sit there in a bikini in front of Chase. Or while sitting next to his mother.

At first she'd tried hard not to eye Chase in the pool the way he'd eyed her, but failed miserably. The wetness of his bronzed skin seemed to emphasize every inch of his muscled strength. As he dunked Drew partway into the water then back up, to the child's laughing delight, his biceps bulged and his six-pack rippled, and the dark, wet hair in the center of his chest ran in a damp arrow to disappear beneath his black swim trunks. Why couldn't the man be growing a paunch and losing his hair?

"Our Andrew is a fish, just like his father," Evelyn said.

Dani yanked her attention back to Chase's mother, thankful Evelyn was watching the action in the pool instead of noticing the way she was staring at the woman's son. Evelyn wore what seemed like a permanent expression of happy pride, and Dani felt gratified and blessed that Chase's parents already adored their grandchild.

"Is Chase a fish?" She tried to remember if she'd ever seen him actually swim, but could only come up with the times the two of them had splashed in waterfalls with shallow pools. Not that she'd be surprised, since he seemed to be good at everything physical. Which started her thoughts down that painful path again, and that had to stop. Chase wouldn't be around to show her his various physical skills, and she again pulled her attention back to Evelyn.

"Oh, yes. Many of the places we lived had lakes. When he was older, he started doing triathlons and trained in the ocean when we lived somewhere near a coast." She smiled, obviously enjoying the memories. "When we worked at big hospitals, he was on a few swim teams and won a number of trophies. He and Brady would swim laps for ever, it seemed, though, of course, Chase lasted longest as he was older."

Brady. Obviously, Chase's brother. "I hope you don't mind if I ask you about Brady," she said quietly. "Chase has never talked about him."

"No, he wouldn't." She sighed, her eyes shadowed as she stared at the pool. "It was a terrible thing for all of us when Brady died."

Dani sat without speaking, hoping she'd continue. Eventually, though, she had to ask her to elaborate. "What happened?" she asked gently.

"We were living in the Congo. Working at a small hospital there. Chase was sixteen, Brady fourteen." Evelyn turned her now serious gaze to Dani. "We knew it must be malaria, though, of course, we'd taken the usual precautions. Took one chloroquine once a week. Had mosquito netting over the beds and used repellent."

Her expression grew grimmer as she turned her gaze to the pool again. "But Brady presented with high fever. Was lethargic. We immediately gave him more chloroquine and kept an eye on him, giving him fluids." She closed her eyes for a moment. "But he got sicker. We tried quinine with the chloroquine but after another couple days, he couldn't eat or drink. We put a tube down his nose to rehydrate him, but knew we had to get him home to a U.S. hospital."

"Did Chase go with you?" Dani could only imagine how scared a sixteen-year-old boy would be when his beloved brother was so sick. Or maybe, as a teenager, he hadn't fully understood how serious it was.

Evelyn shook her head. "No. And that was a mistake. He was in the middle of mid-term exams, had his friends there, and we were blindly sure that, once in the States, Brady would get better." She turned her brown gaze on Dani, and tears filled her eyes. "But he didn't. Turned out he had a strain of malaria resistant to chloroquine. The malaria went into his brain and it was over."

"I'm so sorry." Dani's throat closed, and she rested her hand on the older woman's arm, knowing the touch was little comfort. What else was there to say? An unimaginable loss for any parent.

Evelyn nodded and wiped away her tears. "It was a terrible time for all of us. But in some ways it was worst for Chase. He never got to say goodbye to Brady. Wasn't there at the end, holding his hand, like we were. It wasn't his fault, but I know he felt guilty and selfish that he'd stayed in Africa to take a test and hang with his friends instead of being there for his brother."

Finally, Dani saw everything very clearly, as though she'd been looking through binoculars and had suddenly found how to focus them.

She saw why Chase was so insistent that Drew not live in Africa. Or any developing country. He'd experienced first hand the worst that could happen.

Obviously, it was also why he hadn't wanted children, ever. Doctoring the neediest of humankind, as he'd so often said, was what he did. Who he was. And he couldn't do that, and be that, with a family he wanted to keep safe.

His rejection of her marriage proposal hadn't been all about him, as she'd long assumed. About having a woman in every port, so to speak, which she'd bitterly wondered after she'd left. It was about his deep caring for others, and she should have known that all along.

"Thank you for telling me, Evelyn," Dani said. "I would guess you're in agreement with Chase that I shouldn't have Drew here in Africa."

Evelyn gave her a sad smile. "There are risks no matter where you live. I'm not sure what the right answers are. I do know Chase didn't particularly like living in the States."

But he wanted her and Drew there. "Do you know why not?"

"We sent him to a boarding school for a year after Brady died, and he hated it. He was too used to living in unusual places around the world with all different kinds of people and couldn't tolerate what he saw as the superficial things important to American kids of his own age." A genuine smile lit her face, banishing the shadows. "I told him he's a reverse snob. That it's okay to want to have nice things and live in a nice house. It's all a matter of balance."

Wasn't that true about life in general? Balance. It was what she needed to find with Chase in their decisions about Drew. Marriage or no marriage.

"Don't look so stressed, dear." It was Evelyn's turn to press a reassuring hand to Dani's forearm. "I know my son can be a bit on the domineering side when he makes up his mind, but things will work out the way they're meant to. I don't know why you kept Andrew a secret from Chase, but after meeting you I would guess you had your reasons. Now that we have Andrew in our lives, you already know we're here to stay."

"Yes." Dani looked at the steadiness in Evelyn's eyes, the warmth, and knew Chase had been blessed with special parents as he'd grown up. Part of what had shaped him to be the special man he was today. "I do know."

CHAPTER THIRTEEN

BY THE TIME they returned from Parakou, the moon was rising and darkness was closing in. Spud had a simple, late meal waiting for them, ready to be warmed.

Swimming was clearly an exhausting activity, as Drew's eyes kept closing at dinner, his face nearly dropping into his plate of spaghetti. With his grandparents chuckling, Dani decided there was no hope in trying to get more food in the child that night. She followed Chase as he carried Drew, barely able to awaken him enough to get bedtime necessities done before he was in a deep sleep.

Dani pulled Drew's covers over his shoulders and kissed his cheek, his little rosebud lips already parted in deep slumber. "'Night, baby boy."

She pulled the mosquito netting around the bed before turning to Chase in the darkened room. He stood there with his hands in his pockets, staring at her with such intense concentration it was almost unnerving.

"I guess we should get back to dinner," she said. "Help clean up."

He stood silently for another long moment before he finally spoke. "Thank you for today. I know my parents had a great time with you and Drew. And I did, too."

"I couldn't believe how much he loved the water. You were right—at this rate he's going to be swimming before his next birthday."

He placed his wide palm against his chest and raised his eyebrows. "Did I hear you say I was right about something? I need to sit down."

"I'm pretty sure I give you credit when you actually *are* right. Which does happen occasionally," she said, trying to lighten the mood, which had weighed heavily on both of them all afternoon.

He didn't even smile, his serious eyes seeming to study her. Maybe he could see what she was thinking. Feeling. Finally understanding.

"I'm...sorry about the Panama thing. It was wrong of me to not talk to you. I just..." He shoved his hand into his hair. "I felt desperate. I don't want to leave without you agreeing we should get married. Without us *being* married."

After learning what she had today about his brother, she understood much more than she had just hours earlier. And the pain of his rejection when she had proposed to him didn't hurt quite as much as it had before.

As she looked into his eyes, she allowed herself to see what she hadn't looked for back then. Hadn't bothered to observe. The vulnerability deep within their chocolaty depths when all she'd noticed had been his utter confidence. His utter determination.

What must it have been like for him to be living his carefree teenage life, focused on school and his friends, only to lose his brother so suddenly and shockingly? The fact that she'd known Chase for over a year and he'd never mentioned it showed her he still carried the pain of it deep inside.

"I'm not ready to make a commitment to marriage, Chase. But I understand things better now." She clasped his hand. "We have a little time before you go to Panama. When you leave…"

He pressed his finger to her lips. "Shh. I don't want to talk. I don't even want you to say you'll marry me right now. We've done too much talking in circles, arguing, trying to figure out what to do and how to do it. All I want is to kiss you and be with you." He cupped her face in his hands and gave her the softest of kisses, and like before, it was too much and not nearly enough.

Too much to be able to walk away, feeling nothing. Not nearly enough to satisfy the craving her body couldn't help but feel for him. The craving she was no longer trying to resist.

She wanted those same soft kisses everywhere on her body.

Need bloomed within her as she wrapped her arms around his body and pulled him close, her breasts tingling at the heavy beat of his heart against them. "The only talking I was going to do was to say, 'Make love to me.'"

His lips curved and his eyes gleamed in the low light. "Now, that kind of talking I'm good with."

He kissed her, soft, teasing, coaxing. But coaxing wasn't necessary. The moment his mouth covered hers, gently drawing her tongue inside to dance slowly with his, she was lost. He tipped his head to one side, exploring her mouth so thoroughly she could barely breathe. His fingers pressed into her hips and pulled her against his hard body. Her heart thumped hard against her ribs and just as she sank deeply into his kiss, fumbling at the button of his shorts, wanting him so much her knees wobbled, his hands dropped to her shoulders and he set her away from him.

She stared at him, confused. His eyes smoldered, dark and dangerous, and the curve of his lips promised all things carnal and wonderful. So why wasn't he touching her? "What—?"

"I found a place for us that's a little more fun than a bed." His voice was low and sexy. "More like what we enjoyed in Honduras. For days, I've been thinking about you and me, there, naked under the stars. Let's get in the car and go."

She couldn't wait to make love with him, and he wanted to go on a road trip? "We made love in a bed plenty of times in Honduras. I'm for that. Your room. Like now."

He laughed, a deep, smoky rumble. "I like it when you're all bossy." He pulled her close again for a hard, intense kiss that was over all too soon before he set her away from him and pulled his phone from his pocket.

She folded her arms across her thumping heart, staring at his phone in disbelief. "You going to call 911 for help? Good idea, because I just might have to hurt you if you don't immediately demonstrate some of your amazing sexual skills."

That low laugh of his, louder this time, seemed to reverberate in her own chest. He pressed his palm to her mouth. "We agreed on no talking, remember?" With that annoying smile still on his face, he lowered his head to nibble her neck, her lobe, his moist tongue touching the shell of her ear. "Unless the subject is sex. So let me tell you what I want to do to you."

His breath slipped across her skin and the rumble of his voice was filled with desire. "First, I want…"

"Less talk, more action." She slipped her hands inside his T-shirt, up the smooth skin of his ribs to lightly abrade his nipples with her short fingernails as she ran her mouth across his jaw. Beneath her hands, his heart pounded and his muscles bunched.

"To strip off all your clothes and see every inch of your skin," he continued in that deep voice so full of sexual promise she about threw him down on her bed to get on with it. "All day you teased me, wearing that little bitty swimsuit of yours. I want to—"

"Get naked and horizontal right this second?" She slipped her hand down into his shorts, seeking the biggest object of her desire.

He quickly pulled her hand out of his pants and heaved a breath. "You always were an impatient cheat." He texted into his phone as she massaged the hard ridge beneath his zipper. He grabbed her wrist again with a breathless laugh. "Damn it, stop."

"You kiss me until I can't remember my name then say stop?" Nearly dizzy with wanting him, she forced herself to step to the bed and sat, but the distance barely slowed the aching heat pooling low in her body. "Fine."

If he planned on continuing his hard-to-get game, he was in for a surprise. On alert, she watched him, ready to make her move. Which would be that as soon as he came close enough, she'd pounce and yank him down next to her.

Yeah. She felt her own lips curve, anticipating what fun it was going to be, wrestling around on the bed and stripping off their clothes. Somehow she doubted he'd keep up the delay tactics and resist.

Except he was still looking at his phone, and her amusement faded into downright irritation. All the teasing all week, even their lovemaking of a few nights ago, had left him cool and in control while she was practically melting for him?

Then the surprise move was his. Two steps to the bed, and he effortlessly scooped her up into his arms. With quick strides he carried her out into the hall.

Okay, maybe he had a good plan after all. She pressed closer, wrapping her arms around his neck and nibbling at his lips. Beneath her hands, his back muscles flexed and tightened. "I hate to remind you," she said, giving his lips a teasing lick that left his own tongue chasing after hers, "but we can't just leave Drew."

"What, you thought I was texting my broker?" He practically kicked open the door and carried her out into the warm, sultry night. "Mom says she'll watch Drew."

Her blood began to pump faster and her body hummed in anticipation. He'd thought to call for babysitting, which must mean he had something very delicious in mind. She ran her mouth across his skin, loving the taste of him, the curve of his jaw, the slight abrasion of his skin.

"If you don't stop, we're not going to make it any farther than the backseat of this car." His eyes glinted down at her, eyelids half-closed, and it wasn't too dark to see that the smile was gone from his face, replaced by a hunger that was exactly what she wanted to see. The same hunger rising within her and leaving her breathless.

He yanked open the door of the Land Rover and practically dumped her inside, before shutting the door and jogging to the driver's side.

The engine grumbled to life and Chase hit the gas, apparently in a hurry. And that was fine with Dani.

Wondering why such an old car had bucket seats instead of a nice, long bench, she attempted to cuddle up close to him, touching her lips to his chin, his cheek, his ear. It wasn't too difficult to ignore the hard plastic between the seats, but the gear shift was darned annoying.

She wrapped one hand behind his head and flattened her other palm against his body, giving him slow caresses that made him suck in his breath. Teasing touches beneath his shirt to feel the smooth skin over hard muscle there. Combing through the soft hair in the center of his chest then down. Pressing against the zipper of his pants, which was currently strained to its limit.

He grasped her hand and held it motionless and tight in his. "You trying to make me wreck the car?"

"No. Just trying to hurry things up." She pressed closer against his shoulder, ignoring the stupid gear shift digging into her thigh. She sucked gently on his throat, every sense tuned to his scent and his taste and the feel of his skin.

"I do have to actually change gears, Dani." His voice was a low growl. "Please move over for just one minute. We're almost there."

Oh, right. The gear shift wasn't just an in-the-way annoyance. "Sorry." She straddled his lap and the bounce of the car on the rutted road pushed his hard erection right where she wanted it. The sensation was so erotic, she moaned. She tunneled her fingers into the thick, soft hair she loved to touch and very nearly gave him a full mouth-to-mouth kiss, but figured that wasn't compatible with him actually being able to see and drive.

"God, Dani." He gave a breathless laugh. "If you

wiggle against me one more time, I'm gonna run off the road into a tree. Do you have some kind of death wish?"

"No." She knew the man could practically drive in his sleep. "Just remembering how much fun we had in Honduras. How crazy you made me back then. How crazy you make me now."

"You're crazy, all right. But I like it."

The car suddenly veered to the right and bounced even more for another thirty feet or so before coming to a jarring stop.

Immediately, his arms wrapped around her, and the kisses between them became frenzied, their bodies rubbing together until Dani thought she might come undone with all her clothes still on.

Chase yanked his mouth from hers, and their panting breaths mingled in the air between them. His eyes glittered in the darkness. "I didn't drive all the way out here to make love to you against the damned steering-wheel. Come with me."

"I just about did."

His quiet laugh filled the car before he shoved open the door. Still holding her in his arms with her legs wrapped around his hips, he somehow managed to grab thick blankets from the backseat and stride with her toward a small cluster of trees.

She quit nibbling his face and neck to see where they were going. Probably would be a good idea to help with the blankets instead of just hanging onto him like a baboon.

She slid her legs off his hips and wasn't sure she could actually stand up. "Give me one."

Together, they laid the blankets over whatever spongy,

soft, and dark plant life was thriving beneath the trees. "What is this stuff?"

"I don't know. Don't care either, except that the minute I saw it, I thought of lying here with you, watching the stars."

"I didn't know you'd gone anywhere since I've been here."

"I haven't."

His eyes, shining in the darkness, were filled with both desire and tenderness, and his meaning finally sank in. "You mean, you thought of me even before I showed up in Benin?" she whispered.

"Thought of you. Wondered about you. Dreamed of you."

His quiet voice slipped inside her heart until it felt so full, it was hard to breathe. He reached for her, held her close, and for a moment the heady sexual desire that had consumed them earlier gave way to a quiet, aching connection. To what they'd had before.

To what they still had now.

He loosened her hair from its band. Pulled off her shirt between kisses. Caressed her collarbone, her shoulders, her back as he slipped off her bra. Pleasured her breasts with his mouth as he pushed off the rest of her clothes.

Then it was her turn. But she couldn't go slowly, as he had. His kisses, his touch had ignited the smoldering fire he'd lit within her earlier, and she made quick work of his clothes until they were both naked, with the cool night air skating across their skin.

She pushed him down onto the blanket and looked into his handsome face. At his shining eyes and sensual lips curved in a smile.

"You make me think of a wood nymph up there, naked and beautiful with your curly hair shining in the dark." His big hands slid up her thighs and his thumbs slipped into the juncture between them, stroking her slick skin until she gasped with pleasure.

"If I recall my mythology, Greek gods liked to play with wood nymphs. Are you a Greek god?" She said it teasingly, breathlessly, but it was, oh, so true that he looked like one, with his gorgeous, muscular physique, his dark hair, his eyes flecked with gold, and the kissable shape of his beautiful lips.

"If I need to be to play with you, the answer is yes," he said on a heavy breath, smiling. "Playing with you is my number-one fantasy."

"Good. Because I'm liking being a wood nymph. Playing with my Greek god." She slowly moved against his talented fingers, the tension coiling and rising deep inside. She ran her hands slowly over his chest, his shoulders, his arms, loving the feel of his skin, the breeze touching her body, the moonlight dancing across his face, his skin, his hair.

"I'm liking it, too." That smile still played about his lips. "It was worth nearly ending up in a ditch as we drove here."

She had to kiss those sensual, smiling lips and leaned over to cover his mouth with hers, slipping her tongue gently inside to touch his. He tasted so good, so wonderful, his skin so warm against hers, his chest hair tickling her sensitive breasts, she wanted to just stay there, draped over him, kissing him in the moonlight. Making up for all the lonely nights she'd missed his moist lips, his warm body, the shivery touch of his hands.

But the slow circles he was making with his thumbs

turned her insides to a liquid fever and the fact that he was naked and right there wouldn't let her draw out the moment any longer. She rose up to sheath him with her wet heat, and the throaty groan he gave in response made her move faster, more urgently. His hands grasped her hips as he moved with her, their gazes locked.

"Dani." His voice a harsh whisper, he suddenly bent at the waist and took her into his arms, reversing their position so she lay beneath him. Their pace quickened, the night air filling with the sounds of their pleasure. His hands were everywhere, gently squeezing, caressing, holding her close, their mouths and bodies joined in a dance that took her back to every achingly beautiful day they'd shared deeply hidden in the mountains of Honduras.

"Dani," he said again against her mouth. She heard herself crying out against his lips, and he joined her with a groan that came deep from within his chest and reverberated within her own.

They lay there for a long time, their breathing slowly returning to normal. The feel of his face buried in her neck, the weight of his body pressing hers into the spongy mattress, his hand cupping her breast, was perfection.

Cool air slipped between them as he shifted, lying just off her, skin still pressed to skin. His finger slipped across her ribs to trace lazy circles on her stomach.

"I want you to know I'm planning to stay in Benin for my vacation time until I leave for Panama." He paused. "If that's okay with you."

"That would be good." Drew would get to spend even more time with Chase if he wasn't working. And she'd have a little while to make sense of all her confusion about the future.

He propped himself on one elbow, his face close to hers. He splayed his big hand over her navel as he looked down into her eyes. "About my wanting you to marry me—"

She pressed her fingers to his lips. "I thought we weren't going to talk about that. I just want to lie here with you and look at the stars. After the next couple weeks, we'll…figure out what's best for everyone."

"I'm not asking for an answer right now. I can wait. But there's something I need to say." His dark eyes had lost their sensual glow and were now deeply serious. "I'm sorry I was so…unpleasant when I said, back in Honduras, that I never wanted to get married and have kids. If I'd known about Drew, you know my answer would have been different."

A sharp pinch twisted her heart as she stared at his somber face. Was that supposed to make her feel happy? What did he want her to say in response? She already knew that was the only reason he wanted to marry her now.

She turned her face to look at the stars, their twinkling points blurring as unwelcome tears stung her eyes. The last thing she wanted was for Chase to see her all teary over him. To feel guilty that, even though he'd said he loved her back in Honduras, he hadn't loved her quite enough.

"It's all right. I understand."

"I haven't finished." He gently grasped her chin between his thumb and forefinger and brought her gaze back to his. "The reason I acted like such a jerk was because it crushed me to realize it was about to be over between us. I knew I couldn't live a regular, suburban life in the States. I couldn't be the husband you wanted and give you the family you wanted. And that hurt like hell."

She pressed her palms to his chest, feeling his heart beat strong and steady. "I figured you were the kind of guy who just wanted to be free. That I wasn't enough to make you think otherwise."

"Not enough?" He cupped her head between his hands and kissed her hard, as though she'd made him angry. When he broke the kiss, he looked down at her with disbelief etched on his face. "Too much. More than I deserved. A woman who was everything—a caring doctor who made everyone around her smile, a woman with an adventurous spirit, a woman any man would be damned lucky to have in his life. And on top of all that, so beautiful you made my chest ache every time I looked at you."

His eyes seemed to look deep into her heart. "I love you, Dani. You're everything I've ever wanted in a woman. And now you've given me Drew. He's a miracle I didn't think I could have in my life, but a miracle I can't imagine being without now."

Her throat closed and she wrapped her arms around his neck to give him a kiss she hoped showed him how much his words had moved her. How much they'd given her hope that a good life for the three of them really might be possible.

Their lips separated, and the emotion shimmering between the two of them caught her breath and expanded in her heart. The clear night, the fragrant air, the softness beneath their blanket, all wrapped them in a quiet intimacy neither wanted to have end just yet.

Chase settled back to lie flat next to her, shoulder to shoulder, fingers curled together as they stared at the stars.

CHAPTER FOURTEEN

DANI FINALLY BROKE the long, relaxed silence. "I'm always amazed at how the Big Dipper looks just the same here as in the States and Honduras," she said, trying to lead up to the conversation they needed to have about Brady.

He chuckled. "Yeah, amazing, Miss Astronomy. Remind me to not have you teaching Drew about physical science."

She playfully swatted him. "You know what I mean. That the world, really, is such a small orb in all of the universe, with billions of people floating together through space."

"Yeah."

She turned her head to look at him. "Your mom told me about Brady."

Silence again stretched between them, this time no longer calm and relaxed. The sound of his heavy sigh mingled with the chirp of crickets until he finally spoke. "Because we moved so much, Brady and I were best friends. We did everything together, even when we made friends with local kids and kids of other doctors and med professionals."

"I never had a brother or sister, and always wished I

did." She squeezed his hand. "I can't imagine how hard it was for you to lose him."

"Yeah. One minute he was with us, the next he was gone."

He turned his head toward her, the softness that had been in his eyes earlier now gone. Replaced by the hard and determined stare she'd become accustomed to when he objected to Andrew being in Africa.

"Now you understand why Drew can't live here. Why, short term, Panama would be safer. Why it's best for the two of you to live in the States until he wouldn't be as susceptible to a serious illness."

"So you'd be okay with our living there and you living here, or in Central America, or in India?" Trying to wrap her brain around how that would work was hard. But his mission work was such a big part of his life, it would be wrong to ask him to give it up completely. Even if he did, he'd ultimately resent it, and very likely Drew would sense that resentment.

Could she give up her desire to do mission work, too? Was it fair of him to even ask? Or perhaps she could convince Chase to compromise, every few years working together in somewhat safer locations like Panama.

"I'd be in the U.S. several months a year." His fingers tightened on hers and his breath brushed her cheek. "It's not a perfect solution, but I know we can make it work."

Could they? Just hours ago she'd been sure the answer was a resounding "No." But maybe, just maybe, an imperfect solution could still be the best solution.

"Now you know about Brady. It's your turn," he said, rolling onto his side, head propped on his hand, his fingers sliding across her stomach again. "You said something about knowing what it's like to have a parent think you're a burden. Why?"

"My parents were college sweethearts. Dad was the only child of a well-to-do family. Apparently there were expectations that he'd concentrate on school, get an MBA and eventually take over the family business."

He touched his lips to her shoulder. "And?"

"Mom got pregnant. And that didn't fit into anyone's plans. They didn't get married, but his family's lawyers set up child support. Which wasn't much because, at that time he was just a student and the court didn't factor in his family's money."

"And he never had much to do with you?"

"No." She shook her head, surprised that, even now, she felt a sliver of hurt over it. "He complained to her all the time about any extra expenses she asked for help with. Sometimes plain refused. When Mom tried to get him to talk to me on the phone, he was curt and got off as fast as possible."

"Did he pay the child support?"

"Oh, he dutifully sent the checks, and his parents even paid for part of my med-school tuition. Which they didn't have to do, and I was grateful for it." His hand moved to cup her ribs and she turned her head to look at him. "But every time I invited them to some school event, they came up with an excuse. Said they were too busy. He married somebody in his social sphere, but never had kids. He and his wife travelled all over the world. Still do, I suppose."

Enough with the self-pity, which was absurd after all these years. She lightened her tone. "Hard to believe I never even got the souvenir shirt that said 'My dad went to Paris but all I got was this lousy T.'"

"So you felt unwanted and unloved by him and that felt like crap. I get why you've been so worried Drew would feel the same way." He cupped her face in his hand, his dark eyes earnest. "You do know I'll always be here for both of you, don't you? Always."

She did know. The man was the most honorable and caring person she'd ever met. "Yes. And if we decide—"

"Uh-uh." He rolled onto her, pinned her beneath him, pulled her hands above her head and silenced her with a kiss. "I know I've been pushing you hard for an answer, but now I'm pulling back. Giving you three weeks before we talk about it at all. Then we'll come back here and have this conversation again."

"Just the conversation?"

His teeth were white in the darkness as he grinned, pressing his body into hers as they sank deeper into the spongy earth. "Well, you know what they say about all talk and no action…" With the sun barely peeking through the curtains, Dani couldn't believe how wide awake she felt. As she stretched, she had to smile at the little aches and twinges from the previous evening's physical activities.

She rolled over and closed her eyes to try to get another hour of sleep. After ten minutes or so it was very apparent that wasn't happening. She stood and pulled on sweats and a T-shirt and peeked at Drew. His sweet lips were parted as he slept soundly and she kissed his head before creeping out the door to make some coffee.

As she expected, the kitchen was quiet and empty, but to her surprise the delicious scent of coffee filled the room. Early-bird Chase must have made it before his run and workout.

Perhaps he was finished and already in the shower.

The thought of finding out and joining him there was more than tempting and she walked down the hall to peek into the shower room.

Darn. Dark and quiet. She smirked at the disappointment she felt. Since when had she become a sex maniac?

She knew the answer. Since being with Chase again.

It was hard to believe an entire week had gone by since his parents had left. A week of fulfilling work and lovely family time. Not to mention all those close and intimate moments with Chase after Drew was asleep.

In mere days the man had managed to make her fall headlong in love with him again. Or maybe the truth was she'd stayed in love with him all this time. In love with his strengths and his commitment to others and those deep brown eyes she sank into every time she looked at him.

And, of course, she loved his knee-weakening kisses. The thought sent her mind back to the shower and the fact that he must still be out running and would need one when he returned. Her heart did a little pit-pat, and it was clear she needed a distraction from her libido. A vibrant sunrise peeked through the window, and she wandered outside to enjoy it.

Streaked gray clouds stood out against a magenta sky, the bright orange ball of the sun casting, as it rose above the horizon, a beautiful pink glow across the savannah. She took a sip of her coffee, letting the taste linger on her tongue, then nearly choked as a movement by a nearby tree startled her.

Chase. Doing rapid push-ups like he was in an army boot camp. Doubtless he'd already been for his run and was engrossed in the rest of his fitness regimen. Thank heavens he hadn't dragged her out of bed to join him.

Next would come squats and lunges and some kind of upper-body work, and he was the worst drill sergeant ever, with no sympathy for anyone's tired muscles. Not to mention that Chase had given her muscles a very good workout last night.

His biceps bulged and deltoids rippled and just as Dani was admiring all those manly muscles, he jumped up and ran to a tree, leaping to grasp the lowest branch to start on pull-ups.

She'd almost forgotten how beautiful his body was. Even during their lovemaking, when she'd seen him naked, run her hands over his solid strength, she'd been so focused on other things she hadn't taken the time to admire him, which had been pretty much her favorite hobby in Honduras.

But now, with the vivid sun silhouetting his wide, muscular shoulders, his powerful chest, his strong thighs, she let her eyes savor him. It was all she could do not to walk over and slip her hands beneath his T-shirt, currently hiking up with each movement to expose his belly button and the line of dark hair on his taut stomach. To feel his smooth skin all slippery from sweat.

Thinking about that made her feel very warm, like she was the one doing all those pull-ups. Better get back inside before she couldn't resist dragging him into the shower or back to bed, which wasn't a good idea with Drew waking up soon. Or before Chase spotted her and made her hit the ground for push-ups and sit-ups of her own.

Now, there was an alarming thought. She backed towards the door, turning to escape.

"Running away scared?"

She looked over her shoulder as he dropped to the

ground and walked towards her in that easy, athletic stride of his.

"No. I'm not afraid of your workouts. You can put me to the test any time." Which he'd done last night. And the night before. Unable to resist his seductive and convincing kisses, she'd completely failed every test. Or aced them, she thought with an inward smile.

"Yeah?" He stopped in front of her and pulled her into his arms. Warm brown eyes smiled into hers before his lips slipped across hers, feather soft.

With his arm draped across her shoulders, they walked together to the kitchen, and Chase poured more coffee into her cup.

"Thanks for making coffee. You sure know the way to a girl's heart."

"I know a few other ways, too."

"You do?" The way he looked at her, the smile on his beautiful lips, had her leaning in for a kiss, stroking her hand down his damp shirt and over the bulging front of his shorts.

"Is that all you think about?" he teased, his voice a low growl. He picked up a covered plate from the counter and slid the foil off. "I was referring to Ruth's coffee cake."

"Well, that is another way to my heart." The cake did smell delicious, but not quite as delicious as Chase.

"I'm thinking this earns me double points," he said.

"It does." She pinched a piece and stuck it in her mouth. "Definitely. So what do you want to use your points for?"

He pulled her close for a kiss, lips clinging before he pulled back, the corners of his eyes crinkled, his lips teasingly curved. She could get used to waking up to this. To the taste of warm coffee and Chase on her tongue.

She poked another piece of cake into her mouth and Chase licked a crumb from her lips. "I'm thinking my points should get me—"

The kitchen door swung open and Trent walked in then slapped his hand over his eyes. "Could you two please keep your romantic moments out of the public areas of the compound? I'm afraid to go anywhere now for fear of having my innocence corrupted."

"Your innocence was corrupted long, long ago, Casanova," Chase said. He moved to the counter and poured a cup of coffee, handing it to Trent. "When are you leaving for your vacation?"

"In about an hour. I'm meeting a friend in Brussels, and we're going to do a little European tour for a few weeks."

"Would this friend be of the female persuasion?" Chase asked.

"Of course." Trent swigged some coffee and rocked back on his heels. "What would be the point of spending a few weeks with a man? Working with you for the past year has been torture enough."

Dani laughed. She'd heard about Trent's reputation, and wondered how much of it was really true. "I hope you have a great time. And that you enjoy your stint in India."

"Thanks." He turned to Chase and reached to shake his hand. "God knows why, but in all seriousness I'll miss you. I hope we work together next time around."

"Me, too."

They smiled at one another with an obviously close bond forged between two doctors who spent their lives doing what so few others did. As difficult as it would be to pull up roots and start somewhere new every year, part of Dani envied their amazing commitment.

"Good thing you're spending your vacation here as I hear the only doc coming to replace both of us is going to be a week or so late," Trent said.

"Yeah. Think they'll give me double pay for working through my vacation?"

"You'll be lucky if they don't pay you in goats and yams."

Both men grinned, and Trent set his coffee on the table to give Dani a warm hug. "You take care of Drew and keep me posted on how he's doing. And best of luck with this one." He jabbed his thumb towards Chase. "Because you're definitely going to need a lot of luck."

"Thanks. I know." She looked over at Chase's smile, her heart lifting with a sweet ache, and knew she already had a whole lot of luck in her pocket.

Trent left, and Chase pulled her close for another quick kiss. "Tomorrow we'll be busy, with just the two of us here. What do you think about taking Drew back to the hotel today to swim and have lunch? I've got a taste for the burgers they serve there."

"Sounds perfect."

His hands drifted down to cup her rear. "I need a shower. Feel like joining me?"

"If Drew's still asleep, we can—"

He grabbed her hand and practically pulled her out of her shoes as he hurried her down the hall. "I'm ready to redeem my double points. Like right now."

Dani took the last swig of her iced tea and chuckled as she watched Chase and Drew play in the hotel pool.

They'd been at it for hours, with only short breaks, and she knew their son would sleep very well tonight.

"And then Superman swoops into the ocean to save Metropolis!"

Chase held Drew's small body between his hands as he dove him headfirst into the water and back up to the surface.

"Again!" Drew swiped his hair and the pool water from his eyes, his grin nearly stretching from one ear to the other. She hadn't realized until she'd seen him all wet how much the child needed a haircut, and made a note to do that tomorrow after work.

She had to laugh at the way Drew held his arms stiffly at his sides like the true Superman, and at Chase's silly comic-book commentary. How amazing that the child who had never liked water being poured over his head to rinse out shampoo now adored being completely underwater. He even liked to jump straight in from the side of the pool, as long as his daddy was there to catch him.

Chase was so good with him that she felt ashamed that she'd ever believed he'd be a distant dad. Yes, there would be physical distance while Chase worked overseas, but Drew would always know how much his daddy loved him, of that she no longer had any doubt.

A few other women sipping drinks by the pool barely concealed the way they eyed Chase, and who could blame them? With his handsome face and bronzed skin over all that muscle, he truly looked like the Greek god she'd teased him about being when they'd made love outside in the moonlight. And he could be…was…all hers.

She stood and walked to the side of the pool. "It's four o'clock, you two. We need to be leaving pretty soon."

"I not done saving Metroplis," Drew said. "Mommy, watch me dive!"

"All right, Superman. Here we go again." Chase grinned at Dani and readjusted his hands on a wriggling Drew before he dunked him beneath the water again.

The grin on Chase's face suddenly died, replaced by a deep frown. He started wading toward the shallowest water, holding Drew up against his chest.

"I not done swimming, Daddy."

"I know. I just want to check something."

The odd expression on Chase's face set off an alarm in Dani's brain. Something was worrying him, and he wasn't a man prone to worry.

Dani's feet landed on the top step of the pool just as Chase stood Drew there. "What's wrong?" she asked.

Frowning, he began to palpate Drew's abdomen, but the child leaped, trying to jump back into the pool. Chase moved his hands to grip Drew's arms and brought his face close to their son's. "Hold still, Superman. I want to see if you've got kryptonite in your belly."

Drew's eyes lit up at the idea. "Okay."

Dani's heart began to thud and her breath grew short. Why, exactly, she didn't know, but something about the way Chase looked made her feel very, very uneasy. She stepped farther down into the pool next to him and leaned close to Chase, staring as he pressed his fingers gently but firmly into Drew's abdomen and flank.

"What's the matter, Chase?"

He turned to look at her, and his shaken expression, the starkness in his eyes closed her throat. His chest lifted as he sucked in a deep breath before turning back to Drew. "Superman, the kryptonite is going to make you unable to move. Why don't you go up and sit in the chair to finish your smoothie. That'll melt the kryptonite and you'll be strong again."

"Okay. I need to get strong!" Drew grinned and hurried up the steps to grab his drink and sit in the chair.

Dani grabbed Chase's arm. "You're scaring me. What's wrong?"

He closed his eyes for a moment and scrubbed his hand across his face. When he looked down at her, his gaze was tortured. "There's a large mass inside his belly. With its location and his age, my best guess would be nephroblastoma. Wilm's tumor."

"Oh, my God. No," she whispered. Her heart stopped completely. "No. He couldn't possibly have cancer."

CHAPTER FIFTEEN

CHASE PLACED THE X-ray cartridge beneath Drew's lower back and swiveled the C-arm of the machine over his mid-section, trying to stay calm and professional. The moment he'd touched that hard mass inside Drew's little body he'd felt like someone had kicked in his chest and stopped his heart, and only the fact that he'd taken and developed X-rays hundreds of times enabled him to function at all.

"Okay, Superman? We're going to take some pictures of that kryptonite in there."

"Okay, Daddy."

His son's huge grin made Chase's throat close. He didn't know how the hell he could manage to keep acting like this was all a big game, but somehow he had to stay strong. Had to make sure he didn't scare Drew by showing the gut-wrenching terror that made it hard to breathe.

"After we take the pictures, Mommy's going to fix you your favorite dinner," Dani said. Chase glanced at her as she held Drew's hand and knew she couldn't possibly be holding up any better than he was. The strain and fear on her face made her look suddenly older, and she stared at him in mute anguish.

The car ride back from the hotel had been quiet. Despite Drew falling asleep in his car seat, Chase and Dani hadn't said much. What the hell was there to say? They didn't know anything yet. Didn't know if it was Wilm's tumor or something else. Something non-malignant. Or something even worse than Wilm's.

The shock of it had left both of them stunned and speechless. He hoped to God the X-ray would give them some idea what they were dealing with, but he had a bad feeling they wouldn't know much more than they did now.

"That's it, Superman." Chase pulled out the cartridge and swung the C-arm away. He lifted Drew's small body into his arms and held him tightly against him, closing his eyes for a moment and trying to slow his breathing. Calm his tripping heart.

He headed into the kitchen with the child. "Let's get you something to eat. Your mom will fix your dinner while I get the pictures developed. It'll be important for you to eat good food to build all your muscles."

Drew snaked his arms around Chase's neck. "I will, Daddy. I getting big muscles like you."

Chase sat his son on a kitchen stool and ruffled his hair, somehow managing to force a smile. He turned to Dani, who was busying herself putting together Drew's meal.

"I'll ask Spud to sit with him while he's eating," he said to Dani. "Give me time to get the X-rays developed then come down to the clinic."

She nodded without speaking, without even looking at him, and he headed off and spoke briefly with Spud. Desperately anxious to see what the X-rays showed, he dreaded what they might indicate.

He shoved the films up into the old light box hanging on the wall and peered at them. What he saw made him sway slightly on his feet, unable to catch his breath. It took a Herculean effort to stay upright instead of slumping down into a chair, and he was leaning his hand against the wall to support himself when Dani walked in.

"What do they look like?" she asked, her voice barely above a whisper.

"See the shadow?" He grasped her arm, tugged her closer to look at the films. "There's a suggestion of a large mass in his left flank. Whatever it is, it's big. I'm guessing at least a pound. From what I can see, though, it doesn't look like it's metastasized into the lungs."

"Oh, God." She stared at the films, and tears filled her eyes and spilled over. "Can you take it out?"

"If this was a kid who lived here, whose life was here, I'd do what I had to do." If Dani hadn't been so naive, so damned carefree, they wouldn't be in this situation. "But who knows what the hell it is for sure? We don't have CAT scans and MRIs and ultrasound. We can't even do a biopsy unless we take him to Cotonou."

"I think we should take him to Cotonou right away."

"Are you crazy?" He stared at her and wondered if she was denying the reality staring them both in the face. "We have to make a plan, this second, to get him to the States for a complete diagnosis. Then surgery by someone who knows exactly what they're doing. And chemo, which he'll probably need."

"Maybe it's not malignant. Maybe it's just a benign tumor."

"Maybe. Are you willing to take that chance? Apparently you like taking chances, as you brought him here in the first place. But I'm not willing to take that chance, because you know as well as I do what these X-rays indicate. That it's a pipe dream to hope it's not Wilm's or some other cancer."

The dread and anger he'd been shoving down for hours welled up in his chest and burst out in words he knew he shouldn't say. Words he couldn't stop. "If you hadn't brought him here, like I said all along you shouldn't have, he could already be in a hospital in the States. But, no, he's here in Africa. And it's going to take days to make that happen."

He jabbed his finger at the image of the mass inside their baby's body. "And if it *is* Wilm's, you also know how fast it grows. How it can metastasize practically overnight."

Tortured-looking watery blue eyes stared at him. "Are you blaming me for this? I love him more than anything in the world." A sob caught in her throat and she pressed the back of her hand to her mouth.

"That love should have told you to do everything in your power to keep him safe. But instead you brought a two-year-old to a developing country."

"You *are* blaming me," she said, anguish and disbelief choking her voice. "He obviously had this before we even left the States. Neither you or I could have protected him from something like this."

"No." He grabbed the films from the light box and shoved them in a folder. "But if you'd kept him where he belongs, Drew would be getting the necessary tests done right this minute. Getting treatment that could very well mean the difference between a good outcome and a bad one." He slammed his hand against the cement wall, unable to control the fury that kept welling up in his chest, twisting with the icy fear lodged there. "Between life and death."

Dani burst into tears and buried her face in her hands.

Damn it, he shouldn't have yelled at her. But she also needed to hear it. Had to know he was right. Had to know she could never put Drew in a dangerous situation like this again.

He sucked in several breaths before trying to speak again. "What's the best children's hospital near where you live in the States?"

"I rented out my house, so we can't stay there. We can choose any hospital anywhere and just stay at a hotel."

"You're the one who knows the best pediatric cancer hospitals in the U.S. Decide on one, make some calls, and I'll get the plane tickets and other arrangements taken care of."

"And I guess I need to call GPC. Try to get someone here to take my place."

"Somebody needs to be available in the clinic until the new doc gets here and knows what he's doing." The thought of not being able to go with them immediately tore at Chase's heart, but they couldn't just leave the clinic empty. Who knew what desperate patient might walk through the door? "I'll take your place here until I can leave."

"You aren't coming with us?"

The shock in her eyes added to the heavy weight in his chest, but there was no way around it. "You know the new doc isn't coming for another week or so. I can't leave the place with absolutely no one here. But I'll come as soon as I can."

Myriad emotions flitted through her eyes as she searched his face. He wasn't sure what all he saw etched there, but sad and weary disillusionment seemed to shadow her eyes. She nodded and turned away.

"I'll make some calls. Hopefully Drew and I will be out of here by tomorrow."

At the Philadelphia children's hospital, Dani sat alone in the harshly lit waiting room as her son underwent surgery to remove the huge tumor growing inside his small body. She'd kissed Drew as he'd sat in the rolling crib they used to take him to the OR, his little face smiling as though he was on a great adventure, and it had taken all her strength to smile back, to wave as if he was heading off to a play date.

The moment he'd disappeared from sight the tears had begun. Flowing from deep within her soul in what felt like an endless reservoir of dread. She thought of the poor mother bleeding to death whose life Chase had saved, and felt a little like that. That she just might slowly die if she lost her baby boy. Intellectually, she knew life would go on. But it would be forever altered.

She flipped through the battered magazines, but gave up on being able to read anything. So strange to be sitting out in this room with other parents and the siblings of patients instead of on the other side of the wall, involved in a patient's care. Absently, she watched little ones play with the toys in the room, loud and giggling, munching on snacks from little plastic bags and reading stories with their parents, completely unaware of what their families were going through.

Of course, some of the surgeries going on that moment were fairly routine, with little risk. But others? Heart surgeries and brain surgeries.

Cancer treatments.

She leaned her head against the wall and closed her eyes. Never, in her worst nightmares, would she ever have thought Drew would have to go through something like this. She tried hard to remember that Wilm's tumor, if that was what he had, was highly treatable. That over eighty-five percent of children survived it. Thrived, healthy and happy, the rest of their lives. And she prayed hard, over and over, that Drew would be one of them.

She shoved herself from the chair to grab a cup of coffee from the smiling, elderly volunteer pushing a cart with beverages and snacks. She moved slowly to the rain-spattered window, staring outside at the gray sky, and wondered if the sun was shining in Benin.

She'd forgiven Chase for being so angry with her. For somehow blaming her. He loved Drew nearly as much as she did, and she knew his outburst, his agitation had stemmed from the same shock and terror she'd felt. People did and said things under stress they normally wouldn't.

She'd even forgiven him for not coming back to the States with them. Or maybe forgiven was the wrong word. Accepted, painfully, what she'd known all along but had buried beneath her love for him. Beneath her desire to believe they could have a future together, however complicated.

His work was his life. Who he was. Without it, he wouldn't have an identity that he understood, and that identity took precedence over everything.

But, as bewildered as she felt, one thing became very

clear. As she'd taken Drew to his first doctor's appointments, to the first of so many tests, when she'd held his hand as he'd cried during the MRI, and as he'd been poked and pinched as his blood had been drawn, she'd known the life Chase proposed for them wasn't enough.

For a short time, in his arms, through his kisses, she'd become convinced it was, and just thinking about those moments filled her with a deep longing. But through all the lonely hours since she'd brought Drew back to the States, she'd come to see that she deserved more.

She deserved a husband who would be with her every day. Through good times and bad times. In sickness and in health, as the marriage vows said. And that simply wasn't possible with him living across the world most of every year.

She rested her forehead against the cold pane of glass. She loved Chase. Loved him so much it hurt. But many of the things she loved about him were the same things that drove him to do the work he did.

He couldn't change who he was, and she couldn't even really want him to, because he was like no one else she'd ever known. A man with so much to offer humankind but not enough to offer her.

"I know this cast feels even worse than the last one, but at least you don't have to deal with that apparatus any more, right?"

Chase leaned over Apollo and checked the new cast he'd put on the boy, which extended over his whole leg now that the boy's wound had healed enough to be covered. "Does it hurt?"

The boy shook his head and smiled. "The 'be happy' song makes it better."

Don't worry, be happy. Chase swallowed hard. That wasn't even close to possible.

Apollo's mother reached under the blankets she had stacked next to the bed and brought out a small fetish she'd most likely made herself, handing it to Chase. "I heard the pretty doctor's son was sick and needed to go back to America," she said. "I wish to give this to her and her son, asking for Sakpata's healing."

Her son. His son.

"Thank you. I'll let her know." Chase took the beaded and painted mud statue from the woman and tried to smile. If only such a thing could really help. But Drew's health—his survival—would come down to modern medicine and a little luck.

Each time he'd treated small children in the clinic, their faces had blurred to look like Drew's. His big brown eyes and his beautiful smile. And through every crisis, every surgery he hadn't been able to take his mind off him for even a second. Wondering how he was doing. What he was going through. If he'd be okay.

Wondering how Dani was holding up through it all.

Chase moved on to the next patient, thinking about his last phone call with Dani. She'd given him the details of Drew's tests, what they showed, what they planned to do. Her voice had sounded calm, her recitation to the point. She sounded okay, but he suspected it was an act. His frustration level at not being able to be there with them threatened to make it nearly impossible for him to focus on his work.

When the hell was the new doctor going to get here?

His cellphone rang and he pulled it from his pocket. His mother. Calling for at least the tenth time.

"I'm wondering if there's any news."

Her voice reflected the same tightly controlled foreboding he felt that had every nerve on alert. "No, Mom. She said she'd call after the tumor was removed. After they do a biopsy to confirm the diagnosis."

"I still think you need to go be with them, Chase. I think you should book your flight."

"I can't do that yet." Surely she knew he felt as frustrated and anxious as she did? But she also knew that if he left there wouldn't be one damned person here to take care of an emergency. And the nurses would have to take care of the hospital patients alone, with a few in serious condition.

"You do know it's okay to put yourself first once in a while, don't you? You need to be there to support Dani through all this."

"It isn't logical for me to go there where there are umpteen doctors of all specialties ready to take care of Drew, and not a single doctor here to take care of these people. You know that."

"That's not really true, Chase. That hospital has their techs who are well trained for things like hernia surgery, and they'd do the best they could if there wasn't a doctor there." His mother's voice grew more irritated, which he rarely heard from her. "You have your whole life to take care of needy people in the world; you have only this moment to take care of Dani and your son."

He stared at the hospital ward, at all the sick and injured patients, and didn't know what the hell to think. How could he abandon them? Yes, the techs could handle most problems if necessary, but it felt...wrong to leave them without a truly qualified surgeon. And yet the place he wanted to be was with Dani and Drew.

He hung up and pulled out his stethoscope to check the next patient.

* * *

"The prognosis is very good, Dr. Sheridan." The surgeon, still wearing his blue cap and surgical gown, sat in the chair next to hers in the waiting room. "I suspect it was, indeed, a Wilm's tumor, but of course we'll have to wait for the biopsy results to confirm that. It was a stage-one tumor, completely isolated in one kidney. With the removal of the tumor, kidney, and ureter, I think only a short course of chemotherapy will be necessary. He's going to be fine."

Dani nearly slid off the chair at his words, tears clogging her throat. Her first thought was to wonder if Drew was awake and wanting her. Her next thought was that she wished Chase was there to embrace in shared relief.

"Can I see him now?"

"He's in Recovery. Still asleep, but you can go on in there so he'll see you when he first wakes up." The doctor smiled and patted her shoulder. "We'll keep him in the hospital a couple of days. Then we'll discuss the next step."

The nurse led her to Recovery and she sat next to Drew, holding his hand, knowing he'd be in pain and maybe confused when he awoke. She'd brought a pillow and blanket to spread on the narrow, but thankfully padded, window seat in his room so she would be right there for him if he needed her.

His eyelids fluttered and he looked up at her. "Mommy?"

"I'm right here, sweetheart." As she squeezed his hand, her own heart squeezed until she thought it might burst wide open. While she knew there was still a slim chance something could go wrong, it sounded like they'd been very, very lucky.

She slowly combed her fingers through his beautiful, thick hair, her heart clutching at the thought that it might all fall out during chemo. She couldn't even imagine it, but would figure out a way to make it seem okay, maybe even fun. After all, he was still so little he might like the adventure of using his noggin as a canvas for non-toxic markers, and managed a smile at the silly thought.

"Is Daddy here?" he asked, his voice sleepy and slurred.

"Not yet." And wasn't that what she'd probably be telling him his whole life? That his daddy would be home whenever he could be there? Maybe soon? Or, more likely, not soon at all.

Tears yet again closed her throat, slipped from her eyes to sting her cheeks, as she told herself it would be all right. It had to be all right. Drew would recover and grow up to be a smart, strong and handsome man like his father. Chase would be there for him when he could be, talk to him a lot, probably send him photos via computer of all the places he was living and all the things he was doing.

And she would be right here for Drew. Every day.

Chase concentrated on his push-ups, trying to block everything else from his mind. Fifty-five. Fifty-six. Fifty-seven.

He never worked out twice in one day. The darkness that surrounded him was usually pre-dawn, not dusk. But he had to do something to deal with the anxious restlessness consuming him.

Dani had said she'd call once she knew anything. Hours and hours ago she'd promised that, but he hadn't heard a word. Kept checking his phone to be sure it was on, that its ringer was turned up, that he hadn't somehow missed her call.

He headed towards his favorite tree, which had lost a few limbs to storms but somehow survived. It stood scarred but still strong, and he leaped to grab the lowest branch. When the phone rang shrilly, he dropped to the ground and nearly fell on his face. Fumbling to snag it out of his pocket, he quickly hit the button.

"Hello? Dani, is that you?"

"Yes. It's me. I wanted to tell you he came out of surgery okay and he's doing fine. It was stage one, so they're sure they got everything. And they expect the biopsy to confirm it was Wilm's, so the prognosis for a full recovery is really good."

His legs felt so weak they seemed to crumple beneath him as he sat on the ground. "Thank God." He swiped his hand across his face and moist eyes, not caring that dust covered his palm. "Are you doing okay?"

"I'm fine." Her voice was calm, cool. "I'll call you tomorrow to let you know how he's feeling."

"Wait." Was that it? She'd barely spoken with him and was going to hang up? "Can I talk to him?"

"He's finally back asleep. He was in a lot of pain and cranky, but they upped his pain meds and he's comfortable now. Oh, wait, he's crying a little again. I've got to go. I'll call you later."

The phone went dead in his ear and he stared at it. He should feel elated. *Did* feel relieved beyond belief that the tumor had been caught early and Drew would most likely recover completely.

But with that relief came overwhelming disquiet. As he sat there in the dirt, he looked up at the night sky.

He wished Dani was looking at it with him. Not from Philadelphia but from here.

No. He stared hard at the stars, shining steadily and brightly. It seemed he could almost see the slow turning of the earth, the stars growing more brilliant and defined as they rotated infinitesimally in the sky, and knew.

He should be looking at it in Philadelphia with her.

He scrambled up and dialed the airline. He hoped to God the new doc would show up tomorrow as he was supposed to. And prayed that the techs wouldn't have problems covering any emergency, if necessary. But right now, there was only one place in the world he belonged. He belonged with Dani and Drew.

"Come on, you have to eat more than that." Dani poked raisins into Drew's oatmeal to make another smiley face, hoping he'd eat a few of the oats along with the raisins he kept picking out. "Dig out his whole eyeball with your spoon, and gobble it up like the monster you are."

"I not a monster. I a lizard, eating my bugs."

He picked out the raisins again, and Dani sighed. She needed to stop fussing over him, worrying about every bite of food. It was obvious he was feeling better every day, and she couldn't wait until this afternoon when he would get to go home.

"I brought some Benin bugs back for you, lizard-boy," a deep voice said.

Dani swung around and stared, her stomach feeling as if it was jumping up to lodge in her throat. There Chase stood, tall and strong, his brown eyes tired but intense, his entire form radiating energy. She wanted to run to him and throw her arms around him and beg him to never leave again.

"Daddy!" Drew shrieked and tried to scramble out of the bed, but Dani quickly put a restraining hand on his chest.

"You can't just leap out of bed with all this stuff attached to you," she said. "Lie still."

Chase came farther into the room and draped his arm around Dani, pulling her close as he sat on the side of the bed. His eyes met hers, and a familiar ache filled her chest. He leaned forward to give her a soft kiss, and he tasted so good she forced herself to remember all the lonely days and nights and her conviction that she deserved more than he could offer.

Chase turned his attention to Drew, leaned down to kiss his cheek. He stroked one finger across the child's forehead to get his hair out of his eyes then cupped the side of Drew's head with his wide palm. But he kept Dani tugged close against him. "You've been through an awful lot, getting that kryptonite out of your belly, Superman. How are you feeling?"

"Okay. My tummy hurts but Mommy says it'll be better soon."

"I'm sorry it hurts. You're very brave, and I'm proud of you."

"Time to change his dressing," a nurse said with a smile as she walked in.

Chase stood, and Dani stood with him, because she didn't have a choice with his arm tight around her body. They took a few steps away from the bed to give the nurse room.

"I'd like to see the wound." Chase studied it carefully after the nurse had removed the dressing, then nodded in satisfaction. He smiled at Drew. "Looks good, buddy. Your mom and I'll be in the hall while the nurse gets you fixed up. We'll be right back."

Chase moved into the hallway, taking Dani with him, and in some ways she felt like she was right back where they'd been the first time they'd seen one another again in the sub-Saharan twilight. But this time she knew she would remember how much she'd missed him this week. She knew she could stay strong.

He drew her farther down the hall to a darkened nook holding a single chair. He slipped between the chair and wall and pulled her to him, looking down at her eyes, his own deeply serious.

"When did the new doctor arrive?" she asked.

"Thankfully, he showed up at the airport as I was about to leave."

"At the airport?" Had Chase left before the new doctor was in place? She opened her mouth to ask but he pressed his fingers to her lips.

"Before you speak, I have some things I need to say." His hands moved to cup her face, his thumb slipping across her cheekbone. "I was looking at the night sky and saw the Big Dipper. And I thought about you saying that we're all spinning around together on this tiny speck in the universe called Earth. I realized I didn't want to be looking at the stars, knowing you're looking at them too, and not be with you, looking at them together."

Her eyes stung and her fingers curled into his shirt, but she didn't know what she was supposed to say. Didn't know exactly what he was saying.

He brushed her lips softly with his, and she wanted to

kiss him longer, wanted to feel his mouth soothe away all the worries, all the loneliness.

"I always said being a mission doctor wasn't just what I did, but who I was." His breath touched her moist lips as he spoke. "I was wrong."

He tucked a strand of hair behind her ear, and she wanted to wrap her arms around him and hold him close. "How were you wrong?"

"It's not who I am. It's just what I do. Who I am is the man who loves you and wants to be with you and share my life with you. Who I am is Drew's father, and I want to share my life with him, too." He pulled her close and buried his face in her hair. "I love you for just you, and I love him for just him. I love you, and all I want is to share my life with both of you."

He looked at her again, and she knew he meant every word. That it wasn't just a brief reaction to the terrifying crisis of Drew's illness but words from deep within his heart.

"I love you, too," she whispered. "So much. But it scares you to have Drew live in the places you work."

"Which is why I'm staying here. Working here. With you. In whichever one of the fifty United States you choose. My mother pointed out that I—we—have the rest of our lives after Andrew grows bigger to work missions around the world. If you want to. Until then I'm sure I can find work here where I know I can make some kind of difference."

He drew her to the chair and gently sat her in it. His eyes focused on hers, he held both her hands and slowly dropped to one knee. "I know I was pushy and demanding before, and I'm sorry for that. But I can't wait any longer for you to ask me again to marry you."

"Chase, I—"

"No, it's my turn now." His hands tightened on hers. "Will you marry me, Dani? I'll do anything you ask of me if you'll let me be a part of your life. And Drew's. On your terms, not mine. I'm asking you because I can't be complete without you. I'm begging you because I don't want to live without you. Please, will you marry me?"

"Oh, Chase. Yes. I will." She felt her mouth tremble in a wobbly smile. "I've missed you so much."

His chest lifted in a deep breath and he closed his eyes for a moment before looking at her with so much love her heart felt almost too full to hold it all.

"Thank you." He stood and pulled her into his arms, holding her close. "I missed you for three damned years and I'm not missing you again for even one more day."

He lowered his head and kissed her, and it was so warm and sweet it was like drinking in happiness.

She wrapped her arms around his neck and pressed her cheek to his. "We should probably go back to Drew's room. I get to take him home today. Except that, for the moment, home is a hotel."

"*We* get to take him back home today. And then we'll get started on figuring out where home's going to be."

With the promise of everything she'd ever wanted within his warm gaze, he took her hand and they walked down the hall to be with their son.

Together.

EPILOGUE

LAUGHTER ECHOED OFF the walls of their new home in Chicago as Drew put on a puppet show for his three doting grandparents. On his hand was a pink pig puppet that was dancing so frenetically he kept knocking down the wobbly, cardboard cutout they'd glued red fabric "curtains" to.

It had been so hard to decide where in the U.S. they should live, but Dani and Chase had finally decided on the Windy City. As Chicago was close to Dani's mother and offered a widely diverse population, they both found work here that they enjoyed, and it was a great place to raise Drew, too.

Along with another little one. Dani placed her hand on her belly to feel the hard kicks the baby kept jabbing into her stomach as she tried to watch Drew's show. Their unborn baby girl seemed to be dancing around as much as Drew's pig was, and Dani grinned at her husband. He grinned back, his lizard puppet making little kisses at her, complete with sound effects.

He turned the puppet toward Drew. "You have any bugs, little pink piggy? I love bugs! I'm gonna lick them up!"

Dani, her mother, and Chase's parents all laughed

at the ridiculous falsetto voice he was using, as well as Drew's comical reaction to the lizard puppet licking and biting him all over.

Evelyn squeezed Dani's arm. "I'm so thrilled we decided to move here for a few years. Think how much we would have missed our Andrew. And our granddaughter too, whenever she decides to meet us."

"Hopefully, very soon," Dani said with a smile, getting up to walk stiffly—waddle was probably a more accurate word—to pour herself decaffeinated coffee and place four candles on Andrew's birthday cake.

"I would have gotten that for you, honey," her mother Sandra, said, rising to busy herself gathering plates from the kitchen. Amazingly, Chase's parents were now employed at the same hospital where Dani's mother worked as a nurse. Unbelievable that a family that had once been scattered all over the world now lived and worked within miles of one another.

With Drew's grandparents in town to care for him when they were gone, Dani and Chase were able to work in El Salvador or Honduras for a week twice a year together. Her mission work and her regular pediatric practice left Dani feeling deeply satisfied, knowing she was making a difference both in the U.S. and abroad. Chase stayed on at the mission another week on his own, which he said was the longest he could be away from his wife. Drew. It was the best of both worlds, as he liked to say, smiling and fulfilled when he returned home to his family.

Drew's pig puppet completely abandoned the cardboard "stage" and began chewing on Phil's leg. With a chuckle Chase stood and walked to stand behind Dani, wrapping his arms around her, his hands splayed across her big belly.

"That lizard's crazy in love with you, you know," he said next to her ear.

"Don't tell him, but I'm crazy in love with him, too." She turned her face to his with a smile. He gave her a soft kiss, but his eyes were filled with mischief. And something else.

"He told me to ask you if he could lick you all over later. What do you say?"

She laughed and turned in his arms, her belly keeping them farther apart than she would have liked. "Tell him yes. I've always had a weakness for lizards."

He lowered his mouth to hers for a long, slow kiss and his lips were a far, far cry from any lizard's. Soft, warm, and, oh, so delicious, they tasted of all he'd given her.

Which was everything.

* * * * *

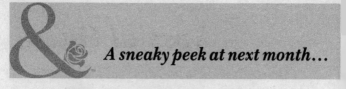